CHOPPERS TO DIE FOR

HOLTZ HAUZEN

authorHOUSE®

AuthorHouse™
1663 Liberty Drive
Bloomington, IN 47403
www.authorhouse.com
Phone: 1-800-839-8640

This book is a work of fiction. People, places, events, and situations are the product of the author's imagination. Any resemblance to actual persons, living or dead, or historical events, is purely coincidental.

First published by AuthorHouse 6/1/2009

ISBN: 978-1-4389-7568-9 (sc)

Library of Congress Control Number: 2009903415

Printed in the United States of America
Bloomington, Indiana

This book is printed on acid-free paper.

Cover design by Greenhaus GFX, Culver City, CA

Contents

PROLOGUE

Dear Jack,

In the mid nineties you and I made frequent contact at military and aviation shows — all over the world. I am still grateful for the publicity coverage your magazines afforded my company's products and systems that we exhibited. Apart from the regular declassified data concerning military systems and various armaments products that we released for military publications like yours, you knew that we always had to guard against revealing technical data of a strategic nature. I always appreciated your professional editorial approach in this regard.

Now, more than ten years later, I want to let you have some insight into the politics and intrigues that has prevailed behind the Apartheid Curtain in the South African armaments industry. I knew all along that you always had a sensitive awareness of the cloak-and-dagger culture that is part of this trade, irrespective of whoever was trying to secretly acquisition whatever military hardware that was available in this marketplace.

Up to now I was always fearful and, to a certain extend I still am, that certain powerful security persons with long arms and longer knives, could silence me. These South Africans have a long track record of successfully bringing to end information leakages of this kind. However, although I wrote this material during that time, I am only now reasonably confident that this information will not be traced back to me. But, because I am not absolutely sure that all these dangerous ex-security persons are by now safely dormant or retired, in jail, or dead, I present this information to you, as a publisher, in the form a novel under a pseudonym.

Since I am not at all a creative writer, this is not nearly Tom Clancy stuff. What I did was carefully dipping the facts into fiction and presented it in a plot form as a story with sub-plots to give you the full picture. Because you are so familiar with the circumstances and structures of the South African Armaments Industry, you will immediately be able to interpret the hidden nuances. You will even be able to recognize those real life persons disguised as characters in this story.

I sincerely hope that, despite my lack of writing skill, this will bring back previous memories and, clear up some developments from that time that is currently prevalent in this continually secretive business. Perhaps other readers may even find this first story from behind the Apartheid Curtain, quite fascinating.

Best regards

Holtz Hauzen
Pretoria. South Africa.

1

DEADLY DECISION.

KEMPTON PARK, SOUTH AFRICA

It was seldom that a man with a conservative Christian background would sit down and take a careful, rational decision to commit suicide. It was even more off-pattern to painstakingly plan the deed in such a way that it would seek to achieve a number of aims. Not only to solve a personal problem in a cold and calculated manner, but also to wreck the technical, cultural, and political systems of a country. More so - when the intention was to prepare for destructive action in a way that would shock the super powers of the world. The location of the carefully planned event had to be chosen carefully, like for the shooting of a spectacular film scene – where there would be a big presence of the international print and electronic media.

Jack du Preez was such a man. All the reasons for his suicide plan were rooted in his workplace, sports club and at home. Conditions in his country gave him all the political reasons and motives to execute his diabolical plan. He took this unusual decision after he thought thoroughly about his set of motives. He carefully planned the event under a password on his laptop. Painstakingly he kept track of local and international issues, developments, and interests. Jack scanned numerous aviation publications and the general media. He also wrote and re-wrote scenarios where the attainment of all his objectives could be knitted into a single moment and at a single cost. His life.

Notching up many flying hours at the major world air shows, afforded Jack the knowledge and to experience a large variety of venues where crowds, from all corners of the globe, gathered. He knew on which days the media coverage of these events was at frenzy. He knew a lot about what was important for his violent finale. However up to now, Jack was not too sure of his own capability to orchestrate the event but his deeply ingrained bitterness rendered him adamant. His life and surroundings did not offer him any good reasons not to set up what he planned to do, or what he deemed a final necessity. He was spiritually cold an empty. His decision was irreversible.

Du Preez thought carefully about the characteristics and merits of the instrument that he wanted to employ to reach his desired evil results. He decided on the eight-ton attack helicopter that was now slowly being towed from the metal hanger into the bright South African sunshine.

Du Preez looked at the approaching machine and suppressed the nagging accusation that tried to escape from his sub-conscious. He felt like a stud farmer who realised that the time has come to terminate the likes of a thoroughbred. Only in this instance, it has to happen prematurely.

Gradually du Preez's plan fell in place without the slightest indication of a hitch. The only thing that concerned him somewhat was the mention of an outsider that may join Africair Corporation's marketing team. Through the grapevine he heard that it would be the well-known defence reporter, Julius Grant. But then again, if he would get in the way, Mark Fisher would take care of him. Fisher was good at sidelining unwanted players.

It was bitterly cold. Under the small wheels that rolled silently on the concrete apron the Martial Eagle dragged a distorted shadow that added to its ugliness. The machine was parked right in front of Du Preez. He looked at the helicopter, resembling a hungry predator in search of easy prey. Du Preez admired the machine. The state of the art built-in electronic attack technology brought a surge of power to du Preez's calculated existence. He zipped his grey overalls against the cold breeze and glanced at the inert weapons strapped to the Martial Eagle's belly. Simulated missiles and rockets were attached to the weapons platform for the purpose of the afternoon's demonstration.

"I hate this bogus junk plastered to the bird's guts." He spoke to nobody in particular while the drone of an approaching fuel tanker silenced his words.

"We will miss the rugby match but I still think it will be fun to fly over the rugby stadium. Most of the people on the stands will today see this chopper in action for the first time."

2

Du Preez turned to the short, stocky, young man behind him. He looked at his red hair swirling in the wind but did not respond.

"Hello Jack."

"Hi Chubby! Yea, sure we will have fun."

Although they had spent many hours together throughout the development and testing of the Martial Eagle, the two men were not close. Long ago Chubby gave up penetrating or understanding Du Preez's reserved attitude. He came to accept the man's emotionally uninvolved qualities.

The two men stood looking at the machine and followed the activities of the ground crew. They admired their competence. All team members knew exactly how and when to carry out their responsibilities. They were tending to the helicopter with an excitement resembling eager ants disposing of a huge dried-out grasshopper. Most of them worked with the development engineers for more than eight years. The machine had become their whole life and demanded many hours from them. Little time was left for family and recreation. In addition, they spent many months abroad, following a demanding programme demonstrating to potential clients and participating in many international air shows.

"To develop and maintain a modern attack helicopter requires a lot of discipline," Du Preez said. Chubby listened intently to his colleague. As newly appointed co-test pilot he accepted that he was earmarked to take over from Du Preez sometime in the future. Over the past few months he noticed that his superior took care to fill him in on the development history and other technical detail of the 'bird' or 'chopper', as Du Preez called their machine. Du Preez's careful tuition strengthened Chubby's view. "By 'modern' I mean a chopper designed around a fully integrated state-of-the-art digital management system," Du Preez continued.

"I believe this baby was bred on the experience that you guys gained during the Angolan Bush War." Chubby tried his best to keep Du Preez at it. They had time to kill. Du Preez walked over and sat on the running board of the fuel tanker. Chubby followed him and squatted on the cold cement in front of the lanky pilot.

"Yes. That war taught us the value of accurate and strong fire-power, let alone factors like day and night high intensity operations, as well as affordability and availability." Du Preez carelessly lit a Camel. "In those dismal days we felt the full effect of the UN's weapons embargo against South Africa. We longed for the capability of American attack helicopters. If we had those, we could have blasted the bloody Angolans, Cubans and not to talk of all the stinking Russians, so sky-high that only their ID's returned to their homes! Therefore, our armaments corporation had to steal technology because we were forced to develop a machine that not only had optimised range and firepower but one that was designed to operate in hot and high altitude conditions. Those circumstances required good ground hover capacity with excess power to put up a good fight against the Angolans with their superior Russian equipment."

"What about...?" Chubby started when Du Preez's cell-phone began to wine increasingly louder.

"Du Preez. Hello. OK, thanks. We will be right over." He slid the instrument back into a narrow pocket on his thigh.

"It's the Control Room. They want to discuss our flight plan for this afternoon's demo. They also have some coffee and breakfast snacks ready."

"Good. I can do with something solid in my basket." Food always elicited excitement from Chubby. He stood up and walked with Du Preez towards the small doorway leading to the company's control tower.

Du Preez and Chubby clattered up the corkscrew steps to the control tower of Africair Corporation. The glass-clad room was warm and the aroma of coffee contributed to the pleasant atmosphere of activity and radio interruptions. Two men with headphones kept busy at their controls while a slender girl tapped very fast on the keyboard of her computer.

"Hi Guys." Du Preez's usual greeting included Rosemary Barnard as she was accepted by all as one of the guys, or perhaps because she was one of only a few avionics engineers in the world who specialised in aero ergonomics. Du Preez could not help to admire her contribution to the development of the man-machine interface of the Martial Eagle. The value she added to the helicopter's user quality made flying a military helicopter an altogether new experience.

Rosemary turned to the pilots, smiled, and nodded in the direction of a tray that carried fresh coffee and sandwiches.

"First things first." She ran her fingers through her short auburn hair. Her hairdo emphasised her smiling blue eyes. She was not Du Preez's type. He preferred brown-haired women who were shorter, and somewhat voluptuous. Perhaps their appearance reminded him of his wife, whose senseless death was the main reason for his deep unresolved anger. Chubby however, admired her for different reasons and always hoped that she would one day be in a desperate mood and that he would be just lucky enough to be around to help her out.

"Hello Rosy. How's my girl?" Chubby who was about three inches shorter than Rosemary, focussed his eyes at her full lips. He thought that, should he want to kiss her, he would have to stand on tiptoe.

She brought him back to reality very quickly, "I am OK, my Daddy, how's mother this morning." She sounded the warning that his advances did not interest her. Chubby blushed and stirred his hands in his pockets. He impulsively got engaged one rowdy evening and did not have the heart to get out of the situation. He lacked the inner honesty that could hurt people.

Chubby tried to maintain his good humour, "Oh, the ol' lady' is still sleeping. Pour me a cup my sweetie."

"D IY," was her only response, while her attention returned to the schedule on the screen. She edited a few figures, some wording and then keyed a printout.

"Who runs the show today?" Du Preez spoke through a toasted cheese and tomato sandwich.

"The Department of Civil Aviation - in conjunction with the South African Air Force. They were directed by the organisers of the Rugby World Cup. Captain Jakes Johnson will be at the sky command post." Rosemary could have guessed what Du Preez's reaction would be.

"You mean Captain 'Jackass' Johnson." Du Preez harboured deep feelings of ill will against his former colleague. They shared unpleasant war experiences in Angola, "I hope he does not mess-up this show as he did with our attack at Serpa Pinto."

Rosemary tried to prevent Jack from repeating an old grudge they all heard many times , "That was then, fifteen years ago. This is a simple fly-past over the country's largest sports stadium filled with ninety-five thousand happy spectators. Nothing can go wrong with this little outing.".

Du Preez was stubborn. "A fly-past like this is nothing else but an airborne mixed steel-salad of fixed wings and rotors. A silly show like this can go horribly wrong Ms. Barnard," Du Preez said despairingly. Rosemary hated his severe mood and pretended to ignore him.

The Senior Controller swung round, removed his earphones, "As Rosemary said, the pattern this afternoon is really short and simple. The first to fly over the stadium at 15:09 will be the rejuvenated old Junkers passenger plane of South African Airways. Nine old Harvard trainers, which in turn will be followed by five Impala trainer jets and four Mirages F100s, will follow. A four-minute break will position the six Puma Transport Helicopters to fly over and then, the next four minutes will belong to the Martial Eagle." He looked at his bored audience chewing on their sandwiches.

"What then?" Chubby hoped he would still be in time to catch a few minutes of the televised final rugby world cup match between New Zealand and South Africa.

"The final countdown to the start of the match will be a Boeing 777 coming over so low and slow that it will fire up the excitement on the stands."

"Why? Sounds like outside of regulation." Du Preez had his own plan for a deviation from the set flight pattern.

"Apparently it is to allow the players to read a message painted on the wings and fuselage of the plane that says, 'Good luck Springboks.'"

"What a lot of sentimental bullshit." Du Preez grabbed another sandwich. Unlike most Afrikaner men, he did not care much for the game of rugby. He lately developed a frame of mind that only had room for retribution.

Chubby tried to ease the mood, "What's the routine for the Jack-Chubby Show?" The young co-pilot glanced at his senior. He immediately regretted his remark. Du Preez would surely respond with incisive language because his mood was growing uglier by the minute.

Instead, Du Preez ignored Chubby. He had something else on his mind. "You said we had four minutes. Can I design my own routine for those two hundred and eighty seconds?" His voice was heavy with sarcasm on account of the short demonstration time allotted to the Martial Eagle.

"No." The answer came from all corners of the control room.

"To blazes with the organisers."

"In those four minutes you must hover, rotate, make a handstand, pull out and disappear into the skies at a south-westerly angle or else you will have a mid-air encounter with that Boeing." The controller was irritated and fed up with Du Preez's mood, "And no deviations from that pattern." He returned to his screen and tapped in the data to confirm flight arrangements.

Hitting that Boeing was perhaps not such a bad idea! But then, a rugby world cup was definitely not the event or venue to execute his 'Big Plan'. All the wrong people would die, Du Preez thought, and warned him-self to keep control of his thoughts when it came to his grand suicide plan.

2.

MOCK-ATTACK.

ELLIS PARK RUGBY STADIUM, JOHANNESBURG

The skyline of downtown Johannesburg stood out sharply on the mile-high ridges of the South African Highveld. The huge yellow sand dumps that elevated amongst the concrete high-risers, was evidence of the Golden City's earlier character as a sprawling mining town.

From the tandem-cockpit of the Martial Eagle Jack Du Preez and Chubby Wilson scanned the skies and the pastel scene below. From the rear seat of the Martial Eagle Du Preez took flight-control. Chubby, in the lower front-seat, was out of Du Preez's sight. The red-haired young man was trained to run weapons-control but had enough experience to take full flight charge from the avionics in front of him, should circumstances call for a take-over. However, the way things ran this morning with Du Preez at the controls Wilson had very little to do but to be on standby. His relatively low responsibility for the morning's outing allowed him to look forward to an enjoyable flip over the huge sport stadium.

The two aviators flew on in silence; listening to the dull drone of the twin Makela engines and the reassuring swish of the main rotor's blades. Below them the scene slowly slid backward en-route to the Ellis Park Rugby Stadium. Chubby wished he had brought his camera along. The vibration-free frame of the Martial Eagle would have allowed him to take high quality photos.

Their attention was focused on the flight plan and the instructions coming from the air command position of Captain Jakes Johnson. They calculated their slot into the fly past envelope and Du Preez kept a careful watch over the altimeter and air speed indicator. He did not want to waste one second of the allotted four minutes dedicated to the Martial Eagle's routine. He wanted to impress the ninety thousand rugby fans, and those amongst them that experienced South Africa's senseless bush-wars. The special manoeuvre that he planned to surprise President Mandela and his political entourage may just scare those snobbish VIP's a little. The thought brought a cruel smile to his tanned face and deepened the scar below his left eye.

"Show time Chubby!"

"Yahoo, Skip."

They approached the stadium, which opened up like a crater filled with flowers below them. They were now close enough to see the departure of the eight Puma transport helicopters from where they were parked above the crowd before disappearing over the opposite wall of the stadium.

"Chubby old man, let's fool around and have some fun with those political boffins down there." There was no humour in Du Preez's voice. It had a metallic crackle, which gave Chubby the shivers and made him frown.

The Martial Eagle slid very low over the rim of the stadium. Chubby took a quick glance at the altimeter. They were way below the flight-plan limit. Then they parked above the centre kick-off spot clearly visible on the deep green playing field. Du Preez dropped the obedient machine another few metres into the stadium and came level with the tops of the goal posts. Chubby felt like a terrified angel who disobediently flew in to watch the game. He sweated profusely. Something was wrong.

"Shit Skip! Are we still on track?"

"Shut your bloody trap Wilson. And keep it shut till this little demo is over. It's an order!" Chubby was knocked into silence by Du Preez's rude utterance. He saw that Du Preez flipped the overriding mute of the external communications system. However, he left the intercom engaged.

The Martial Eagle hovered for less than thirty seconds, and then moved slowly sideways towards the grandstand. Du Preez air-parked the machine on eye level right in front of the presidential suite. The glass-covered cubicle shook like a fish bowl standing in a heavy draft. Chubby had trouble keeping quiet. His thoughts hollered silently at a high pitch, "Oh hell! This bastard is out of his mind!"

Du Preez enjoyed the expressions of surprise and bewilderment on the faces of the rugby officials, organisers and President Mandela. The huge frame of Dr. Louis Luyt, President of the South African Rugby

Federation, rose and he waved his arms as if trying to frighten a hungry vulture from a helpless lamb.

Cold shock ran through Chubby when he noticed that the instrument flashed the weapons-engaged signal. The twenty-millimetre nose-canon of the Martial Eagle was now enslaved to Du Preez's helmet sight and followed his every head and eye movement. From where the nose-gun hung pointing forward, it now dropped down thirty degrees and turned sharply towards the stand.

Du Preez slanted his head to the left and flashed a sadistic smile while slowly saluting the VIP's. Chubby heard him shout over the intercom, "Hello and goodbye President Mandela ... Blam! Blam! Blam! Blam! And to hell with you and your black comrades! See you later Nelly alligator!"

Chubby froze, "Skip, this is a bloody sick game you're playing! Drop it man. Are you out of your mind?"

"I told you to keep your whining trap shut, you little red chicken."

Anger filled Chubby Wilson and something deep inside him gave way. The crowd roared with admiration. The media later described The Martial Eagle's manipulation as an "animated salute to President Mandela from the country's technology flagship."

Du Preez reversed the agile helicopter back to the centre of the grounds, made a handstand manoeuvre and then ripped it vertically out of its parking position with thunderous motors and cracking rotor blades. He missed the oncoming, low flying Boeing, carrying its message of good luck, by a breathtaking margin and disappeared into the hazy sky that covered the city.

"Hell! Are we going to hear a lot about this senseless stunt of yours?" Chubby still shivered from the angst of an impending crash.

"Say's who, Ginger Boy?' Du Preez sounded calm and matter-of-factly.

"Just get that radio back on and listen to what Captain Jakes Johnson has on his mind," Chubby said, starting to regain his composure.

"Agh! To hell with that ol' arsehole."

They took their course towards Africair's landing strip. Chubby heard Du Preez sing to the tune of the well-known nursery rhyme, "Who's afraid of that big bad Johnson ...big bad Johnson."

Du Preez clicked on the radio, "Hello, Jakes old boy! Reporting - completion of Martial Eagle's contribution to the Rugby World Cup's curtain raiser. It was a show with a difference by the world's most super attack helicopter!"

The organisers were left with the task to convince everybody that it was all a display of excellent organisation, technical discipline and a show of South Africa's first world aviation capability.

3.

MANDELA'S RUGBY JERSEY

ELLIS PARK RUGBY STADIUM, JOHANNESBURG

The team of hosts, who were agitated by the disruptive demonstration of the Martial Eagle eventually succeeded in bringing order to the presidential suite at Ellis Park Rugby Stadium. It was now time for the World Rugby Cup Final's kick-off. In the locker rooms the teams were warmed up to near exhaustion and dressed in their rugby gear. By the time Dr. Marlene Brooks had succeeded in isolating President Nelson Mandela from the rest of his entourage and hosts, he had just enough time left to slip on a Springbok rugby jersey and cap over his shirt and tie. He was ready to go onto the field and meet the finalists. The president's communications advisor gave a sigh of relief when she escorted the grand old man down to the exit tunnel. From his cell on Robben Island he could never have pictured this day on the Ellis Park rugby grounds, which witnessed so many historical test matches.

"I feel a little stuffy in this rugby jersey." The grey-haired president tugged at the green and gold garment with the embroidery of a Springbok antelope and protea flower as emblem.

"Sir, you only need to wear it for a few minutes. Perhaps if I take off your tie you will feel more comfortable. I will be waiting right here and when you return you can slip it on again, once you escaped out of that green jersey."

"Thank you Marlene. You are always sensitive about the small but important things in my life and, don't worry my sister, we will emerge from this with dignity." Nelson Mandela smiled at his attractive consultant. Little did they know that the Springboks would be victorious and the President had to don the jersey again later when he awarded the Rugby World Cup to the winners.

"Thank you for trusting me with your image, Mr. President." Marlene squeezed his arm. Mandela smiled with a slight wink and strode out onto the field towards the opposing teams while an unprecedented cheer filled the grounds of Ellis Park, like never before in its long history. Marlene watched the president walking onto the field, with his now familiar amble. His outstretched hands greeted the players and officials.

Marlene switched on her cellular phone to talk to the chief organiser. An incoming call beat her to the dialling button.

"From where I stand here in the suite of the Press Club I can see you clearly through my binoculars." It was Julius Grant, her partner in their communications agency, "Everything still running as planned?"

Marlene was irritated with her colleague's untimely call, "Yes. What else did you expect?" The stress of the moment got to her.

"Just, a little concerned. That's all. Talk to you later." Grant left her with the silent instrument still clutched to her ear. She felt remorseful about her sharp remark and tried to convey her regret by waving in Grant's direction, hoping that he still had her in the field of his binoculars.

4.

INVITATION TO DEATH

STADIUM PARKING LOT.

Gareth Williams was late for his appointment at the Ellis Park Ruby stadium. He underestimated the heavy traffic from his hotel which was located in a northern Johannesburg suburb. Somehow he assumed that moving around in South Africa was just as relaxed as when he was a team member of the touring British Rugby Lions, ten years ago. The promise to visit the top test rugby stadium of South Africa again, after so many years, filled him with excitement and nostalgia. He reminded himself to stay humble during the afternoon. At all times he would have to refrain from reminding anybody of the last-minute try he scored on that same field. On that occasion it was the final test match and not only did the British Lions win the match but the test series against the South African Springboks.

Williams particularly looked forward to meet his former rugby opponent, Herman de Witt, now a wealthy business tycoon, who invited him and sponsored his visit. Perhaps the message he carried from the British Ministry of Defence for the South African Minister of Defence, Joe Modise, was the reason for his hospitality. However, De Witt who was now Chairman of the Board of Africair Corporation would not be too pleased to hear that only indirect benefits would develop in favour of his company from a future British weapons contract. Apart from his business errant, Williams hoped that there would be enough time to meet all the other old rugby friends. He also would like to bump into Julius Grant again, so that he could whisper in his ear the rather intriguing message that he carried. A skilful issues-writer like Grant would need only half a word to understand the sensitive nature of military business between their countries.

Williams' old Lions rugby blazer lay folded on the passenger seat. He made sure that the parking vouchers, entrance-ticket and invitation to Africair's suite were in the inside pocket. There was a long queue to the entrance of the crowded parking lot and the parking was slow. He grew impatient and every so often glanced at his Seiko. He did not want to miss any of the ceremony that usually preceded a final rugby match of this kind.

Eventually Williams nudged through and parked the rented Toyota on stand ninety-three. From the glove compartment he took the red Avis folder and made a note of the parking bay number and the car registration before slipping it into his blazer pocket. It could become a nuisance if he had to hunt for his car after the match and the cocktails that normally followed these occasions till late in the evening. Williams looked in the rear view mirror and decided that his hair was still in good order. He grabbed his jacket, slid from behind the steering wheel and pushed the key into the door lock.

"Mister Gareth Williams - from London?"

Williams swung round and smiled at three men who appeared from behind his car. "Yes. Good afternoon. I suppose Herman de Witt sent you chaps." He looked at the bearded man standing in the middle, "Are you gents the welcoming committee?" and laughed at his own remark. Williams was a jovial person.

The bearded man answered with a heavy Afrikaans accent, "I suppose in a way you can call us that. As a matter of fact, I have brought something very special for you." He stood close and in front of Williams who looked a little amused.

Too late Williams saw the silencer of a nine-millimetre Parabellum in his big hairy hand. He heard the muffled shot, before the bullet penetrated his heart from a distance of six inches. The projectile gushed out of his rib cage and shattered the side window of the Toyota behind him. With a thud the lead-pointed bullet lodged into the passenger seat.

The two men, who stood close to the bearded man, grabbed Williams by the arms, opened the door through the broken window and seated him behind the steering wheel. Williams' head flopped backwards against the headrest. They slammed the door shut, jumped into a red Volkswagen cargo van, which in the meantime drove up with the sliding door wide open. Within a matter of seconds the assassins reached the exit of the parking lot. With little regard for the oncoming traffic they drove over the concrete median of the busy street. Amidst angry honking and screeching brakes from the oncoming cars, they sped off in a westerly direction with tyres that churned up a blue haze from the tarmac. It all happened so fast that it took a while for some of the excited rugby fans in the parking lot to realise what actually happened.

5.

Winners and Losers.

Eastern Johannesburg Village

The birth of the Rainbow Nation of South Africa was magnified by their victory of an international rugby final. President Nelson Mandela, donned in a green and gold rugby jersey, stood with raised arms and fists in the cold evening air of Johannesburg's Ellis Park. Francois Pienaar, the tall captain of the triumphant Springbok rugby team, stood beside the smiling president. Pienaar held the newly won World Rugby Cup with outstretched arms above his head. The thunderous roar of the ninety thousand spectators rolled over the Golden City's skyline, and dubbed the twilight with a throbbing sound.

"We are the champions - - - we are the champions." Their team's favourite song rose upward likes a spontaneous anthem. In the homes, bars, clubs and cars of forty million people, all over the Republic of South Africa, the culturally divided nation for once had a proud reason to unify in their celebrations.

With disbelief, the rest of the world's rugby nations witnessed the event on television and two hundred million viewers around the rugby world saw how the South African Springboks triumphed over the All Blacks team from New Zeeland. The Springboks ran a victory round and displayed the Rugby World Cup to a face-painted and flag-waving crowd. The Rainbow Nation was elated, proud and loved their team and charismatic president. A night marked by crazy parties, toasts, dancing, and singing began. On the streets inside South Africa's borders, from north to south and from the East coast to the West coast, festivities began. The revelry was the pinnacle and grateful deliverance from almost eight weeks of rugby excitement and match anxiety.

At his huge home on the eastern side of Johannesburg, Johann Kurtz rose from his easy chair and silently left his television room. He pushed his large hands deep into the pockets of his blue slacks. In his own reserved way he felt as if he just enjoyed a movie with a happy ending. Kurtz ambled towards the liquor cabinet in a softly lit lounge. He poured a four finger Johnny Walker, and added a good measure of ice.

Mark Fischer, his guest and subordinate, followed him. Fischer preferred another beer and snapped it open. He refrained from making any comments on the game and waited for the older man to talk. Fischer slowly poured the golden bubbly into a porcelain mug that depicted a German beer garden.

Their eyes met. "At least we are now officially the world's rugby champions. Perhaps it will do South Africa's general morale some good. The country bloody well needs it now." Kurtz took a good sip from his scotch.

"It will do absolute bugger-all for our international aviation business." Fisher fisted a subdued burp. He was well aware that his remark watered down the excitement of the moment. He had difficulty hiding his deeply ingrained antagonism about the general state of affairs of the country, his workplace, his home and future . . . Their glance conveyed an understanding between the two experienced aircraft-engineers. They had been working together in the military-aircraft business for more than fifteen years and over time developed a mode of communication that demanded few words.

"Listen, Mark, I know we are all in the pits because the British did not accept our Martial Eagle as an appropriate gun-ship for their attack helicopter needs. But although we lost the tender, there are still a few options left. In fact we are very close to 'secretly'," Kurtz made inverted signs with two fingers, "pick up some trade-offs to supply components for the British contract. Apart from pursuing the many other business opportunities that exists in the world attack helicopter market."

Mark Fischer gave his boss a long indifferent look. Over the years he also developed a dislike in Kurtz's business and management style. Sometimes his antagonism showed and the sensitive CEO of Africair Corporation noticed this. Fischer hated the way Kurtz sometimes played his cards so close to the chest. Particularly with regard to those matters that touched on Fischer's area of responsibility. Although Fischer steered the company's international marketing program, he always felt that his CEO had his own hidden marketing agenda.

From time to time Kurtz would come up with a surprise like now. Fischer wondered why, for heaven's sake, must he I hear of this new development or so called 'business opportunity' in this casual manner. Like here and now at his home while the television is blasting out the highlights of a silly rugby victory. His response reflected his stifled inner feelings, "Sorry Boss, I think I must have missed out while reading the latest marketing notes. What 'trade-offs' are you referring to?"

"No, there was nothing about that in the notes." Kurtz sensed Fischer's hidden indignation, "Why do you think I gave up my seat at the stadium? So that Gareth Williams could watch the rugby at Ellis Park this afternoon?"

Fischer knew Gareth Williams from the British Defence Ministry quite well. He had to entertain him more often than he cared to remember and aired his frustration, "That's obvious. Despite the fact that we got sweet blow all out of the UK contract, we abused the conceited little Englishman many times to gain special information so that we could strengthen our bid against the American's attack helicopter. Or perhaps you felt that we owed him something. I suppose it is just natural for you to be a nice to the guy for old time's sake. Or maybe you're hoping that in future some new business may come forward. In any event, perhaps this may happen only long after the two of us have been ousted from the industry as a result of Mandela's enforced affirmative action."

Kurtz raised his thin eyebrows. The scotch strengthened his authoritative manner. He glanced at Fischer and detested the cynical and sometimes negative outlook that the astute engineer developed over the past few years. Perhaps it was the effect of the company's continuously unsuccessful attempts to sell South Africa's eight-ton attack helicopter in a highly competitive and demanding international marketplace.

"Something did come up, though. As you know, I was allocated a seat for this match, right next to that of Defense Minister, Joe Modise which I made available to Gareth. I am sure that he had time enough during the match to whisper the important message from Sir Michael Riffkind, in Modise's ear. Williams requested an environment that did not allow for too much formal discussion. He merely wanted to personally pass on the British MOD's message to Modise without being lured into a discussion. I thought this match would be an ideal opportunity to do exactly that."

"You were very clever, boss." Fischer's sarcasm nibbled at Kurtz's tolerance but he chose to ignore it.

"Furthermore, I can no longer stand the sympathetic remarks or questions about why we lost out on the British deal. That's why I preferred to sit here and watch the game on the telly. On the other hand I am not that much of a rugby fanatic. And so are you. Still, I appreciated you spending the afternoon with me." Kurtz hoped that Fischer would take his leave sooner than later.

"What's the message?" Mark tried to pretend that he knew very little about the real reason for the English official's visit. On the other hand he did not expect an outright or clear answer. Not if Kurtz kept to his normal business style.

Johann Kurtz poured himself another dark tanned scotch. He grappled ice out of the bucket with his large hand and slowly dropped the cubes in his glass, "I am not completely informed but I could make a good guess." Fischer knew this was where Kurtz's 'management-by-lies' style would kick-in; Kurtz lit a Rothmans, inhaled deeply and coughed. "But what I presume is that, to soothe the relationships between John Major and Nelson Mandela, we may be called upon to supply some components - in conjunction with an English company of course."

Fischer admired Kurtz's believable lie. He had some knowledge of the content of the message Williams had to deliver but decided to use the opportunity to play out his game of deceit. "What components?"

Kurtz stroke the rim of his glass with his hairy middle finger. "Perhaps, landing gear." Fischer's expression made him add, " ... or even some real-time avionics."

"What? South African made components, for an American Cayuse or Cobra? Somebody must be farken dreaming. Perhaps you can bullshit one of our recently elected politicians who are still new in our business but nobody else. In any case, it sounds like a petty cash option to me."

Fischer could not hide his despondency. And the beer did nothing for him. Perhaps it made him a little aggressive. Suddenly he felt tired and wanted to call Janet to join him at an Irish Keg Bar. She is crazy about rugby. Her old man was an international player who represented South Africa in the Fifties. Perhaps a long night of Springbok victory celebrations will put his girlfriend in one of those rare erotic moods. He needs to zap-off all his frustrations. Perhaps then he would be geared again to bear the boss and a totally new set of circumstances on Monday.

"You must not make the mistake to underestimate minister Modise. That ex-MK-man is a soldier with real courage. And he is clued up too. He also has a keen eye for business. During the past year he paid several visits to London and had many long discussions with both John Major and Riffkind. He also worked his backside off to support our marketing efforts at the past five international military and aviation shows. You know that. No ways a guy like Gareth Williams could, or even would try to bullshit the old man. Gareth is too polished for that. I am still convinced the message will be a good one. It might at least spell out a future strategy or promise a potential   contract - perhaps even in another armaments discipline." Kurtz felt that this was as close as he could get to speculate on the real purpose of Williams' visit. It was enough information for Fischer, at this stage.

Fischer recognised that his boss was, as usual, not outright open with him. Bloody bastard! The thought nearly slipped from his bitter tongue. The message, that was really the so-called 'Williams-plan" had to be prevented at all cost. Disgust rose like bile in his throat but he kept a rational pose.

Kurtz signalled to Fischer to recharge his mug. Before he could decline, the phone rang in Kurtz's study.

"I suppose it's a call from my neighbour who will be elated out of his wits with the results . . . and very sozzled by now. This is going to be one very long and giddy night."

While Kurtz spoke on the phone Fischer returned to where the television sounded the irritable six-o-clock news sting. Most of the newscast was dedicated to the South African rugby world cup victory. The elated remarks of the captain, President Mandela and other sporting dignitaries summed up the joy of the nation.

Fischer, however, was uptight with anticipation. He assured himself that the newscast could not yet carry an item on Gareth Williams' fate. He suddenly was unsure of how he would respond should the news break on the Englishman's 'accident'. Fischer stressfully wondered how he would stand up to the impending reality that the subversive actions of his political affiliation would bring about.

Kurtz picked up. On the line was Africair's head of security Fredrick Kramer. He opened with an apology, "Sorry to bother you sir, but I have rather disturbing news."

Kurtz sounded his jovial mood, "No man, and it's good news! Didn't you hear? We gave those All Blacks a good thrashing. Although with a slight margin of only three points, it was good enough to make us the world champions. And to think that in '87 and '91 we were nowhere!"

"Yes sir, but . . ." Kramer tried to be polite to his boss but could not keep the stress out of his voice.

Kurtz sensed the tough security man's anxiety, "What's bothering you Fred?"

"Sir, I'm calling from the Ellis Park Rugby Stadium's security room. I just spoke to officers from the Central Police Station. I wanted to confirm all the available facts before I called you."

"What the hell went wrong man? Something happened at the factory? Why are you still at Ellis Park? The game stopped more than an hour ago. Are you . . .?"

"Your guest, Mr. Gareth Williams from the British Department of Defence, is dead, sir!"

A long silence lingered. The bland statement jerked Kurtz upright. The fuzziness from the scotch and his elated spirit left him instantly. He slowly placed his glass in the centre of the green blotter on the desk. He slid sideways on to the desktop, his left leg swinging.

"Are you there sir?"

"Yes - - - yes." He tried his best to keep an orderly mind.

"Fred, tell me what happened ... how was he ... killed?" Kurtz could not picture a dead Gareth Williams. He was a fast-moving energetic man, like the rugby player he ... was.

"The facts are very skimpy at this stage, sir. I was told that he was apprehended in the VIP parking lot by two or three thugs. Apparently he was shot at point blank range just as he got out of his car. They left him, bleeding profusely in his car while they sped off. By the time a passer-by managed to call an ambulance and the police from her cellular phone, he had already died of a chest wound."

"How did you hear about the incident?"

"As you know sir, with all the important guests at the chalet, I was on duty with one of my men. A police officer found our invitation card, with other personal identification documents, on Williams. A senior police officer brought us the message with a request for more information about Williams. Although the attack took place only minutes before the start of the game, we only heard about it towards the end."

"Who communicated with the defence minister?"

"In the absence of our public relations chap, I informed the minister, sir."

"And what was his reaction? I mean, what did Minister Modise say when you gave him the news about Williams?"

"With shock of course, but he immediately took charge of the situation."

"And ...?"

"He asked to be informed of as much background as possible and then dictated a short response for the purpose of media enquiries. He also mentioned that he would like to talk to you as soon as possible."

"OK, I will come right over."

"That would be near impossible with all the outgoing traffic, sir. In any case, the minister has already left. I suggest you call him an hour from now at his home. I do know that he will be a guest of the Pretoria Rugby Club at their celebration function after nine this evening."

"Will do so. Ask John Molape to call me."

"You mean the public relations manager, sir?"

"Yes man, who else?"

"Right now Molape is on his way to Dubai, sir. His flight left about an hour ago"

"To do what?"

Fred Kramer's responsibility was to scan the overseas visits of all staff, from a security viewpoint. He had knowledge of the itineraries of all personnel travelling abroad and the objectives of their trips.

"He has an appointment with 'The Gulf News' and saw it as an opportunity to lobby other Gulf media to facilitate publicity for our participation in the next aviation show in Dubai. From there he will be going on to Kuala Lumpur to talk to the media about the Lankawi Air Show in Malaysia."

"Sounds like another of his well planned jolly outings. He should be concentrating on the Malaysian media alone at this stage. OK. Fred, keep in touch and stop calling me sir all the time."

Johann Kurtz dropped the phone and sat quietly in the dark study. He fumbled for a cigarette and for a moment the flame from his Dunhill lit up the lines of his troubled face. A long intense red glow followed. He stood up slowly and thought about a thousand things simultaneously. A portentous concern started to develop deep inside the big man's chest. It made him horribly uneasy.

Now he had to tell Fischer about this and he could only guess at the tirade of remarks that would follow. "What a bloody mess! And on a night like this where there will be no room for any form of sober thinking," he said aloud.

When Kurtz returned to the television room the newscast was just about to be concluded. He guessed that most of the cast was dedicated to South African's victory.

"Still at Ellis Park," the suave anchorman read from the teleprompter. "A British subject was shot and killed in what was apparently an attempted car highjack in the Ellis Park field's parking lot. It is believed that the person would have been the guest of the Minister of Defence, Mr Joe Modise. They were to share a hospitality suite at the rugby this afternoon. Minister Modise expressed his shock and forwarded his condolences. The name of the deceased will not be released until his next of kin has been informed of his unfortunate fate."

Kurtz was relieved from the task to break the news to Fischer. He looked intently at the younger man whose thick eyebrows were tied in a knot. He was clearly uncomfortable with what he heard.

"My, my - so dear old Williams could not deliver his message. And there goes our last British option for more business to save the country's aviation industry," Fischer mocked with a coarse voice. He displayed no shock or emotion. It added to Kurtz's growing discomfort.

"To hell with you man! A dear friend of ours just died. Dammit!" Delayed shock caused Kurtz's trenchant reaction.

6.

DATE IN DUBAI.

SHERATON HOTEL, DUBAI

From where he stood in his room on the tenth floor of the Sheraton Dubai hotel, John Molape followed the city's activities below him with relaxed dark eyes. The brown tinted pane of the wide window presented him with a soft sepia picture. The scenery lacked the brilliant reflection of the blue channel and the white sandy surroundings. His mind was equally at ease and he was not thinking about anything in particular.

His eyes shifted from the slow singles game played on the hotel's tennis court to the large white yacht moored in front of the hotel's side entrance. It was well past six yet outside the Saturday evening still glimmered with the Gulf's desert heat. There was very little traffic in the street below. It was as if the people of the city, and its cosmopolitan visitors, waited for relief from the mid-July temperature promised by the impending darkness.

The huge South African scratched his densely curled head with a thumbnail and wondered how long his guest would keep him waiting. His natural sense of humour made him smile wryly at the perception in his country that there was such a thing as 'African Time'. Black people were always accused of being late for appointments because they had their own perception of urgency. If that was true, then the few experiences he had in the Gulf States taught him that there was such a thing as 'Arabian Time'.

"We black South Africans may have our own values as far as the clock is concerned," he mused, "because my traditional upbringing taught me that to always be in a rush, is a sign of immaturity or rather bad self-control. But these desert people sometimes have problems with their calendar!" Molape smiled at his reflection in the mirror as if he shared his whispered remark with a dear old friend.

Molape enjoyed the calm of the Dubai creek and followed a lazy skit as it drew a long trail on the surface of the bay. He could not help but admire the lush green parks and shady spaces between the skyscrapers, which lined the causeway. It was difficult to believe that this was a desert, transformed drop by drop through hydroponic irrigation systems into lush green scenery. Molape turned his attention to the new camera equipment that he bought at a bargain price in the nearby souk. He was a keen photographer who won a few awards while he was still a reporter and news photographer for 'The Sowetan', South Africa's largest black daily newspaper.

The sound from the doorbell brought Molape back to the business at hand. With a few long strides he reached the door of the suite and opened the heavy door widely. He looked down at a frail man with a heavy black moustache and gold rimmed spectacles. His white Arab dress surrounded him with an air that called for respect.

"Mister Molape? We spoke on the phone. The name is Assad from the Gulf News." He was soft-spoken and carried a Fleet Street accent. It betrayed Akbar Assad's journalistic background.

"Yes, good afternoon Mr. Assad." He stretched out an open hand.

Assad measured the tall man from his toes to his broad smile, which displayed exceptionally strong white teeth. His appearance impressed him. He could not help but notice the expensive dark brown trousers and shoes that blended softly with the mustard coloured Polo shirt and dark complexion. Molape was an attractive man with fine taste and the magnetism of a sport star.

"Thank you so much for the effort to meet me on a Sunday evening … but please, do come in." Molape led the way to the lounge area.

Assad followed and sat down on a couch, which allowed him to enjoy the scenery. He slowly moved his gaze from the Creek and locked eyes with Molape.

"Coffee?" Molape moved towards the phone on the desk. His security chief, Fredrick Kramer, briefed him on Arabian customs. He advised him never to invite an Arab gentleman for ' a drink'.

"Yes, please."

Molape ordered and seated himself opposite Assad. He placed his feet neatly on the green patterned carpet in accordance with Arab custom and leaned slightly forward with his arms resting on his knees. He was eager to tell Assad as much as he could about Africair and the company's business objectives in the Gulf States.

"My apology for being late, but I just could not leave the re-run on television. I mean the final game for the Rugby World Cup between your country and New Zealand. Congratulations. The Springboks are now the world champions. I suppose you feel good about it?" Assad tried to break the ice.

"Yes, I suppose so. But like most black South Africans I am a soccer fan. For this reason I can't wait for the African Soccer Cup series, which will take place next year. There is a possibility that the series will be played in my country. That is, if we are chosen to host the series." With democracy restored in South Africa and as a member of the ANC, Molape felt good and somewhat proud to refer to South Africa as 'my country'.

Assad had enough of the sporting angle as an opener for their meeting.

"You wanted to brief me on your company's participation at the Dubai Air Show during November." Assad slowly slid a wire-spine notebook from the side pocket of his garment and placed it on the table in front of them.

"Yes." Molape reached for his briefcase and handed Assad an illustrated booklet. "I brought you a copy of our latest portfolio and would like to talk you through it."

Blatant free promotional stunt, Assad thought. He had drawers full of company and product brochures. "Yes, thank you. But tell me what new products or aviation systems are you going to introduce?" His sense for hard news broke through.

"Well, you will remember that we introduced our eight ton helicopter to the international market, and displayed it for the first time here in Dubai."

Assad's gaze traced the city skyline, "The Martial Eagle?" He still remembered how the ugly machine flew low over the show crowds. To cries of amazement it pulled out of a barrel roll, shot up in the sky and came down through a loop - - a first in aviation history for a helicopter of that weight.

"Yes!" Molape flashed his huge smile.

"That must have been two years ago. Yes, I can remember vaguely. I was with the London Sunday Times then. But I did attend the helicopter shows at Middle Wallop and Farnborough where I saw its flight demonstrations." Assad flicked his gold ballpoint pen and searched for an empty space in his notebook. He was still waiting for something worth his while to jot down.

The coffee arrived and for a while the men busied themselves with the fine porcelain, pouring and stirring.

"I can remember writing about the announcement that you did not qualify for the UK tender to supply about ninety heavy attack helicopters for the British Forces." Assad kept on stirring his coffee absently.

"Yes." Molape pulled a face.

"Our bid was unsuccessful because we were not permitted to integrate American Hellfire missiles on the Martial Eagle's weapons platform. Lots of international political games ruled us out of the race. Not so much a lack of state of the art technology."

Assad listened to Molape's drawn-out account and wondered if he would be a reliable first contact for what he had in mind. He decided that it would take time. But he was patient and careful.

"Tell me. Why did you name your helicopter the 'Martial Eagle'?" He tried his utmost to sound interested. It was particularly difficult because of the detailed briefing he got some weeks ago from his covert network's agent. He knew just about all there was to know about the Martial Eagle's state of the art technology. The young Arab was asked to be particularly interested in any recent developments and the names of the key role players who were responsible for the development of this formidable machine. He also had to evaluate Molape as a potential source or leak to obtain technical information about the Martial Eagle. For that reason alone, he was prepared to listen to the talkative communications manager of Africair.

"Well, when our gunship progressed from the development stage to start with test flights we referred to it as our demonstrator. The project and marketing manager, Mark Fischer, then wrote a competition, calling for an appropriate name." Molape noticed Assad's bored expression.

"So, that's how it came to be named the Martial Eagle?"

"Quite an appropriate name, I would think. In the southern parts of Africa this is a powerful and savage bird with terrifying talons. It is indigenous to Southern Africa and feeds on small mammals, reptiles and birds. The wing span of the Martial Eagle is more than two metres, you know."

"My goodness!" Assad smiled with surprise. Like many Arab men, he was interested in eagles.

"The name was acceptable because Fischer could compare all the other characteristics of this species with his attack helicopter's capabilities." For a moment the image of Fischer with his, sometimes, severe attitude flashed across Molape's mind.

"So, your helicopter was not successful in the UK. Has it since undergone further development? Do you see a market for the Martial Eagle in this part of the world? Who would be your potential clients? Have you obtained your government's approval to market to any Arabian State?"

Assad sat forward with his notebook on his knee. For the first time he sounded like a serious journalist who wanted to get the detail and get the hell out. Like he wanted to rush off to his word processor and file his story.

Assad's pose misled Molape completely. He was sure that he captured the small journalist's curiosity. This guy will be a good media contact, he thought. I can smell some good coverage coming here. If so, we must give him special treatment. The Gulf News carries good circulation and has a wide syndicate network. I will even invite him to visit our factory in Johannesburg. The thought made Molape smile.

7.

THE LONDON AGENT.

SOHO, LONDON.

London's streets were shiny-damp. The curve in Flitcroft Street, Soho, disappeared in the mist that hazed the Saturday afternoon. The July weather contributed to the absence of elbow space in the crowded bars of the Old Town. The situation was even worse in the Silver Fern Bar, where a telecast was about to run the Rugby World Cup final between South Africa and New Zealand. The occasional opening and slamming of the front door as newcomers dropped in, did not allow enough time for the fresh, damp air to dilute the smoke-filled bar-atmosphere.

Douglas Collins who just walked in, wondered how to find his way to the crowded bar counter. He lacked the rudeness of someone like his brother-in-law, who always quickly found his way to wherever he wanted to go. The smell of smoke and liquor, slightly fragranced by the perfume and after-shave of a cheerful group of young men and women who stood close to him, swept Collins' concern from his mind. The place was cosy. He shook the dampness from his short umbrella, slowly rolled and clipped the ringlet. He gradually found his way to the counter, caught the barman's eye, and ordered two Johnny Walkers with ice and club sodas on the side.

With the two tumblers neatly parked on the teak bar top he awaited Brian Boddington's arrival that was always late for an appointment. But he always turned up and never failed to draw the attention of patrons when he arrived. For him, it was no effort to secure the best spot in any London bar. It is always easy to force consideration when you are loud, halfway intoxicated and move around robustly in a wheelchair.

Brian Boddington rammed open the Silver Fern's squeaky doors with a jarring bang. Although it was not loud enough to stop or silence the high-volume hum of the bar-talk, it did turn a good many heads away from the television cast where the camera zoomed in on the rugby captains. They were tossing for the privilege to choose the playing direction. The Springboks got the better choice and for the All Blacks this should have served as an early warning signal about the outcome of the game.

The huge man, obviously discontented to be tied to a wheel chair, glided soundlessly down the swiftly opening path towards Collins, where the scotch begged to be sipped. Boddington was in a determined mood and sober. He noticed that he caught Collins off-guard.

"How are you doing, brother Brian?" The bar noise muffled the half-hearted greeting from Collins. If there was one thing that Boddington could not stand it was to face his brother-in- law when he was sober and soured.

"Hi Doug! What the hell is this all about?" When in an abstinent mood, Boddington was a severe man to deal with. However, Collins tolerated his moods, purely out of understanding how difficult it had to be for an attractive and once virile man to deal with the unfortunate outcome of a helicopter crash. It happened only days before he was due to return from Vietnam. During 1970, Boddington's helicopter was hit over a particularly dangerous area. His Bell-Cobra crashed into a forest and slammed this man of six-foot five into a wheelchair for the rest of his life. The career of a most accomplished "Snake Driver" as the pilots of the Cobra AH-IG Attack Helicopters were called ended abruptly.

But Collins had a most unusual mission in mind for Boddington that would allow the pension-strapped man to earn a handsome fee.

"First say hello to our Johnny Walkers. They have been waiting here very impatiently for nearly an hour." Collins was such a habitual, smooth talker that he became comfortable with the facts that he distorted so easily.

"To blazes with you Doug. It's not my fault if you arrived too early. Also, the ice cubes in these glasses is far from being watered down. Listen, this evening I am in no mood for your bullshit stories. In any case, I hope we are here for more reasons than to watch the finals of the Rugby World Cup. If not, I must've underestimated the seriousness of your hang-up about the silly game of rugby that you imperialists invented and forced onto your colonies. May this tame, touch-type of ballgame never take root in the States." The Houston drawl in his baritone voice was obvious.

"Exactly brother. Do you think rugby would be the only reason why I would invite an American to this bar, with its New Zealand sentiments plastered all over the walls? We'll come to the main point on the agenda a little later, Brian. It is just about kick-off time…"

"Pass me the booze and let me suffer through this game in silence please – if that would be at all possible. If I were an Englishman I would have been ashamed to watch a sports final between two of my former colonies. Especially if my people were the inventor of the game but played it so lousy that we were ousted long before the semi-finals. You Brits are such a useless lot of bastards! You were unable to walk over the Americans; you lost the war against a small band of Boers and made a spectacular mess of every form of governance in India. Then the Americans had to come to your aid to save your balls from the Germans in war two. When Vietnam raged you bloody stiff upper-lipped islanders looked the other way. No wonder that the only shitty pleasure that you can have on a summer Saturday, is to watch how your offspring do what you couldn't achieve. I bet you would give your super royal balls to be in this lime-light."

Collins listened undisturbed to his trenchant but still sober brother-in-law's attack of word-diarrhea. He pretended not to have heard the swear words and provocation. It was in any case not his intention to land them in yet another silly, drawn-out argument. It happened so many times in the past. There was only one way to move Boddington into an acceptable frame of mind. Get him half-drunk. Then his bitterness about everything that he regarded as detrimental to his life, his mind, and his emotions would be smoothed-over. Smooth enough to allow him to be even open-minded to new opportunities.

"Sure, I did not only invite you to enjoy this afternoon's rugby with me. In that respect you are right. As far as the history is concerned, leading up to this moment in time? To me that is inconsequential. Stop your aggressive, overbearing American brazenness, drink this smooth Scottish whiskey and watch the game." Collins hoped it would still the tremble in the claw-like hands that were tugging at the tires of the wheelchair.

Collins reached for the scotch and lifted his slightly shaking glass towards Collins. His mumbled "whatever'…" was drowned by the noise in the bar. The taste of the Johnny Walker made Boddington wondered why he was so embittered towards his English relative. In actual fact, Collins was a successful businessman and could be useful to him, especially in his dismal circumstances. The drink eased his decision to change his grumpy mood.

The big screen showed that the South Africans opened up the scoreboard. Just to sound a little amiable Boddington asked, "Who would you like to walk off with the cup?" The bar became extremely noisy after the successful converter and he was not exactly interested in the answer to his question. So he signaled for another JW.

Douglas Collins did not answer him. He tilted his head and pulled up his shoulders. He just wanted to stay sober enough to wheel Boddington out of the bar after the game. He also wanted desperately to involve him in his potentially lucrative project. But he wanted to do it in such a way that Boddington, in a half-drunken state, would not find enough reason to argue or resist. He cautioned himself to carefully pace their whiskey intake.

The Johnny Walkers made it bearable for Boddington to watch the game to its conclusion. Outside, the rain had stopped and Collins wheeled Boddington at a brisk pace towards their favorite Chinese restaurant. They called for a de-boned fried duck with toppings and side orders.

"Brian, I need your professional help. And I need it desperately." Collins tried to see how much focus was left in the eyes of the battered "Snake Driver".

The crispy dish brought Boddington to a state of relaxed, sobriety. He pushed back the wheelchair and laboriously wiped his mouth. He burped loudly and looked quizzically at Collins. "How can a disabled Cobra pilot, assist a successful aviation marketing agent like Mister Douglas Collins?" Another loud burp followed his sarcastic remark.

Collins maintained his pose and ignored the mockery. He was pleased that the situation developed exactly as he wished for. The moment was right to present his proposal to Boddington. "Your assistance and co-operation could land you a neat half- a-million."

Boddington slowly lowered his liqueur, "Half a million what?"

"American Dollars – what else?"

"Bullshit!"

"OK. So you're not interested?" Collins pretended to lose interest in their conversation

"First tell me more." Boddington became serious and stretched forward to accept the Pall-Mall offered by Collins, hastily lit up and blew the first hazy fumes in total disregard of the other guests in the restaurant, towards the ceiling.

"It is all about helicopters. Attack helicopters. Heavy stuff you know. Real gunships that can destroy tanks." Now he had Boddington's full attention.

"In your game, who's buying and who's selling?" The cigarette trembled slightly between the ex-pilot's bony fingers.

"The market for attack helicopter replacements is currently really big. The main forces of the world need about eight hundred over the next four years. And that is not counting the potential needs of Mainland China. This is a conservative estimate from our marketing research agency in Seattle." Collins waited to see if he had succeeded in drawing Boddington into his speculation.

Collins knew that he hooked Boddington, who still kept abreast of the latest developments in the aviation industry, when the pilot said, "And I suppose that about half of that will be traditionally supplied by American aircraft at about fifty million apiece. Man, you're right there. We're talking mega-money."

"I agree, but there are a few competitors for the Americans. And these bastards are only confusing the marketplace and making things difficult for us. I mean for me." Collins pulled a face.

"It doesn't seem to be a problem to you. Not if I judge your role to secure the American contract for McKinley-Arthur to supply those ninety Warrior-machines to the UK." Boddington wondered just how much commission Collins took home. His company, World Aviation Promotions, or WAP as it was generally known, was the sole marketing agent for the American helicopter manufacturing company. McKinley-Arthur's attack helicopter, the Warrior, was favored above several contenders.

"I did not play such an important role to secure the order for the Warrior as you would think. Helicopter needs are defined by the pilots, as you surely would know." Collins tried to downplay his role.

Boddington pulled a face, "Yes. That is where it starts but it does not end there. Then the ranks start to play a role. I'm talking of those guys with the Milky Way on their shoulders. They determine what the poor chopper pilots will fly. By then, it is to hell with all user and tactical demands." Boddington stomped out his cigarette and shredded it vigorously in the small glass ashtray and shook his head, "Eventually an acquisitioning land on the politicians table. And then, smooth agents like you simply buy these decision-makers."

"Perhaps you are right. But, as you said, the politicians are the real decision-takers. For them, factors like international interests and relationships start to play a non-technical role. By then there is just about no chance for a little agent like myself to 'buy' anybody." Collins started to develop the scene for Boddington to understand how he could play a role in a future transaction.

"Little agent! My eye! Picking up fat commissions and other forms of remuneration? Living like you do and playing around in all the world's most expensive fun places." Boddington looked at his relative from his expensive shoes, suit, and stopped at his tie. Then right in the eyes, "Looking at the size of politicians' salaries I would say it should be easy for you to palm a few hands with currency to shape their minds."

Collins did not respond to this remark. "Sometimes one can influence the course of events to ensure that certain bids succeed or fail." Collins cleared his throat and tried to evaluate how Boddington received his remark.

"Is that how you clipped the wings of the South Africans' Martial Eagle bid - for the Royal Air Force?"

"Not exactly." Collins coughed and avoided his eyes.

"Then how did it come about that they lost the British contract. I mean, your British stripe-suited guys were their friends throughout the years of their Apartheid-regime. Despite the demands you placed on those pigheaded Afrikaners to change their inhumane political structure."

"Other political priorities played a role in the British Cabinet's decision not to buy South African-made helicopters..." Collins coughed again and offered another cigarette to Boddington, before he ordered black coffee.

"Oh? Despite the fact that now the country's whole political dispensation has changed? Thanks to old Baldy De Klerck who decided that Uncle Mandela can walk out of jail a free man?" Boddington liked to mock his English relative's awkward political viewpoints.

"Despite that – yes". Collins looked at the patterns on the tablecloth.

"And that, despite the fact that as president, nelson Mandela made all the right international moves? Said all the right things? Committed him to an unwavering attitude of reconciliation? And paid personal visits to Bill Clinton and John Major?" Boddington tried his best to understand how the South Africans lost the deal … or rather how the Americans, with the help of Douglas Collins, won the transaction.

"Those were routine political calls. In no way could President Mandela or the new political players influence the UK-decision." The coffee arrived. Collins asked for an artificial sweetener.

"What then swerved the decision in the Americans' favor?" Boddington sensed what was coming.

"I'm not sure. But my guess is that a lot of reasons of a higher strategic order played a role." Collins did not want to reveal how much he really knew of what went on behind the scenes.

"The papers and aviation magazines said it was because the Martial Eagle's missile-system did not measure up to specs. Was that the real reason?" Boddington could talk about aircraft all night long but he sensed that Collins wanted to steer the conversation into a more conclusive direction.

"Yes and no. The Martial Eagle's weapons-platform, as you would know, is designed to carry any type of missile system. So it could have been possible to integrate the American Hellfire system, which the UK preferred, with the systems of the Martial Eagle." Collins knew more about the technical requirements of helicopter acquisitioning than he was prepared to admit to Boddington.

"If you were such thick buddies with the new black government of South Africa, why didn't you just whacked the stuff on board the Martial Eagle and -- and Bob's your uncle?"

"Because you Americans imposed a weapons and defense technology embargo on South Africa as result of that much publicized Philadelphia court case. That's why."

Boddington pulled a face, " OK, but don't forget, that court case was all about those sly weapons smugglers from South Africa's defense industry, who illegally incorporated American components into their missile systems. And, later on they covertly shipped some of that technology to Sadam Hussein! And what's more, their illegal Apartheid government looked the other way."

"That has not yet been proved beyond doubt, you know." Collins wanted to avoid legal trivialities at all cost.

Boddington became irritable again, "Now what was the reason then?"

"As I said, there were strategic reasons of a higher order." Collins had to turn the argument his way now.

"Tell me about it." The Ronson lit up Boddington's lined face.

"Well, some people call it international interests," Collins started.

"Yes, and others call it 'Pentagon thinking'." Boddington's divided loyalty, as an American, who gave much of himself for a much-disputed war, came through.

"Whatever. There is a school of thought that claims that the comprehensive and highly competent South African defense industry kept Apartheid in power for at least fifteen years longer than necessary." Collins also lit another cigarette.

"Despite the political turnaround, I believe their industries are still going strong." Boddington regularly visited air shows and saw the South African technology on display.

"Yes, and there are still some well-founded fears that their capabilities will land in the hands of white right-wing elements who could apply it to restore apartheid or establish an Afrikaner homeland." Collins hoped that he gained ground.

"Hell that could start a new Bosnia-type theatre." International conflicts always interested Boddington.

"Personally, I doubt if that would easily happen. Not all Afrikaans-speaking people are right wing minded or even white, you know. The chances of a restoration of an Apartheid Government again are just as slim as America ever having a black president. "Collins regularly visited the Republic of South Africa under different pretences to find out about his main competitor, Africair's, capabilities and price structures.

"Then there is no reason to fear their prowess. I do believe their defense industry is responsible for more than fifty thousand jobs."

Collins had to swing the arguments to such an extent that it would strongly motivate Boddington to accept his request for assistance. As dangerous and with all the legal risk as it might be. "That may be true but there are other factors to be taken into consideration, which can have far more serious consequences than to maintain a few jobs."

"Like what?"

"The same capabilities which kept Apartheid in power, or could be of consideration to a right wing element, could also be made available to friends of the new black rule in South Africa. They need to reward their old friends for their assistance during the years of the ANC's struggle." Collins looked intently at the man in the wheel chair.

"What are you trying to tell me Doug?" Boddington's approach became warmer.

"Well, we all know who their friends are, Brian."

"You mean like Castro, Kaddafi, Arafat, Sadam, Syria, North Korea and a host of corrupt African leaders?"

"Exactly." Collins slowly nodded his head.

"Shit! That means that if they mismanaged their capability, their defense industry could become a bloody dangerous threat." Boddington lifted himself with his elbows and adjusted his seating.

Collins leaned forward, "Like you said, I don't think the Pentagon will be particularly happy or at ease with Castro or Sadam having some of the world's top attack helicopters and or longest range howitzers in their arsenals."

Boddington rubbed his hands, "Hell man! You're right. With the South Africans' latest base-bleed ammunition, the Cubans can reach up to fifty-five kilometers. By floating those guns towards Florida, they could make a mess of the surroundings at Key West and Miami and for that matter also Cape Kennedy. Or for that matter - any of the many military installations in Florida."

"And just think of the possibility of those projectiles carrying you know South African made light nuclear warheads!" Collins saw that his arguments brought real concern to the ex-helicopter pilot.

Boddington stroked the wheels of his chair. "Just think where those other characters can place a few shots. Hell Doug! This can create a whole new costly cold war scenario all over again. This side of the wall"

"That is exactly why America, as the world's only super power, should not favor any large military orders for the South Africans. It can only mean sustaining their industry, which will continue to arm the politicians whose objectives do not always concur with those of the United States and its allies." Collins tried to drive the argument in solidly.

"Is there another big order or bid in the pipeline?" Boddington began to wondered where he would fit in.

"Yes. I'm afraid so. And the closing date for bids will be announced shortly." Collins took the ticket from the waiter and reached for his credit card.

"And the clients?" Boddington's eyebrows shaped in a question mark.

"The Royal Malaysian Air Force. I believe they are shopping for forty gunships and you know what their sentiments are and to whom they may pass on such dangerous hardware."

Collins saw how Boddington's smile lit his face as this train of thought dawned on him. "What or how can I make a contribution to keep those South Africans out of the market place?"

Bingo! Collins thought. "You can make a considerable input by causing some disruption that may sink the Martial Eagle's next bid."

"And this could mean another big sale for you?" Boddington did not lose sight of the total picture.

"Yes - if we are successful with a Warrior bid." Collins poker-faced him.

"This 'disruption' you talk about, is it dangerous or risky?" The big hands trembled.

Collins slowly nodded his head, "Yes."

"And will it serve the good interest of our respective countries?" The big hands tightened on the thin rubber wheels

Collins was still in agreement, "Yes."

"Is that how I can land a million dollars?"

Collins shook his head sideways, "Half-a-million dollars."

"Then tell me all about it and where you see me fit in. I'm all ears." The big hands steadied.

8.

THE COMMUNICATIONS ADVISORS.

ELLIS PARK RUGBY STADIUM, JOHANNESBURG

The huge rugby stadium was littered, cold and deserted. Most of the floodlights were turned off. Only a selected number were left on to allow enough light for the cleaning-up operations. It was close to midnight and there was still much activity going on in the tournament organizer's office-suite. A dozen or so administrators were busy at tasks too imperative to be left until the following Monday. Dr Marlene Brooks stood behind her desk and carefully gathered her documents and placed them in her briefcase. She gave her cleared workstation a last glance as if she could not believe that the weeks of rugby-dominated activities were done.

"The game was a grand opportunity for us to boost the image of President Mandela. And it's a job well done. Even if I have to say so myself," Marlene said to a few members of the organizing staff. She was a popular public relations consultant, and well liked for her calm and efficient manner. Marlene stopped at each person's desk for a few last words of gratitude and farewell. She thanked and greeted them with a smile, a hug and kind word of good wishes.

"Are you OK as far as transport is concerned?" Phillip Busch, the secretary, asked her with an affectionate smile. Over the past weeks he came to like Marlene Brooks. He found her most attractive and admired her firm figure and exquisite taste in clothing. He guessed her age to be in the upper-thirties. As far as he could establish, she never married. But he was too careful to ask. He allowed his fantasies to run wild around this distant woman.

Brooks smiled, "Thank you Phillip, but my colleague, Julius Grant, phoned me a moment ago. He was a guest at the media chalet where he enjoyed the afternoon with his old colleagues from his newspapers days. I arranged to meet him at the main gate."

Lucky man, Phillip thought and said as he moved closer to her, "OK Marlene. Thank you for the privilege we had to work with you. I hope we find another opportunity to tackle a project some day. This was tough but very satisfying."

"It was indeed." She pecked him on the cheek. "Take care now, will you?"

Phillip heard her firm steps receding on the cold cement floor of the long hallway that surrounded the pavilion. He sat listening to the fading rhythm and felt an emptiness growing in him. "There goes quite a lady," he mused.

Phillip picked up his pen and added a few words to his report. He stopped halfway through a sentence, leaned backward, and meshed his fingers behind his balding head. "It will take me a long time to get you out of my mind Doctor Marlene Brooks – you bright, beautiful woman of my dreams. Oh how I wish you were mine!"

MARLENE'S PRETORIA APARTMENT.

Marlene Brooks saw Grant's green Range Rover parked on the curb. He pulled up as close as possible to the main entrance and patiently waited for her. She ran to his sports utility truck while inhaling as little cold air as possible. Grant leaned over and opened the door for her. She made a quick dash for the passenger seat. The motor ran quietly and soft music murmured from the player.

"Hello Julius. It is really very kind of you to pick me up. You just spared me from walking in the cold night air to the officials' parking-area." Marlene noticed the pleasant lines on his face and his high forehead while he carefully navigated his way back from the paved pedestrian area into the street.

"I suppose this is what four-by-four vehicles are made for; to illegally jump the pavements." She tried to tease him despite an intense fatigue that suddenly threatened to overtake her. She was completely drained and welcomed the warm interior of the Range Rover. Marlene unbuttoned her coat and longed for a hot shower and her bed.

"However, it requires, quite a big capital investment to have this extra illegal parking capability, I should say," Grant continued the small talk with a smile. Marlene saw in the glow of the dashboard instruments how his eyes wrinkled with mischief. He always tried his best not to sound like a stiff upper lip Englishman. Yet, she was too tired to continue the chitchat.

"This was a demanding and stressful day." Marlene kicked her shoes off and rubbed her nylon-covered toes. 'Fortunately I managed to side-step all the invitations to celebrate our World Champion Status"

"As far as I can gather everything went well and it sounds like it was a huge success. May I congratulate you on a job well done?" Grant reached for her hand.

"Thank you, Julius for the many times you helped me out -- although this was not even your project." Marlene squeezed his hand lightly, trying to add sincerity to her tired voice. Marlene still regretted her abrupt manner on the phone earlier in the day. She appointed Grant as an associate communications advisor about a year ago. To this day she never regretted her decision. His capability as a communications strategist and his extensive international lobbying and networking experience with the media added much value to her agency, Meyer, Brooks and Associates. He would never really replace the likes of her ex-partner, Arnold Meyer, who was killed during a media visit to the Angolan border war front. But, he brought a new type of capability to the agency. Also, Grant could never fill the empty space that's left in her heart since Arnold vanished so mysteriously. She looked at Grant hoping to see something that would reassure her that she was right. A quiet strength seems to radiate from Grant's' studious manner. Or could he?

Grant caught her eye and wondered what she was thinking. He responded smiling, "Thanks, but don't mention it. At least it gave me the opportunity to meet President Mandela, and I appreciate that tremendously. By the way, what did the President say about this big rugby hype?"

The streets were emptying and Grant was able to make good time in the direction of Pretoria and Marlene's apartment. "Well ... he was a little hesitant at first to wear the number six-rugby jersey. But when I convinced him that it would be seen as a gesture of his support for the Springbok team, he agreed. He was quick to add that he would also score points with the world's millions of rugby fans and the many white

South African supporters. While Nelson Mandela was jailed on Robben Island, he made it his business to keep himself well-informed about the development of the cultures of Southern Africa." Marlene admired President Mandela's ability to walk out of an imprisonment of more than twenty-seven years, into the glaring limelight of the world with a clear focus on the demanding and challenging agenda of his country.

Marlene's sighed and lowered the backrest of her seat. She was physically and mentally so exhausted it left her with little enthusiasm to go over the day's proceedings.

Grant, however, seemed to be ignorant of her being pooped-out "I think that was a smart little PR-stunt to get Mandela to wear the Springbok jersey and cap!" He hoped that by keeping the conversation going, she would not drop-off to sleep. He always enjoyed her pleasant company.

"It was not a 'stunt' as you called it. That, my dear partner, was part of a well-planned communication strategy. To build the image of the president of a new democracy is not a task that you achieve with 'stunts,' Mister Grant. And I don't need to tell you this." She pretended to be annoyed.

Grant smiled and then turned serious, "What can the President expect in return for his strong association with the rugby sport and the Springbok emblem?"

Marlene pressed her tired mind into action, "Perhaps not much. But if you take into account that the President's bottom word for a new and successful multi-racial nation lies in 'reconciliation', it places the onus on a lot of our people who harbor huge differences of opinion, culture and the like, to switch to a comparable frame of mind." She rested her face in her hands and said with some annoyance in her voice, "Dammit, Julius. Don't try to pull me into an academic discussion. Not now, my dear friend. I feel as crisp as yesterday's tomato salad."

Grant looked at her, smiled, and tried to sound understanding, "You are only suffering from a little fatigue irritation my partner. In a few minutes I will drop you off at your place. Do not even bother to take a bath. Hit the sack right away and sleep it off."

"Good idea," she murmured and dosed of.

At the entrance to her apartment complex Grant brought the Range Rover to a jerky halt. He did this on purpose hoping to wake her up and hurried over to the passenger side to open the door for her. Grant read the tired lines on her normally smooth complexion, and took her briefcase. He took the sleepy woman's arm and leisurely walked her to the well-lit foyer where he cared for the formalities at the security desk.

She looked up at him, "I feel a little rested now. Care for a late night sip of something?"

Grant felt excitement building up within but decided otherwise, "Rather not, thank you. I can do with some sleep too. Although I had a relaxed afternoon with the boys…"

"See you tomorrow then?" Marlene was thankful and stifled a yawn.

"Call me tomorrow, when it suits you. Perhaps we can grab a brunch or something?" Grant had an exquisite spot just out of town in mind.

"That sounds great. Thank so much again for everything, Julius" She smiled at him and lifted her slender finger from the elevator's hold button. The closing doors separated them. She left him in the foyer, alone with a good mood of anticipation for the following day.

On his way home Grant listened to a late newscast. The reference to the murder of Gareth Williams came to him as a tremendous shock. He met and knew the popular government official and could still remember the interview he had with Williams in London as a reporter with "The Guardian."

"There must be something seriously wrong here, he thought. This was not just another attempt to highjack a car, as the report suggested. With Williams' role, responsibilities and knowledge, there must be something sinister behind his death." Grant pictured Williams lying in a cold Johannesburg morgue. He said with sadness in his voice, "Hell, my friend, to come all the way to South Africa and die such a senseless death! Can there be any purpose behind it?" and decided to make it his business to find out why Williams was killed.

It was well after midnight when Grant arrived at his high-walled home in Sandton. He waited patiently for the electronically controlled gates to slide open. They moved too slowly to his liking. He kept a constant watch in all directions during these moments of vulnerability. His fingertips rested lightly on the butt of the cold caliber 7.65 Walter PPK in the glove compartment. This was routine entrance procedure to his property. The crime statistics of the new South Africa reached an all-time high. He decided long ago to be a careful, instead of a brave, man.

Grant parked the Range Rover in front of the main entrance, feeling too sleepy to park his favorite vehicle in the garage. At the front door his old cat, Kieter, waited for him. The large Siamese cat with its stuck-up personality gave the impression that he was doing them a favor by sharing the huge mansion with him and his son, Peter.

"I suppose you need a drink -- or even a midnight snack." Grant sat on his haunches in front of his aged feline companion. Kieter stretched his lean body and stood staring crossed-eyed at Grant.

"Hello old guy. I was gone all day and, as you can see, most of the night. What's this? Not a word from you?" The cat purred at the touch of his cold hands. Kieter stroked against Grant's legs while he opened the heavy front door. He picked his cat up above his head and looked the huge Siamese strait into one of his cocked eyes.

"Are you annoyed with me old man?"

"Meow."

"Will a glass of milk resuscitate our friendship?"

"Meow."

"OK. A small tot of the best 'cow-wine' in the world and then off to bed. Old guys like you and I should not be out drinking at this time of the night, you know."

Grant draped the eighteen-year-old cat over his shoulder, locked the door behind him, and headed for the refrigerator. He waited patiently for Kieter to finish his milk. Grant cradled him in his arms, and went upstairs to his bedroom. The huge bed looked irresistible. He put his old pet on a pillow, kicked off his shoes and crept under the warm cover. As usual he tried to picture his wife Anna and how she looked and acted before their fatal accident. But, instead, a picture of Marlene developed through a hazy, cheering football crowd.

9.

An Astute Chair.

Kempton Park, Johannesburg

One by one the members of Africair Corporation's board of directors turned up at the company's large wood-paneled boardroom. They joined the top management team, which was already there waiting for them to arrive. Small groups congregated, and talked with lowered voices as if attending a church service. The groups helped themselves to tea and biscuits. They talked about the economic conditions but mostly about the previous Saturday's rugby match - and the death of Gareth Williams.

Glynis Botha, Johann Kurtz's secretary received the board members with a friendly smile. She made sure that they all had their agendas to work from and offered her assistance. She dutifully invited the external directors to call on assistance should they wanted extra copies of documents or had calls to make.

Johann Kurtz and Doctor Herman De Witt, the chair, arrived last and closed the door behind them. De Witt was a razor-sharp manipulator of agendas. He always insisted on a meeting between him and Kurtz before entering the board room. De Witt hated any sort of surprise that may pop-up during a meeting. Kurtz insisted that at all times a firm consensus must prevail on all matters, between himself and Johan Kurtz. De Witt regarded this as the fundamental starting point for him to run operations in the direction he wanted matters to develop and materialize. More so when, it came to strategic and sensitive matters – like the circumstances surrounding the death of Gareth Williams.

Ever so often De Witt would say to Kurtz, "We must not allow the board members to drive a wedge between us. You and I must at all times agree on all crucial matters. That's how we can influence and manipulate the board's decisions. It is our responsibility to proficiently steer all issues towards an outcome and conclusion that will be to our satisfaction. In this way we will successfully all achieve our objectives. Including, our covert intentions." .

Over time Kurtz began to understand how De Witt rationalized matters so that that a 'satisfactory' results may have meant that which was perhaps good for the company – but definitely supported his hidden agenda. At times Kurtz was not particularly happy with the way matters developed or worked out.

Miss Glynis thumbed back her heavy rimmed glasses with its thick as bottle bottom lenses that always slid down her beak-like nose. She sensed the importance of De Witt's early morning caucus meetings and always made preparations in Kurtz's office for these sessions about two hours before the start of the official board meetings. This morning, however, the two of them wanted to start their discussions much earlier. She presumed that the board had to address a few sensitive items, of which some were crucial to the survival of Africair. Like Miss Glynis, the atmosphere was notably tense and she always found it difficult to handle work-related stress and was ill at ease.

De Witt formally opened and addressed the board meeting in English, "Good morning ladies and gentlemen." Since President Mandela took over the government, most large corporations rapidly switched their meetings and correspondence from Afrikaans to English as medium. The new black Minister of Industries progressively replaced the white government officials, who represented the shareholding of the Government on the board of Africair, with black directors. De Witt welcomed the new directors with a cautiously formulated statement. "The language of the aviation industry is English and so are most of our board members." While talking he made eye-contact with the new members in the manner of a headmaster at a term-opening, "English is also an international business communications tool. Perhaps this is one of the few excellent legacies the English gave to the world - a practical communications tool." He trusted that his remark would sound as if he was making an assertion based on a great deal of executive insight.

De Witt also wanted his remark to serve as a good justification to some of the unrelenting Afrikaners on the board, as a good reason why it was imperative that they conduct their future business in English. He applied his ability for slyness to create a feeling of cohesion amongst the white and black people who had to use a language other than their mother tongue. The Afrikaners ultimately accepted that it was De Witt's way of contributing towards the reconciliation attempt that was evident the New South Africa.

However, in the meantime, this was not the state of affairs in the private companies where De Witt served as the chair or a board member and where the majority of the capital and shares were in the hands of Afrikaners.

The point on the agenda, which brought about the most discussions and conflicting views, was the company's unsuccessful bid of the Martial Eagle's for the lucrative UK attack helicopter contract. "Africair failed to gain the British Royal Air Force order for ninety-one attack helicopters because we were hampered by an American arms embargo. Instead the order went in favour of the American attack helicopter, the formidable 'Warrior'. The loss in potential turn-over runs into millions of dollars," said De Witt in a weighty voice.

The larger part of the meeting was then dedicated to a review and discussion of all possible facets of technology, performance results and political implications that could have caused the failure to secure the bid for the South African aviation industry. After many hours of deliberation, it seemed as if every possible angle was touched upon.

De Witt listened intently to all the viewpoints raised by the members of the board and top management. He cleverly steered the line of discussion in a totally new direction when he asked, "Apart from the unavailability of American technology to integrate onto the Martial Eagle's weapons platform, are we sure that we handled all levels of our communications correctly? I am, for instance, referring to our media communications?"

Johann Kurtz's preset reaction to defend the company's communications manager followed, "I hear what you say, Mr. Chairman but, to my mind, John Molape and his public relations team facilitated exceptionally good coverage for the Martial Eagle in a number of defence and general publications."

Kurtz's remark was a set-up for De Witt to suggest that management be authorised to outsource communications assistance. "I agree. Mr.

Molape and his team are really doing well under the circumstances but, they also need somebody who is experienced and has a good track record, to operate successfully at an international level." De Witt looked good, exercising their pre-meeting consensus tactics. He pretended to listen to the board members who supported Kurtz in his defence of the communications team. The black board members, led by deputy chairperson, Mary Nxumalo, were very enthusiastic in their support of Molape. He and the larger part of this department, like the company's human resources department, was a showcase of affirmative action, or black empowerment as was referred to in certain circles. The staff of Molape's department consisted of eight black assistants, three Asian officials, and two white staff members. It closely resembled the demographics of the New South Africa. The black members of the board wanted to make sure that no reflection indicated that the communications department had not done a proper job to date. They also feared an accusation that a sub-standard communications performance was the reason behind the Africair loss of a potential contract of millions of dollars in international revenue.

Remembering what Kurtz told him the previous Saturday afternoon, Fischer knew what was coming, and did not like it at all. He sincerely hoped that the idea would somehow fail to come to fruition. So he also responded with affirmation on the good work done by Molape and added, "To call in outside help will only increase our already astronomic marketing costs. And apart from paying a big fee to consultants, they will want to earn commission based on a successful sale. Most of these marketing support services are asking for that nowadays."

De Witt was obviously concerned about the support for Molape, "Ladies and gentlemen, I am not at all suggesting that Mr. John Molape and his team did not do a good enough job. Of course they are successful in the important areas of the communications discipline. Including how effective his team is with their public relations and how they conduct a proper internal communications program."

De Witt made eye contact with each member seated at the large oak table. "What I am really saying is, because we lost out on the UK contract, we should not overlook a single opportunity to improve all our odds to win the bid for the Malaysian attack helicopter contract. What I am suggesting in fact, is that we strengthen and complement the grand effort by Molape and his team." De Witt was careful not to sound one little bit critical of the results of any of the black additions to Africair's mostly white Afrikaner management and operational teams.

De Witt turned to Fischer, "Winning the Malaysian contract is imperative for Africair. We need to adjust our marketing budget to include the fees and commission that you are referring to. In the end it could be built into the acquisition expenses for the client. We must also make sure that we re-evaluate every facet of our marketing approach to ensure success this time around."

The objective approach of deputy chairperson Ms. Nxumalo came forth, "Mister Chairman, I think that every board member is well aware of the fact that we have limited financial and other resources to maintain a long and costly international marketing campaign. But if we lose out on the Malaysian deal, then we may well be forced to re-evaluate our position in the marketplace for the eight-ton attack helicopter class. This is so serious; it could mean the closure of the attack helicopter manufacturing plant."

Kurtz, who was persuaded by De Witt to support his imminent suggestion, added to the chairman's argument, "It will result in a job loss of at least six hundred top-qualified and experienced engineers with their technicians and assistants.". Kurtz hoped to at least, motivate Fischer into accepting the chairman's suggestion by pointing out the potential calamitous consequences for Fischer's colleagues.

Fischer's thoughts were not aimed at the question at hand. He beamed a laser-like stare at Kurtz. Over time he developed a state of mind that rendered him ice cold towards his colleagues. He could not care a hoot about their future. He used them like high precision tools to pursue the objectives of his Right Wing Movement. One such a human tool that he hoped to manipulate was Jack du Preez. Fischer was sharp enough to understand the test pilot's embittered motives and found them most convenient and helpful for the Movement's purpose. He was also determined to gradually frame Molape and his team.

Dr. De Witt drove his argument home, "Because these types of contracts always run into billions and are always politically sensitive, they draw a lot of attention from the media. I am convinced that we need to step up our well-planned strategy to handle issues and incidences in the international media - more so in the aviation publications." De Witt sensed that his board understood his concerns.

Kurtz continued his support, "Mister Chairman, although we ran a well planned product-advertising campaign for the Martial Eagle, I tend to agree with your views. We were never really on top of all the issues, which always came by way of a surprise from the media. I think, from an operational point of view, it may be worth our while to call in expert advice to strengthen Molape's team in this regard."

De Witt lightly stroked his grey pointed beard. He paused to give his suggestion good timing, "May I accept the Managing Director's remark as a suggestion that the board appoint an outside communications agency with a good track record? And may we agree that their main focus must be to support our media communications program to secure the Malaysian contract?" Only the ticking of the large grandfather clock paced the silence that followed.

Nxumalo ended the pause, "Any suggestion from you or the board members as to whom we should consider?" With her remark she expressed the board's accord.

De Witt knew that the members did not have time to consider any potential candidates. He planted his well-prepared directive, "I think the agency that handles President Mandela's public relations program is doing an excellent job under difficult and sometimes sensitive circumstances." He knew his suggestion would go off well with the black and Indian members of the board and followed, "What's good for our President should certainly be good for our company".

Several board members wanted to know the name of President Mandela's public relations consultants. Kurtz carefully worded the board members' question by asking, "You may ask - if this agency is so good, why are they not well known?"

"Yes ... yes, who are they?" The questions came from all directions.

"It is a firm with an excellent track-record, called Meyer, Brooks and Associates." De Witt said it in a way as if he understood their lack of knowledge, "I do not need to tell you, ladies and gentlemen, that the hallmark of a professional communications agency is to put the agenda and name of their clients first and not to promote themselves in doing so.

For this reason nobody can blame you for not knowing who really runs the President's public relations programme."

It was business insights like these that made people tolerant with De Witt as Chairman of the board of Africair Corporation. However some of the younger board members had an outspoken dislike in De Witt. To them he embodied everything of the old South African order. He was a white male, with grey hair and an Afrikaner. They were of the opinion that he enjoyed too many years of white privileges, which also made him immensely wealthy. In their eyes his time was up and over for good in the history of South Africa. Nevertheless, they also conceded that De Witt was not only an astute chairperson but also a brilliant businessperson. Until the company was out of its difficult operational phase they had to put up with him. It was early days. Yet they knew there would come a time in the near future when further political developments would oust him from his privileged position.

De Witt, however, also gave evidence that he was positive towards the general aims of the New South Africa. Being wealthy he could go to great lengths to afford many lucrative opportunities to members of the emerging black South African elite. Some board members realised this fact. Those who decided to utilise his useful networks to speed up their careers as business people resolved to endure, for the time being at least, his occasional overbearing mannerisms and innuendo's of male and racial arrogance.

Fischer, however, respected De Witt for another set of reasons. He was aware of De Witt's obscured Afrikaner sentiments and therein saw hidden possibilities for their political interest group's objectives. He also knew that De Witt favoured him, considering the many one-on-one 'inside' discussions they had at several previous strategic planning sessions. Although the appointment of an external communications expert could hamper their group's plans, Fischer was sure it was the De Witt's way of apparently supporting the marketing team. But he also had a gut feeling that the old rascal had something else up his sleeve.

Fischer listened to and thought about De Witt. On the other hand, he trusted the Chairman as a shrewd political player who knew when and whom to support and the old silver fox always had a hidden agenda. Fischer was sure he also had something from his past to hide. All these wealthy old Afrikaner-types who financially sponsored the objectives of the National Party and its vicious Verwoerdian Apartheid policy always had some personal objectives to hide. Whatever it was, De Witt also had his own aims in mind. The wily old fox read the signs of the times and was careful not to show his conservative affiliations. He wanted the best of all possible worlds. Fischer knew through his affiliation with the far-right movement that De Witt was a member of the Afrikaner Broederbond, the organisation that employed all possible means, short of criminal activity, to further the wellbeing of its members.

Fischer was never regarded as a candidate for this powerful secret Afrikaner organisation. Although he was considered as a good 'Boer', he could never be rated as a 'Super Afrikaner.' Because he divorced his wife and lived out of wedlock with Janet, his consideration as a member of the Bond was regularly black–balled by those members who were ministers in the Dutch Reformed Church. That was why acceptance by the far out Right Wing Activists appealed to him. It was easy for Fischer to respond to their supplication. It suited his temper and would afford him an opportunity for sweet revenge.

While Fischer was musing about his place in the current political make-up of the Afrikaner culture, the board discussion developed to the point where it was left to Herman De Witt to initiate negotiations with Dr. Marlene Brooks, head of the public relations agency. De Witt wrapped up this point on the agenda , "May I thank the board members for their support for the suggestion that Africair approach Meyer, Brooks and Associates. We will instruct them to devise a communications strategy that will assist the company through a thorough international media-lobby program." De Witt looked particularly pleased with himself.

The meeting concluded with the board calling upon the members of Africair's management team to employ a keen approach when they reviewed all technology capabilities, client-relationships, and the anticipated hidden political by-plays pertaining to acquiring the Malaysian helicopter contract.

The meeting adjourned and a soured Fischer joined them for the traditional lengthy lunch.

10.

Inquisitive Directors

Management Dining Room, Kempton Park

After the board's morning session and an abundance of superb South African wines and traditional rich food eventually created a very relaxed and jovial mood in the management dining room of Africair Corporation. Throughout the luncheon the main topic was the rugby match and the magnificent outcome for South Africa.

Remarks were plentiful about how President Mandela beamed with pride while wearing the green and gold rugby jersey. He was praised for his association with a mainly white-dominated sport. This gesture sounded a definite message of goodwill to the white South African minority. They even speculated that Mandela's siding with the Springbok emblem, always seen by many as a symbol of the practise of segregated sport, served as an indication that this is now something of the past. The words of the captain, Francois Pienaar, sounded a fitting promise of an earnest effort by all South Africans towards reconciliation when he gasped over the stadiums loudspeakers, "There are not only forty million people out there to support us but we had one nation behind us." During the relaxed circumstances, nobody referred to the death of Gareth Williams.

De Witt and Kurtz, however, planned to pay due attention to the gunning down of Williams during the afternoon's session of the board meeting and therefore preferred soft drinks instead above the superb wines. They were cautious to not stir up too much unease about the occurrence. Yet they wanted to make sure that the board members leave the meeting with a tolerable perception about the incidence. De Witt relied on the casual mood of the members, which he allowed to develop by intentionally allowing an unusually longer session for pre-lunch drinks. In this way he hoped to smooth over this sensitive point on the agenda.

Back at the table, Mary Nxumalo was the first to respond on to the sombre point on the agenda, "Mr. Chairman, we all heard or read about the unfortunate death of Gareth Williams. We also know by now that he was actually from the British Ministry of Defence and would have been the guest of our Defence Minister, Joe Modise. I spoke to Joe last night; he told me that there were no official reasons to meet Williams at the Africair chalet on Saturday. It was to be a courtesy call."

Dr. Herman De Witt nodded all along to confirm what she understood was acurate.

Nxumalo continued, "But, I fail to see why we must discuss the matter at this meeting. The fact that they would have met at our company's chalet would have been a mere coincidence brought about by their respective programs and is not an official Africair matter. Not so? "

De Witt was comfortably relieved and saw Nxumalo's remarks as a good opportunity to portray the matter as one of rather inconsequential importance "Yes, Ms Nxumalo, you are right. The reason why I requested for this point to be brought to the table is that I do not want the members of our board to be unsure of the circumstances surrounding this unfortunate incident. I do not want any of you to be embarrassed when you find yourself in a situation where speculation around Williams' death is the subject of discussion."

"Still, questions could and will be raised why he was invited to our booth." Nxumalo stuck to formality.

De Witt stroked his pointed beard fast and firm. He prepared the right answer meticulously, "First of all, Mr. Williams was a former Welsh and British Lions rugby fly-half who toured this country during the middle sixties. I had the privilege to play for the Northern Transvaal province as a prop-forward against that touring side. As a senior official in the British MOD we, that are Minister Modise, Johann Kurtz and I, met him several times while we prepared the Martial Eagle's bid for the consideration of the British Defence Force." De Witt tried to avoid everybody eyes by bouncing his focus from the walls behind the members and the table top, directly in front of them.

"So there was no real reason to talk to Minister Modise?"

"There was no official purpose at all. I just thought, to strengthen old rugby and official ties, it would be the right thing to include him on my guest list for the finals." De Witt glanced at his wristwatch.

"If that is so, why bring the matter forward?" Nxumalo was adamant on this point and clearly suspected that something was being kept from them. She thought that she perceived a white conspiracy of some sort. She showed that she was not at all contented that the matter was tabled as a mere point for clarification. De Witt uneasily wondered how much of the real background to William's' presence and his death she derived from Minister Modise the previous evening.

"For official reasons, I deemed it necessary to discuss the incident at this meeting because of Williams' position. Because we failed in bid for the British helicopter contract, speculation already started in the media about the reasons for having Williams as our guest. Indications are that there is perhaps something sinister about the whole issue. As I said, the purpose of discussing it here was to clarify the situation for all our members." De Witt fumbled for words and it made him touchy.

"Was there really anything worth questioning going on?" The request for information came from Moosah Patel. He was an attractive Indian and an extremely successful hardware trader.

De Witt looked him straight in the eyes, paused and said slowly and on a firm note, "None whatsoever. I would like to give this assurance to the board."

Nxumalo said, "I came to the same conclusion after I spoke to Joe," her familiar first name reference to Minister Modise indicated her special relationship with a particularly influential member of the cabinet and it impressed the other board members.

De Witt on the other hand, was immediately relaxed, felt on top of the state of affairs and hastily threw in the closing remark, "Thank you ladies and gentlemen. Shall we move on to the next point on the agenda?"

The rest of the agenda consisted of commonplace items and were dealt with expeditiously by a less interested and by a now, drowsy board who longed to get back to their homes and social routines.

After the meeting De Witt and Kurtz slowly walked to the official parking lot. Their expressions were serious. "Do you think Nxumalo is suspicious or suspecting anything?" De Witt firmly gripped door-handle of his silver grey Mercedes 500. He was still somewhat uncomfortable and it showed.

Kurtz said in a near whisper, "Perhaps, yes, but I don't think so. For the simple reason, that Modise knew nothing about Williams' intention to deliver a message to him – of the possibility that it is the British Defence Department's intention to covertly favour us with some of their other armaments acquisitioning. By talking to Modise she could not necessarily have gained any knowledge of such intentions. You will remember that it was not our responsibility to brief Minister Modise about this highly confidential message that Williams had to deliver."

De Witt relaxed somewhat, "I must agree. Minister Modise was until that moment in no way aware of the covert plans that Williams had to brief about. Perhaps, he will be drawn into the new developments at a later stage. Let's leave it that way. Heaven knows how we should take this matter further? In a way we stand to lose another good opportunity to sustain our armaments capability. Perhaps fate decided today that the Williams Plan is not for us." It was unusual for De Witt not to rely on his own intellect to be in control of the outcome of clandestine business of any kind.

—Kurtz pushed his hands deep into his pockets and looked at De Witt sliding his thickset body behind the wheel. Rolling down the tinted window he said, "Johann, you look very troubled. Don't be. Get it out of your system man."

Kurtz leaned forward, "Williams is dead Doctor. What concerns me most is that someone knew something. Perhaps in a way our discreet effort to get a foot in the door of the British acquisition office was timely sabotaged"

"Like who would know what?" The astute Chair upped the window in short intermitted jerks, indicating his haste to close their discussion.

"I mean like somebody very close to our inner circle that was also well informed and had the intention and means to stop Gareth Williams."

De Witt held the window open with only his light blue eyes visible. He started the Mercedes and turned off the radio, still looking at his CEO. "Do you have any inkling who that could be?"

Johann Kurtz leaned back and stared at the bright streetlight and the myriad of white moths that danced around it in the cool evening air. He stooped again and looked the old man straight in the eyes, "Not the foggiest, sir".

De Witt scratched his beard furiously while he looked up at Kurtz. "We, have some serious thinking to do. See you later Johann." The upward whine of the window also closed their discussion.

With his hands still deep in his pockets, Kurtz followed the growl of the V8 engine as it left the parking-lot of Africair. The factory site joined the Johannesburg International Airport and a departing Boeing 747 gradually muted the beat of the Mercedes.

Kurtz walked slowly to his car. He felt uneasy because he was not yet able to shrug off the whole matter as De Witt suggested. Something arcane was developing amongst the people of Africair. He felt that a growing apprehension eroded the excellent work culture, which was at a peak during the Apartheid-era. He sometimes thought that there were evil networks developing amongst some of the workers and management. Perhaps even between management and members of the board.

"My dear doctor, at this stage I doubt a lot of people. Including you sir". The sub-zero winter coldness swirled his words into vapour.

11.

Death of a Darling.

Johannesburg - Kempton Park Freeway.

The morning traffic was congested as usual and moved at a snail's pace towards the central business district of Johannesburg. This morning Grant selected his aged Jaguar XJ-Six to take to the streets on his way to the offices of Meyer, Brooks and Associates. His mood and work agenda somehow played an important part in his choice of transport to the office. His times of departure from the office and arrival at home depended on the needs of his clients. He did not follow a strict routine. Peter assured him, "Dad, your irregular programme and diverse means of transport is perhaps a build-in secure strategy against car hi-jacking."

Grant smiled as he thought of his twenty-five-year-old son's obvious fear for his safety. But he understood the reason for his fears because currently an average of thirty cars per day was snatched from unsuspecting drivers in Johannesburg City and just about as many lives were also lost during these acts of car-jacking and the ensuing violence. Peter warned him that, "Driving expensive vehicles like you do, and driving on a notorious route to your office every day, is setting yourself up for trouble. You must remember Dad that these thugs are experienced with what they do every day. What's more, they plan their attacks very carefully."

Grant just winked at his son and promised to be careful, "OK, my son, I will keep my eyes open and inform you regularly of my movements, especially, on those evenings when I will be home later than usual."

Peter was still not happy, "Don't joke about the danger involved. We must apply all the available technology to alleviate our senseless stress and worry, you know. That's why we have cell phones and security systems. OK Dad?"

Peter's mature concern filled Grant with pride. If only Anna could see him now how he became such a grown man. Whenever something reminded him of his late wife, it coloured his mood blue for most of the day. It was nearly four years since her death, and the ache still lingered deep inside him and at times threatened to burn him up.

The traffic slowed down to a standstill. To break the dreaded train of his thoughts he turned up the volume of his car radio. To his surprise he heard a reporter conducting an interview with Marlene Brooks. It was a "behind the scenes" item. She outlined what it took to run President Mandela's public relations programme. The interview was in Afrikaans and Grant formed a vivid picture popped up in his mind of her attractive face and pitch dark hair.

Grant's own knowledge of Afrikaans was limited and he only used it when he spoke to his son. He also did so when he wanted to amuse Peter with his awkward expressions. Sadly, his usage of Afrikaans broke down since his attractive wife died. Grant pictured his wife – like she was on that fatal night that would end it all for them.

"Here my thoughts are back with Anna again." Grant spoke to himself and detested it when his memory went into a replay-mode. He still harboured a vague guiltiness about falling asleep last night with a picture of Marlene on his mind. Lately he was thinking more and more of her, outside of their work relationship. "Damn cunning demons. How will I ever get you out of my system?"

Grant willed his thoughts back to Peter and the conversation they had yesterday morning. "You will only come to terms with mother's death and put your mind to rest, once you stopped blaming yourself for that awful accident you had." Peter said

The winter morning's fog suddenly seemed to settle in his eyes. He thought of the time when they had their first open discussion of Anna's death, when he broke down and sobbed like a child. He confided his feelings of guilt while the young man sat listening and good-naturedly allowed him to empty his bottled-up remorse. After listening to him Peter said gently, "It was proven beyond doubt that the oncoming car was going in the wrong way and on your side of the lane." Peter had placed his arm round his shoulders and drew him closer.

Grant recalled how awkward he sounded through his tears, "Yes, but I had too much to drink at The Star's cocktail party. If I was really sober perhaps I could have avoided the fatality of the accident. My reactions were too slow and that made me responsible for your mother's death." He walked away from his son and stared through the window of his study. The miserable grey of winter had dried up most of the huge lawn and it somehow reflected the quality of his life. He felt utterly miserable and wondered if he would ever emerge from this seemingly everlasting winter. In vain he tried to hide his tears from Peter.

Peter walked over to his dad and hugged him, "Is that why, since that night, you never touched alcohol again?"

"Yes." Grant heaved an irrepressible sob.

"Why? You were always a responsible drinker. There is no reason to penalize you in this way." His mother is dead but his father was always a moderate man and Peter viewed his change in habit as an over-reaction. "I don't think you should continue limit yourself in this way, Dad."

Grant thought for a while, "I am also doing it for your sake. I am taking into consideration your religious reason why you do not approve of the use of alcohol. Perhaps I hoped to convey to you how dreadful my life turned out since your mother's death and how sorry I am for what I have done. And I do not want to hurt you any more in any way." Grant regained control and turned to look at Peter.

A long silence followed. Peter looked at his dad, still holding on to his arm, "Thanks, my dearest and noble old Englishman-of-a-Dad. Thank you for being, so considerate, but you have no need to side with my decision in this regard, or show your grief to me through any manner of conduct. I think I know what is going on inside of you." He spoke softly and held on a while longer. Peter tried to lift his mood with a smile in his voice, "It will also do your health a lot of good. I mean, your favourite Scotch-on-the-rocks, now and then. My abstinence is based on fitness reasons – and not because of religious principles. Just remember who turned water into wine." Peter quickly turned around and left the study with long strides. He said in a rather loud voice, "But right now I am going to turn hot water into some nice strong coffee, instead." Grant heard the sob in his son's voice.

The persistent honking from an irritable commuter brought Grant's mind back to the traffic that started to move again. In the meantime the interview with Marlene Brooks was over and Kris Kristofferson sang, 'For the Good Times'…

"Don't look so sad,
I know it's over,
But life goes on.
And this Old World
Will keep on turning.
Let's just be glad,
We had some time
To spend together ..."

Grant felt a little embarrassed that he did not follow the interview with his partner and decided to pretend that he never heard the radio item. Perhaps it would not be altogether untrue. Twenty minutes later the Jaguar dipped into the parking garage. Grant took the escalator to his office on the twentieth floor.

12

Generous Colleagues.

Johannesburg Central Business District,

Grant walked into his office at his usual brisk pace. His stride accommodated the slight limp from his restructured foot. It took half-a-dozen painful operations and many frustrating months on crutches in an effort to loosen-up and remodel his left ankle that was crushed during the crash on the freeway exit. Grant hung his tweed jacket over a chair and booted his computer. Out of habit he first read his e-mail and then scanned the news media on the Internet. Then he surfed into the financial news and updated himself with the wire-services' headlines. To this he added the top stories from New York Times, Washington Post and Los Angeles Tribune. Lastly he paged the main London dailies and the other major oriental news-networks and military magazines. He kept at it for about an hour. It stilled his need to be informed as far as the latest news headlines were concerned. He developed this habit when he was still a news reporter.

Grant twirled the Seiko that hung loosely around his wrist and checked the time. It was already ten minutes past nine. He stretched his long legs before him and buzzed Connie Heyneken on the intercom. She was always on time at her desk. "Good morning there! *Meneer* Grant. *Gaan dit goed?*" She knew about his little Afrikaans knowledge and liked to tease him by throwing in a few Afrikaans words now and then.

Grant immediately responded with, "Hello Sweetie, how are you doing?" He knew she hated it when he called her 'Sweetie.'

"Just fine Julius. Did you enjoy your hectic weekend?" There was some envy in her tone.

"I must confess it was a rather demanding break," Grant liked the energetic young woman.

"Are you finished with your news-update?" Connie was quick to learn his office-routine.

"Yes my dear. It is always fun to read the American and English papers before they do. With us being so many hours ahead of them, and thanks to the Net, we meet the day head-on while they are still fast asleep."

"What do you mean?"

"Well, for instance when I read the Washington Post on the Internet here in Johannesburg, it is still four in the morning over there and most of those fat cat American lobbyists are still in bed dreaming of yet higher fees. So I beat them and the guys in the White House to their own news."

"OK, I know that we are six hours ahead of them but, just remember that right now we are six hours behind the guys in Singapore and some smart little communications boffin has read your news while you and your cat were still dreaming of your fat fees! Or perhaps that racy-thing you charmed after the rugby-party." Connie snickered.

"We are just so bloody clever this morning, aren't we?" Grant shot back.

"When can I come in to listen to your adventures or rather discuss the day's program, your diary and the list of phone calls to be made?" Her voice sounded inviting.

"Let's make it around nine-fifteen." Grant's voice became formal.

"OK, *Meneer*."

"And Connie…"

"Hmm?"

"There are no fat fees for me and there was no racy thing this week-end." Grant wanted to get on with the day's work.

"You will change your mind about the fee in a matter of minutes. The boss wants to talk to you. Marlene wants you to drop in, even before we start our overview." Connie sometimes allowed her pre-knowledge about matters to show.

Grant frowned. "Will do." He shook his head while taking up his note-pad and cheap ballpoint pen.

"Talk about woman-power . . .," he muttered as he ambled down the hallway towards Marlene's roomy corner-office.

She had a corner office with a magnificent view of downtown Johannesburg. He took a seat and waited for her to finish her phone call. While she spoke he noticed that she still looked a little drawn. Grant could see that she needed more rest and he felt a strange sense of compassion for Marlene. He was glad that they decided not to go out to lunch the day before. When he called her on Sunday morning he gathered from her tone of voice that she was still absolutely worn-out. Instead he insisted that she should stay at home and enjoy a good Sunday rest. Grant controlled his disappointment and waited for Peter to return from a church service. Grant invited him to a brunch at a small Italian restaurant in the Rosebank Mall. Like Anna, Peter was actively involved in church affairs. Even as a student he was always tied-up in all sorts of revival programs. Grant felt a twinge of guilt for lacking at least a basic interest in what his son really believed in. He was also sad about the many opportunities they missed to be together in a father-and-son manner. That's why he cherished the day's outing with him.

Marlene started to end her phone conversation and Grant's attention returned to her. Somehow he enjoyed looking at her. She gesticulated in an eloquent manner while talking and Grant was tempted to just sit there and take pleasure in her beauty, but instead he pretended to peek at the now familiar headlines of the morning papers on her desk. He did not give her conversation much attention. It sounded like she was talking about a new project for the firm. She replaced the handset and scribbled a few notes.

He opened their meeting on a light note, "Good morning, Doctor. How is the Impresario of Meyer Brooks and Associates doing this morning? May I again congratulate you on your success of the weekend? Having President Mandela as the star of the show, I suppose it was not too difficult to land on all the front pages, like you did." Grant waived at the newspapers but did not mention the radio interview.

"Listen Julius, stop teasing me. That was one, how do you always say, 'helluva' communications exercise and I found it not the least bit entertaining." She smiled at him and for a moment her face lit up.

"I suppose you will call a debriefing session, like you always do. Perhaps we will gain from an evaluation of the things that went wrong and those that went right. I always believe one must know why your performance was not up to standard and also why you succeeded." Grant was still not sure if Brooks knew how he preferred to operate. Perhaps he annoyed her with his obvious male pushiness and somewhat old-styled bossy manners.

"Yes, I suppose in public relations practice there are always three rules for success when it comes to giving attention to detail; Review, review, and once again review."

"You are right there, Marlene, but without a sound strategy to direct actions you can do a lot of things perfectly right for all the wrong reasons."

As far as the practice of communication was concerned Brooks believed that she and Grant shared the same professional values. This gave their partnership the added advantage of a superb understanding between colleagues. They seldom argued about the approach to follow in dealing with complicated communications issues. They may, however, sometimes differ on the most effective method to reach the same objective. Despite his assertive approach, Grant made her feel at ease. Since he joined the firm some months ago, she felt more secure. For the first time in many years, since the absence of Meyer, she did not get the proverbial 'Lonely at the top' feeling. The thought made her blush.

Grant noticed this and wished that he could read her thoughts. "And?" he asked.

She noticed that he looked at her in his caring way and gave him a little uncomfortable smile. She thought, this is a sensitive man. I must watch out when I am with him.

"Oh, it's not important. I just thought of something. Perhaps we may talk about it sometime later."

Grant did not want to embarrass her any further and kept the conversation formal, "What did you want to discuss, Marlene?"

"We were asked to take on a new assignment. I was wondering about the weight of your workload before I offered to take on this project." She looked at him with wide brown eyes.

Grant thought for a while, "I noticed that the work for Mandela took up most of your time. Are you still comfortable with your commitments or do you need my assistance?"

"For the time being - not really. Perhaps, when special events like last Saturday crop up, but then again I can rely on the inputs of just about all our staff. No, I don't think so, Julius."

"Well, if you are not in need of my assistance as far as the Mandela-program goes, I think we may consider taking on a new project. Let me tell you where I stand now as far as my order-book is concerned." Grant briefly brought Marlene up to date with a mining project that was on the verge of completion. It would soon allow him time to take on a new venture. So I will be concluding the project for De Beer's Diamond Mining Company shortly," he said.

Does this go for all the issues around their Russian partners and the questionable African diamond production and marketing project?"

"For the time being – yes, however I think we have addressed only the more crucial incidences. To a large extent the issues around the cartel has been put to rest. From here on their internal communications department will be able to tend to the run-of-the-mill events. I did, however, arrange with the executives concerned to audit their progress at regular intervals and report any of the anticipated complications in the diamond industry that may crop up."

Marlene's eyebrows jumped, "Like . . . ?"

Grant stared for a while at the city scenery, turned to her and said, "Sometime in the not too distant future, the media will become aware of the inhumane and appalling conditions under which diamonds are excavated in certain African states. Then a wave of media generated compassion will break loose. And that could hurt the operations and business outlook for regulated and well managed diamond mining concerns"

"Will their communications persons have the aptitude to keep it up?" Marlene was always concerned about her client's interests.

"They do have a team of well-qualified and experienced communicators there. I think, with some assistance during critical issues, they will keep it up."

Marlene saw an opportunity to show her appreciation for Grant's contribution. She knew by now that compliments made him uneasy so she said in a roundabout sort of way, "Good. It did, however, suit De Beer's strategy to employ us as outsiders to facilitate some of the more sensitive matters as far as their international issues are concerned. Those normally bug the large conglomerates. I want to congratulate you on the fine job you did, Julius. Recently I received a personal call from De Beer's C.E.O. He expressed his gratitude and mentioned your fine contribution."

"That is what we get paid for. To effectively handle the issues that may explode into international incidences." The Englishman said in a matter-of-fact manner.

Her flattering made Grant uncomfortable and he wanted to steer the conversation away from himself. "Tell me about this new project. What is it all about?" Grant preferred those communications tasks where he could apply his strategic skills and international media networks. He sat back, folded his arms over his broad chest and waited for her response. Silently he hoped another project of the De Beer's magnitude would be in stall for him.

"I am afraid that at this stage I do not know much. But from what it sounds like, this will perhaps be an unusually complicated project."

Grant leaned forward, "In what respect?"

"I know very little about the armaments and aviation industry. What I do know is that due to a lull in Sub-Saharan conflicts, the South African industry is in a serious downward trend. We were called to assist with the marketing strategy of an aircraft manufacturing company." Marlene sounded vague.

The words 'armaments' and 'aviation' immediately grabbed Grant's attention. "I believe that just about all the aircraft manufacturers around the world are in a cut-throat state of competition. Who's the potential client? There are not many of those in South Africa."

"Africair Corporation. You must have heard the name before."

"Most definitely. The Government has the controlling shares in this venture. Africair supplied in all the needs for the South African Air Force during the years when the UN-sanctioned arms embargo against this country prevailed."

"Tell me more." Marlene walked to a side table and poured coffee into two large mugs that read 'Yours' and 'Mine.' The latter was slightly bigger.

Grant continued," Apart from upgrading Mirage Fighters and Puma Transport Helicopters, they also developed an attack helicopter, called the 'Martial Eagle.'"

Marlene was not totally ignorant of the status of the South African aviation industry, "Yes, then you will also remember that they recently lost out on their bid to supply attack helicopters to the British Army. Apparently the deal was eventually worth a cool $4-billion. The order went in favour of the American 'Warrior' helicopter."

Her knowledge surprised Grant because he made it his business to keep himself informed about those strategic industries that played a significant role in the country's economy.

Marlene handed him 'Yours.' "Well, I received a phone call this morning from that company's chairman, Doctor Herman De Witt."

"Heard that name before," Grant muttered.

"He told me that Africair is in a do-or-die situation in bidding for another important order."

"What do they want us to do for them?"

"Again, I am not sure. De Witt said he wanted to recommend to his board that Africair acquire our services as an outside communications source to assist their marketing effort. They will discuss our appointment at their board meeting. De Witt also told me that apart from our normal retainer fee and production cost, we would, like their international marketing agents, also be entitled to a one-percent commission on the final acquisitioned contract figure. Whatever that means?" Marlene looked quietly at Grant. She clearly did not grasp the huge financial implication of such an additional commission payment to their fee.

Grant rose halfway out of his chair and brought his face close to hers, "What! Are you sure that's what their chairman offered us?"

"Yes, partner, what is so unusual about that. It only tells us how serious they are to succeed with their bid, this time around. That is if I understood De Witt correctly."

"Good Lord, Marlene! In the public relations world this is unheard of. Do you realise the potential revenue for this firm, should we assist them to pull off the deal? My dear Doctor, if that happens we will be creating a totally new approach to the fee-structuring approach of international communications business." Grant slowly lowered himself into his chair while swiftly calculating in his mind what one percent on the price of an eight-ton attack helicopter could add up to.

"No Julius, I do not have the faintest idea of what that could come to. I realise this is an unusual extra form of income for the firm. I therefore decided to see this form of payment, when the job is completed, as a special bonus. You and I will share that amount on a fifty-fifty basis."

Grant stared at her in disbelief. He slowly shook his head and said in a scratchy voice, "Marlene, we are talking of millions here. At the production cost of an attack helicopter and when an order runs into dozens of these killer machines . . . I think you need to reconsider your offer of sharing that particular huge income with me. Whatever basis you have in mind, I suggest you take all that money and retire most comfortably from the pressures of living the life of a public relations practitioner." Grant sweated a little and for some reason felt very uncomfortable. Large amounts always scared him. He wrote many stories where big money caused big troubles.

"No Grant. I have made up my mind. We will share that income and both look at the possibility of a comfy life. Don't forget, you are the one who will have to originate and make all the inputs. And - perhaps run some personal risks too! I am not going to discuss my decision any further. Ever!" Marlene banged a small fist on the desk that made her bangles jingle. To Grant it sounded like the closing hammer of the stock exchange with Christmas music in the background.

"And . . .?" Grant decided not to take the matter any further. Actually, his discomfort slowly changed to excitement. He felt like somebody who had a small-odds lottery stub in his wallet with a guaranteed big second prize. Provided the tender for the sale was a success!

"Once their directors buy into the idea, we, or rather you will have to attend a briefing session."

"OK let me know when they are ready." Grant stood up and placed his chair carefully back in position.

Marlene nodded at her electronic diary. "I will be in Cape Town most of this week. I told Hermann – er - Dr. De Witt to call your directly once he is ready for the briefing. I gave him all your contact numbers."

"Right, Marlene. I will evaluate the situation and come back to you with a structured budget." The business side of things was always important to Grant. This time, however, he knew the numbers will be very different. With a smile he passed on to Marlene a saying that he learned from his father, "My old man always said - happiness is a positive cash-flow.

"Taking the promise of a very high commission into consideration, I suppose we could very well become very happy indeed," Marlene said without enthusiasm while realizing that despite growing up without a caring father, money was never a shortcoming in her life.

"Let's not count our chicks . . ." Grant's voice trailed. He felt a little embarrassed about his hopeful anticipation, "at least we will end up comfortably poor"

Marlene smiled and nodded to him to sit down again "This project may take up a lot of your time. It will also entail a lot of travel abroad."

"Yes, it sounds exciting," Grant admitted. "But my gut-feel says – we must stay on the alert at all times."

They discussed a number of issues pertaining to Grant's remaining projects. It took them the best part of two hours before they were done. Grant returned to his office. His thoughts strained to run wild. Now this was the sort of thing that warmed his blood. It also dissolved his routine Monday blues. It sounded like a job to look forward to. Out of the blue he wondered if and how the death of Williams fitted into the picture. "If it does, this is not your usual type of PR-job, old boy," he said to himself.

13.

CLIENT'S CALL.

JULIUS GRANT'S JOHANNESBURG OFFICE.

For a long time Grant sat in his office - deep in thought. He felt elated but at the same time developed an uncertain feeling he could not pin down. Perhaps it was the vagueness surrounding the new client that, little by little, grew a stressful frame of mind in him. Part of his anticipation also carried with it the feeling of uneasiness and then he recognised it as the sensation that usually accompanied him when he got involved in a clandestine-type assignment. These mixed expectations were not new to Grant who, till now, enjoyed for a long period a relaxed and well controlled inner stance.

He failed to notice Connie Heyneken where she stood leaning against his office door. She waited for him to snap out of his pensive mood, but actually enjoyed watching him. A warm feeling of affection towards the attractive Englishman filled her. Was it good old compassion for the loneliness that emanated from him or was it something else? Connie shrugged off the thought that she dared not define. Perhaps he would notice how she preened for hours before coming to work. He may even notice her new mini-skirt and blouse with the subtle low cut. The man is surely not that busy, she mused.

"You ready for me now, Julius?"

"Hi, Connie." Grant broke away from his thoughts. He slowly swivelled his chair in her direction but kept his gaze on the Johannesburg skyline. Outside a cold noon breeze tugged at the new South African flag above the entrance to the adjacent police headquarters. The sun shone brightly and the winter temperature gradually climbed from zero to the low twenties. The frosted lawns in the park opposite their building slowly melted. The green from the grass gradually developed out of its white cover like a snapshot on Polaroid-film. Soon the grass would turn into a wintry yellow, he thought.

Connie Heyneken carefully sat down opposite Grant. She made sure that the way she crossed her legs would be most pleasing, seen from the angle that he would look at her. Grant admired her presence and movements. He looked at her long golden hair, her full red mouth and pleasant smile. He noticed how her blue outfit enhanced the colour of her eyes. For an instant Grant wondered what would happen if she would lean a little forward. He needed not to wait. She sat forward to place her notebook on the desk and he looked at how her full figure rose as she did so. Grant smiled, it reminded him of the bread rolls his mother prepared for the oven. For a fleeting moment he dropped his eyes, lifted his gaze, and still smiled because of his silly comparison. Bread rolls and breasts. He must be falling off his trolley or ageing very fast now. Grant hoped she would understand that although he was not going to comment on her appearance, he did find her company pleasant. She would know that he is not really dead...yet!

"OK, what does our schedule look like?" Grant tried to concentrate again.

"Let's run through it." Connie tried to hide her disappointment with his sudden businesslike manner. She had hoped that he would start by making small talk. On a Monday morning he sometimes did. However, now he seemed eager to get stuck into things right away. She wondered how much Marlene told him about De Witt. On the other hand, she hated it when they talked for hours behind a closed door.

Connie ran through his commitments taking them right up to the last day of the month. Grant took notes as she read from his schedule, asking questions as she talked him through his program. He shook his head at the growing demand for his time.

"Now for the calls?" Grant waited.

A long list of routine names and numbers had to be followed up. Together they worked out the priority sequence of the calls. Grant had the habit to schedule his priorities to fixed times on his daily program. That way he took care of the really important things first.

"Who's this Miss Botha and why is she so urgent?"

"I don't know. Never spoke to her before. Actually she called just minutes ago. She wanted you to call her back around six this evening."

Grant frowned, but could not think who the caller was. Connie misread his thoughts and a faint uneasy feeling resembling a light bout of jealousy touched her heart. "Perhaps this could be somebody new whom you met over the weekend during all the fun and football madness?"

The tone in her voice caused him to look up at her. He heard her concern and smiled with an impish look, "No-no. I met nobody in particular. I was just trying to remember who it could be. I will call her at six." By now Grant was ready for the normal Monday surprises.

Ms. Botha was the secretary of Dr. Herman De Witt. She greeted him in a formal, abrupt manner and connected him immediately to the Chairman of Africair.

"Powerful little first lady. She must be pissed-off because I did not need to beg her to get through to Mister Super Afrikaner," Grant thought to himself. In future Connie Heyneken will have to put De Witt on the line directly or else he is going to commit another male chauvinist indiscretion. Grant hated bitchy types but he also hated meek-minded women. "Dammit Grant, you are developing into a real grumpy old bastard - if forty-something is considered as old. Watch it old boy!" He spoke with his finger on the mute button.

"Good morning Julius." De Witt sounded like a real big Afrikaner money boffin.

Being married to an Afrikaans girl and living in the South Africa for a good few years, Grant was well acquainted with the Afrikaner culture. He was one of a minority of English-speaking South Africans who intimately knew about the Afrikaners' ambitions and aims. Sometimes he both respected and feared the control and influence of their networks. One should never underestimate the powerful link-up between organizations like the Afrikaans Business Institute and secret organizations like the *Broederbond* and its youth wing, the *Rapportryers*. As a journalist he tried many times without much success to infiltrate the agendas of these organisations. Journalists of the Sunday Times had more luck and even uncovered their membership lists. He did, however, come across enough inside information that sometimes made his hair stand on end. Because these movements were always male-driven, Anna could not offer much explanation about the frame of mind of their members. She grew up in a home where politics was only dealt with on voting days. However, like most every Afrikaner, she was fully aware of their immense authority.

"Thank you for being so prompt Julius." De Witt said. "Marlene told me about your background and it sounds as if you will be just the right person for this job." De Witt stated

Grant immediately took a dislike in his brash manner but remained polite and decided not to sound too eager yet also be a little tough minded, "It all depends what the 'job,' as you call it, will add up to."

Grant heard that he surprised De Witt. Perhaps the old man was of the opinion that he was going to work with a public relations man without a mind of his own. If De Witt was under the impression that people in the communications discipline were always obliged to be unruffled, smiling through, and super-nice-persons with faultless human skills, no matter how much dung slapped the fan - he had another think coming. "I'll cut the old goat down to size," Grant thought.

Nevertheless, De Witt glibly switched his mode. He sounded a little cautious and irritated. He accepted that Marlene Brooks gave Grant a clear instruction to take on the communications assignment. She did, however, warn him that Grant was very experienced and strong-willed. He had participated for many years in international journalism and business communications projects. She also gave him a brief overview of some of the most well known assignments Grant concluded most successfully.

"Mr. Grant, can we call for a meeting at the corporate office of Africair? We will give you a full briefing on the issues that we want you to manage for us." De Witt sensed some tension. Grant felt a little better when he succeeded to impel De Witt to refer to him as 'mister' Grant. Now he could call the rules of etiquette.

"Call me Julius or Grant. I always prefer to run a project on professional lines but in an informal manner."

De Witt did not offer Grant the same privilege. Somehow Grant just knew that he, in any case, would not like to get too chummy with the chairman. He had an inkling that the nature of the assignment will not allow for too much closeness between them.

"Sounds to me like the right way to start with our problem. I will ask Ms. Botha to synchronize our schedules with yours so as to arrange comprehensive information and planning sessions. This will be held at Africair's corporate offices."

Grant asked a few general questions just to get some outline of what the project could entail. He tried to ascertain what would be expected from him but De Witt's answers were hedged. On the other hand, Grant had enough general knowledge of the defence industry to get some indication of what the project would demand from him.

"Now I am really beginning to look forward to this 'cloak and dagger' adventure." He said to himself. Although Grant could not guess what he would be up against, he vaguely expected to run head-on with the most ruthless sales forces of military equipment in the world – and the representatives of their equally notorious clients. He had knowledge of the armaments sub-culture that sometimes dealt severely with those who put obstacles in the path of set objectives. There existed a complicated network that relentlessly pursued the potential of commission earnings. This just might become his nightmare. Grant knew from his news-reporter days that the consequences could be fatal for those who opposed or threatened the potential of their earnings.

Grant called Marlene, "I spoke to your friend, Dr. Herman De Witt. He sounds like a real Boer-in-a-china-shop. Nevertheless, the issue may develop into an interesting set of circumstances. In fact, it sounds like a real 'dirty tricks' adventure is about to kick off."

Marlene heard the tease in his voice but was just a few seconds too slow to moderate her response, "He is not my friend. He is a business acquaintance that I happen to know for a number of years. In addition, you will find out that once he gets to know and trust you, he can be a very agreeable man. Perhaps this will be just another communications project. I am sorry to kill your hopes of becoming a communications hero - if ever there is such a thing."

Grant ignored her somewhat sharp response, "I hope you're right. He did not sound like someone who cared about making a good first impression. See you tomorrow." Grant sounded equally stern. He was surprised that he struck a sensitive cord. For a few moments he wondered just how well Marlene knew Herman de Witt. He quickly shrugged off his feeling of unease. However, he could not explain the uncomfortable forewarning.

Grant shrugged and slowly punched in Peter's office number.

14

TOP MANAGEMENT-TEAM

AFRICAIR'S KEMPTON PARK BOARD ROOM.

Grant accompanied Marlene to her car, where it was parked in the basement of their office building in a bay with her name on it. Grant refused the same treatment from the janitor. He did not like to advertise his whereabouts to strangers. Perhaps, he thought, now that he was suddenly involved in the shady world of the armaments business, it could be regarded as a good security-measure.

Marlene was on her way to the Johannesburg International Airport to catch an early flight to Cape Town. She looked forward to her regular communications meeting and was particularly excited to work with President Mandela. The meeting was set to take place at Tuinhuis, the official presidential residence of the Republic of South Africa. By many it was regarded as the country's White House. The stately old home had a Cape-Dutch architectural style and served for many decades as the official home of many South African Governors, Prime Ministers and Presidents. Marlene and the President met here on a regular basis accept when she accompanied the President on his many travels abroad or when circumstances called for her communications assistance during the many official visits by dignitaries.

Grant on the other hand, was this morning equally keen to attend the first briefing session at Africair's corporate office. He was particularly interested in the opinions of the designers and manufacturers of South Africa's attack-helicopter, the Martial Eagle.

They exchanged last-minute business details. Grant squatted at the open car-window, "How long will you be out of town?"

"About three days." Marlene stroked the steering wheel of her Mercedes 300 and looked Grant straight in the eyes, "Those peepers of yours tell me that the Martial Eagle project excites you." She was right, and he hoped that she missed the new feeling towards her that he tried to hide. She continued,

"I hope you have fun. It is still quite a man's world and Dr de Witt said you are bound to run into a strange culture, with equally strange characters." She smiled at him and showed some concern, "My schedule is rather loaded with business and social commitments, but I also want to take some time to do shopping at Cape Town's Waterfront. I believe there are a few new outlets that recently received their new summer fashions. Nevertheless, my mobile phone will be on line. Let's keep in touch Julius."

Grant smiled a farewell and stood looking at her as she sped out of the parking garage into the morning dusk. He was surprised how much he detested her departure. However, his excitement over his new assignment grew and he murmured. "Now, go and grab that Martial Eagle by the neck, old boy."

Grant walked to his car and thought about Marlene. He remembered saying to Peter once, "I suppose a man goes really overboard with your genuine feelings of love only once in a lifetime. If that first love somehow ends, and you meet somebody new, I suppose you would then dedicate your affections in a more mature sort of way. That is if the new woman in your life allows you to do so. If so, the second time around could be the best ever." Grant tried to deny his awareness that Marlene took up more and more of his thoughts, and tried to deny this by saying out loud, "You are still very much alive in my thoughts Anna. Death does not mean the end of love" he tried in vain to still a vague guilt feeling.

Grant took the eastern freeway to Africair with thoughts that focussed on the Martial Eagle. He covered a lot of systematic thinking and tried to define his role in this new venture. During the past two evenings he spent many hours at his computer and roamed the Internet. He pulled up many articles on the developments around Africair's international business and its main competitors. He found a few inconsistencies in the way that Kurtz and other spokespersons responded to the media. It seemed as if most issues raised were not clearly thought through by management, "On the other hand, perhaps you guys just did not prepare all that well for your media interviews." Grant said while looking at the large road-sign of Africair that spanned the main gate.

A security officer, with a huge paunch that strained at the buttons of his blue uniform, ambled towards Grant's car. Grant dropped the window and the cold air burned his cheeks. The man stooped and brought his bearded face close to Grant's. His red complexion glowed through the white stubble on his cheeks and a faint liquor smell forced Grant to lean back with his elbow on the centre armrest. To Grant, the man looked like an evil Christmas Father, who would find endless joy in dishing out gift-wrapped landmines on Reconciliation Day. His eyes gave Grant a watery glance and he signalled for his ID.

Earlier, Glynis Botha notified security officer Christian Faber of Grant's arrival. She and Faber have been in the employment of Africair for close to twenty years. They met when she was a junior typist and he a transport-helicopter pilot. Faber was always a robust man and capable of turning a bar's furniture into firewood in a single night. His hedonistic lifestyle caused him to lose his job. One night during the African Bush war, a platoon of wounded infantrymen desperately need assistance after a border skirmish with Angolans. Faber crash-landed the Puma transport-helicopter on arrival and wrecked the aircraft and its urgently required medical cargo. Many unfortunate young bush-war soldiers died that night. It meant the end of his Air Force and flying career and over time he became a drunkard. Some years later, Mark Fischer recognised Faber one evening in a sports bar. He took the man home and promised him a non-flying job if he could contain his intake. Faber recovered satisfactorily enough to be appointed as head of aircraft security at Africair's plant.

Miss Glynis told him urgently, "Please do not hassle the man Faber. Honour whatever form of ID he presents to you, even if it is a British passport."

"OK! OK! OK!" Faber grunted and slammed down the intercom. He looked at the junior security guard that leaned against the control gate, spat through the grid of the steel gate and hissed, "Bloody old bitch of a spinster. She thinks her backside smells like daisies now that she's the big guy's secretary. What the skinny old cat needs is a decent screw but she is too ugly to even excite a farken blind drunkard."

Faber flipped through Grant's British passport and without reading a single word grumbled, "You're OK and A for away mister Grant! Follow the signs to the main building. You will find a parking spot there with your name written all over it." His paunch nearly filled the whole window as he stood up straight and gave Grant a mock salute.

The receptionist smiled warmly at Grant and asked him to take a seat, "Miss Botha is on her way down. She will escort you to Mister Kurtz's office.

Grant looked around Africair's large reception foyer and looked at the trophies and paintings. The theme was understandably aviation artefacts, statues, and certificates of good performance. A large collection of medallions was locked away in a glass cabinet. People in Air Force uniforms and blue Africair-overalls walked in and out of the busy reception area. Almost everybody spoke Afrikaans.

Miss Botha arrived. Grant was amazed at her length and the spectacles that gave her eyes the appearance of skinned litchis. She was equally bland in her manner and he followed her to the elevator and down the long hallway to Johann Kurtz's office. Kurtz walked up to Grant and greeted him with an outstretched hand and a warm smile, "Please to meet you. I am Johann to everybody. May I call you Julius?"

"Sure do. And it is good to meet you, Johann." Grant immediately felt at ease.

They exchanged generalities and Grant knew they would get on well. Glynis Botha served tea while Kurtz took time to brief Grant about the current organizational status and the people he would have to work with. Grant liked the straight and objective manner in which he referred to his colleagues. Kurtz was quick to establish a sound reporting relationship between them. It took Grant only a few minutes to understand that the tall man was firmly in charge of Africair, its six thousand employees and the more than two hundred sub-contracting firms.

In less than an hour later Grant had enough reasons to appreciate Kurtz's concise induction and overall neat management approach. It told him that he had a good and reliable client on his hands. He knew very little about Kurtz's personally and regretted for not trying to find out more about this man who right away made such a good impression.

However, Grant was confident that Kurtz would likewise respect his own keen professional approach. "Johann, I want to thank you for allowing me to feel at ease, here at Africair. I appreciate your outright manner and the way you structured our relationship. I believe you will also understand and tolerate my set of rules regarding the level at which I would like to serve you and Africair's objectives. I assume that you contracted me in to honestly tell you, from a communications point of view, what you must hear and do, and not what you and your staff instead would like to hear. My opinions and attitudes may at times annoy some of Africair's people but, it will be up to them to accept or ignore my recommendations - or get rid of my services. I am not the type who easily compromise when it comes to doing things the right way. What I am saying is, our fledging good understanding may die, right here, if you would feel uncomfortable with the way I prefer to do things."

Johann Kurtz looked at Grant as if he saw him for the first time. Grant's approach added a personal dimension to the factual security report about him that was presented to them the previous day. He stood up from behind his desk and walked over to the large windows that had a clear view of the company's main hanger and runway. He could find no fault with Grant's approach and turned to him, "You are on Grant. I can work with a no-nonsense approach. Let's go through to the boardroom and meet the management team."

-oOo-

The members of the management team were eager to meet the celebrated journalist. They compared their first impressions of Grant with what they formed about him at a previous briefing from their security chief, Fredrick Kramer.

Kramer's report reflected his secret police training; it was drafted in the typical apartheid-based security manner. He presented more background about Grant than was really necessary for this management meeting. Kramer hoped to impress the management with the important role that he still played in the circle of security networks. The security departments of various state agencies still employed many officials who also served under the Apartheid Regime but, black officials from the African National Congress' [ANC] ranks were steadily replacing the old cadre. Kramer knew that his days were counted and he feared the foreseeable day when he would receive his marching orders. He was insecure because he was afraid that the new democracy in South Africa would cease to appreciate the importance of the country's well-developed security information discipline. Kramer wanted to convince everybody that his work still mattered a great deal. However, he was a man with strong principles and a clear thinker. He would not ever consider a distortion of the facts he revealed.

Kramer made his presentation in his usual credible manner. He could not get used to the idea that people were no longer in awe of security people and that the needs for strict security ceased. "Our friends at National Intelligence, the Directorate of Information of the South African Defence Force, and the South African Police, assisted me with this comprehensive background on Meyer, Brooks and Associates. It also contains a rather intimate profile of Julius Grant."

Kramer's audience mentally prepared themselves for his longwinded and formal delivery. He took a lot of time to fill them in on the communications firm. He told them that he did not have much background on Dr. Marlene Brooks. She was the only child of a Greek father and Afrikaans mother who grew up in a mostly English community in Barberton, a small mining town situated in the Lebombo Mountains of the Mpumalanga Province. Her parents were shopkeepers and she lost her father at a very young age. Apparently she always had enough money to complete her studies as well as travelling frequently abroad. She obtained a doctorate degree in communication sciences from the University of South Africa. In the same year she founded a small communications firm and later joined up with Chris Meyer to form Meyer, Brooks and Associates. Meyer was related a family who were powerful liberal politicians in South Africa. His agency handled many controversial accounts that did not favour the Apartheid Regime. There was a rumour that Meyer was a member of the ANC, which was then still a banned political movement.

The government of P.W. Botha, who exercised strict media control, followed a continuous informational program to convince the general public and the media of the need for the South African Defence Force to be engaged in a lengthy border war. From time to time they took opinion leaders, industrialists, and selected media writers on excursion to carefully selected war zones. During these tours their guests were exposed to the objectives of the enemy and given reasons why enlistment was inevitable to keep the Russian Bear from crossing the homelands borders. During one of these border visits, a group of five civilians and two members of the armed forces, who acted as guides, were ambushed.

A helicopter patrol came to their rescue but enemy fire wounded one of the infantrymen and two civilians. Chris Meyer, who was the most severely injured, never regained his consciousness and died three days later in a military hospital in Pretoria with Marlene Brooks at his bedside. Understandably, the incident received wide local and international media coverage. Brooks was apparently very careful and formal during her interviews with the local and international media. A liberal Sunday paper speculated that the incident was a set-up to kill Meyer, who was since his days as a student, at loggerheads with the apartheid politicians and government. Therefore, it was understandable why the new government officials of the Department of Communication entrusted certain facets of the communications program of President Mandela to Meyer, Brooks and Associates.

Kramer continued, "To this day Julius Grant is the holder of a British passport and has not yet applied for South African citizenship."

"Bloody Pommy," Fischer murmured.

Kramer ignored the remark, "Grant was born in London, as the only son of Derrick and Cynthia Grant. His father was a well-known staff member of the military magazine, 'Jane's Defence Weekly and his mother was an American citizen from Orlando, Florida.' Grant started his career as a journalist with 'The Guardian' in London. Later he was appointed by Reuters and transferred to Johannesburg in the capacity of military correspondent.

"Julius Grant probably knows more about this country's past military activities than most other journalists. I suggest that we do not underestimate his insight into military equipment and other sensitive matters." Kramer placed a slide on the overhead projector and beamed a head and shoulders photo of Grant.

The security official continued, "In South Africa he worked with and later married Anna Joubert. She was a well-know beauty, very bright and started her career as a journalist for the Afrikaans daily newspaper, 'The Transvaler.' You would remember that the then South African Minister of Information once objected strongly to her editor about a series of articles that she wrote. She questioned the moral grounds of apartheid as a system of minority government. Soon after the birth of the Grant couples only son, Peter, Reuters decided to transfer Grant back to London.

Less than two years later they returned because Grant became so fond of the South African lifestyle and climate that he resigned from Reuters and joined the editorial staff of the Johannesburg-based newspaper, 'The Sunday Times.'"

Rosemary Barnard, a senior avionics engineer giggled and remarked. "Perhaps, his not a 'Pommy' anymore and only needs to get the citizen paperwork done."The group laughed while Fischer scowled.

Kramer spoke over the snigger that followed, "Grant's happy marriage ended tragically about four years ago. His wife died in a horrible car crash on the Johannesburg-Pretoria freeway. A Mack truck pushed them off an exit-bridge and left the scene of the accident. The truck, reported stolen, was later found in Soweto. The police, who had very little evidence to follow, never found the driver and closed the case. However, Grant was driving their car that fatal night and there was speculation that he was under the influence of alcohol. Somehow the authorities failed to test his blood-alcohol content. However, the circumstances under which the accident happened proved it was the result of the truck driver's thoughtless driving."

"So, we have a widower on our hands." Molape stated the obvious just to break Kramer's monotonous presentation.

Kramer used this opportunity to display his knowledge of the "entity" as he liked to refer to a person mentioned in his reports. "Yes, and Grant does not have a firm relationship at this stage. Recently Grant received a comfortable inheritance from a wealthy British family member but he still prefers to continue with his career. He and his son lives in the northern Johannesburg suburb of Sandton their upper class home."

Kramer tried to lighten-up his briefing. He flashed a picture of the Gauteng Provincial Rugby Team on the screen. Cheers went up from the ardent supporters. Then they noticed the red circle drawn around one of the players. "Some of you will perhaps know that his son Peter, was till recently the regular fullback for the Gauteng Lions. He missed his Springbok colours and an opportunity to play in the Rugby World Series due to a serious knee injury."

Kramer's last bit of information caught most of them by surprise and he set off a snap debate whether Peter Grant was really the best fullback in South African rugby. However, in the end they all agreed that he performed well as a defence player and that his kicking to the goalposts was superbly accurate. "He was always worth at least ten points in every match," said Rosemary Barnard, who was an ardent supporter of the Gauteng Lions.

When Kurtz brought the arguments to rest, Kramer added, "Some of you may also remember Peter Grant in another role. As a student he was involved in multi-racial religious crusades at university campuses. His group tried to bridge the racial divide that existed between the youth of this country by co-finding the non-denominational movement, 'Jesus in Jeans.'"

Somebody said, "Amen."

"But that is not where our relationship with Peter Grant ends. He is in the employment of the consulting engineers, Aircom Limited, who designed the integrated communications systems of our transport helicopters. We later modernised this system for the Martial Eagle." Kramer knew this bit of information would jolt the audience into attention. At least it quieted them into comprehending the Africair-Grant-relationship.

"That makes a lot of sense," Kurtz remarked. To him the involvement of the Grant family seemed to become increasingly suitable for Africair. Perhaps Dr. Hermann de Witt was not so off-centred when he suggested Grant's firm to be appointed as their communications consultants.

"At least the father and son moved in circles that are close to our industry," said Rosemary Barnard.

Now Kramer was in his element. He continued to pour out a massive amount of detail on Grant's career to date. Most of it was interesting but of little importance. He also touched on Grant's religion because he knew how important religious commitment was to his Afrikaner audience. For them, matters of a man's faith were always a crucial yardstick.

The security expert concluded, "On all accounts we can safely say that Grant is not a religious person, perhaps even agnostic, despite his son's convictions. But, by all accounts, he is a very ethical person."

The group was quiet for a while. Then Fischer offered his snide summary, "What a combination! Here we have an international communications boffin, who does not attend church, has a Christian-principled son who informs him at home about the intricacies of aviation technology. So this Julius Grant, based on his advice and super morality, will show us how to market our attack helicopter to Muslim clients in the Asian Pacific. My! my! my!"

Everyone in the room was used to Fischer's acid remarks whenever anything looked like the slightest threat to his position or capability. They also knew that he was registered with an Afrikaans church but he was not known as an active member.

15

THE POMMY, THE BOERS AND THE MARKETPLACE.

AFRICAIR'S KEMPTON PARK BOARD ROOM.

Kurtz and Grant walked in silence down the hallway to the boardroom that was well prepared for a planning session. Two overhead projectors were aligned at screens that were positioned diagonally in the corners of the room. A video projector hung from the ceiling and was aimed at the larger centre-screen. Two flip-chart easels, with a range of colour pens, told Grant that the place was rigged for some original assessment and planning. A uniformed attendant served coffee and biscuits at a side table. Several men and a woman stood in a semi-circle chatting and drinking coffee. Their topic was rugby players and their individual performances. Their laughter and quips ceased as they all turned towards Grant and Kurtz who entered the room.

Kurtz introduced Grant to each member of the group. Mark Fischer, the project leader, was tall and attractive muscular man. With an unsmiling army-like manner he looked down at Grant, and gave him a hint of reluctance before they shook hands. His manner reminded Grant of an interview he had at a Farnborough Air Show with a very snobbish Royal Air Force General. John Molape the director of communications on the other hand, received him with a loud, jovial greeting. They shook hands, following the three-grip African routine. Fredrick Kramer, head of security and intelligence, was a short stocky man with a handshake like a body builder. In his eyes, however, Grant detected caution. Gert Smuts the director of finance wore tinted glasses which sat awkwardly on his narrow face. Willem Niemand was in charge of production and appeared bored with everything around him. He hated meetings and longed to be at the assembly plant -- the world he knew and where he was always in control. Rosemary Barnard, chief aviation engineer of ergonomics, gave him a firm handshake, smiled, and pleasantly acknowledged his acquaintance. She was attractive with a determined, but sophisticated presence.

Fischer turned to Grant and said out of the corner of his mouth, "Let's turn to the most important thing on the agenda for today. Let's have some refreshments. The tea break is the only exciting thing that happens here at Africair." Grant could not miss his sarcastic tone and wondered what fired-up Fischer's gall.

"Thank you." Grant decided that he would maintain a courteous approach until he sorted out the personalities and the inside politics that were clearly prevalent at Africair. Like the rest of the team he carried his tea to the outsized yellow-wood table in the centre of the room. He was seated next to Kurtz.

Kurtz shuffled the papers in front of him while he waited for the group's attention to centre on him, "Colleagues, Mr. Grant invited us to call him by his first name." He turned to Grant, "Welcome, Julius. We are looking forward to have you as a member of our Malaysian marketing project. We hope you will find your time with us most interesting and successful." Kurtz was adamant that the Malaysian deal should not go the same disastrous way as the British bid. He continued, "Our team was briefed yesterday about your firm, Meyer Brooks and Associates." He did not add that Kramer also gave them an overview of Grant's career and profile, "So I do not need to spend time on introductions. So, let's tend to the business right away."

Grant responded out of courtesy. It was important for him to create a good rapport, "I am pleased to meet you, lady and gentlemen. Thank you for allowing me to be on first name terms with you all." Grant's baritone voice contributed to his calm, confident manner, "I am looking forward to working with you and I intend to make a meaningful input to this most important marketing project." While he spoke he again felt the hunch that this was going to be a stormy flight for him.

Kurtz took-up the reigns, "We will be joined by our chairperson, Dr. Hermann de Witt, at around noon. In the meantime we want to bring you up to date with important industry and financial facts, regarding the Martial Eagle. Then we will have an 'exciting' tea break, as Mark calls it," he gave Fischer an evaluative glance, "before we tend to the developmental, manufacturing and marketing facets. Grant, you are free to interject questions at any time."

Grant prepared himself well for this briefing. He was aware that all eyes were on him. From his inside pocket he took a small wire-bound notebook and a pen. He slowly paged through his notes and it seemed for a while as if he was unaware of their presence. Grant looked up and said, "I would prefer to listen to the various presentations before asking any questions, Johann."

"Good," Kurtz turned to Gert Smuts to talk about the financial implications of the project. Apart from the manufacturing and other operational costs, Grant was surprised at the size of the Malaysian order and the income that could be generated from this deal. He made a few quick calculations in his notebook. If he could play a decisive role with this project, and they win the contract, it would certainly mean the end of Marlene's and for that matter his and own financial concern. For the rest of their lives they would really not need to work again! Goodness, what then? What will I do with myself? He willed his thoughts away from his lottery-type of wishful daydreaming.

Willem Niemand's used diagrams on slides to make his production presentation. It was as dull as ditch water and he did not allow time for questions. He asked to be excused and could not depart fast enough from the meeting.

They took a tea break and Kurtz steered Grant in the direction of the restrooms, "Grant, let me show you where in this place, the big knobs hang out!" Grant smiled. He liked the man's humour and decided that they could even become friends.

When Grant and Kurtz returned to the boardroom the members of the management committee were still talking at the coffee bar. Kurtz took Grant to a side-table covered with brochures, videos, and heavy volumes with technical data on the Martial Eagle. Grant took up a glossy publication and slowly paged through it. Kurtz was clearly at a loss as to decide where to start with Grant's induction regarding the technical capabilities of the Martial Eagle. It was like trying to explain in a matter of hours, the Bible or rugby to an alien who just arrived from another planet, somewhere in the universe.

On their way back to the boardroom Grant sensed Kurtz's frustration with the way the presentation was dragging on and made a suggestion, "Johann, perhaps we could start where I ask questions about the facts pertaining to the 'Martial Eagle' that I am not sure of. As we proceed your people can fill me in on the things I need to know."

Kurtz scratched his cheek, "OK. As a writer on aviation topics I suppose you do have a lot of knowledge about the industry."

"Maybe so, but you must understand there is a lot of technical, marketing and political info which is imperative for me to know. I need that background, before I can even dare to sit down and structure some strategic thinking. Let alone come up with a sensible action-plan to support your marketing objectives."

Kurtz turned to the team, "Chaps, let get started."

They carried their cups to the table where the notes, files, and transparencies waited. Molape took a plate with cookies and placed it close to his freshly filled cup.

Kurtz said, "Julius suggested that he start asking us a few questions. Once he is done, I think there will certainly be some more detail that we will need to pass on to him."

Grant opened by asking, "Apart from the technical and marketing side of things, would the chairman need to inform me about anything else like - - - political, international relationships, etc.?" Grant's first shot caught Kurtz unprepared.

The way in which Kurtz responded gave Grant the impression that the CEO of Africair was not too content with De Witt's involvement with the company's management and operational matters. "Not really. On the other hand, he normally does not wait to be asked. He will barge in whenever it suits him or if he thinks it is necessary."

Grant brought the team's attention back to the task at hand, "OK. Perhaps I should start with the operational and technical aspects. Up to now for nearly three years, you managed the communications on your own. Why did you call in the assistance of an outside agency like ours at this stage?" Grant sensed animosity from some of the management members and wanted to identify and overcome any form of constraint right from the outset.

All eyes shifted to Kurtz, instead of Molape, to answer, "Let me make it clear, Grant, it was not done because we thought our own communications team, headed by our colleague, John Molape, was not up to the task. We thought that, after our failure to secure the UK attack-helicopter order, it would be wise to take a fresh look at our marketing and communications strategy. We were advised to consider involving someone like you to evaluate our approach from a different angle."

"Who gave you this advice and recommended Meyer, Brooks and Grant?' The answer to this question was most important to Grant. He could not help but remember the hesitation in Marlene Brooks' voice when he asked her a similar question. Somewhere, he vaguely felt, there was a link, going back to long before tall he phone calls were made. Nevertheless, he could not put a finger to it.

Kurtz tendered a hedged answer, 'Odd question Julius. Nevertheless, it came from our chairperson. You must understand that he is an astute businessman and made quite a meaningful contribution in the past to elevate Africair to the international player that the group is recognised for today."

Months ago Kurtz became aware that there was an information leak from someone in the management committee to Hermann de Witt. He had good reason to be suspicious, but was not sure who the possible candidates were. Confirmation that management discussions and standpoints were relayed to the chairperson came when he deliberately threw some 'noise' into the system. He once mentioned during a management meeting that Africair was seriously considering taking over the maintenance capabilities of the state-owned South African Airways.

De Witt, who was also a director of the SAA, contacted him in less than twenty-four hours. His late night call started as a friendly ' touch sides' type of chat. Soon, De Witt came up with his typical, twisted angle, "Johann, during a luncheon with the head of South African Airways, he told me that they are considering spending millions to upgrade their logistic support services. I told him it was an interesting development, but of no consequence to Africair. Our investment and business strategy must focus only on the military aircraft sector. Is that not so?"

Kurtz agreed with De Witt, but said that one should always be open to all possible business opportunities. De Witt walked all over his idea with a long argument of the risks involved in such a venture. Kurtz, however, made his remark in an effort to cover up the trap that he had built into his speculative remark to the management committee. His suspicion that there existed a leak in his management team was now confirmed. He had to single out who had the benefit of a direct line to the Chairman.

Grant saw the hesitation in Kurtz's eyes and watered down his question, "Maybe Dr. De Witt will tell us more about that. However, I am most interested in your industry. As you may have gathered by now, I am quite keen to place my specific communications capabilities and networks to your benefit. However, I will need your direction in many matters, which is very new to me. Nobody knows this game better than you do. May I then express my eagerness to become part of your team? I hope the company will profit from my association with the Martial Eagle team." Grant's short introductory words won a place in the minds of a usually cold and calculating committee who clearly, had a no-nonsense approach.

Kurtz assured Grant that he was most welcome and that the team was looking forward to working with him, "As long as you will be as serious as we are to clinch the Malaysian attack helicopter deal."

Grant turned their attention to the marketplace. He wanted to start from a premise where he could gradually get on top of the situation. "What does the attack helicopter market look like right now?"

Fischer saw himself as the most knowledgeable person on this terrain and eagerly shared his information. He lectured Grant on the various types of helicopters in the marketplace. He screened transparencies on the overhead projector showing the different types of helicopters acquired by the world's defence forces. He also gave a breakdown of the helicopter fleets in operation around the world, and the expected life cycles of the various types. Fischer was well informed.

Grant had difficulty hiding his impatience. His only body language was the tapping of his pen against his fingers, with an occasional glance at the wood-panelled ceiling.

Eventually he answered Grant's question, "Not taking the needs of the United States and Mainland China into account, the number of helicopters in the eight-ton class due to be replaced by the air forces of the world, tops at about nine hundred. This is based on a survey done in 1992, and should there be an absence of new conflicts, that many aircraft need to be replaced in the next ten to fourteen years. But we have learned from our intelligence sources that the potential for conflict could erupt most likely somewhere in the oil-production regions between Western Allies and those forces who secretly back terrorism. That would most certainly change the picture regarding future demand for attack helicopters that can operate successfully in arid terrain. And the Martial Eagle is developed for exactly such environments"

"At a price of about thirty million dollars apiece, we are talking about a huge market," Grant said and again made a few sums in his small notebook. The immediate and long-term financial picture improved by the hour.

"That may be so but you must remember there are four major suppliers or bidders for this market and the competition is tough and politically driven." Fischer selected slides of the models of the main contenders.

"Who would be the toughest competition for us?" Grant knew there was only one answer.

"Well, the Americans of course. About four hundred of the machines to be replaced will traditionally be American replacements. It is not well known, but many American helicopters, including attack helicopters, will be called back for the replacement of a sub-component. That will keep the Americans somewhat occupied enough to allow us to concentrate on the balance of the marketplace. That leaves us with a potential of about five hundred."

"Is the ninety odd machines of the lost UK contract included in this figure of about nine hundred?" Grant saw how his reference to the unsuccessful UK order made Fischer wince.

"Yes."

"That leaves us then with four hundred and ten?"

"I guess so."

While Grant was trying to estimate the real-time count in the current marketplace he clearly remembered a disastrous media conference that Fischer conducted in The Hague just before the UK contract was awarded. At that stage the South Africans were still very confident that Prime Minister John Major and the British government, would award the massive Royal Air force attack helicopter contract to the South Africans. Their over confidence rested on the acceptance that the British would do so out of loyalty to an ex-commonwealth partner or at least as an earned form of political recompense to president Nelson Mandela's government. The Africair team, supported by government officials, was confident that South Africa made good by becoming a democracy with black majority rule. They were certain that Britain would have no other moral option than to reward South Africa by entering into a long-term contract. All indicators pointed to the certainty of their acquisition of Africair's Martial Eagle. Based on this confidence about an impending order, Fischer smirked at the European press during the media conference in The Hague. He implied that the Dutch Air Force's choice of attack helicopters would be forced by what the British decided to buy. "And the Brits are going to buy the Martial Eagle!" he told the media.

However, a few weeks later Britain had a cabinet reshuffle and the new minister of defence swayed the contract in favour of the American Warrior. Days later the Dutch government got word of the impending demise of the Fokker Aircraft Manufacturing Company and for a number of good political reasons shelved their own attack helicopter plans.

Grant said in a careful manner, "Minus the thirty helicopters which the Dutch government postponed indefinitely, I suppose that leaves us with a narrowed-down potential of around three-hundred-and-eighty choppers?"

Fischer did not respond. He disliked the sound of the dwindling market figures and he also did not want to be reminded of his incompetent handling of the Dutch media. He hated to acknowledge to himself that they really needed a seasoned international business communicator.

"Who are the defence forces that make up this market and that we have quantified here?" Grant asked.

Fischer looked at Kurtz who slowly nodded his approval for the information to be passed on, "The Indian forces need about sixty, the Gulf states about eighty, Thailand twenty, Singapore forty, Indonesia thirty five, Turkey sixty-five, Taiwan forty five and Malaysia the rest. The last of these machines should be delivered before the year 2010."

"Which market is our priority here?"

"The thirty-five to forty choppers for Malaysia. Whoever wins their contract must start with delivery by the end of next year."

"And who's our main competition?'

Kurtz liked the way that Grant referred to 'us', 'we,' and 'our.' It showed that he subconsciously committed himself to Africair's objectives.

"Again, the Americans with their bloody Warrior! - who else?" Fischer could not hide his frustration or dislike of Americans.

Grant paged his well-worn notebook and shifted in his seat to ease the pain in his left ankle, "What about the British and European helicopter manufacturers?"

"The British did not support their own industry and the European helicopter manufacturing consortiums are in all sorts of financial and labour dilemmas right now," Kurtz said with a calculating expression in the strong lines of his attractive face.

Fischer continued, "Add that to the fact that the total European defence industry is now dealing with all kinds of business traumas. Their attention is now directed at the unification of their industries. It is a primary objective of the European Union."

"Their industries are not capable of supporting NATO forces to address threats like Bosnia, Kosovo and other similar types of conflicts in Eastern Europe. Their priorities lie elsewhere at this point in time."

Grant listened to the remarks coming from all sides of the table now. It was clear to him that the Africair executives were thoroughly up to date with the contemporary developments on an industrial and international political level.

"The picture you are painting gives me the impression that, to win the Malaysian attack helicopter contract, will be less of a competition than what you experienced with the bid for the British needs. Is that what you are saying?" Grant twiddled his pen like a propeller.

The whole team was quiet and weighed their experience in the light of what lay ahead for them. To go all out for a bid to supply helicopters to meet the needs and specifications of an air force required an enormous lot of energy and paperwork.

"The amount of work and care will not be less. The physical weight of the tender documents for the English contract alone exceeded four tons. Can you imagine what it took from the ME-team to prepare our bid? It would be asking a lot from the chaps to go through another exercise of this kind. Don't be surprised if they lack enthusiasm and falter here and there. It could mean we might again loose the contract on a minor technical point," Fischer sat back and clutched-out of all further discussions that followed.

Grant looked at him with an amazed expression. The way Fischer blurted out his pent-up cynicism sounded as if he would be pleased if they were to fail. Grant decided to negate his attitude, "It must have been a helluva job for the British acquisition team to work through and evaluate all that material," he said as an afterthought.

"Yes, and to think there were five major contestants," Molape said with a right cheek balled out where he parked a cookie.

Grant looked at the huge black man with his permanent amiable expression, smiled at him and thought that he need to make and stay friends with this man. If Molape has any hang-ups about external communications consultants it could complicate matters.

Grant responded, "Now I can understand why it took the MOD so long to come to a decision. And to think how we guys at the media pestered and gave poor old Minister Riffkind such a hard time to come up with a decision." Grant shook his head slowly from side to side as if he genuinely felt regret.

The room was quiet while the management team waited for Grant to compose his next question, "Johann, I assume we will tend to the technical side of the Martial Eagle at a later stage. Therefore, I have still one more general curiosity. I am referring to the death of Williams. I interviewed the man once. Could his death have any negative bearing on the future business of our attack helicopter?" Grant purposely threw this seemingly unrelated question at the meeting to read their reaction but sought in vain for the eyes of his new associates.

An uneasy silence followed. Everybody was suddenly making notes or paging through their documents. A few tight coughs followed. Kurtz wished that Grant had asked him this question earlier when they were alone in his office. Grant's expression turned to amazement as he looked at the people around the table. A moment ago they were all still very knowledgeable and outspoken about everything.

Kurtz cleared his throat, "What about Williams, Grant?"

"A few years ago I met him in London. He played an important part in the formulation of British armaments acquisition policy. He had strong convictions about acquiring defence equipment for British forces from outside of Britain. He had a list of countries, which he saw as preferred sources - and that included South Africa. At that stage this country already developed a comprehensive armaments industry that could supply complete defence systems. South Africa had enough capacity to supply its own forces and export simultaneously. Williams was of opinion that Western allied countries should be prepared to ignore the voluntary non-buying arms embargo against South Africa. They argued that that would prevent us from supplying to Eastern allied countries. Williams told me that if Britain bought weapons from South Africa, they could indirectly control South Africa's weapons deliveries to countries that do not agree with the United States, the UK and their allies."

"Yes Grant, but that was all cold war stuff. Everything has changed now. For that reason Britain was not obliged to buy helicopters, or anything for that matter, from us." Kurtz hoped to end this line of speculation, "This could lead to a lengthy discussion. At some later stage we can talk about Williams and his connection to Africair."

As Kurtz spoke, the door of the boardroom swung wide open. The short round frame of Dr. Herman De Witt filled the opening, "That won't be necessary, Johann. I will give Grant the background right here and now." He habitually talked down to everybody. It was his old fashioned idea of displaying power.

Kurtz drew up his shoulders, "Good afternoon Mr. Chairman. As you wish . . ."

De Witt did not return the greeting, "Williams was a dear acquaintance and rugby buddy of mine. I brought him to South Africa as one of my business guests to attend the Rugby World cup final. I trust the reports on the incident, which came from the police, and Kramer's security teams are correct. Williams was the unfortunate victim of an attempted car hijacking. All I can say is that I deeply regret bringing that fine Englishman to this crime-ridden country. I think Mr. Grant does not need to concern himself further with Williams and his relationship with Africair." De Witt spoke as if he did not notice Grant's presence.

Grant, however, had enough patience and thought, "Somehow I will get to the real answer, you boorish old buffalo."

De Witt turned to Grant, looked at him as if he saw him for the first time. They shook hands and the bottle-shaped man added pressure to their clasp, as if trying to measure Grant's strength. Without hesitation or greetings to the other members present De Witt continued his play of one-upmanship, "The best way to get acquainted with the 'Eagle' is to take a closer look at her. At this moment she is sitting in front of hanger number five, whirling her feathers in the warmth of the winter sun. Let's go and introduce the Martial Eagle to Mr. Grant."

Without waiting for a response to his flowery announcement, De Witt turned on his heels and walked towards the elevator.

16

THE MARTIAL EAGLE.

AFRICAIR'S TESTING AIRSTRIP, KEMPTON PARK

Herman de Witt sat in the passenger seat next to the driver of the Volkswagen van that transported Grant and the senior members of Africair's top management. They were as always keen to witness the flying demonstration of the company's flagship, the Martial Eagle. They travelled swiftly on the airstrip towards a large metal hanger that served as Africair's assembly line for attack and transport helicopters.

Grant saw a wide range of pictures and video-footage of the Martial Eagle in action during the morning's presentation. Despite the vivid material he was exposed to, Grant was excited as he saw the big helicopter's menacing profile where it was parked about seven hundred metres from them. The lazy midday mirages danced on the flat concrete surface and distorted the profile of the Martial Eagle. The visual illusion continuously changed the shape of the helicopter so that the machine took on a mean, menacing look. Grant thought that the current advertising campaign's punch line was extremely appropriate. It read, "Sometimes our business gets a little ugly!"

They pulled up alongside the Martial Eagle and despite his bulky appearance De Witt hopped out of with a boyish liveliness. The rest of the group disembarked orderly and walked towards the machine. It stood there undisturbed on the apron like a huge prehistoric bird that appeared to be fast asleep in the African sun. Grant was impressed with the physical dimensions of the Martial Eagle. It was much larger and taller than he imagined.

De Witt came to a standstill a few paces from the Martial Eagle. It was as if he realised that he reached the barrier of his influence. He turned towards Mark Fischer with a body language that begged him to take over the introduction to Africair's technical achievement.

"Mark, please introduce our iron bird to Grant." De Witt looked at Grant while he spoke. Grant stood with his hands in his pockets, looking at the helicopter without noticeable interest. He was somehow tempted to needle the obnoxious old Afrikaner magnate.

Mark Fischer walked over to the pilot who was talking to a technician on the far side of the machine. The noise of the surrounding area was mainly the reason why Jack du Preez did not notice the arrival of the associates, "Are you ready to give us a short display with a few rolls?"

"Why not? It always gives me pleasure to impress the big Boffins." The seasoned pilot with his creaky smile teased Fischer with his snide remark.

"We also have here a communications man whom we need to impress with our machine. The big guy called him in to promote our machine in the international arena. Now give this farken so-called media-expert, who knows a little about helicopters, an impressive performance."

Jack du Preez looked straight into Fischer's cold eyes, "Will his involvement also promote our ultimate objective?"

Fischer took his question in with some thought, "I am afraid not. If anything, he will be an annoyance to us. He may even become a serious obstruction. Just keep your eyes and ears open when he is around. But don't worry. In time I'll take care of the bloody Pommie." He gave Du Preez a meaningful look, "Let's go Jack."

"Watch my smoke Boss!"

They walked round the Martial Eagle and Fischer introduced du Preez to Grant, "Pleased to meet you Mr. Grant. Next time around I want you to experience some of the fun in the tandem seat ahead of me." Du Preez's smile hid his mocking impudence.

"As a matter of interest, I had a little helicopter experience during the Falklands War. I would like to take up the front seat, if you please sir."

Du Preez was at once surprised and impressed, "Yea, yea. But we will need to plan ahead for such a sortie."

Grant drew the reaction he was looking for, "OK buddy, don't make too much of it."

"It's a date mate!" Jack du Preez did not sound sincere at all. Grant tried to read his mood but did not understand Du Preez's lack of humour and enthusiasm.

Du Preez shook hands with De Witt, Kurtz and the rest of the top-management team. In turn they all made some remarks to the lanky pilot or questioned him about performance results. Another minibus drove up and dropped-off the co-pilot of the Martial Eagle. He was a short, thickset man in his mid-twenties. Chubby Wilson handed the taped flight-plan to Du Preez and they scrambled up the side of the Martial Eagle. They slid like a choreographed pair into the cockpits and the bulletproof canopy closed. As they settled in, the party moved well out of the main rotor's draft range. They listened to the slow whine of the twin Turbomeca-Makila engines as they increased revolutions.

Fischer cupped his hand to Grant's ear, "Those exhaust outlets from where that beautiful sound comes from are fitted with infra-red suppressers to minimise the possibility of detection by heat-seeking missiles." Grant nodded and realised that he will have to familiarise himself with the technical detail of the aircraft if he wanted to become credible with his engineering-minded clients.

Fischer continued, "The four main blades are fully articulated and spans sixteen metres." Grant also realised that it was imperative to know the technical jargon if he was to spend the next few months on promoting and lobbying for the Martial Eagle effectively. He would need the knowledge when talking to the specialised writers of the military and aviation media.

The increased noise made further conversation impossible. The group saw how the main rotor accommodated the eight-ton machine with its fully laden weapons platform with ease. It swiftly lifted, swung to the left and, cleared the hanger dangerously close while it rapidly gained altitude.

Several engineers and technicians, dressed in light-blue overalls, trooped out of the large hanger. They received advance notice to prepare for the special display requested by De Witt for the management team and their guest. The group watched the machine with concern and pride. Grant saw that Rosemary Barnard joined them. For the first time he noticed how attractive she was. Rosemary was perhaps in her mid-thirties. Her lean figure fitted well into the tight skirt and blouse that she wore. Her auburn hair, which she wore in a bob-like style, shined in the midday sun. A few men listened to her with smiling faces that also carried respect and admiration. Whatever she said to them they found extremely funny and drew their spontaneous laughter.

Fischer followed Grant's gaze, "You are looking at one of the most brilliant engineers in the aviation industry. She was responsible for the design of the man-machine interfacing capability of the ME."

"Oh . . ." Grant felt a degree of discomfort being caught staring at Rosemary and did not know how to respond to Fischer's remark. "She also plays an important role during international aviation shows. She is good at informing potential clients about the reasons why the ME is a state-of-the-art flying machine. She adds real value to our exhibition gizmos and is a sure-fire marketing tool."

"That's interesting." Grant wanted to conclude the discussion. The way Fischer referred to a colleague as part of their show kit told him something about this crude man he was trying to label.

"You will meet her often during the marketing and communication briefing sessions . . . and abroad at the shows of course. But, watch-out! She's smart but also a racy little flirt."

"Hmm!" Grant owed Fischer an answer. He really did not have that kind of interest in her. He just noticed her because she was the only woman around, in a world dominated by a lot of boring bloody men!

"And, Grant, like you, she is a single person . . ." Grant thought about Fischer's remark and wondered how much more this man knew about him.

Grant wanted to bring the discussion back to a technical level, "What sets the ME apart from any other attack helicopter in its class?"

"Naturally it was designed with a high mobility warfare scenario in mind. We focused on its capability to execute integrated operations at all levels."

Just then the machine caught the group by surprise with a thunderous roar as it scaled a large black wattle tree at the edge of the parking area. It swooped over them with its helmet-sighted cannon swerving from side to side. It followed the head movements of Chubby Wilson who sat in the front cockpit where the attack command is located. Du Preez flew dangerously low over the group and the hanger. Grant noticed its narrow features and full weapons-loaded platform. It was indeed an ugly and menacing killer.

Kurtz closely watched Grant's expression, "She was designed with the specific purpose to detect, surprise and kill . . . tanks"

"Bloody Russian tanks in Angola..." Fischer interjected, "... and we did not hit a single one of them. Thanks to old FW de Klerck, and his Foreign Minister Pik Botha." Grant could not miss the dissatisfaction in Fischer's voice and attitude.

Kurtz tried to counter his bitterness, "There will be other tanks. Let's leave that to the clients who are going to purchase our product." Fischer scowled at his boss. Grant made a mental note of what he saw and heard.

Du Preez took the Martial Eagle through a tight flying envelope. He did a handstand, flew sideways and rotated. Then he elevated to a thousand metres from where he manoeuvred a barrel roll. More elevation took him to the start of a perfect loop. The display was concluded with a fly-past at a one meter altitude, swirling cold air through the onlookers. It roared upwards at an incredibly steep incline and then silenced out of sight to the landing area.

17.

A BRILLIANT AVIONICS ENGINEER.

AFRICAIR'S RECREATION CLUB, KEMPTON PARK.

De Witt took charge again, "Gentlemen, we will now be accompanied by the senior development staff and test pilots of Africair to the management dining room for a light lunch." They took seats in the van and had much to talk about on their way to the company's recreation club.

At the club they all freshened up in the neat restrooms. Grant's cell phone beeped. It was Marlene, "Hi, Julius. Can you talk now?"

"Yes, if the background noise would not bother you too much?."

"What noise? Are you still in the factory?"

"No - not really. But right now I am busy in an awkward little place, called The Boys Room. But sure go ahead." He thought he could hear her blush.

She became formal, "OK then, I will be short and to the point. I have an appointment with President Mandela tomorrow. The Football Union of Malaysia wants to invite him to the opening of their new national soccer stadium on the island of Langkawi. This may coincide with the Langkawi International Air Show. Will you please find out the details while you are at Africair?"

"Will do so - Kurtz mentioned this earlier. But I need to find out more."

"Thanks Julius – please call me as and when it's more convenient."

"But I am in the convenience..."

"Bye, bye - you naughty boy - Dammit." Marjory laughed while ending the call.

Grant was the last to leave the restroom. He joined the rest of the group in the elegantly prepared dining room. At a side bar members of the staff in white uniforms served cocktails. Grant decided to join the group where Kurtz and Fischer were talking to De Wit.

Kurtz, true to the polished executive that he was, greeted him, "Can I order you some refreshment, Julius?"

Fischer used the opportunity to cut in with a mocking remark, "Make it an advance order for a good quantity of double whiskies and sodas, Boss. You know how these media guys can hit the hard stuff." He mocked a drunk-like chuckle.

Grant gave him a calculated look. He could not miss the man's sarcasm and it preoccupied him for a while. He thought that it was nevertheless time to show teeth to the trenchant project leader, "I am afraid that I do not have the same capacity as you helicopter guys to go on a fast and furious binge in the middle of the day. Make mine a Diet Coke." For a while Grant had Fischer out of his hair. But he surely did not gain a friend.

Grant took his soft drink from the counter and walked off to join the rest of the general managers. Just then the double doors swung open and a group of about nine men entered the room. They were the heads of the various developmental systems of the Martial Eagle. Kurtz walked over to greet them and made sure that their glasses were charged. He then brought them over and introduced them to Grant. They spoke for a while with Grant who asked most of the questions about avionics, electronic warfare and weapon systems. Their youth and dedication impressed Grant.

Kurtz took Grant by the arm, "Julius, you met Rosemary Barnard this morning. Let she tell you more about the man-machine interfacing of the Martial Eagle." They walked over to her.

Her smiling eyes made Grant feel at ease. They quickly developed an enthusiastic discussion, which continued at the table where he took place beside her. Grant smiled at her and said in his honest way, "I know very little about what you call 'man-machine-interfacing.' Tell me more but please use layman's language." She did so and Grant found her explanations most enlightening. He also found her general approach professional and pleasant. Before the end of their lunch he knew that he liked her. Perhaps he could rely on her to explain to him later on why he developed such a strange foreboding sensation around the intricate corporate politics that he picked up during the day.

In an effort to draw in the rest of the group's knowledge Grant asked, "But surly during combat, you won't need to barrel-roll or loop with an attack helicopter. Why then take the risk, like you did this morning. I believe you do this routine also at the air shows. Is that necessary Jack?" he glanced at Du Preez.

Before Jack du Preez could answer, Fischer's tendered a snide remark, "I can see that you still have a lot you to learn about our discipline Mr. Grant. Of course you do not need to execute manoeuvres of that nature but, Jack du Preez just tried to show off the ME's performance capability." Grant ignored Fischer, turned and smiled at Rosemary Barnard.

Chubby Wilson decided to correct Du Preez's lack of courtesy with a proper answer, "Knowledge of the flight performance specifications of an attack helicopter, or any helicopter for that matter, is of vital importance to a pilot. And I am not just talking about firepower, carrying capacity, range capability and so forth. I am also thinking of tactical manoeuvrability. You need to know all about its pitch and gearbox limits, mass limitations and engine ratings. Add to these factors like, its payload capability and flight envelope limitations. By this I mean knowing how it will behave during a sideslip and hovering manoeuvres. And perhaps most importantly, you need to care about temperature and altitude influences."

Grant decided that Wilson might be a responsive and reliable source to learn more about the operational characteristics of the Martial Eagle. He started to look forward to his new assignment.

After lunch De Witt could not let the moment pass without addressing the group. He did so while liqueurs were served. He used the opportunity to mention Grant and welcomed him as a member of the team. Grant noticed that Fischer was the only person who did not join in the light applause that followed.

De Wit concluded, "All of us around this table will be flying to Cape Town in a matter of a few days. We will be accompanied by some junior staff members for a marketing and planning session. We will all be staying at the Arniston Lodge, which is situated close to the Overberg Aeronautical Test Range. I am sure all of you, except perhaps Grant, have been at the test site before or know where it is."

Grant had a vague idea of the location. At least he read once that it was close to the most southern tip of the African continent. He also knew that most of the South African armaments systems under development were tested at the Overberg Test Range. All these tests were shrouded in secrecy - especially the testing of missiles with a long-range nuclear capability.

De Wit continued, "At that session Julius will present us with his communications strategy and action plans to support our marketing effort over the next twelve months."

The group, which was now too large for the boardroom in the main building, moved to the auditorium situated close to the clubhouse.

Kurtz asked Rosemary Barnard to do a presentation. She walked up to the podium where she took time to arrange her audio-visual material. Grant sat in the front row with De Witt and Kurtz. He enjoyed the good opportunity to look at her. The knee-length black skirt complemented her well-shaped legs. A string of pearls contrasted nicely with the red blouse.

"Our Chairman, and the rest of the team, heard my presentation a few times. But on the other hand it is always good to renew old truths. More so for those of us who are getting long in the teeth and short on - memory?" She pulled a comical face and the group enjoyed her remark.

"Today I will take it from another angle. I am doing this with a view to the role that Julius will be playing. He gave me his perspective during lunch. I want to concentrate on the main selling points of the ME."

Grant listened to and appreciated her sharp grasp of the essentials. "The design of the airframe facilitates an optimised flight range of one-thousand-two-hundred kilometres depending on the weapons assigned for the sortie. This machine is also designed for hot and high altitude conditions. It has an excellent out-of-ground-effect hover capability with sufficient excess power. Add to this its fully integrated digital system with a 1,553 avionics bus and a 1,760 weapons bus. Combined with a cockpit that is designed to allow excellent external vision, with separate windscreens for each crew member, we have a winner in the marketplace." Barnard was at ease with her facts. She poured a glass of water, "Any questions?"

Grant took advantage of the moment, "Tell us more about the so called state of the art technologies of the Martial Eagle."

"A good example is the Colour Liquid Crystal Displays in the cockpit. This allows for optimum Man-Machine-Interface. To this you can also add its sand filtering system. With this facility we beat the Warrior. I think you will recall how the latter had problems with dust during the Gulf War."

Grant' general knowledge impressed the group when he asked, "And what does the sand filtering do to the Martial Eagle's engine performance?"

Barnard was equally impressive, "Although it is a highly sophisticated system, it formed part of the design from the outset. We implemented the system without any compromise whatsoever to the aircraft engine's performance." She continued, "From a maintenance point of view, it has very low requirements. And the components have a high level of reliability. The Martial Eagle offers ease of replenishment in field conditions. It requires minimal equipment from Ground Support."

Grant shot her another question, "I know, from reports, that the Martial Eagle was developed for bush-war conditions in Angola. But how will it perform in weather conditions in other parts of the world, like Afghanistan, Iraq and Iran?"

Barnard thought for a while, "It offers good all-weather operation in day and night conditions. Sophisticated sensors and sighting systems allow for this. The support of a fully integrated binocular, full-visor Helmet Mounted Sight and display system contribute to its all-time operational capability."

Grant raised a touchy subject, "There is wide-spread speculation that American missile manufacturers are prohibited by an embargo to supply weapons for the Martial Eagle. It is also not sure if and when this embargo will be lifted. What is your alternative to this shortcoming?"

"Bloody Yanks." The muffled remark came from Fischer.

Kurtz offered the answer, "The American prohibition is understandable. I believe it is a temporary one. In the meantime the South African scientists are close to completion of the development of the Makopa Missile. It will have a range in excess of 8, 5 kilometres and offers good capability against modern armour as well as explosive reactive armour. I am talking of a penetration capability in excess of 1,350 millimetres."

Grant was unsure, "Will it be a cost-effective alternative?"

Kurtz strung his fingers together, "I believe so. Eventually it will be an alternative to what the competitors have on the market."

"Will it compete with, for example, the American Hell-Fire Missile?" Grant wanted to make sure. Facts like these play an important role in a marketing communications programme.

"The Mokopa's design does not only offer flexibility but also options in terms of Radar and imaging infra-red seeker heads." Rosemary Barnard helped Kurtz out with this more technical answer. Yet she kept her promise to Grant to stick to layman's language.

De Witt rounded off the discussion with a very sensitive political remark, "International interests sometimes dictate to countries to buy from an independent perhaps unidentified source. Backed by strategic reasons they do not want to shop for missiles in America, Europe, Germany, Russia or China. South Africa's reliable and battle-proven systems present exactly that alternative."

The presentation drew to a close. Kurtz invited the team for cocktails at the club. Grant excused himself. He wanted to find out more about President Mandela's attendance of the air show in Malaysia.

From his car he phoned Marjory. He gave her the detail that he obtained from Kurtz after the meeting. He confirmed that President Mandela received an invitation from Dr. Mahathir bin Mohamed, Prime Minister of Malaysia. Madiba, as President Mandela is fondly referred to, would be a Guest of Honour at the forthcoming air show on the Island of Langkawi.

18.

CAPE TOWN CALLS.

SEA POINT, CAPE TOWN

The incessant calls of the seagulls, driven by a hunger that developed during the long May night's dark hours, woke Marlene. She lay on her back and traced the dimly lit interior of her Cape Town hotel room with sleepy eyes. She hoped to once again, slip back into the wondrous, hazy world where dreams are sometimes a pleasant reality. All she had to do was to refrain from thinking about her Monday programme, and her appointment with President Mandela. Marlene chose to listen to the screeching calls of the birds instead. She hoped that by doing so, sleep would once again be hers till the wake-up call sounded. On the beach, in the morning mist, the sea birds searched frantically for a first meal between the rocks and pools that were filled with fresh sea life during the night's high tide.

New sounds started to fill the early dawn. At street level the traffic became alive with the movement of heavy diesel trucks and busses. Cocky motor cycles whirred between passenger cars and overcrowded taxis. They all rushed their occupants to time-clocked factory gates and workplaces. Hotel staff talked noisily in the foyer as they welcomed the early day team who were responsible to start up the kitchen for breakfast and to deliver early coffee and newspapers. The hotel's escalator made a noisy first trip carrying down early morning fitness devotees to the mist-filled sidewalks. Joggers selected a route that paralleled the stormy, rocky beach at Sea Point. The noise of filling bathtubs and the faint smell of freshly cooked bacon, eggs and toasted bread filtered through to the hallways of the hotel.

Marlene was left with no choice than to start the day. She swung her long well-tanned legs from the bed as the phone rang. It was her wake-up call. Without answering she lifted and dropped the receiver back on the cradle and stood up. With outstretched arms, she looked at her lines in the full-length mirror that covered one wall of the room. What she saw made her feel good. For years now she maintained an ideal weight for her five-foot eight. She made a concerted effort to stick to her diet. She treated her appointments at the Health and Racquet Club with the same importance as business commitments. The short pyjamas screened her full breasts as she placed her slender hands on her hips and turned sideways to trace the firm line of her tummy. This was the part of her body that she was most concerned about. It motivated her to a dedicated life of moderate consumption and dutiful workouts.

In the well-lit bathroom she snapped on a shower cap and leaned forward to study the texture of her skin. She saw the first signs of wrinkles around her eyes and upper lip in the cruel mirror before her. This was one facet of her personal care she felt she neglected. She decided to remind Connie Heyneken to program her visits to 'Faces from Africa' as a recurring appointment on her electronic dairy. As she stood back and followed the lines of her shoulders and arms she looked at her hands. For the first time she spotted a light coloured freckle that developed close to her wrist. Marlene rubbed at it and thought out loud, "Suppose I must accept some signs of ageing but I still look pretty much the same as when I still had you around my dear Meyer. How long has it been since you left me? How I wish that we had a last word for each other – before it was over for you. All the time since you were ambushed in that godforsaken Angola feels like weeks. Damned Cubans! Damned senseless border war! It killed the one man that risked his all to hopefully urge for an end to an impossible silly war." Marlene spoke to her reflection in the mirror, which started to become hazy with fog.

Marlene stepped into the shower and found comfort thinking how they made passionate love the evening before he left. With misty eyes she revelled under the tepid water that spurted with a tingling force on her smooth body. Minutes later she was dressed in a knee-length skirt and chiffon blouse. Her choice gave full recognition to her well-contoured lines. With expertise and delicate taste she added a shade of makeup. It complemented the colour scheme of her garments and gold jewellery. She made sure that the content of her briefcase was in order, and took the elevator to the first floor where breakfast was served.

While Marlene waited for the fresh fruit, toast, hardboiled egg and sliced tomato that she ordered, she made a few calls to her office and other business commitments from her cellular phone. Lastly she called Grant at his home. She wanted to know how the briefing went at Africair. Grant reported on the people he met and the marketing and technological data that was passed on to him. He also confirmed the role President Mandela would play during the Lankawi Air show in Malaysia. She brought him up to date with the interviews and meetings she had with the rugby and soccer unions.

By the time her breakfast arrived she had her day's program well worked out and confirmed. Marlene enjoyed concentrating on her meal since she was well prepared for her working session with President Mandela.

The rented Audi Marlene brought her to the parking area at 'Tuinhuis.' She walked up to the impressive entrance of the old Cape Dutch home with its sprawling gardens and well manicured lawns. She could understand why the name of 'Tuinhuis' stuck, even under a new black majority government. It was the Afrikaans word for 'garden home'. Marlene passed several uniformed men standing around on the wide veranda. Eventually a short, attractive black woman received her at the heavy stinkwood entrance. Her attire had a hint of ethnic colour and taste.

"Good morning Dr. Brooks. Please come through."

She led Marlene through an equally large and impressive foyer with typical Old Dutch furnishings. There were heavy-framed paintings of various South African scenes and landmarks on the walls. The touch of Maryke de Klerck, wife of the last white president of the country, was still tolerated by officialdom. Marlene thought that the first two years of majority rule had perhaps other priorities than to spend time and money eradicating the signs of the previous white-led government. President Mandela's ANC Party had to tend to more important things than to physically changing the environment. Altering names, pulling down monuments or neglecting existing white cultural things would certainly follow but was not yet important at this point in time.

They walked down a long hallway and entered a medium-sized conference room. The solid yellowwood-topped table made provision to seat six people. In the centre of the heavy table was a thirty-inch high, statue carved from wood. It depicted a naked Xhosa girl holding a calabash. It was the first African artwork that Marlene noticed in the old homestead, which witnessed many historical moments.

Marlene once read that it was in this same room where PW Botha and FW de Klerck discussed, for the first time, Mandela's release from the jail for political detainees on Robben Island. PW Botha was mostly concerned what the implications would be, should Mandela be released from the prison. Little did they know that they would become true historical giants by eventually turning the forceful tide of Afrikaner nationalism!. It was FW de Klerck, however, who took the brave step and directed the National Party to a destination of compassion and true human dignity. He and Nelson Mandela eventually received the Nobel Peace Prize for their efforts.

"The President and his secretarial team will be with you shortly, madam and tea will be served, once the president is seated." The receptionist gave Marlene a pleasant smile.

"Thank you, you're most kind." Marlene said "and may I compliment you on your most beautiful dress," it brought a radiant twinkle her eyes. She threw back her head and laughed loud and heartily in recognition of Marlene's compliment. It filled the room, whose walls perhaps never heard anything this pleasant since it was built many decades ago.

While she made small talk with the young woman, her thoughts were busy with the agenda before her. This meeting would be the first since she saw the President at the Ellis Park rugby stadium. She had to admit that she was a little nervous to hear his comments on the manner that she handled his appearance before such an enormous crowd. He may have had second thoughts or critique from his party members, despite the good media coverage that he received. Marlene was well aware that those party politics played an important role in the New South Africa. There were many interests and hidden agenda's to keep track of for possible reaction. Marlene realised that she was not too informed and was actually in need of someone to paint her a comprehensive picture of what went on inside the black-dominated political groups. It would also be important to know about the concealed political aims of the labour unions, the youth brigades and individuals like the president's ex-wife and current opponent, Winnie Mandela.

Just then Marlene could hear the familiar drone of the President's voice as he and his secretarial staff came down the passage towards the conference room. As usual, when she was in the presence of President Mandela, it filled Marlene's with excitement and pleasant expectations for the discussions ahead.

19.

MEETING WITH PRESIDENT MANDELA.

PRESIDENT'S MANDELA'S OFFICIAL RESIDENCE

President Mandela walked into the room with his typically dignified composure and limping stride. He wore his unique, and now trade-mark, overhanging shirt, with an ethnic batik pattern of green, black, red and purple. He was relaxed and smiled pleasantly as he stretched out both his hands and took hold of hers.

"Good morning Dr. Brooks, I hope you did not have to wait too long for the old man this morning." He laughed pleasantly for the popular reference to himself.

"Not at all, Mr. President, I have just arrived, thank you." Mandela stood a few inches taller than Marlene, despite the high-heeled shoes she wore.

The President took place at the top of the table in the chair that had a longer backrest than the rest. His two secretaries took place on his left side while his personal aide sat to his right. They positioned their notebooks and pens neatly in front of them and smiled at Marlene. The President folded his hands and looked at Marlene with a smile. He had no writing materials with him. Over the past fourteen months Marlene had frequent meetings with them and she always found it most stimulating. Taking care of certain facets of the President's communications program she would always regard as the highlight and most gratifying moment of her career.

"And how is my special communications advisor doing today?" the President asked.

"Oh just fine Mr. President. And how are you keeping?"

"Well, you can guess how it goes with an old man who has too much work to do. Luckily I have my good and competent friends around the table support me. And like you, Marlene, they succeed most brilliantly in their task. They allow the old man to look good and I come up tops every time." Mandela elbowed his aide and laughed.

"With someone like you, Mr. President, it is not at all a difficult task. In fact, it is a most pleasant experience. And I am sure your staff will agree." They smiled and nodded actively.

"Now you have made my day and may I return your compliment. I want to thank and congratulate you on the excellent service and advice that you rendered to my staff and me throughout the event of the Rugby World Cup. Your surprising knowledge of the game of rugby and your contacts with the rugby administrators and some of the stern old Afrikaner guys, who runs the game, impressed me." Mandela winked at his staff, "Your correct sensing of the rugby supporters sentiments, helped me to communicate in a special way my passion for reconciliation amongst the people of our country."

Marlene could not help but to admire the sincerity of President Nelson Mandela. A well-known historian once said that South Africa was fortunate to always have had the right man at the right time to lead the country. She did not always agree with his statement but this time, she was sure, that those words were true.

"Thank you Mr. President, but I only tried to do my duty, for which you are paying me well."

Mandela looked her in the eyes, "Last night I addressed a function hosted by the champions of our defence industry. Someone from the Denel Technology Group, whose name I can't remember right now, stated a true thing when he said, you can never pay a good loyal worker enough but you are always paying a bad worker too much."

"Perhaps you are paying me too much Mr. President." Marlene could not keep the tease out of her eyes and the President enjoyed her remark.

"On the contrary" and he looked for the support of his staff that was silent up to now, "how can you reward, in monetary terms, your advice that I had to wear a rugby jersey and Springbok cap at the opening ceremony of the final game? Everybody agreed that it made the day. I had all the rugby players and supporters of the country behind me. Although I must admit that, at first, I thought it was a bit of an unusual thing for the President of a country to do." Marlene wondered by herself if FW and not to mention old PW, would ever have exchanged their striped suites and silly black hats for a rugby jersey.

The kitchen staff wheeled in a large trolley loaded with silver, porcelain, cookies and biscuits and the President invited hem, , "Ladies and gentlemen let's enjoy what the kitchen has prepared for us."

The mood was relaxed and Marlene hoped that President Mandela enjoyed their work sessions as much as she did. He once referred to her as his communications consultant of 'fun projects'. The musical sounds of silver teaspoons on cups and saucers contributed to the jovial atmosphere. President Mandela nodded to his aide, who started the meeting with a short recap of the President's image building strategy. He also reported on the completed tasks to date and gave an interesting and accurate evaluation of the popularity of the President. He based his assumption on well-researched media clips, which was pulled from weekend and daily local and international publications.

"Marlene, when we established our working relationship you said from the outset that you will tell me what I, as President, must hear and not what I want to hear. I know that I can rely on your objective evaluation at all times. What do you think of our progress this far?" The President placed his hand under his chin and tilted his head to one side like he usually did when he was intended to listen carefully to an opinion.

Marlene's overview was received by eager nods of agreement. Her criticism was noted as well as her appreciation for the support of the President's communication staff, "Please Mr. President, convey my appreciation to them."

"Marlene, I will do so in writing and sign their letters personally." He looked at Marlene and she knew that he was a man that honoured even his smallest promise.

As usual the President was dynamic in all his dealings, "And what about the way forward?"

"I am afraid, Sir, we started something that will not be easily stopped again," Marlene looked at her notes.

"Meaning?"

"Meaning that, you will get requests to do the same for other types of sport." She said

"Yes, perhaps so, but then only when it is on par with a world event like the World Rugby Cup." The president turned businesslike and sharp as usual.

Marlene said, "We will have to judge each request on its merits, Sir. For instance I have here a request from the South African Soccer Union for you to officiate at the finals of the African Cup, later this year."

The President looked at her reflection as he saw it in the highly polished top of the wide yellowwood table. He came to trust her judgement and he also admired her inner strength. The culture of the black race would not simply allow a woman to even contemplate to go against the slightest wish or opinion of a male, let alone if this male was the chief of the tribe or even the chief of all chiefs, the President of the country.

"Soccer is a more popular sport in South Africa than rugby. The majority of supporters are blacks and their numbers are perhaps ten times of that of rugby. But, yes, I must concede we need to look at these invitations carefully. We must maintain a sensitive inclination towards all sentiments and interests of the diversity of our wonderful people. We must respect the importance of their objectives." True to character President Nelson Mandela displayed his superior ability to grasp and integrate the needs of a country that was immensely diverse and demanding. It required the wisdom of ten modern Solomon's to bring about the level of understanding and tolerance, which he said is a prerequisite for a peaceful environment.

"Do I have your approval, in principle, to work on a draft program that will include your involvement in the African Soccer Cup? Taking into account that, as was the case with the Rugby World Cup, South Africa will again be called on to be the hosts of the series?" Marlene carefully asked this question and did not expect the President to give her an outright answer, based on a snap decision. What she did have in mind, however, was to register the importance of an upcoming event and what the consequences for his image could be.

President Mandela surprised her, "When I turned in the night after we secured the Rugby World Cup, I was really happy for Francois Pienaar and his Springbok team. As a soccer fan, I tested my soccer skills as a young boy against my mates in the dusty streets of our township. We played with an old grass stuffed soccer ball. I always wondered what we could day do to boost soccer in our country." He looked at his staff who silently nodded in agreement, "Marlene, you have my approval to go ahead with such a project. But, only on one condition; the professional level of all the arrangements must be of equal or better standard than what we had with the Rugby World Cup."

"Yes and thank you mister President." Marlene could hardly contain her excitement and sense of achievement. This decision of the President meant a new and exciting task for her. It also held a financial promise in fees for Meyer, Brooks and Associates. But the most important reason for her excitement was the fact that the president skipped the formalities and called her by her first name. Popular belief has it that if ever he call you by your first name, it is a clear signal that you have won his total trust. Never before has her name sounded so good. It sounded much better than the title of "doctor". And she can still remember how her newly gained qualification demanded respect and esteem, because the title of doctor carried no gender connotations. Marlene realised that this new assignment would be an additional responsibility for their agency – but an exciting project.

"However, Marlene," and the twinkle in his eyes brought back the informality, "for the soccer players of South Africa, and their supporters I also want to wear a soccer jersey during their big moment. You know, like I did for the rugby fans."

"Yes - without a doubt, Mister President." Marlene took a file from her briefcase, made of black ostrich leather that, Meyer gave to her shortly before his death. He said, "May this bag always carry documents that will help you along your path of accomplishments. I believe it will help you to blaze a successful trail to the future." Perhaps this is happening for her now. Marlene forced the untimely recollection out of her mind.

"Is there something else we need to attend to?" President Mandela looked at the huge grandfather clock and indicated that they reached the end of the session.

"Yes, Mr. President. I must give you a timely warning of an upcoming event, which will take place later this year in Malaysia."

"Yes, yes, I have been alerted that I will be a guest of honour of Prime Minister Mahathir at the opening of the Lankawi Air Show. Apart from attending the opening day of this international air and maritime show I will also need to attend to important discussions regarding trade relations and technology transfer, especially as far as the aviation industry is concerned." Marlene admired his clear and focused zoom into his set commitments.

"I know about this invitation which you are referring to sir," Marlene confirmed.

The President was however unclear on a point, "But, I do not understand why you are bringing up this matter now. This falls outside of your terms of responsibility, Marlene." His polite manner hid his impatience – as more important political matters needed attention.

"You are right, Sir. But during that same week, when the air show will be running and our helicopter, Martial Eagle, will be on display and performing flight demonstrations, the Malaysians are staging a comprehensive sport festival. As part of the program they want to invite a soccer team, representing South Africa, to play in the grand opening match. This match will be part of the inauguration of a new sports stadium. The Malaysian Olympic Sports Committee wants to invite you as a guest of honour alongside other heads of states and royalties." Marlene presented her request as comprehensively and quickly as possible. She tried to be factual and to the point.

"By now we are used to the parallel occurrence of sport and politics. This is the first time I hear of a mix between sport and defence products. But I can see that the Malaysians want to grab the opportunity of my presence in their country to serve their sport plans. I sometimes wish our own people wanted to learn from the Malaysians. They have a burning desire to be a fully developed nation by the year 2020. Their dreams condition them to utilise just about every opportunity that comes their way." He thought for a while and everybody around the table remained quiet, then turned to his personal assistant, "Thandy, what does my diary and confirmed commitments say?"

Thandy was a top communications student from Maryland University at College Park, Washington, DC. She had Professor Larissa Grunnig, one of the world's most prominent public relations academics, as chair for her master's degree. As communicator she had an edge in her field that was not common in South Africa. Her close-to-photographic memory never failed her. "There will be time available for you to accept an invitation of this kind, Sir."

Marlene judged it wise to throw in another argument, "In Cape Town alone, we have about three hundred thousand Malaysian descendants. They have given so much to this country by way of their culture and other contributions."

"In what way?" asked a member of the President's staff.

"Well, they produced academics, writers and poets, excellent and wealthy business people. People from Malaysian decent were also outstanding athletes, and even politicians who are now members of our Government. But, I suppose you know that lastly, they gave us cuisine like bobotie and other dishes and, the Afrikaans language has many words and expressions that are borrowed from Malaysian origin."

The president interjected, "What Marlene is trying to suggest that if I agree to accept the Malaysian sport invitation it will not only strengthen our cultural ties with that country but it will also be meaningful for the Malaysian communities of our country. "

Marlene cautiously said, "Yet, Mr. President, we must not lose sight of the fact that the main purpose of your visit to Malaysia will be to assist our defence industry to secure an order for attack helicopters for the Royal Malaysian Air force,"

"Thank you Marlene, but you are now touching on very sensitive matters which are not really for the agenda of this meeting." President Mandela focused the meeting and Marlene's responsibility in a most subtle way.

The charismatic old President rose to his full length to confirm that the meeting was over. He turned to Marlene and said slowly but in a firm tone, "Apart from the soccer project, also get busy with the social commitments of my intended Malaysian visit."

"Will do, Mr. President," Marlene responded readily.

They all shook hands in the African manner and left the small conference room. Marlene could not wait to tell Grant about the new developments. She was filled with excitement by the prospect of working on the Malaysian soccer invitation. She realized that their respective projects would mean that she and Grant would be simultaneously in Malaysia. This could become quite a pleasant outing, she thought. What she did not in the least contemplated was the possibility that this project could turn into an international disaster and put her and the life of President Mandela in danger.

20.

PROMOTING WORLD PEACE.

KENSINGTON, LONDON

The rain stopped and gave Douglas Collins a chance to push Brian Boddington's wheel chair through the entrance to the pilot's apartment building in London's Kensington district. By now a feeling of wellbeing prevailed, brought about by the hearty meal and wine the two brothers-in-law enjoyed. It framed their minds to talk in a more relaxed manner about what Collins had in mind for Boddington. Or so it sounded from their casual remarks about the rain and traffic.

Boddington's wife was in New York. She attended her mother's eighty-fifth birthday. For years now, the old lady managed to get all her daughters from all four corners of the globe together at every birthday celebration. She looked upon every birthday as "my last birthday on earth." This gave Boddington the opportunity to do things on his own from time to time. He actually enjoyed the absence of his wife, who always fussed around and sometimes annoyed him unbearably. He lifted his cup and silently took a sip of coffee in honour of his dear old hag of a mother-in-law. By now she was most likely walloping in champagne, sentiment, snot and tears. She would have all the sympathy from her middle-aged daughters. Thank God they are all on the other side of the Atlantic. They would all join her tearfully and hope that longevity and medical cost would not erode too much of her fortune. They all hoped that what was left and passed on to be shared equally amongst them, would count to a significant amount. They have worked hard all these years, putting up with her tediousness in the hope to be awarded for their endurance. And, oh yes, not to forget their heartfelt compassion. Brian could not remember how many times she repeated the intention of her will over the past decades. However, this evening it gave them unlimited time to discuss their business uninterrupted.

"Coming back to this 'disruption' that you want me to cause. What must I do? Throw sugar in the Martial Eagle's fuel tank and force it out of an air show - or, what?" Boddington smiled at Collins to signal his light humorous attitude. He sensed that the matter must be of the utmost importance to him. Otherwise why the hell did he go through all the trouble of sharing his only past-time, watching a good rugby match on the telly with his American brother-in law? He could have had a much better time somewhere else at a good old London country club with his wealthy buddies.

"Yes," Collins looked him straight in the eyes.

"Yes, what?" Boddington sat upright in his wheel chair and leaned forward to await Collins's answer.

"Meaning I want you to incapacitate the South Africans' helicopter. I want you to put them completely out of the race for the Malaysian bid." Iniquity shone in Collins' eyes.

"What! Are you really serious? No bullshit? You must be joking or I must be bloody drunk. Or perhaps you are pissed beyond reason, Douglas!"

Collins did not respond while Boddington wheeled to the liquor cabinet, selected a medium-priced French port and two small glasses. He returned to his seat. Silence followed while he filled the glasses.

Collins explained his request, "All I am asking you is to apply your knowledge of helicopter technology to do something to their machine that will affect its performance negatively during the Lankawi Air Show - which takes place on this island two months from now. Failing that, the Malaysians may go ahead and buy their attack helicopter fleet from South Africa. The Malaysians will most likely try to manipulate the South Africans into a joint venture to manufacture parts of the machine in their country. On the other hand the Americans will not be interested in an aviation or manufacturing alliance where they have to deal with a minority shareholder. So, the only way to keep those Africans out of this bid is by arranging for something to go wrong with their chopper - perhaps horribly wrong." Collins said and carefully took the first sip from his port.

"Sounds more and more like straightforward sabotage to me - and people could get hurt you know!" Boddington downed his port with one gulp.

"Yes, if that is the price that someone has to pay." Collins slowly nodded his head to emphasise the seriousness of his remark – and anxiously awaited Boddington's response.

Boddington kept quiet and wheeled towards the small kitchen. It was time to brew a big jar of strong coffee. A lot of thinking and planning lay ahead for them. Running glibly through their plan would not do. Tomorrow would bring reality and then, whatever this night may bring forth; their arguments had to be able to stand the test of reality. He returned with the coffee and a large plate covered with an assortment of salted biscuits, pates and cheeses. Expertly he prepared the coffee table and set out the necessary cutlery, plates and arrangement of seasonings to complement the midnight snack. Collins could not help to admire his brother-in-law for being so independent and capable of looking after himself in the absence of his wife. He also turned out to be a reasonable host.

"Douglas, you always said to be a successful marketer or salesperson, you need to know the product or system of the opposition just as well as your own. Am I right?" Boddington got down to serious business now.

"Yes, but what are you getting at?" Collins studied the deep lines on Boddington's face over his steaming hot cup. The damaged pilot aged prematurely.

"If you want me to let something happen to the Martial Eagle, I need to know absolutely everything about that chopper. You could therefore just as well start with all that you can tell me about the African bird. Leave it to me to decide what is valuable for me to know." Boddington was an ardent reader of flight magazines that specialised in helicopters. He already had some background on the South Africans' Martial Eagle. But he needed to get behind the marketing politics and intrigues.

"I will tell you as much as I know. Let's take a look at the technical details that allows the ME to be considered as an option in the marketplace. OK?" Collins mentally arranged his knowledge.

"Do you also have information in print?" Boddington interjected.

"Yes, and - over time I picked up enough of it, also at international air shows." Collins could sense the man's vibrant interest and commitment, although he has not yet clearly stated his intention to accept the challenge.

"OK Douglas, but without being difficult, I will have to get hold of the real technical data. I am talking of data packs or technical directories, which comes right out of Africair's design-office. But please let's not belabour the point. Tell me what you know." Brian Boddington could not remember how long it was since he had been fired up to talk about the things he loved most in his life. He could dwell forever on defence aircraft and in particular helicopters. For the sheer satisfaction to be once more involved in something close to his heart and mind, he would even undertake to snuff out that bloody South African's whirly-bird for good.

"OK brother. I have very reliable operational networks. In good time I will pass on to you a set of original design documents, coming right out of the Martial Eagle's nest. That I promise to you." Collins anticipated this need long ago. The fat fees he paid were already fuelling his networks to provide him with what they needed. They were so efficient, that there was no chance of tracing the acquisition of these highly secret documents to his address.

"Sounds very clued-up, and reassuring to me brother. But what can you tell me in the meantime about the ME. I am most interested in its performance capabilities." Boddington realised that he was enjoying their conversation.

"Then I will start at the point where it matters most -- what the user could expect from the ME's performance." When it came to keeping his cool with a view to succeed as a marketer or 'sales person' as Boddington called him, it was hard to beat Douglas Collins.

"Shoot!" Boddington poured himself a fresh cup of coffee and settled into a listening mode.

"I am sure you have met Rory Cowan of 'Defence Helicopter'. It's a Shepherd Press publication." Collins was aware that Boddington was a keen reader.

"Shit man, who does not know that? I met him once. He is a well-known professional engineer and test pilot who were trained at the Royal Naval Engineering College at Manadon. He also did a spell at the Empire Test Pilots' School at Boscombe Down." Boddington was in his element.

"Maybe you are right, but Cowan took that chopper for a test flight during the previous air show at Farnborough, and I had a very interesting discussion with him afterwards." Collins enjoyed the eagerness in Boddington's eyes.

"How come?"

"Well, I tried to motivate him to write an article about our agency and of course the reasons why the Warrior should win the UK bid over the Martial Eagle." Collins said.

"OK, but we all know that the eventual decision was politically based. Nobody cared stuff-all about what the pilots, or 'users' as you call them, preferred. But, go ahead. Tell me what his impressions were. I have great respect for the man, and enjoy reading his reports. One can take his opinions to heart." Brian Boddington wished for the night to last forever.

Collins prepared himself a few biscuits with a variety of toppings. While he chewed, he spoke from the side of his mouth, "Cowan did this test flight in a brisk south-westerly wind at Cambridge. According to him, the overall impression a pilot has when he descends from the seven-foot high cockpit of the ME is that of a very powerful machine that is easy to fly. The design philosophy of the aircraft embraces simplicity, which makes it easy to operate from the moment you touch the start buttons, through all the manoeuvres and even down to a rough landing."

"Did he mention starting procedure and time?"

"The ME can start and depart in less than one and a half minute. Engine starting is automatic with a choice of ground power."

"Good!" Boddington smacked his lips and rolled to the sideboard from where he took an unopened pack of Rothmans from his wife's stock. He smoked any brand, particularly those he could get for free, "What did he say about ascent and descent?"

"You can pick her up at a rate of 2,500 feet per minute and let her spiral down at 3000 to 4000 feet per minute, and still maintain easy control."

"I heard you can fly her with one hand, leaving you with enough room to detect an attack." Boddington offered a cigarette to Collins who declined and preferred his own brand.

"Apparently the cockpit is spacious and uncluttered. The colour digital displays of the instrument panel and the standby instruments are adequately positioned. The low sills of the windows afford unimpaired views to both sides and the front." It was clear that Collins new the ME inside out. He quoted Cowan just for the sake of giving a pilot's point of view to Boddington, whose attention he hoped would not wane at this stage. He filled him in on many technical details and answered all of Boddington's questions fairly accurate.

While Collins ran through his mind for more data to disseminate, Boddington threw him a last but important question, "As you described this chopper it sounds as if her exhaust fumes create a permanent halo above her rotor. There must be something suspect he must have observed. It is always the case with all experimental aircraft, not so?"

"Let me think. Ah... yes. He mentioned that the inertial navigation system tended to trip 'off-line' on engine start. This again, had a negative influence on the auto pilot, especially at low altitudes."

"You know, Douglas, an attack helicopter spends most of its life at around 50 feet or less…" He allowed his thoughts to trail and Collins did not interrupt, but waited patiently. "…if the auto pilot lets you down while you have your mind tied-up with the execution of an attack, even just a few seconds will erode safety margins to the point of unavoidable disaster."

Collins saw through his idea and enjoyed the feverish glint in Boddington's eyes. He stood up and walked to the window. Outside the dawn was breaking and the weather was still miserable. He turned around and faced Boddington.

Boddington's fists pummelled the wheels of his chair, "That is what's going to happen. The ME's auto-pilot is going to bring her down." Boddington wheeled his chair around with a jerk, rolled towards Collins and looked up at him, "You know what I think? I could do the world an unaccountably big favour if I prevented the Afrikaners who are now working for the ANC, to pass on their capabilities to those other potential enemies of ours. I am referring to Castro and that bloody Kaddafi. Not to mention Saddam Hussein and all his towel-headed neighbours. Should I be successful to stop Mandela to provide his old chums and sympathisers, from the days of their struggle, with what they need, I may even become some sort of a bloody silent hero after all! It will stop those bastards to muck around and add a new dimension to their terrorist activities. Perhaps I could even be making a grand contribution towards world peace." Boddington's mind was made up and he wheeled back to the coffee table.

The fact that Collins would earn a lot of commission and he only a lousy five hundred thousand dollars for his trouble, is of minor importance, he thought, "I want $250,000 up-front money in my personal account. How soon can you oblige?"

"Who talked about up-front money?" Collins wanted to cement his commitment thoroughly. He had difficulty in hiding the pleasure he derived from his wickedness.

"Get out a here, Collins. You're wasting my time!"

"Then you will do it? You will snuff out the Martial Eagle?"

"I said get the hell out and go and make that deposit. I will be watching my bank account on my pc-banking." Boddington nodded in the direction of his monitor that ran a screen-saver displaying a series of military helicopters.

"$200,000." Collins' natural business talents played its role.

"$250,000 - or get the hell out of my life."

"OK. Before noon you will read the deposit on your telly-bank."

"It's a deal. I'll give you my bank details." Brian Boddington's mind was already hard at work, devising various options of how to make possible the destruction of the Martial Eagle.

21.

FLIGHT TO JOHANNESBURG.

FLIGHT FROM DUBAI TO JOHANNESBURG

A frail looking Akbar Assad dressed in a pin-striped suit looked ill at ease where he sat in the business class of Emirates Air's midnight flight from Dubai to Johannesburg. He leaned against the oval window and looked down at the intermittent Dubai harbour lights and hear how the under carriage of the Boeing 747 snapped into its bays. The brightness from the modern sector of the city moved out of sight as they rapidly gained height and set course for Johannesburg. Below, the full moon blanketed the Arabian Desert in a creamy cashmere tint. Assad quickly fell asleep and missed out on the last round of refreshments before the cabin crew darkened the passenger area.

The early morning greeting from the cockpit brought Assad back to reality. A light breakfast was served before the landing at Johannesburg International Airport. He waited for his turn to freshen up in the small restroom where he shaved, tended to the neatness of his full-size black moustache and returned to his seat.

The southbound flight to the Golden City took just over eight hours. As their flight crossed the Limpopo River the decent started and Assad felt how a somewhat tenseness increased in his chest. It was his first visit to South Africa. His uneasiness was the result of the anticipated strangeness of everything that characterized the country's diverse cultures. The mountains and rolling yellow grass landscape below amazed him. Large valleys were covered in hazy grey, early morning mist. The sky was brilliantly clear and held the promise of a pleasant winter's day. The captain predicted a ground temperature around freezing point that could climb to the low twenties towards noon.

Assad passed through customs and picked up his baggage at the carousal. He arranged with John Molape of Africair Corporation to meet him. While he waited for the delivery of his large bag, he again thought about his agenda and the real purpose for this visit.

Assad expected the week ahead to be crucial. He expected that his career as a journalist to take on a totally new and unfamiliar dimension. He knew his visit also held the promise to open up the potential of increasing his experience as an investigative reporter. In addition, it could confirm his capability to generate an additional source of revenue. The first responsibility of his mission was to report for The Gulf News on the capabilities of South Africa's aviation industry. Simultaneously he would evaluate the possibility for joint ventures and counter trade between the United Arab Emirates and the Republic of South Africa.

Assad realized that his tenseness was the result of the undercover purpose of his reporting. He had to establish the significance of John Molape as a possible secret connection to retrieve sensitive attack helicopter technology. A covert network, referred to as The Agency, approached and recruited him some weeks ago with the promise of an additional income from syndicating news items to them surreptitiously in his private capacity. Just before his departure he received a very short instruction with regard to his first assignment. He simply had to use his position as a journalist to establish if he could recruit someone at the Africair Aviation Company to help with obtaining specific secret technology information.

Following their first meeting in Dubai with John Molape, he relayed the communications manager's name as a possible source in Africair who may be an appropriate contact to provide the necessary technology information. Since he received Molape's invitation to visit the Martial Eagle's assembly plant and after he made arrangements for this official editorial trip to South Africa, The Agency somehow knew about his program and contacted him. Shortly before his departure, he received a supplementary background on Molape, compiled by The Agency's South African set-up. Assad was instructed to study and immediately delete the report which was transmitted to his e-mail address under cover of a password. He made sure that he could recall all of the material, "Your choice seems, at first impression, to be a promising one. M is a person who grew up with the attitude that the white people of the country created, through their political power, an unfair advantage for themselves to accumulate wealth. His parents, who were both teachers in the Apartheid regime's Department of Bantu Education, nursed this approach. They were looked upon as law-abiding citizens and were not regarded as partisan to the political struggle of the black people. They were, however, embittered by their standing as second class citizens."

The report continued, "M was known as a quiet dedicated student who never caused trouble of any kind and who stuck to a well-defined behaviour of submission. Molape's parents constantly reminded him to bow to the country's white power. They also warned him that, he should stay out of racial aimed politics. This could jeopardize their careers as public servants in the Department of Bantu Education that was created by Hendrik Verwoerd, the architect of Apartheid. Instead, they encouraged him to strive to qualify himself as a journalist. They were confident their son would find a position with a government-funded publication. That way he could earn a reasonable income and find one of the few opportunities that were available for blacks to be somewhat prosperous. It would allow him to acquire some of the 'good things' that white technology and its commercialized life style offered. Molape's parents assumed that an Apartheid regime would always be in command.

The report ended with a last promising observation, "M apparently believes that the dawn of the new South Africa holds a promise for black people to also become materialistically minded. The new country's acceptance of the practise of affirmative action to eradicate the gap between privileged whites and the disadvantaged blacks elevated his opinion. John Molape saw it as an opportunity to catch up with the level of material wellbeing that his parents would never be able to achieve." The Agency was reasonably confident that Molape could be corrupted. His instructions concluded with a guideline, "You will be informed about your available budget for Molapi, and how to apply it. This will be forwarded to you with the payment of your next monthly advisory fee."

Assad was thankful for the so-called 'advisory fee'. It calculated to about four times his salary and would indeed boost his life-style. Assad smiled as he walked through the arrival gate.

22.

FREELANCE WORK.

JOHANNESBURG INTERNATIONAL AIRPORT

Molape waited patiently for Assad in the overcrowded arrival hall of Johannesburg International Airport. He was well ahead of the scheduled time and watched how several flights arrived within minutes apart. He could not help to question if the country had the capability to stage a world event such as the Soccer World Cup of 2010. As hosts, they did not too bad with the Rugby World Cup's visitors. But then again, the magnitude of the soccer turn-out would place a much higher demand on the country's infrastructure. Molape was optimistic that international politics and the sentiments around the soccer sport would eventually give South Africa the opportunity to be selected as hosts for the world's best teams. Despite the fact that Nelson Mandela's country became the democratic champion of Africa, to date the Soccer World Cup had never been awarded to this African country.

Molape was on the lookout for a short dark skinned Arabian in a white robe, so at first he did not notice Assad. Only when Assad pushed his baggage trolley towards him, he recognized his guest dressed in his neat business suit. He looked so much different from the time that they have met previously when he wore his traditional flowing white attire and headgear. They shook hands, exchanged greetings and moved out of the noisy hall into the cold morning air. Assad shivered from cold and excitement as they walked briskly to where a company car and driver waited for them.

Their first stop was two miles down the freeway at the Holiday Inns. It was also close to Africair's premises, which bordered the airport. While Assad registered at the reception desk and followed the bellboy to his room, Molape made breakfast arrangements.

Molape pushed the cutlery aside, "Today we will meet the key people of Africair and visit the assembly line of the Martial Eagle. For lunch we will be going to the Sandton Hotel with Julius Grant, our international communications' advisor." Molape did the briefing while Assad ate and made notes in Arabic. Now and then he would interrupt with a question.

"Will I be able to talk to the engineers and technicians of the ME-team?"

Molape hesitated for a while. It was company policy that only a few selected and well-briefed senior management members granted interviews to the media, "I will see if we can make an exception in your case - especially with a view to the content of your article."

"Good." Assad's moustache stretched out as he smiled at Molape, "I have set aside two days for Africair. The rest of my time will be with about four other companies in the aviation components and services business."

Molape was tempted to ask him who they were but refrained, "Once you have covered the Martial Eagle, will we meet again, before you leave?"

"Oh, yes. I am leaving on a midnight flight next Monday. Perhaps we can have dinner somewhere and round things up before my departure." Assad looked at Molape to signal that such a meeting would be imperative to conclude his visit.

Molape made a note in his dairy, "Fine with me."

"Of course I will also have to make contact with representatives from my paper and the Emirates government." Assad made it clear that he did not expect to be chaperoned for the full duration of his tour.

"Why would the Gulf News be so interested in the Martial Eagle? I mean, compared to the other general media, you are not satisfied with the normal news releases, fact sheets, photos and captions. It seems as if you need some really comprehensive technical detail and prefers to take your own photos." Molape wanted to warrant the special attention he gave this journalist.

Assad was immediately on guard. He reminded himself to be careful not to arouse the suspicion of this bright young man. It may cause Molape to close up and until the time is right, he may also want to guard the information for which he is paid so handsomely.

"Well, I must agree that I do sometimes come over like a technical writer of an aviation magazine, but the reason is that I have to answer to my Chief Editor. He was once the editor of a trade magazine and still requires from his editorial staff a multi-source approach when they are writing anything for him. When it comes to financial and technical things, he believes in offering the informed reader a little more than just a general news article."

"I can't find anything wrong with that, but how do you feel about this approach as a journalist?"

"Perhaps I need to please the boss. But on the other hand I have a feeling the choice of an attack helicopter for the United Arab Emirates, and perhaps other Arabian states is important. I also believe that the average citizen should know why a certain machine would be suitable for the forces. As a matter of fact, I am leaving shortly for Europe, the UK and the United States. My plan is to look at and also write about their attack helicopters." Assad surprised himself with the fluent lie and hoped that he convinced Molape with his account.

"Well, as a journalism student I had a professor who always said we should rather over-service a story with facts and leave it to the sub-editor to cut the writing to fit the available editorial space." Molape wanted to signal to Assad that he had some knowledge of what goes on in a newsroom.

Assad thought the moment was right to move a little closer to Molape's personal interests, "As a matter of fact, my editor is so serious about technical detail that he sometimes appoints special correspondents to supply us with material." The bait splashed before Molape and for a while he was quiet. Assad allowed him to think about the possibility realising Molape could let the opportunity pass.

Instead he asked, "Would you like me to suggest to you the names of freelance journalists here in Johannesburg for consideration by your editor?" Molape was not sure where this discussion was taking them.

"Not really. He allows his writers to decide whom we would like to assign or help us with information gathering." Assad searched Molape's eyes to see if he could be lured into the trap.

"Well ..." Molape scratched with his pen in the dense hair above his right ear "... I do have some writing experience. But then again, if I do it for you, I will have to do it for all the other media guys."

"I suppose so, if they pay you a writer's fees like we would."

"You mean apart from the normal news releases I write and issue, you would pay me to write a special story for your paper?" Molape's dark brown eyes glinted eagerly.

"Yes, and we will make it worth your while. And you don't have to work too hard at writing the story. All you would need to do is to supply me with the facts I call for and I will do the final writing." Assad was pleased with the way their conversation developed. He did not expect that the opportunity would present itself this early during his visit.

"Well, I am interested. Where do we take it from here?" Molape leaned back in his chair, chewed on his pen and looked expectantly at the lean Arab.

"Before I return to Dubai we can work out a reporting arrangement."

"And also the payment arrangement?"

"Yes. And it will be enough to make you smile ..." Assad looked at his slender hands. He was afraid Molape would pick up on his satisfaction. Got you, Mister Greedy, he thought. This will be a handy extra source for you to catch up to your wealthy white colleagues with their beautiful homes and shiny German cars.

Molape eagerness came through, "Good. Let's drive over to Africair."

23.

THE EAGLE'S NEST.

AFRICAIR'S FACTORY, KEMPTON PARK

"I am pleased to meet you, Mr. Assad." Mark Fischer moved towards the easy chairs arranged around a coffee table. Before he sat down he opened the curtained windows of his large office. Assad and Molape took place opposite Fischer, who tried his best to come over as relaxed and amiable as possible. He did, however, not fool Molape. He knew from reports that Fischer was not easy to get along with and lacked the pleasant qualities required to maintain a good business relationship

"Please do call me Akbar. Everybody else does." Assad smoothed his moustache and his smile showed regular teeth, which appeared brilliant between his brown lips.

"OK Akbar. Call me Mark. Let's stay on first name level. John gave me a backdrop to the aim of your visit. Please tell me how we can help you?"

"Well Mark, my mission is quite simple. With a view to the oncoming air show on the island of Lankawi in Malaysia, I would like to compile as much information as possible on the Martial Eagle. I will be attending the show for 'The Gulf News' and want to be a jump ahead of the regular technical media guys."

Fischer became serious and leaned forward, "I suppose there's nothing wrong with a pro-active approach but, I am sure you will appreciate that some information is confidential and we would not like our competitors to read about those."

"Oh yes, that I understand all too well, Mark." Assad knew that to get what he really wanted will be tricky and he will have to take utmost care.

"But apart from that and any indication of to whom we are selling or how such efforts are progressing, there is still enough to write a whole book about the Martial Eagle." Fischer leaned backwards in his chair as if he believed the whole approach was structured. Assad may go ahead to compile the facts. He knew that the corporate security team would shadow him and make sure that they will stay out of the sensitive areas in the assembly plant.

Molape sensed Fischer's concern for security and tried to alleviate his fear of negative consequences, "I discussed with the Head of Security, Fredrick Kramer all the detail of the route that Akbar and I planned to follow during his visit."

"OK John. Go ahead and show Akbar the best attack helicopter that any country's defence force can ever think to buy." Fischer had to drop his sales punch-line.

"In my article I will also let the spotlight fall on other attack helicopters, Mark." Assad hoped that this remark would avoid a too tight-fisted attitude towards the information that he was after.

Fischer pulled a face, showing irrelevance, "That I can appreciate Akbar. But there is nothing that excites us more, here at Africair, than a little competition." Fischer winked and still failed at being amiable, "Let Molape show you our little factory."

The sheer vastness of the Africair Corporation's manufacturing facilities overwhelmed Assad. This was not his first visit to an international aviation manufacturer's plant. But he had to confess to himself that he could not, in his wildest imagination, picture what enfolded before him. He did not expect anything this comprehensive anywhere in Africa. Assad now had grounds to believe how serious this country's previous government was with its aviation and armaments industry.

When the design team made its presentation on videotape and overhead projector he felt unattached. It all came over as ice-cold facts. It was detail, which he could have picked up in the Gulf News library or on Internet. Now, as he stood there aware of the factory smells and heard the activities of manufacturing all around him, the massive scope of the operation was an undeniable reality.

"John, I must confess, this is all very impressive. You must please allow me to ask some awkward questions today. We may also need to go through this visit much slower than we anticipated." Assad looked earnestly at Molape while he wondered if the black man knew that his briefing in Dubai warned that he might come across technology that would surprise him. Yet, he had to concentrate mostly on what The Agency wanted to know. But he was honestly not prepared for what he saw. Assad pretended that the overwhelming impression of the state of the art technology called for his slower uptake. His true reason was to make sure he did not miss an opportunity to pick up the useful information he was after.

"I do realise you do not have all the time in the world during this visit. And I know you want to visit a number of other South African defence industries…" John Molape said as they travelled with a golf cart through the hangers where the manufacturing of the Martial Eagle took place, "…but I will do my best to accommodate you."

"Yes, but my visit to this plant is of prime importance …for the purpose of my series of articles on the development of the world's large attack helicopters." Assad took his automatic Konica from its poach and made sure that the film loading was in order.

"Assad, you may only use your camera if the security baboons behind us are comfortable with what you intend to photograph." Molape surfaced his view of displeasure for the old style security systems which were still in place.

"Thank you for the early warning, John. It is this kind of censure on all media people …and communications persons like you that make our official lives miserable. It does not help our efforts to demystify the armaments industry at all! More so as it was the culture of your previous government to keep their entire defence capabilities top secret." Assad was aware of Molape's quick glance. He must be careful not to let too much slip out of his pre-knowledge on the South African state of affairs. He was well informed of the developments up to the time of the unbanning of the ANC and Mandela's release from prison.

"You are right Assad. Nothing beats the sluggishness of the white operated security networks of this country. It will take some time to wrench us free from their tight grip on the dominance of security structures in the various government controlled institutions." Molape lightly pounded his fist on the golf cart's steering wheel as they entered an enormous steel hanger.

They travelled along the designated route towards a box-like drawing office in the centre of the main hall. Through the tinted windows, Assad saw an open plan, office layout. The well-lit workstations were tightly furnished with slanted drawing tables, computer screens and printing units. About thirty engineers and technicians were at their desks. They were so caught up in their work and discussions that they paid no attention to Molape, Assad followed by Christian Faber, Head of Security, as they entered the exceptionally well air-conditioned room.

Molape stood at the entrance and looked at the scene before him as if he was not sure where to start. Behind them Faber stood like a mountain in khaki clothes. The slight eye movement from Molape signalled to Assad that the security escort was also on the scene.

"Let me introduce you to the chief designer, who will show us around." Molape tried to ignore the huge security guard that followed their movements with reddish, watery eyes. However, his unruly white beard that covered most of his face caught Molape's attention.

"Are there only the two of you on this visit?"

"Yes, Mr. Faber." He did not bother to introduce him to Assad.

A middle-aged man with a short white jacket and half rimmed glasses took them through the section and tried to describe with as little words as possible what the responsibilities of the design centre was. He spoke in a monotonous voice and with a heavy French accent. Assad new that, over a period of two decades, the South African armaments industry head-hunted highly qualified engineers from all over the world to extend the skills of their own trained personnel. Some of these foreigners were lured by the exceptionally ample compensation. As they experienced the easy-going lifestyle and the moderate climate of South Africa they grew accustomed to their new environment and liked it. The opportunities for a wide range of outdoor recreation, beautiful scenery and wildlife, made it easy for them to convert their work contracts to that of permanently employed positions. Their children adapted to the white culture, settled and became South African citizens. As European kids, it was easy to grow-up in the white sector of the country.

"Can I state with certainty that the Martial Eagle has progressed, as an attack helicopter, past the development stage and that you only need a large order to kick into the production phase?" Assad saw how the Frenchman became a little uneasy. Molape nodded in the affirmative.

"Yes I think you can say that. However, the culture here is to continuously strive to upgrade its technology." The design engineer clearly did not enjoy Faber's presence and hoped that they would take leave as soon as possible. His body language signalled that he had pressing matters to attend to and would like to get on with his task.

"Can you tell me about the new capabilities that you are working on now?" Assad had his notebook ready.

The Frenchman controlled his haste, took off his glasses, and folded them slowly before he dropped them into his breast pocket. He glanced at Faber, then at Molape, looked at the people hunched at their workstations and then became abrupt, "No I cannot." He turned around and walked off without greeting or looking back - signalling that their visit was over.

Assad could not repress his feelings of anxiety, which were brought on by the possibility of a lost opportunity to find out more about the technology secrets of the Martial Eagle. He felt as if the visit to Africair was a waste. As a matter of fact, his new bout of stress stemmed from the sinking feeling that the whole idea of coming to South Africa was a misfire. This was supposed to be a scouting mission laden with promises of rich rewards. If he had only a pinch of success in snatching some meaningful information it could make a world of difference. Then he needed not to rely too heavily on Molape to supply information on request. Now the opportunity was gone. Just like that and because of a person who was used to work under the suffocating threat of secrecy!

"I do have some tea and sandwiches for you and your guest, John. Would you like to join me?" They turned and smiled at the slim girl with the warm expression of amusement. Her auburn hair fell to her shoulder as she posed her question with a slight slant of her head.

"Akbar, may I introduce you to Rosemary Barnard. She is the engineer who is in charge of the man-machine interfacing of the ME."

Assad gave her his broad moustached smile. He felt relieved. Here was perhaps an opportunity to stretch his time to find out more about what was going on in the nerve centre of the Martial Eagle's factory.

With the formalities over, Assad made a fresh attempt, "Can you tell me more about your discipline?"

Rosemary Barnard winked, "Most certainly. Come to my little kennel and we can start with the coffee or tea if you want." They laughed at the reference to her workplace as a pet's shelter.

24.

Stories need Facts.

Africair's Design Centre.

Assad listened intently to Rosemary Barnard and made notes while she spoke about the complexities of the avionics in the cockpit of attack helicopters. From time to time she called up simulated readings on the computer screen to describe the functional facets of the system she designed. The edge of her technology secured an adequate status of information for a pilot to fly and attack with the Martial Eagle helicopter. Faber in the meantime apparently lost interest in his monitoring task and was paging through a helicopter magazine. His attention was temporarily diverted. He knew Barnard was trained to inform visitors and potential clients during international exhibitions. She knew her job well and would not let sensitive technical detail slip out.

The small workstation became crowded as a messenger arrived and asked her to sign for the reception of top secret documents. She complied immediately and dropped the folders next to Assad on her desk. The young Arab journalist was a trained fast reader and with one glance picked up the title of the portfolio, of which there were four copies. His hair stood on end as he grasped the importance of its contents: "New Design for an Air to Air Warning and Surveillance System for the ME Attack Helicopter."

Rosemary Barnard continued with her presentation but Assad had difficulty concentrating on what she tried to explain. He had to get hold of one of the copies of the newly arrived document on the desk behind him. If he could succeed, it would impress The Agency immensely. Although his body language told her that she had his undivided attention, he did not comprehend her explanation of how the avionics system worked.

"May I take a new notebook from my briefcase please?" Assad's request drew a glance from Faber.

"Why, sure" Assad turned his back towards Faber who returned his attention to the flight magazine. Assad took several notebooks, brochures and publications from his briefcase and placed them on top of the pile of top-secret documents. Then he delved laboriously into his briefcase again and came up with a clean wire-bound notebook. Slowly he picked up his publications and made sure that he also took the top copy containing the design of the new warning and surveillance system. Assad stuffed the booklets in his briefcase and hoped that nobody, especially Faber, so close behind him, noticed his intention. Assad's heart throbbed so violently that he could hardly speak. He turned back to Barnard and Molape and said with a croaky voice, "You said that the avionics of the ME is now in a mature stage, not so?"

Rosemary Barnard glimpsed at the pile of newly delivered documents on her desk. She knew the contents by heart, as she was an important contributor to the team who developed the system, "Just about. A few minor adjustments and we are there. As a matter of fact, a full blast production program can begin any time now." Assad knew she was smooth-talking herself out of this tight spot. He also knew enough about aircraft development that the sooner you could come by new technology data, the lesser the chances were that any mole activity could be exposed.

"Ms. Barnard, I think you will understand, as a complete tenderfoot on this subject, I will need to fax you a copy of my article before I present it to my editor. Otherwise I will stand the chance of making a fool of myself . . . and mislead my readers. Will you please be so kind as to assist me with my copy material?" Assad was aware of Faber clutching into the discussions again. The fat, bearded man was particularly pleased by the idea of having an opportunity to scrutinize Assad's article before it went to print. He started to experience Assad as a very professional writer who did not want to upset his source of information. Faber knew enough of the communications discipline to understand that every journalist held in high regard the source of a good story.

Assad and Rosemary spoke for a few minutes longer to work more facts into the article. Assad looked up from his notes and could not hide his admiration for the attractive woman's skill, despite the fact that as an Arab man he was seldom exposed to women in pioneering positions. She could be useful at a later stage, he thought. She indicated that their interview was over. He expressed his gratitude and intention to continue with the factory visit. Just then he felt the heavy hand of Faber on his shoulder.

"Mister Assad, we need to talk." The young military reporter knew this was the end of the line for him. Faber would ask that he accompanied him to an office where they could search his briefcase. This would mean incarceration in a security-controlled cell of the intelligence department of South Africa - a department still regulated by the old style yardstick.

"About what, Mister Faber?" His jumping Adam's apple was the only sign of the stress that gripped his throat and bulged in his chest.

"About, authorizing the draft of your article. You must fax and mark it for the attention of Mr. Frederick Kramer only and nobody else at Africair. He will bring it through and discuss it with Ms Barnard. Is that clear?" Faber brought his face close to Assad, who could smell the alcohol on his breath.

Assad wondered how to hide his relief. He nearly shat himself and now suddenly wanted to kiss this ugly old Afrikaner, "Thank you for this guideline Mr. Faber. That will add more credibility to my reporting."

For Assad the rest of the visit to Africair was just an uncomfortable formality. He saw six Martial Eagles on the assembly line in various stages of completion. He spoke to the project managers of the various systems. Like Rosemary Barnard and Mark Fischer, they carefully hedged their answers.

Around noon Molape received a phone call from Grant who asked to be pardoned at the luncheon. They decided to arrange for a meeting with Assad at a later stage. Molape tried to reschedule their programme. "Perhaps we can have lunch at the Management Dining Room," he suggested.

Assad was anxious to scan the document he took from Barnard's desk and to report his find to The Agency, as soon as possible, "Thank you John, but I think I should rather go back to the hotel, unpack properly and take a short nap."

"That's OK by me. Let me take you back to the Holiday Inn."

"Good, then we can meet around seven-thirty for dinner this evening."

"Sounds great. Let's go." Molape steered the golf cart in the direction of the motor pool. A driver took Assad back to the hotel.

There was a message with a phone number waiting for Assad at the front desk. It simply read:"Call Yusaf ASAP." Assad never heard or met a Yusaf before. He did not have the slightest idea who this person could be.

25.

A DEATH THREAT.

SANDTON, JOHANNESBURG.

Julius Grant drove swiftly to his home in Sandton. He harboured mixed feelings. The long briefing at Africair and the Martial Eagle's flight demonstration was aimed at bringing him fully up to date with the situation at Africair and its marketing objectives for the attack-helicopter. Besides feeling irritated with De Witt's obnoxious presence he was also sure some information was absent or purposely withheld from him. But then again it would be a little unlikely to expect that anyone would be prepared to give him an insight into the undercurrents of the corporation. Perhaps he was the victim of his intuition. He sensed just too much restrained remarks; glances and body language that made him accept that everything was just fine at Africair. Grant was sure a few important issues did not really become visible. There was an undercurrent, barely below the surface, in the scenarios they introduced to him.

Grant said to himself, "Damn it! Some facts or part of the backdrop is still missing. On the other hand, Kurtz did mention it was imperative that we should have an 'in depth talk.' He indicated that a meeting between us would follow. The man said 'I am waiting for your call so that we can set up a discussion, Julius.' This is an invitation that I need to follow up. Rather sooner than later. I will call him first thing tomorrow." It was his habit to talk aloud to himself when driving alone.

Grant was so deep in thought on the day's presentation that he did not notice how the northward bound traffic out of Johannesburg slowed down. Normally it frustrated him out of his mind. He preferred to leave the office after seven in the evening when the traffic flowed smoother. Right now it was a mess of metal and fumes. The city slowly emptied from the high ridges of Johannesburg's business district. The traffic moved like hot lava down the slope of a volcano.

He turned up the volume of the car radio and listened to the beat of UB-40's music. It reminded him of the good times he and Anna had together, "Darling, we always had only good times." Grant new it was a lie. They also had serious bad times. But when it came to memories around Anna he, somehow, made a special allowance for the less pleasant memories to fade because his compassion for her made this type of self-deception acceptable. His love for her even allowed him to twist a few things, to be accepted as the truth. Perhaps that is what fond memories are made of. Where does rational truthful thinking ends and love begins?

The monologue continued, "Bugger it Grant. Stay with the job at hand! You will meet with Kurtz, hoping that he will be a reliable alliance. Perhaps that is not too far-fetched. He could provide insight into the undercurrents, which could make your master communication plan float. But if you ignored the man he may sink your best efforts with one glib remark."

Grant was surprised at how quickly the time passed. He was already at the exit from the N2-north, which would route him to his home. He realised that his subconscious and active planning blocked out the regular traffic delays, music and the radio announcements. Instead, a clear and meaningful communications plan developed from his thinking. He was in a hurry to get to his laptop and punch out the master-plan, which took shape in his mind. A plan, which, he was confident, would contribute immensely to gain the Malaysian contract for Africair's Martial Eagle.

Grant stopped at the huge green metal gates of his home. Kieter, his old Siamese cat, waited for him in the driveway. He applied the normal security-routine with caution and drove through the gates that closed slowly behind him. He thought how easy it would be for a person to slip in behind the car and hide in the dense shrubs of the garden. By the time he gathered his briefcase and notes on the Martial Eagle, his cat waited for him alongside the old Jaguar.

"Hi old Kieter-cat, this is a nice surprise. You do not normally greet your old Daddy at the gate." Grant looked upon Kieter like a family member – as one of his children, "How're things here at home-quarters? Killed any important long tailed rodents or seduced some feline beauties from the neighbourhood?"

Kieter gave Grant a subdued meow and brushed with force against his legs, waiting to be picked up. "Come, let's see what there is to drink, you grumpy old bloody cat-a-ma-thing. Tell me, what Peter's up to."

"Meow"

"OK. That means yes, or no, or I don't know. Bloody stupid old crossed eyed cat," Grant said with affection.

"Meow"

"Shut up cat! You talk too much."

Grant hung his coat in the foyer. Somehow he got the feeling that everything was not in order. Maybe that was why Kieter waited for him at the gate. It was not his habit to do so. Perhaps the Siamese tried to pass him a message. He was sure something unusual happened today in their residence. He shrugged off the sensation and took milk and a diet coke out of the fridge. Kieter waited for him at his bowl. "Here you are old buddy. Perhaps I need to put you on a diet. You have become a real fat cat you know!"

Grant walked through to his study. The phone rang, "Must be Brooks or Peter," he thought. The feeling of discomfort still lingered. Was that a whiff of sweat he picked up? He lifted the receiver of the simulated antique phone on his desk. He never liked the instrument but somehow decided to keep the bland fake model. Anna sometimes displayed a touch for interior decorating that he did not agree with.

"Hallo. You're talking to Julius Grant. How can I help you?"

A monotonous, taped voice, clearly from a recording machine, answered Grant, "Mr. Grant, if you want to know what is good for your health you will distance yourself from Africair and its Martial Eagle. Stick with your stories about money matters and the mining industry. Do not interpret this pre-recorded message as a challenge or as an opportunity to become a hero. Stay clear from all facets of the armaments industry. Your further involvement can be bad for you. Get out of this now and nothing will happen to you. The choice is yours. Don't disregard this friendly warning. Gareth Williams ignored us and look what happened to him."

A clicking sound was followed by the even tone of the line gone dead. Grant still held the receiver to his ear when he heard how Peter's BMW raced up the driveway. He was trying to recall what the message said. There was a distinct Afrikaans accent and a vague familiarity to the voice that amateurishly tried to sound dramatic. He was sure he had heard that voice recently. But he could not put a face to it.

Peter Grant swung the huge front door ajar and dropped his briefcase and car keys on the umbrella stand, "Hi Dad. Where are you? Trying to scare me like you did when I was a kid? Dad, are you OK? Yoo-hoo?"

"I am in the study Peter."

"Hi! Pop. Are you OK? You look a little perturbed, you know. Had a tough day at Africair?"

"Yes, and I am OK - for the time being, though."

"What do you mean by that?" Peter switched on the hallway lights and followed his father to the kitchen, "What's going on Dad? Are you feeling ill or what?"

"I am OK Peter but there are people somewhere in this city of ours who just now sounded me a warning to the contrary. Somebody said that if I continue with my Africair association, it could be very bad for my health - or perhaps with fatal results!"

"What! Did somebody actually threaten you with death?"

"Yes. I think so. And the person sounded serious."

"Are you sure it's not just somebody's silly idea of a practical joke?"

Grant filled the kettle with fresh water, switched it on and turned to his son, standing in the kitchen door. He had one hand in his pocket and leaned against the white painted frame. The young man filled the opening and Grant looked him in the eyes while trying to remember what the voice said.

"I do not think so Peter. The voice said if I do not heed its call, my fate could be the same as that of Gareth Williams."

"Who is Gareth Williams and what happened to him?"

"He was a senior official with the UK Ministry of Defence. He was killed on the day of the Rugby World Cup final, at Ellis Park. The news media said it happened while his car was high-jacked."

"Oh yes, now I remember, but I still do not see the connection."

The kettle started to whine and Peter walked over to the wall unit, took out large brown mugs and prepared coffee. They went through to the television room while they stirred their coffee and thought about the storybook-like call. They had difficulty comprehending the message properly. Flopping down in easy chairs, they ignored Kieter's calls from the kitchen for more milk. Father and son looked at each other. The mysterious phone call was the first incidence loaded with far-reaching consequences since Anna's death. Only, this time cessation of life was clearly predicted and would not come as a nasty and unfortunate turn of events.

"I fail to understand what's going on, Dad."

"I am also still a little fuzzy about the whole damn affair. I will have to figure this out. If only I knew where to start."

"What now, Dad?"

"I don't know son. I planned to work on a strategic communications plan for the ME this evening. Now I am threatened to get out before I've even started. Somebody must be well clued-up to sound such an early warning. Could it be somebody at Africair who's afraid my presence will interfere or uncover his or their agenda?" Grant sipped his hot coffee.

Peter sat upright, "Who else? I think it's more likely that you have come in the way of a group's objectives. I doubt if you are up against a one-man show."

"Perhaps you are right. I will need to do a lot of thinking. Suddenly a cut-and-dried communications project, which promised to be a lot of worthwhile fun, wants to turn sour. By fun, I mean international travelling, beautiful showgirls and all the delightful trappings of the aviation-world-on-show. Not to mention the exciting financial rewards. This now threatens to become a real scary cloak-and-dagger adventure. Grant's eyes widened.

"A mission that is up against dirty tricks, deception, etcetera?" Peter became wary of his father's project, "Get out of it while you can Dad."

"Hell son, I am intrigued and not easily frightened. You know in my career I ran quite a few risks while tracking down some scary stories."

"This sounds terrifying to me. I still think you should not get further involved in this type of South African styled James Bond games, Dad. It is just not the type of thing you are wired to handle. It is totally out of your line of business. It sounds like something for trained spies to tend to and not for dignified journalists who turned communication advisors."

Grant slowly placed his mug on the coffee table. He looked in silence at Peter and appreciated his son's concern, "Perhaps you're right, but I cannot just fade, you know."

"Well, Dad, I trust you will take care and approach this whole matter with caution and utmost responsibility. And please do not hesitate to trust me in this matter or call for my assistance." Peter stood up. The uneasiness shivered up his spine. He had difficulty to hide his concern for his father, "Unfortunately I need to go out this evening. We are working on a new development to improve the composite material of helicopter rotor-blades and its influence on electronic systems - if any. I told you about this. Can you remember?"

"Yes, yes. I do. OK son, please go ahead. I have lots of thinking and a few calls to make this evening."

"Sure you do." Peter ran the stairs up to his room to freshen up. A few minutes later Grant heard the growl of his BMW as it hurried through the gates.

26.

BURNING MIDNIGHT CANDLES.

GRANT'S HOME, SANDTON, JOHANNESBURG.

Grant walked through to his study and sat down behind his desk. Kieter jumped onto the highly polished desktop and tried to look him, as straight as was possible, in the eyes. He had an accusing look. Grant stared back at him, "You know, that funny feeling I got before the phone rang? Well I have it again. Right now! Somebody else was in my study today. The blotter you are standing on was moved off-centre from where I am sitting now. The centre drawer of the steel cabinet is not properly pushed back. The housekeeping people will only be in by tomorrow. So who did it? And why did you allow this to happen? Hey fat cat?"

"Meow."

"OK Cat, let's see what else have been disturbed in this room." Grant carefully went through every arrangement on his desk, cupboards and drawers to find for more little indications that somebody searched his study. At times he was not quite sure but as he went through his documents he became more and more convinced that his documents were not exactly as he had left them. His search was twice interrupted by phone calls from Peter's friends. He scribbled the messages and phone numbers on his blotter. After about an hour of careful scrutiny Grant stood in the middle of the room and looked about him. Whoever entered and sifted through his things got by the security systems, the locks and did a careful search job. If this was a normal household with regular cleaning and a spouse tending to the home making, like Anna always did, the faint trails would have been erased. And he would have been none the wiser. He would have carried on in his naive way thinking this was just another communications project. The faint evidence of intrusion and the phone call convinced him the way forward would not at all be normal.

Grant cradled the huge overweight cat in his arms and went back to the kitchen. He fixed himself a cheese and tomato sandwich and heated a large helping of chicken-flavoured cat food for Kieter in the microwave. Grant complemented his own snack with a large apple and another diet coke. Grant returned to his study and booted his laptop. He loaded a new disc and opened a file under a:\stratplan.africair.

He sat back and did a mental routine before he started to formulate the strategic framework for his comprehensive communications plan. He tried to visualize and formulate what the preferred end-result should be. The completed action plans and tasks would all be aligned to bring about the desired results. Grant started off by pretending this was just another communications task. He decided to take the threat into consideration only after he completed his strategy and plans. He would then consider the next careful step. Right now, here in his study this evening, he was still free to do his planning.

For some time the only sounds were the tapping on his laptop that filled the large study. It played a rhythmic game with the clicking of the old grandfather clock behind him. Later on Kieter curled up close to him and contributed to the peaceful scene with his loud purring. This part of his planning was most important. The rest of the plans and actions would hinge and focus on the end results. After some time he had a defined objective on the screen which he referred to call a 'work-target.' This meant he would adjust his objective or alter his definition as the planning developed. He would continue in this way up to the point where he would be reasonably sure he had integrated all the role-players' needs to make the ME's marketing plans succeed.

Grant read his 'work-target' definition out loud, "The conclusion of a contract between Africair of South Africa and international partners and alliances to supply to the Malaysian Air Force with thirty-five attack helicopters, each fitted with electronic warfare and weapon systems that will meet the detailed specifications of the client. The systems will be integrated to address the perceived threat, which the aircraft client defined. The contract will include a fully-fledged pilot and maintenance crew's training package. A logistic support programme will cover the life cycle of the helicopters up to the stage when a first major upgrading and modernisation of the gunship becomes a consideration."

Grant swivelled his chair, looked up at the high metal patterned ceiling, shifted his eyes to furnishings, trophies, framed pictures on the wall and eventually rested on the telephone before him, "I think we must accept that this room and phone are bugged. Perhaps, the whole bloody house, for that matter! Whoever was capable to slip past our security system had the whole day to rig this place!" Grant realized he was whispering to himself.

Grant raised himself abruptly, took his mobile phone from its charging base. He walked through the front door and out into the cold night air. He stopped at the fishpond in the middle of the large sprawling lawn. The garden was well lit by strategically placed floodlights, which also enhanced the beauty of the garden. The full moon peeked over a lane of Cyprus trees, which stood tall alongside the garden wall. Grant did not notice the beauty or how cold it was. He entered Peter's speed-dialling code, "Hi Dad. Checking up on your little boy eh?"

"Yes and no. Peter I am convinced that there is a possibility that our phones and perhaps the house are now bugged. In future let's talk on our mobile phones and do it outside our home. A few calls came through during the evening. They were all for your attention and I took messages, instead of passing on your mobile number as usual. This may sound childish, like something from a youth novel. But I suddenly realized that the games played under the apartheid regime are still at the order of the day. Let's make sure first. Maybe this is all a hoax, or a silly joke like you said."

"No Dad. I do not think you are overreacting. Remember how I cautioned you earlier. I am glad you are taking this whole thing serious. I will be home shortly. Bye."

Grant returned to his study with a fresh cup of coffee. He took to his laptop again and it was well past midnight when he heard Peter return. Before he closed the screen he called up the password facility to cover his file. For a while he looked at the pulsating cursor in the empty space of the password frame and then typed in a single word: "Choppers."

It was close to two in the morning when Grant and Peter decided to retire. They postponed the evaluation of Grant' strategic plan to a late breakfast the next morning. Grant hoped with clear heads and in the light of day they would be better equipped to consider his next important step.

27.

WHITE BACKLASH.

KEMPTON PARK RUGBY CLUB

By the time the Grants prepared to go to bed, the meeting of the Technical Committee of the White Afrikaner Concern was about to come to a close. The WAC, as the media had labelled them, was in the words of a leading black editor, ". . . yet another concealed far-right conservative Afrikaner group that cannot adjust to the demands of a New South African dispensation. They will do anything in their power to restore the old establishment of white Afrikaner domination. Even to the detriment of the majority of South Africans who will have to pay dearly for their aims."

Mark Fischer was the chairman of the meeting. As usual they held their gatherings in a medium-sized breakaway room of the Kempton Park Rugby Club. About thirty Afrikaner men were in attendance.

Fischer stood up to address the meeting, "Friends, we have spent a lot of time on this cold weekday evening to think and talk about a very serious and sensitive matter. Before we close tonight's gathering may I summarise the points we agreed upon. I do not want to invite any further reactions to this evening's proceedings and deliberations. I also do not want to run through our decisions glibly, because I know we had our differences and objections. I am only doing this for the sake of clear understanding because from now on a number of serious thing are going to happen."

Fischer used the silence that followed his opening statement to make eye contact with his audience. He took a sip of water from the glass in front of him.

With a sincere tone in his voice he continued, "We are all white Afrikaner brothers who are concerned about our future in this part of Africa. This evening we agreed to disagree but we also kept to the understanding that we will unite in those objectives, which will conserve the future of the White Afrikaner in this country. And let me tell you, most of us have nowhere else to go in this world. The Afrikaner made its last trek. The wagons stopped here. This is where we are going to stay. Of course, I do not refer to those Afrikaners who became part of the so-called 'chicken-run.' Tonight they find themselves as outsiders in countries like Australia, England, Canada, the USA and New Zealand. No, I am talking to you men who are not prepared to become outsiders in our own country. Our forefathers paid with their blood when the Zulu's and English tried to take our land away from us. Our aim is to develop a very important and effective minority in this country that will not fall victim to a black majority government."

For a moment Fischer thought he sounded like Eugene Terreblanche, the right-wing leader of South Africa, now spending time in prison. The men were emotional enough. He must try to switch his approach to a more rational level and continued, "As an engineer in the avionics industry, I have been around technical matters all my life. I have had little or no exposure to party and international politics. I am also not at all at home with theological arguments about God's good intentions to place the white man here on the Southern tip of Africa, with a Christian mission as early as 1652. And with this remark I am not inviting arguments about the real historical reasons why the Dutch positioned Jan van Riebeeck and his staff, here on the stormy shores of the Cape of Good Hope. But what I do know is that I am seriously concerned with the Afrikaner's continued existence as a nation. Therefore you cannot fault me on my patriotism towards my people, and what should be our country." His audience smoothed over this awkward spot in his speech by applauding him warmly.

"Thank you brothers but let's get down to the facts. We are all members of the White Afrikaner Concern or, WAC, as the media has labelled us." Fischer tried to sound like the competent engineer and project-manager that he was. "Our leader appointed us as members of the WAC's Technical Committee. Our mission is to explore our discipline for opportunities that can be utilised to sustain the future of the white Afrikaner under a government that was formerly our enemy. We need to become not only a significant minority but an influential constituent to be respected in the future South African culture. An element of the social structure that has sharp teeth who, at all times, should not be ignored by the ruling blacks on any of the levels of this country's government. We all know that our situation developed as a result of the so-called 'enlightened' direction in which FW de Klerck steered the Republic of South Africa. Some people see him as a great man in the making of the history in this country. Some of you regard him as a traitor of the nation." Lengthy applause followed.

Fischer drank some more water and looked at his followers over the rim of the glass, "Thank you my brothers. The following is in my view what we agreed upon. Mr. Secretary, please correct me if I am wrong." Fischer picked up his notes and realized he would have to be brief because it was well after midnight. The drawn expressions of some of the men told him they kept their pose only out of respect for the cause.

"When we started the development of the Martial Eagle nine years ago we wanted to equip the South African Air Forces with a weapon-system that could counter the massive build-up of enemy forces on our Angolan border. I refer to those nations who supported the struggle of the blacks in South Africa. The Martial Eagle was developed to become our Russian tank-killer. By the time we completed the development of this formidable attack helicopter, the international pressure succeeded in changing the political environment of our country. With the result that this country now has a black majority government. Our weapons-systems were supposed to be engaged in an all-out war against our enemy. Now that selfsame enemy has become our new government, not by overpowering our weapons capability but by overpowering us through an election. So now we are the subjects of Mandela's ANC regime. That means all our efforts and dedication over all these many years . . ." Fischer paused for a moment and with a far-away look stared over the heads of the men, ". . . had just come to nothing."

"Yea! Yea! What a lot of bullshit! That farken bald-headed de Klerck dropped us head first into the stink!" came a remark from the back of the group. It aroused a murmur from the audience with more comments that depicted personal frustration and agreement with Fischer's comments.

Fischer waited patiently for silence, "What's more, when we were at the point of launching a final onslaught on the Angolan capital from the land, air and sea, the Americans looked the other way and we became the bloody international fools of the world."

"Yea - yea! Farken scared bloody Yanks. They were still frozen over as a result of the little men from Vietnam who mucked them up good and solid!" The same chanting voice opened the jeers and disgruntled noise from the back of the floor. Fischer tried to pick up who was leading the choir of bitterness. The voice sounded familiar.

He continued with his summary, "Now we are in a situation where we have developed and integrated First World Technology into our attack helicopter. That capability will now fall into the hands of the ANC's old supporters and friends - their allies from the days of the 'struggle,' as they called their terrorist actions from the past!"

The voice from the audience came loud and gruff, "now we've got real farken trouble.'" This time Fischer spotted the chanter. It was Christian Faber, the retired helicopter pilot and maintenance mechanic, who now had a contractual appointment as a security guard at Africair Corporation. His round figure bobbed around as his comrades slapped him on the back. His yellow teeth stood out from his full white beard as he laughed from the sheer joy he experienced from the applause he received.

Fischer realized that he should avoid furthering the emotions with his address, yet continued, "Brothers, believe it or not, the new friends of South Africa are now Castro, Kaddafi, Arafat, Hussein, the leaders from Iran, Pakistan, North Korea, Syria and so forth. We all saw them when they attended Mandela's inauguration. And to think on that day we flew our only two Martial Eagles past the inauguration ceremony to honour of the very people we intended to dishonour with our supreme weapons capability."

Fischer saw how Jack du Preez, the test pilot of the ME, slapped his hands over his ears and rested his elbows on his knees. He stared at the pattern on the carpet under his feet. Faber shouted, "Farken bloody baboons," but everybody else in the group was quiet. They grew weary of his heckling.

The group waited for Fischer to complete his summary, "Our most important decision as a group was to ensure that the weapons capability does not land in the hands of the countries that I mentioned. We decided to do all we can to thwart any actions or possibility that would result in a transfer of our technologies, equipment or any form of intellectual property regarding our military. Our decision may even please the Americans and their allies. That is, if they are serious about controlling these fast growing new pariah states. Shortly Mandela's chums will have the whole South African military supermarket to satisfy all their needs for weapons of mass destruction!"

Somebody shouted, "Like hell they would!" The group roared with laughter at the awkward turn history took.

"We took this decision so that we, as Technical Committee, could make a significant contribution to achieve the objectives of the White Afrikaner Concern. But let us look at the wider issues that have a bearing on our situation."

Fischer picked up the glass, saw it was empty and slowly replaced it on the table, "We all saw how Mandela's charisma swept the politicians and media of the world, off their feet. He has also drummed up the sympathy and support of a large percentage of Afrikaners."

The meeting was quiet. Amongst them there were those who silently admired Mandela. He did not harbour any bitterness, despite the harsh treatment, legal inequalities and a twenty-seven year jail sentence he had to endure. Fischer continued, "We also heard his announcement in London when visiting Prime Minister John Major, that he will hand-over the leadership to Thabo Mbeki after the 1999 elections. We know why the Old Man is so confident too. It is quite clear that the old National Party has no hope in hell to become a proper opposition that will win any seats in Parliament. That means after 1999, we will have a one party state in South Africa. So the political face of South Africa will look pretty much the same as it was in the Apartheid days. We will have the same tree with different monkeys!" Fischer's last remark was intended to be humorous but nobody seemed to get it.

Jack du Preez stood up, "We agree Mr. Chairman. We also know the sentiments of Thabo Mbeki. He will not be as tolerant and as accommodating as the Old Man. He will do with this country just as he likes. And he would like to see 'black' written all over everything."

"That will also mean supplying weapons to those buggers who were mentioned!" The heckler was Christian Faber.

"We must apply our skills and opportunities in a most meaningful way to disrupt the course of events." Fischer realized they had actually repeated the meeting. The intensity of the arguments made everyone sit up straight, "For that reason we as an action group decided to design an effective plan to address this matter. And whatever we come up with, I can guarantee you my brothers, will rock the world. Prepare yourself for fireworks from hell." Fischer thought for a moment that his approach was too threatening, but the cheers and howls told him he had their support.

"This committee will report back one week from now. Same time, same place."

A huge Afrikaner with a short beard thanked Fischer on behalf of those present for his guidance and wished the committee God's blessings.

"For those of you who are in the mood for a night cap, I have arranged with the club manager that we can go through to the Daniel Craven Pub." Craven was a Springbok scrumhalf and a world famous rugby player. He was a professor at the University of Stellenbosch. This institution, apart from its academic prestige, was looked upon as the cradle of South African rugby. Dr Craven, an arduous student and thinker of the game, wrote many books on the technique of rugby. Many of his writings were accepted as guidelines by the rugby playing countries of the world. The bar was recently redecorated with huge photo montages that displayed all the glorious moments of how the South African recently became Rugby World Champions. A centre-piece was an after-party pose by the Springbok Captain and President Mandela with the trophy. Behind them there stood onlookers who were all well known political, business, and sport dignitaries. Over the President's right shoulder a stern-faced Dr Hermann de Wit faced the camera.

About half of the group accepted Fischer's invitation. The rest, especially those who had some distance to travel, shook hands and left. Besides, they knew the days of good police contacts were over. To be trapped nowadays by the police of the new South Africa with too much alcohol content in the blood resulted in big problems.

28.

TALK IS CHEAP.

DANIE CRAVEN BAR, KEMPTON PARK RUGBY CLUB

Most of the men that stood with charged glasses in a tight circle around Mark Fischer were members of the Technical Committee of the WAC. The small, cosy bar quickly filled with cigarette and tobacco smoke.

"We can talk men. I know the barman - he can be trusted. As a matter of fact, he works as a clerk for Chris Faber. I personally gave him permission to moonlight here at the Club. He is a bright young guy and one day he may become one of our chartered accountants." Fisher nodded towards the short young man who stood behind the wooden counter who continued to wipe the countertop without looking up.

Frans Smit, the man who thanked Fischer after the meeting, started their discussion, "During the meeting you gave some indication of a 'grand plan' to create havoc to draw attention to the cause of the WAC. Could you tell us a little more?,"

Fischer had a lot of respect for Smit who was a radio communications expert and a captain in the South African Air Force's strategic planning department. He lit a Camel and said, "Yes Frans – I will give you a little more detail. However, I must warn you these are only tentative ideas and should be carefully revised before they can become vaguely effective for what we want to achieve."

"OK but it will still make good conversation though." Beer foam settled on Smit's red moustache.

"I developed these ideas with the help of Jack du Preez. Perhaps Jack should give us his version or point of view on what could be done." Fischer looked at Africair's test pilot.

Du Preez was a man of close to six feet four. He was a very attractive person who always seems to be in a brooding mood. He was known as a courageous pilot but not a fine narrator. Du Preez clocked thousands of hours in fixed wing and rotary aircraft - most of those hours were under war conditions on the Angolan-South African border. Everybody knew that this silent man carried a veiled bitterness which he never talked about. Those colleagues who were close to him knew it was as a result of a serious personal trauma.

Du Preez held a chilled diet coke - he was a moderate smoker who seldom used alcohol, "Well, let me be as brief as possible. We thought of a plan with which we could solve a number of problems or accomplish a number of our objectives simultaneously or whichever way you want to look at it. We also want to accomplish these objectives, with one swift operation. We all know what some of those objectives are – but we can talk about that later," Fischer added.

There was a pause while the glasses were recharged and Du Preez continued, "A few weeks from now we will be at the Lankawi Air Show, in Malaysia. We want to utilize during that show our flying demonstrations and routines to carry out our plans. We want to stage a massive display of destruction to draw attention to the objectives of the WAC. In the process a few of our black politicians and other internationally known persons will be – ah –at risk." Du Preez wondered if he revealed too much of their plans. Also his plans!

"It sounds if you will also be stirring up serious havoc amongst the Malaysians?" Smit was immediately hesitant and on guard.

Fischer sensed Smit's concern, "Yes and no. But we want to use it as a backdrop to make to send a message that sure our objectives must be taken seriously."

"Why there - on the Island of Lankawi?" Smit was still very cautious.

Du Preez decided not to elaborate further, "For a lot of reasons. The geographical situation will complement our plans – and it will also coincide with the proposed signing of a contract for Africair to supply thirty-five ME's to the Royal Malaysian Air Force. As all of you know that to stop such an agreement is one of our main objectives. The Malaysians want to buy into our helicopter technology for the sole purpose to find a way to supply our machines under cover to other Muslim controlled military markets."

Smit was persistent, "What do you mean by the 'Muslim Markets'?"

Fischer displayed his marketing flair, "It is known that countries like Saudi-Arabia do not want to become too dependent on American defence exports. But they also do not want to jeopardize their relationship with the Americans. So if they buy from a Muslim country, like Malaysia, they hope the USA would tolerate their acquisition. But what they in actual fact want to do is to be somewhat free from American dominance to be a link for some of their other – eh - associates. They know that South Africa is just about the only country in the world that has a comprehensive armaments capability and who are not directly linked to American defence manufacturing."

Faber said, "Not taking into account the technology that the guys in our armaments industry stole from those dumb Cowboys!"

Fischer gave him a sharp look, "Christian, you are now on dangerous ground. Rather shut-up about things you know very little about."

Smit tried to make sense of their discussion, "No right minded person can live with such a possibility - hell, things are perhaps more meaningful than we thought." He liked to talk and think about comprehensive strategic matters.

Du Preez suddenly lost interest in the turn of the conversation. He was not in the mood to fool around with Afrikaner views on morals or Christianity. Instead he thought of the beautiful woman waiting for him. It would be pleasant to slip in bed behind her small, full body. Nothing could beat that on a cold night like this. He wasted his time to talk and speculate with these bloody "Armchair Afrikaners." They like to talk but do not have the guts to do anything about their bleak future.

Fischer sensed Du Preez's mood and decided to spill the beans, "In short, we want to utilize the flight demonstration at Lankawi to direct our air to ground missile capability to clinically take out the main section of the spectator's – where Mandela and Mbeki will be sitting in the Grand Stand as guests of honour to Dr Mahatir, Prime Minister of Malaysia."

A tomblike silence followed. The men around Fischer shifted their weight from one foot to another, taking deep draws on their smokes or big long swallows from their beer mugs

Smit broke the silence, "Will Mbeki definitely become the next president after Mandela?"

"Most likely – and the Old Man will still be busy grooming him to become the new President of South Africa. It is also expected that

Mandela will announce that Mbeki will be taking over of the ANC leadership. He may do so at the next ANC annual congress."

Smit experienced a dry throat despite the beer in his hand, "What will happen then?"

"Then we will demolish the surrounding areas to keep security busy while our escape plans kick in." Du Preez said and thought of his planned suicide would be his own way to escape from the havoc, hatred and the bitterness that always burned like sulphur within him.

The thorough silence that followed again was only disturbed by someone who swallowed audibly.

"Goodness gracious! This is awesome – and what if you hit Malaysian Royalties and politicians as well?" Smit became really uncomfortable about the whole scenario. The thoughts of bewilderment which racked his mind also plagued the minds of the other bystanders. Perhaps for the first time their fantasies around manipulating their political and cultural sensitivities became a shockingly reality. To talk was an easy speculative luxury to indulge in but - to originate realizable plans of action was something much more demanding than they anticipated, The consequences of from executing such plan was – horrifying.

Du Preez was bored and fed up with their lack of grit, "That's precisely part of the plan guys. It will become an important chapter in the history of that Malaysian country and it will keep them busy for a long-long time."

Smit suddenly wanted out and looked for an escape route out of this scenario that started to sound too fundamental for his liking, "Excuse me for asking guys - but do you think you have enough hair on your balls to pull this off?"

More silence and swallowing followed.

Du Preez looked at Fischer who slowly nodded in the affirmative. Then they both turned to Smit and, like in a staged duo, responded simultaneously with a loud, - "yes!"

29.

TWO LONELY PEOPLE.

APARTMENT IN KEMPTON PARK, SOUTH AFRICA

Jack du Preez was one of the firsts to leave the now, not so cosy, Danie Craven Bar. He walked across the dark parking area towards his silver-blue Toyota. It was parked under a large blue-gum tree. He approached the car watchfully and hated himself for leaving the car in a dark, secluded spot. When he arrived it was not yet five and the sun were still glowing in the west. Now it was almost three in the morning and it was bitterly cold moonless night.

Du Preez unlocked the car door and thought he caught a movement behind an adjacent tree. He stood still for a while and then decided to move swiftly, by slipping behind the wheel and locking the door in one movement. The Toyota started immediately and he backed up very fast for about fifty yards. He swung the sedan around and with spinning wheels left the parking lot. Once in the near empty street he chased down the double lane and exceeded the speed limit by far.

Du Preez lived through a lot of anxiety and fear in the many cockpits he had flown in. But somehow he always felt on top of the situation and could manage those threatening feelings of apprehension. But on the ground he felt totally out of place. For the first time he realized the games they played had become serious schemes and obligations. Perhaps that was what made him so jumpy. He thought, "What the hell - maybe I should end everything in a more uncomplicated, traditional way".

Twenty minutes later he entered Lillian Pretorius' apartment. He knew she would be asleep and he moved quietly to the bathroom where he undressed, took his gown from behind the bathroom door and brushed his teeth. Du Preez had a double set of everything in her apartment although his own home was only about ten kilometres down the road. He lived in a quiet suburb fitting for people of his income level. Du Preez longed to be with her. Even if she would not feel like talking to him this time of the night, her closeness would still his disrupted mood.

He slipped in the warm bed behind her and was grateful for the added comfort that the electric blanket contributed. The moments before he fell asleep were always the most dreaded time of the day for Du Preez. He always had a constant battle to keep his thoughts from imaging his wife. Ugly pictures of how she was brutally gang raped and killed by burglars constantly plagued him. They took her life ... and the life of their unborn baby girl. . He had difficulty in blocking out the photos he saw in the police file. These pictures stuck in his mind like a frozen image on a computer monitor and he could not exit from it. It was as if all the programs ran the same frozen picture. Oh - how she looked in that cold drawer of the morgue. He never saw the baby. He refused to. He did not even want to know if it was a girl or a boy. When the mortician told him that it was a perfect little girl he staggered and then fell to his knees and, with his head on the floor, he cried – like a little girl – while all his inner ability to be a compassionate human being died.

Afterwards the earlier memories of this devastating turn in his life also stuck in his brain. He had just completed the last flight display of the Martial Eagle at the Paris Air Show at Le Bourghe and was on his way to buy some French perfume for his lovely Linda. The call on his cell phone made him rush to Charles de Gaulle Airport where he was placed on standby. The slow hours, which dragged by until they touched down in Johannesburg, and the twenty minutes drive to his empty home and then to the morgue turned his overwhelming shock into deep sadness. Later the bitterness set in. Still later, he was filled with a growing hatred from which he could not rid himself. Then his emotions hardened and grew cold – and he actually died within. Eventually he made a truce in his mind about the senseless killing of his family. He firmly decided that he was fed-up with South Africa and its development of a one-way political system that he was sure would end up – a switch-over from black oppression to white oppression. He viewed the overwhelming power of Mandela and his ANC party as just another form of new Apartheid with blacks calling the shots this time. Same tree, different monkeys - as the guys referred to the new political dispensation.

As an orphan brought to South Africa from a post war Germany, Du Preez had no family. He grew up in church sponsored orphanages, got a BSc degree in engineering, became a pilot and travelled extensively. Du Preez could not think of a single place in the world where he would like to live. A new commitment, even with the lovely Lillian lying here beside him, would be impossible to sustain. He was tired of Jack du Preez. He lost his last best friend when he lost himself! Jack du Preez was set to kill and end his own life. "Before some bloody black criminal does it to me," he promised himself. But he would make sure that for Linda's and his baby's sake his revenge would at least be spectacular. He owed that much to his girls.

Du Preez once shouted, "My end will also be the end of a lot of you bloody ANC baboons – and your dreams of becoming stinking rich by embezzling government funds and taking in kick-backs from lobbyists and supplier's agents - will go up in stinking smoke!" as he drove in the noisy Johannesburg traffic, dodging the reckless taxi-drivers who raced each other to get a slice of the over-traded commuter market.

About two years after the death of Linda, he met Lillian Pretorius at the rugby club's ladies bar. She was a divorcee who accompanied her younger brother to a junior league match. Du Preez caught her eye - she smiled and then everything developed incredibly fast. After the game she went with him for a drink while her brother met up with his friends for a beer. She was clearly very lonely and he was heartbroken and bitter. The evening ran at the pace of a one-night stand. They got to her apartment and made passionate love till dawn. They slept from exhaustion all Sunday morning, woke up and made love again –and again.

The very next day they both were unsuccessful in reaching each other. He was flying and she assisted with a dental operation. Du Preez drove straight to her home without calling beforehand. Minutes after he walked in the door they made love again. They followed this pattern for the past four months. Their togetherness and love-making made up for the emptiness within them.

The soft light on Lillian's side of the bed flickered on and she turned towards Jack, smiled and said softly, "Your meeting of the 'Live Pilots Society' took a long time and - I became a little worried." She spoke in a sleepy voice - teasing him.

Jack looked at her, nodded and opened his mouth to reply - then he saw how she started to unbutton her pyjama top. It slid open to reveal her full softness. He tenderly touched her while she took his face in both her hands and kissed him on the tip of his nose. She rolled on top of his naked body and became aware of his prominence underneath her.

30.

THE EVIL CHRISTMAS FATHER.

BERTRAMS, JOHANNESBURG

Christian Faber moved from behind the bulky trunk of the blue gum and smiled at the frantic way Jack du Preez left the parking lot. He relieved himself, and zipped his wide khaki trousers and walked over to his battered Volkswagen. The 1980 model actually belonged to his only son. The young man died some years ago, somewhere in Angola. They never found his body. He had to rely on operational reports to find out what became of his son and three comrades.

Faber could never bring himself to the point of selling the faded old Volkswagen. It was his last link and memory, like some video footage, that constantly reminded him of his son. Many times, especially when he had too much to drink, he would sit for hours in the car and cry while listening to the music tape that his son left in the player. What grieved him most was that he could not remember if he ever told his son that he actually loved him.

Faber grew up in a culture where emotions and feelings were never displayed -at least, not at all by men. Affection was just a little something that died shortly after a honeymoon. The only sparks of romance later expressed by spouses signalled the intention to mate with the hope to produce another child. His wife was in her early fifties and he could not remember when he stopped bedding her. Not that it was important because to have sex at his age you need to start with an erection, something he could not produce with the best will in the world.

The huge man got out of the Volkswagen which he parked under a street lamp in front of their small home. He looked at their run down fence and poorly kept garden. Faber walked round to the back of the six-roomed structure where a light was on. He unlocked the kitchen door and welcomed the warmth, which radiated from the ovens. His immensely overweight wife stooped at the off-white stove where she arranged some biscotti to be dried out. Her home made baking made a considerable contribution to their tight cash flow. However, it required her to be busy in the kitchen at all hours of the day and night.

"How about some strong coffee and - a warm biscotti old wifie?" Faber slurred.

The big woman did not stop at her task and she heard the slur in his voice. Once she served him, he will sit in his chair for hours and tell her how he will one day do something on his own to revenge the life of his dearly lost son. Their only son was average sized; common faced, lacked a personality and had difficulty to perform at school. But over the years Faber developed a fictional memory and referred to his son as someone who was as intelligent as Einstein, with the body and courage of Rambo.

"Today I took the first step to scare the snot out of somebody who is working against the plans of the WAC. I did it on my own, Ma and - that was only the beginning. After a few good scares I will personally switch off his lights. At that stage he will long for the darkness of eternity," Faber hiccupped and rolled his bloodshot eyes.

Ma heard him faintly with one ear only. Over the years she heard so much drunken talk from Faber that she did not even stop to properly consider what he tried to tell her. But to avoid the repetition of a statement she regularly threw in some thorny questions.

"And what did Fischer say?"

"Say about what, Wifie?"

"About what you did - stupid!" A strong bulky arm opened the oven.

"Listen you old cow, don't you call me stupid hey! Here sits one of the few men in the WAC who is prepared to do something on his own - for the honour of the Afrikaner nation." Faber scratched his white beard furiously and his face deepened to a darker shade of red.

"OK. Pipe down. Does Fischer think you did a smart thing? Does he agree it made you a real Afrikaner hero?" Ma emptied the pan of dried biscotti on the cloth-covered kitchen table.

"No - actually he said nothing." Another stretched-out burp followed.

"How come - big Boer hero?"

"Because, [hick] I didn't tell him about what I did - stupid old cow."

Ma Faber stiffly stood up straight and placed her fists on her broad hips - her limbs were rigid and aching. Ma's massive bosom strained against the buttons of her red and white flowery-patterned dress. As always, she had problems tolerating Faber's insults, "I have a feeling you made another of your silly mistakes and I don't think you should try to do things on your own. What is it that you have done?"

Faber looked at his huge hands and the grime under his fingernails, "There is an Englishman with the name of Grant and I only set up a recorded phone call to scare him a little."

"Scare him about what?" Ma Faber wiped the sweat from her brow with the apron.

"That, if he does not disappear from the scene - we will do the same to him as what the Leader asked us to do to another Englishman who tried to be smart."

"Is it you – or the brandy talking now? Who was this other Englishman and what did you do to him?" Ma Faber leaned forward and pushed her round sweaty face into his.

Faber looked at her with glazed-over eyes while he staggered somewhat on his feet, "This is men's stuff. There is nothing for you to know about anything. Get on with the baking and get some sleep."

Faber's voice trailed off as he stumbled noisily towards the bedroom. He yawned and at the same time passed a long, drawn-out smelly fart. His weight made the bed creak and bounce. Instantaneously he started snoring. However, what he did not realize in his drunken state was, that his premature warning led to action that actually saved Grant' life.

31.

NOBLE MOTIVES.

JOHANNESBURG.

Grant and Peter pushed their empty plates aside. They enjoyed a large English breakfast, which Peter prepared. Grant had printed out an extra copy of the communications strategy that he drew up the previous night and gave it to his son so that they could run through the outline of suggested actions.

"You will realize of course that this document still needs many specifications around timing, costing, support material and so forth…," Grant made a few side notes with a red pen.

"Yes, but I can see your single-minded approach runs like a live wire through the whole program." Peter was used to act as a soundboard for his father's strategies. Over time he learned that his questions, some out of ignorance – actually helped Grant to shape his tactics. He also found out that his father had the patience and allowed him to criticise or question his ideas.

Grant remarked, "The bottom line is that we want the signature of an authorized Malaysian official for an order of thirty-five Martial Eagles - delivered over a period of not less than eight years. That is the ultimate delivery capacity of Africair at this stage."

"Dad, when will you be presenting this to the top management of Africair?"

"Shortly -their chairman indicated that we would do it at a resort somewhere in the Western Cape. My presentation will be part of a three-day workshop and marketing planning meeting. I also need to talk Marlene through these proposals first. Apart from all the detailed planning it will take me some time to structure the fee to be charged by our agency."

"And when do you see her again?"

"She is still in Cape Town but, should be back the day after tomorrow."

"Besides the regular retainer fee, material production costs and of course travelling and hotel accommodation, what else do you need to take into account?" Peter was not always sure if his father took the right step by going into the communications consulting business.

"The basics are easy to calculate but it is the potential exceptions that need the real thinking and calculating." Grant said with the pen stuck in the corner of his mouth.

"Like what?" Peter was still concerned about his father's lack of accountancy experience.

"Well, there are a lot of factors to take into account. But the most important is the clause in our contract that entitles us to a percentage of the total contract concluded - that is if the project leads to a successfully closed deal."

"Good gracious Dad! Even if that commission is based on a small percentage, it could mean millions!"

"Yes, it sure does." The thought steadily pleased Grant

"Would that also mean a bonus for you, personally?" Peter thought that he may have underestimated his dad's experience in business matters.

"If you want to call a percentage of a percentage a bonus, then the answer is positive." Grant smiled and wrote a large dollar figure at the top of the page.

"From your point of view, would you want to estimate what it could do to your personal bank balance? - not thinking for a moment that you have any cash flow problems." From where he sat Peter tried to read the figure Grant scribbled at the top of the page.

"At a conservative price...," Grant took a pocket calculator from his briefcase, tapped in a few characters and altered the amount he guessed. He looked up at Peter with a straight face, "... my bank manager will have just about a one million dollar reason to let out a shriek instead of his usual bland smile."

"Dad?" Peter could not believe his ears.

Grant mused, "I would enjoy seeing the bloody old sour goat's face - should I be so fortunate to make a deposit of this size."

"Is that your driving force to go through with this project? Despite the warning you received last night? Is it money? Is that it Dad?" Peter's religion brought him to unambiguous views on materialism. He never brought anything remotely around faith into a discussion with his father. They had a heated argument many years back when he was still a student. It was all about his involvement with the controversial 'Jesus in Jeans' movement that students of his university promoted during holidays. They never completed the argument and Grant was of the opinion that Peter went overboard with his religion. Peter on the other hand, thought that his parent was harbouring sceptic views – so that somehow they would never be able to come to an understanding.

Grant closed the file in front of him, "No - the chance to be successful with this or any other contract, with the Americans as main competition, is fairly remote. Perhaps this will also turn out to be another misfire - like the UK contract. But I have other concerns."

"What are those reasons?" Peter wondered why his dad was so fired-up with this project.Grant brought up his reality value around the Africair objectives, "It will take the whole morning to convince you. But in short - if South Africa loses its edge as far as aviation technology is concerned the country becomes just another first world element that will be lost for this part of the continent. Here at the southern point of Africa we are geographically remote from the rest of the world and its markets. North, east and west are thousands of miles away from us and south there is nothing but - a huge chunk of ice. We are desperately dependant on air transport to keep this economy growing and maintaining our civilization. Can you just imagine if the flow of airlines to this remote southern part of the African continent starts to dwindle, what it will do to the future of this country? Let alone its hopes to take advantage and develop further on one of the few legacies which the armaments industry of the previous government left to the economy of this new country?"

"You have a lot of earnestness for South Africa. Is it something that Mum instilled in you?"

Grant looked with kind-hearted eyes at his son, "Perhaps -but then again there are young people like you who need to have reasons to believe in a future here in South Africa. On the other hand - I do feel pity for what happened to the majority of the people of this country. I also believe that we, who were shaped and privileged by a different and more favourable set of circumstances, should be prepared to share and help those that have the capability to excel."

"As usual, I admire you noble motives, Dad. As long as the resources of the so called privileged population, do not get cannibalized to the point of widespread bankruptcy. Then they will not be able to help themselves – let alone supporting the advancement of the less privileged of this land." Peter sounded firm.

Grant was somewhat surprised by his son's slight outburst "Like in what way?"

"Like, in taxing the earning population right out of our pants and - pushing us out of high-earning jobs. Not to mention the alarming rate at which crime and losses are rising which I fear the new government of the country is not able to curb. If this continues, people will just leave this country in droves -even those who were born here will move somewhere else. When their great grand parents emigrated from Europe to Africa, they did it for many reasons but - they also did not expect their offspring to become so patriotic that they could not repeat history in an exodus mode."

Grant started to pack his briefcase and became serious, "In a way you are right, son. The numbers leaving the country right now are already alarmingly high. South Africans are now like Greeks and Jews - you come across them everywhere in the world. Even Africair is concerned about their loss of skills at this stage because it could mean that if they acquire a large order they may find that they do not have the skills to execute their commitments."

"I suppose you have read the quip on the back page of the Financial Mail, about what's the difference between an emigrant and a refugee?" Peter asked.

"No, what's the difference?" Grant always did selective reading and skipped things like sport, social gossips and the like.

"The difference lies in - timing."

Grant smiled, "Have you got such plans, Peter?"

"It all depends..." Peter stood up and twiddled his car keys around his thumb.

"You and your company are, from a technological point of view, important to Africair with your supply of rotor blades and electronic equipment. I think..." and Grant felt the threat of an ever greater loneliness looming, should his son decide to leave the country, "... that you understand quite well why I am concerned and motivated to do all I can to assist in cutting this deal."

"OK Dad - you convinced me. Go ahead with your plans but, allow me to call in an old and trustworthy friend who runs a small but very successful security service in Durban. I will ask him to sweep our home for bugs and to upgrade our burglar systems. It will be my contribution to the added value of your property. And - I will never forget that you refuse to take any boarding fee from me." Peter winked at his father.

Grant thought again about the threat he received over the phone, "I will approach this whole adventure with more care - trust me."

"Have an exciting day, Dad."

Grant engaged the security system and locked the front door behind them. They stopped to stroke Kieter where he basked in the early morning sun. Their cars ran with misty tailpipes down the winding driveway. The vapour swirled over the frost covered lawns as the steel gate came in motion and allowed them to follow their different directions into Johannesburg.

Grant hoped he could dedicate the rest of the day to complete his strategic presentation. He called Marlene in Cape Town and brought her up to date with the latest developments. She in turn told him how pleased she was with the sudden enthusiasm with which her Malaysian soccer plans were received. They decided to meet for dinner on her return to Johannesburg. He was tempted to tell her about the mysterious call but decided to let it be. Thinking again about it this morning, made the call sound a little childish. He wished he had recorded it. He usually did when he talked to the media. He could not help to think that he had heard that voice before. It had to belong to someone at Africair, but he failed to tie a face to the accent.

32.

A FRIEND IN NEED.

BUSY SHOOTING RANGE, HILLBROW, JOHANNESBURG,

Grant could feel a rush of adrenaline through his veins that brought a sharp edge to his mood and he knew he had to contain it. In this mood his assertiveness could easily turn into aggression. Perhaps that was why he chose the Range Rover to commute to the office because, the superbly engineered vehicle, which he thought was the ultimate in cars, fitted his mood. To absorb his surge of energy he dialled the shooting range at his pistol club. He was set to better his personal best on the target. Since Anna's death he joined the club and was surprised to find out that he was in effect a crack shot. He became member of the club's first team and was earmarked to become a member of a team to go on an international tour.

The shooting range was fully booked and he promised to call later for a practise session. The booking clerk mentioned that everybody suddenly wanted to learn how to use a firearm and said it was a result of the rising crime and increased sales of handguns.

Peter left the range and walked into his office shortly after ten. He found Connie Heyneken eating a breakfast snack she bought at the cafeteria. She hid her bulging cheeks behind her hand and nodded him a greeting. Julius winked her to follow him to his office.

By the time she swallowed her snack, retouched her make-up and stepped into Grant's office, he had his working papers spread out on his desk.

"Have you got any plans for this evening Connie?"

His tone failed to let her hope that he wanted to date her - "I should be so lucky and he so desperate," she thought, "No Julius, why?"

"I want you to take the next half hour and reschedule my program for the day. I would appreciate it if we could close our doors for the rest of the day and work on the strategy I drafted last night. I also want us to keep at it, even if tomorrow's daylight finds the two of us here. OK?"

An evening with Julius - even if it's official and here in the office, sounded exciting to Connie, "Right you are Julius. I will reschedule and we should be 'A for away.'"

"Knew I could rely on you to manage our time." Grant said.

She left him with the pleasant smell of her perfume lingering however, Grant was so absorbed in his task he was not aware of the aroma, which he usually welcomed - because it was mostly absent in his man-alone-world.

Grant was a stickler for detail. He passed his notes on to Connie as and when he completed the pages. She had the capability to type at an incredible speed and her sound knowledge of Afrikaans as well as English allowed her to correct his grammar as she worked through his data. Grant sometimes refrained from dedicating enough time to his way with those words that were intended to serve his ideas. Around lunchtime she carried in sandwiches and tea. He wrote with his left hand and held a sandwich in the other. While he munched, he made phone calls to correlate facts and figures he retrieved from the bank, the accountants and travel agencies. On a few occasions he had to call Peter to confirm certain technological realities that had a bearing on his plans. It was past seven in the evening when he completed the last page of his presentation.

"Please make us twenty copies of this document and bind it with those fancy plastic spiral binders." Grant always sounded awkward with administrative detail.

"OK Julius, It will take me about thirty minutes. I will compile them and leave them on your desk ready for you to pick them up in the morning - if you are in a hurry to leave it's OK by me." Connie dreaded his reply.

Grant ran through his cabinet and said over his shoulder, "Not on your life! I still need to make a couple of very important phone calls – so by the time I am through, you should be done. Then I would like to take you down to old Hin Woo's place for a sweet and sour something or perhaps you would like a pizza at Gingillio's?"

Connie stared at him in disbelief and felt excitement rising in her, "Eh ..."

Grant turned and looked at her, "Sorry - I suppose you need to rush off to one of your late gym classes? - or perhaps meet up with one of those hunks who are regular members of your fitness club?"

Connie hated when she blushed, "None of the sort and - I do not have 'hunks' as you call them trying to flirt with me at all." She thought by herself, "Damn, I am twenty-five, and still act like a bloody silly little high school girl'.

Grant smiled, "OK, so if you do not have to please a 'hunk' perhaps you would not mind going with this old skunk?" They both laughed at his silly remark. Connie winked at him and walked off to the process-room.

At the fourth ring Kurtz picked up the phone in his spacious home-office, "Johan Kurtz here." He started off in Afrikaans. As soon as he recognised Grant' voice he switched to English. His many years of service in the UK and elsewhere abroad allowed him to loose some of his typical South African accent.

"If it is not a suitable time for you to talk now I can call you later but I would prefer if it could still be this evening - to be honest, rather sooner than later." Grant asked.

"No, no, not at all Julius. As a matter of fact, I was expecting to hear from you earlier today. I drew up and circulated an agenda for our ME strategic meeting next week in the Cape. I entered your presentation as a main item. It is imperative that your strategic plan should be as close to a final document as possible. It will be moderated as we go along, though. In the meantime I would like to hear the basic outlines on which you are structuring your plans." Grant picked up the urgency in Kurtz's voice.

Grant suggested, "As a matter of fact I am just about ready - I just need to make a few additions and also discuss the project - especially our fee and other financial implications, with my partner, Dr. Marlene Brooks."

"Then you must have worked like hell on this one?" Kurtz was surprised at his consultant's enthusiasm.

"Yes, I did give it some stick." Grant suddenly realized he was tired from the previous night's lack of sleep and the long hours at the computer.

Kurtz invited him, "Please, go ahead. I am in any case working on a section of our bid for you-know-who and will be at it till late. How can I help you?"

The fact that Kurtz did not refer to the Malaysian bid by name gave Grant the sign that he was not at all at ease with his telephone security, "What I wanted to discuss, should, on second thought, be done personally. Perhaps I can arrange an appointment with you tomorrow." Grant hoped that the CEO of Africair caught his message.

"OK, I will ask Miss Glynis to arrange something - good night." The line went dead.

Grant was still staring at the instrument and wondered what to think of Kurtz's abruptness when his cell phone rang. He swung round to take the instrument off the battery-charger on the cabinet behind him.

It was Kurtz, "OK, Julius, now we can talk. I am standing in my garden and calling you from my mobile. If a man wants to talk about sensitive matters, this is for the time being the safest way." Kurtz sounded business like.

"Why 'for the time being'?" Grant was curious.

"Because right now the technology in this country has not yet caught-up with the developments that will allow for the bugging of cell phones." Kurtz said.

"Yes, I suppose technology will eventually strap us down completely. The 'Big-Brother-is-watching' syndrome, you know." Grant dreaded what electronic communication could hold for the future.

"As you said Julius, the worst is still to come. But what's bothering you?"

Grant cleared his throat with a drawn-out rasp, "I'll come to the point, just hold for a minute." Grant placed the instrument on his desk while he closed the door of his office.

He returned to the call, "Are you still there? OK. I got a pre-recorded phone call from someone who - ordered me to stop my involvement with Africair or suffer drastic consequences."

"Like a death threat?" Kurtz sounded guarded.

"I was told outright that if I ignored the warning, I could go the same way as Gareth Williams went." Grant was still wondering who the caller could be.

There was a long silence. This was the moment that nearly stressed Grant out of his mind. The following moments would suggest if his gamble on Kurtz as the right person to trust was a wise choice. He may have misjudged the man - despite his enormous experience of human nature and his sixth sense, which allowed him in the past to trust or distrust somebody quite correctly.

"Julius," Grant could hear how Kurtz lit a cigarette on the other side of the line, "We need to talk personally about this call ... and about Williams. Eye to eye. What you said is troubling me immensely. I have reasons to believe we are up against something here that we will have to approach very carefully. I am sorry but I cannot just laugh this off as a mere prank by somebody."

Grant sighed – and nearly said out loud - bingo! "I was afraid I am at the point of making a fool of myself. Where do we begin?"

"Tonight I still need to finish the paperwork that's sitting on my desk. Tomorrow I have to pass it on to old man De Witt for consideration. I will first have to drop it off at my office. I would prefer to meet you tomorrow morning at your place. And by that I mean your home, if that is possible?"

"What time?" Grant hoped to catch up with lost sleep.

"Around ten?"

This would afford Grant some shut-eye, "OK. I will be at my home. Perhaps we can share a brunch together." Grant gave Kurtz directions to reach his home and asked the CEO of Africair to call him a few minutes before his arrival, so that he could activate the electronic gate at his home. Suddenly he realized that his home could also be somewhat insecure. Perhaps he would suggest that they got to his Country Club instead.

33.

Working Overtime.

Gingillio's Restaurant, Johannesburg

Grant opened the door of his office and heard Connie wrapping up at the far end of the hallway. He walked slowly towards her while she switched off the lights in the process room and cradled the documents in her arms. She walked up to him and he noticed the enticing swing in her step. Her silhouette against the soft exit light showed her beautifully shaped figure and legs. As she walked towards Grant he was surprised at the sudden excitement he felt to enjoy a late night snack with her.

"QED, Sir. You owe me a pizza for this."

"I will do one better. I will also buy you sangria. Let's see if Gingillio's is still open." Grant took the documents from her, slid them into his briefcase and followed her out of the building.

Gingillio's restaurant was within a five-minute walk from their office building. A chilly draft swirled down the one-way street and Connie clutched her large bag while taking Grant' arm. They walked at a brisk pace yet Connie took Grant's slight limp into consideration. It was past eleven when they were seated and ordered. The young man who waited on them showed signs of a long shift and lacked enthusiasm so Grant decided to leave him a handsome tip.

They ordered pasta and sipped sangria while for the moment they were quiet. On several occasions Connie had dinned out with Grant and members of their office as a group. However, now she felt a little uneasy to be alone with Grant under similar informal circumstances. They looked at each other and smiled. Connie was thinking of something to say or ask but Grant beat her to it.

"You know what? This morning I tried to book a spot at the shooting academy but they could only accommodate me over the weekend." Grant relaxed and seemed pleased with his opening bat.

"This is about the third week in a row you have missed out on your pistol shooting practice – perhaps one of these days the club will drop you from their team!"

Grant looked a little concerned, "Yes, I am afraid you are right but, things were a little hectic and out of routine lately. Perhaps as far as my inclusion in the Gauteng Pistol Team is concerned - it will have to wait until the Africair-project is completed."

"Would you care to take me along to a practice session one evening? I heard you are quite a marksman. I would also like to learn more about firearms and how to handle them." Connie requested.

It took Grant some time to answer her. He looked at her petite figure and wondered why would she want to do that? He was not even sure why he joined the pistol club after the death of Anna. He hated to believe that it became a means to rid him from a numb self- guilt which refused to settle inside him. He said, "Those are dangerous toys and should not be handled by little…," he wanted to say "little girls" but realized his sexist remark could spoil the evening. He did not want that to happen by letting her think he was talking down to her. He fluently twisted his sentence to save the situation, "…by elegant hands like yours."

Grant reached for her hands, which she held over the table towards him. He closed his long fingers around hers, squeezed them and then let go. She hung on to his fingers for a while and then sat back, running her fingers through her shoulder-length hair. She had a full mouth and a soft smile and Grant realized for the first time how beautiful his assistant was.

"So? Will you take me along then? Or is this a no?"

Grant conceded, "Let's do it as soon as we can arrange a booking, preferably this weekend."

Connie was delighted, then a thought struck her and she made an unhappy face, "I need to go with my parents to Bloemfontein in the Free State this weekend. My father will be attending an international conference for heart surgeons. I have to accompany my mother to friends and relatives in that dreary old Free State town."

"Then we must do it some other time." Grant tried not to sound relieved to be off the hook. He did not value the shooting academy as the place for a social outing. And as far as training in handguns was concerned, there were many clubs in town she could join and be trained in the art of self-defence.

Connie tried to keep the small talk going and looked him searchingly in the eyes, "The pace at which we work nowadays does not leave much time for this sort of thing, does it?"

Grant looked at her and smiled but also hoped that he did not create the impression that the evening was perhaps an opportunity for an after work flirtation, "I am afraid that is so. Furthermore, although we are very professional and businesslike in the office and really work together as a super team, we do not know much about each other. Do we? I mean from a personal point of view, I know very little about you and I have been with the firm for close to a year now." Grant sat back to allow the young waiter to arrange their huge pasta helpings and side orders.

Connie teased him again with her smile - she enjoyed being in the company of this very attractive and mature man, "Well, we can start off by exchanging our life stories. What do you want to know about me?"

Connie looked At Grant. At first she thought he was a bit of a stoic type but later she learned he had an honest way with words and people and came over mostly in a positive manner. He was also an excellent writer and very logic in his approach. Sometimes, however, he could sound a little short tempered. Then again at times sadness clouded his eyes and he would become very quiet and deep in thought. Could it be that he was still thinking of his deceased wife? He never referred to her. She heard stories about their accident and how he was injured and possibly responsible for their misfortune.

"At least I know now, you are the daughter of a heart surgeon. But what does your boyfriend say if you are not available on an evening like this?" Grant saw the guarded look in her eyes and he knew that he touched a raw nerve.

"Nothing - we broke our engagement about three months ago." Connie twisted the pasta around her fork.

Grant searched for a suitable word, "Perhaps the young man was just not up to your standard?"

Connie wanted to put her heartbreaking experience in perspective, "We were a number of young people who shared a communion.

Unfortunately one of our co-inhabitants was too strong competition for me. Or rather for my boyfriend's self control. One evening, I came home earlier than usual and found them fast asleep in our bed. By the time they woke up, I was carrying my belongings out to my Fiat."

Grant wanted to ease away from her sad personal experience, "Where is home for you now?"

"I moved back in with my parents in Pretoria. They allowed me to move into their garden cottage again. They did not comment about our breakup - in any case, my boyfriend never impressed them. Judged by their easy acceptance of the whole spectacle, I think they were relieved that our affair ended."

Grant felt embarrassed that his question led to her frank admittance, "Are you over all this now?"

Connie thought for a while with eyes that glistened, "I think so. Perhaps my ego was more damaged than my heart." As she said these words, she felt how objectiveness settled inside her. At once she knew this insight would also mean the last of her hurting reflections and disillusionment.

The small talk returned. Connie Heyneken told Grant how she started to go to the health club as a means to fill her evenings. She also took up photography, which complemented her love for outdoor living. They laughed as she told him about embarrassing situations from her days as a student. On a more serious note she told him about her achievements in gymnastics when she was still at school.

Grant relaxed and he told her about himself - perhaps even more then he cared to admit was necessary. He even opened up to her about his marriage to Anna and the fact that he and Peter now lived together in his big Sandton home. He refrained to tell her about his guilt feelings around the accident in which Anna died and the fact that he was slightly intoxicated on that tragic night. Instead, he told her about Peter's achievements as a student and rugby player. Connie sensed how proud he was of his son.

Connie said she knew about Peter's sport achievements and his involvement in the student religious movement called, 'Jesus in Jeans,' "I met Peter once very briefly – but I did not realize he was your son, Julius. He was well known amongst students – and also very popular as captain of the university's first rugby team. He was considered a good catch, you know so - I am amazed to hear that he is not married yet."

Grant sounded indifferent, "Yes. He is still very much a single man – with a girl friend who is an undergraduate at Oxford University. I think time and distance is taking its toll because it sounds as if their relationship seems to be cooling down. But, yes, I enjoyed watching him play. However, his religious activities left me cold and at times we were caught up in heated arguments about faith. Peter thinks I am spiritually cold to the level of being near agnostic. To date I could not convince him that I sincerely believe that it is enough for me to accept that there is a supreme location at the absolute midpoint of the universe, heaven if you will, from where God rules all. He insists that the means of access and entrance into heaven, wherever it may be, can only be achieved by believing in Jesus."

For a while they spoke about the role that religion played in their youth. Their conversation lightened again when they laughed about silly things that happened in church, which caused Connie to struggle with pent-up giggles, to the utter annoyance of her stern parents.

"Phew! Look at the time. If you stay with your parents, it means that you still need to travel all the way to Pretoria at this time of the night." Grant felt bad for being so ignorant about not knowing where her home was. He was concerned because the Johannesburg-Pretoria freeway was most certainly not the place to travel alone in a car in the middle of the night - especially so if you are a vulnerable young woman.

"Yes, it is a little scary. I once had an unpleasant experience when a car full of men drove alongside and harassed me on the way home one night. Fortunately we caught up with a police car that became aware of the game they were playing. With a few siren sounds and the flashing of its roof lights, they lost interest and sped off. But don't worry - I will brave it. I can complete the trip in under an hour."

"I am terribly sorry for not thinking about this. Why didn't you tell me? - I feel like an utter irresponsible fool," Grant was annoyed with himself.

"Don't worry about me Julius. I will be all right."

"No you won't. I insist that you stay over with us this evening. We have a big house with an extra room with a bathroom that you can use.

Tomorrow you can rush home and freshen up if you must. I will be in the office only after lunch." Grant did not tell Connie about his appointment with Kurtz at his home.

"Are you sure Julius?"

Grant thought he perhaps sounded a little overbearing, but he wanted to compensate for his indiscretion, "Most certainly - let's pick up our stuff in the office and go to my place."

They stood up and Grant slipped his credit card to the waiter. The young man smiled at the sight of the generous tip. They returned to the office where Grant made sure he had all the documents he needed for his discussion with Kurtz.

Connie stopped with her bag and briefcase in the doorway, "There was a message from Peter on the answering device. He said he had to leave for Durban and will only be back in the next day or so. He also said that apart from his business errands, he will talk to his friend about the security of your home?" There was a question in her voice.

Grant's eyebrows jumped - this was awkward. Now the two of them would be alone in his huge mansion. Grant tried to sound casual, "Oh yes. He wants to upgrade our home security system. He thinks it is outdated and not reliable." Grant felt uneasy for not telling her the real reason.

By the time they left the office it was well after midnight. Grant was tired and longed to get to bed as soon as possible.

34.

CARE KILLS THE CAT.

GRANT'S HILLBROW MANSION

Connie followed Grant to his home in her car. She was impressed with the large mansion and sprawling gardens as they followed the paved driveway to the double front doors. Grant walked over and opened the car door for Connie. She took her bag from the rear seat and they walked slowly up the few steps to the veranda. Grant fumbled for the keys and looked carefully around him. Connie noticed his searching look.

"Is something wrong?" For some reason she whispered to him and immediately felt a little foolish.

"No. I was just wondering what happened to Kieter," he said aloud.

"And if I may ask, who is Kieter -your butler?"

Grant smiled, "Kieter is my eighteen-year-old Siamese cat. He normally greets me at the door. But I suppose he is out doing some consultation work." His voice sounded mischievous while vapour from his breath swirled in the cool night air.

"A cat doing consultation work?" They entered the foyer. Connie noticed the large cashmere carpet and welcomed the warmth of the house.

"Many years ago Kieter had this big restrictive operation you know. Despite this unfortunate experience he still likes to check up on the females of the neighbourhood from time to time. I just accept that as he is no longer making an active contribution to bring joy to their hearts, so he must act in an advisory capacity to the young males."

Connie found his story very funny. She laughed contagiously as they walked to the large lounge, "The spare bedroom is upstairs right next to Peter's the adjacent bathroom has a shower, robes, towels and so forth. Can I lend you a set of my pyjamas?"

Connie smiled, "Thank you Grant, but I have here in my bag a light track suit and enough cosmetics to see me through. But could I hope for a spare toothbrush?"

Grant thought for a while, "Ah, yes. In the vanity cupboard of the bathroom you will find amongst others an unopened toilet handout from Singapore Airlines. In there you should find many things - also a toothbrush."

"Thanks." She squeezed his arm.

Grant asked, "Would you like something to drink? I am going to make some hot chocolate."

"No thank you Grant. I am OK. A hot shower will be just the right thing to put me to sleep."

They moved upstairs and grant switched on the lights in the hallway and the guestroom, "Thank you for all your assistance today. And I am very sorry for the inconvenience that I am causing you."

"Don't bother - it's my pleasure, Boss." He enjoyed the tease in her eyes.

"I am quite hopeless in the kitchen - when I make coffee I tend to burn the water you know. But I will be able to prepare you some tea and a sandwich in the morning - say around seven thirty?"

Connie laughed and assured him she was all right and they said good night. Their glances reflected for fleeting moment the awareness that they were alone in the huge house. Too late they realized, with Peter out of town, that they perhaps had not made the best arrangement for the night. But it was too late now. Grant smiled and turned back to the kitchen. He shrugged off the awkwardness of their situation. Damn - it's not as if I wanted to sleep with the kid, he thought.

While he waited for the milk to heat Grant walked through the dimly lit ground floor rooms, calling for Kieter. The old cat sometimes had the stuck-up notion to hide somewhere when strange people arrived, especially when they were female guests. After a while he gave up, poured his hot chocolate and took it to his bedroom.

Halfway up the broad hardwood stairs he stopped cold in his tracks as he heard Connie's continuous high-pitched yell. Grant placed the ceramic mug on the steps and rushed up the last flight, leaping three steps at a time. Her cry came from behind the closed bathroom door. It was locked. He stood back and rushed forward. On the second attempt the door gave way and banged loudly against the wall. The copper doorknob disintegrated the plate-glass mirror that covered the wall. While glass splattered across the marble floor he rushed to Connie where she crouched in the empty bath. Her golden hair was bundled into a shower cap and she was naked.

Grant's violent entry and breaking glass increased her distress and she cringed while breaking into a near hysterical cry. At first he could not see what caused her fear. The shower door stood ajar. Grant froze at the sight before him. From the showerhead Kieter hung like a soap-on-a-rope with a note that dangled from his tail. Grant stared his cat stared - deeply shocked while near uncontrollable anger rose in him.

"Oh my poor cat! Why my poor old Kieter? You bloody children of the devil - whoever you are! For this I will personally cook your balls in public! You - bastards!"

Behind him Connie sobbed loudly and Grant regained his self-control. For a moment he was so shocked at what he saw that he forgot all about Connie's distress. He kneeled beside her and picked her up like a child - she felt unbelievably soft and light as he carried her to his bedroom. Connie clung to him and her long fingernails bit into the back of his neck. The whole situation took on a movie-like scene as he saw their reflection and her nakedness in the mirror opposite him. He held her with one arm and pulled back the bedspread - lowered her onto the bed and slipped off the shower cap. Her long hair flowed across the blue pillow. He carefully loosened her arms from his neck and covered her up to her chin. He leaned forward, held her and whispered soothing words close to her ear - as if she was a little girl.

Once she calmed and stopped shivering, Grand whispered , "I'll remove Kieter and bring you something to drink, Connie - just wait a few minutes my dear I won't be long."

Through tears Connie begged, "Please don't leave me now - just hold me for a while longer. Who would want to kill your poor innocent cat? Who's the cruel person who killed your Kieter? Oh! - your poor old cat." She cried like a child who sympathised with the loss of a friend's favourite doll. Grant stroked her hair and the rage inside him was slowly replaced by sadness as his thoughts dwelled on his pet. It was like the death of a member of the family - like Anna…

Connie stopped sobbing and allowed him to go and untie Kieter. Rigor mortis had begun to set in - yet Grant carried his cat out of the door with his lips close to his ears. From a linen cupboard in the passage he took a small blanket, knelt down and undid the message from Kieter's tail before he lovingly covered his cat in the chequered wrap.

Grant read the note where it lay on the floor next to the sad bundle:

"Mister Grant,

It seemed that you think we are not serious. We decides to start with your kat. Next in lines could be your son . . . or even you!

Get out of Africair business or get killed!"

Grant reread the unsigned hand-written note and noticed the grammar and spelling mistakes.

"Bloody bastards! When will you stupid people realize that the days of old-style games are over! God helps us and I hope it is for good." Grant stuffed the note in his jacket pocke and placed Kieter on the dryer in the laundry. Perhaps he would ask a veterinarian to incinerate him – on the other hand, Peter may want to bury him in the garden like he did with all their previous pets. At the liqueur cabinet he filled a glass half with scotch and went upstairs again. In the medicine chest he found some sedatives. Grant filled another glass with water and helped Connie swallow the tablets.

She was still trembling and while he held her close to him suggested that she take a sip of scotch. She took one gulp, pulled a face and pushed the glass away. The blankets lowered with her movements. She was unconcerned about her full round breasts pressing against Grant. He closed her up again and arranged the pillows under her flowing hair. She closed her eyes and tears ran down her cheeks, to which some colour had returned.

Grant sat on the bed and emptied the rest of the glass with one swallow. It was a long time since he had used alcohol. He stared at the curtains while behind him Connie started to breath evenly. He then went downstairs, filled the glass with another large tot of Johnny Walker and sat for a long time in the dimly lit television room. After a while the whisky warmed and relaxed him.

Grant vividly remembered the morning of his birthday when Anna came into the room with his favourite breakfast. She placed the tray before him and from a large milk jug, a friendly fluffy little head popped up and greeted him. He can't remember why he named the little cat Kieter - he only remembered his cat's many loving mannerisms. Eventually his thoughts came to a standstill and the he started to cry softly – over his cat, Anna - and his lousy, lonely guilt-filled life. "Jesus I am miserable!" - his thoughts went out to Peter whom at that moment he missed very much .

It was close to daybreak when Grant kicked off his shoes and tiptoed up to the spare bedroom. He dropped onto the bed and sank into an irregular sleep filled with sad dreams.

35.

THE GAUNTLET DROPPED.

GRANT'S HILLBROW MANSION

Around seven Grant went down to the kitchen to prepare something that could look and taste like breakfast. Connie was still fast asleep so he waited for the sound of her steps on the stairs before he started with the toast. She appeared in a red and white tracksuit and looked amazingly fresh after the night's unpleasant ordeal. She walked up to Grant and held him close. Grant gently held her.

"I am sorry that I overreacted so violently last night." She stood back and a slight flush covered her cheeks. She remembered Grant seeing her totally naked last night - yet he did not take advantage of the situation. As a matter of fact, apart from the short outburst of swears words, he was a symbol of self-control and maturity and she loved him for that.

"No my dear, it is I who brought you into this mess. I am so sorry - will you please forgive me - please?" Grant rubbed the stubble on his chin and felt desperately in need of a shower - perhaps a long hot suds-filled bath would revive him.

"There is nothing to forgive. I am very sorry about Kieter and I can see you are very sad too. But I also think you are in some sort of trouble. Do you want to share it with me? Perhaps in some way I can help - I am also your friend you know. Maybe you are in need of a friend now." Her eyes shone while she tried to smile.

Grant felt trapped -he could not dance out of this spot, "Yes, I begin to think something seriously could happen to me if we implement my Africair strategy." He slipped two slices of white bread into the toaster.

Grant looked at Connie, "You typed the whole strategy yesterday and saw my recommendations. It is clear that we are in a minefield of razor sharp competition – and defence systems are always sensitive stuff to deal with. The armaments industry is a maze of secret agendas and a real back stabbing business with clock-and-dagger interests. Millions of dollars change hands in commissions, bribery, kick-backs and heaven knows what other types of beneficial schemes." Grant sounded as if he lost some of his enthusiasm –perhaps he was just dog-tired.

"Why are we then into this type of business? Why can't we just walk away from it?" Connie could not hide her new found concern for Grant.

Grant ran his fingers through his uncombed hair, rubbed his shaded chin continuously -the itchiness bothered him."For a number of good reasons – and you know some of them."

Connie wanted to know what he had in mind, "Apart from collecting a really fat fee, what else is so important for you to be involved? I think it must be a good one - for I can see the determination in your eyes - despite the fact that you must be exhausted. Connie stood closer again and searched his eyes.

Grant warmed to Connie's sensitivity and he held her for a moment. Behind them the toaster popped, "Let's eat something." Grant said and they sat down opposite each other at the small nook - realising that the atmosphere was now so much different than during the previous meal they had together in the restaurant.

Grant dished up the eggs and bacon. "The main thing is that the aviation industry is of vital importance to a country like South Africa, because we are so geographically isolated from the rest of the world." He gave her the same arguments as he did for Peter the previous evening.

Connie added a little marmalade to her toast, "So, what you say is that if the technical facilities, needed to maintain aviation traffic to and from South Africa degrades, discontinues or even disappear, this country will surely backslide into an underdeveloped state at a fast pace?"

Grant poured himself more black coffee and slowly stirred in sweeteners, "Yes I do think South Africa is 'backsliding', as you put it - and I am concerned about it. I hope to do my part to retard the process. A lot more needs to be done at various levels to turn the situation and head the country in the right direction."

Connie licked the tip of her finger."Like what?"

Grant decided to let her in on his fears for the future of South Africa, "Mandela's government will have to seriously stabilize the internal situation. Otherwise we will lose skills and foreign investment. We desperately need a firm grip on the rampant crime that ruins this country. On the other hand government spending will have to be brought to acceptable levels.

Grant continued and commented on, as he put it, the one potential good infrastructure legacy that the Apartheid government left behind, "The new government unfortunately made a serious mistake by relaxing the effective border control measures that allowed for a well guarded north boundary of the country. Consequently there is a growing, uncontrolled influx of foreigners from all over central and North Africa into the country. They come here, committing crimes to stay alive and are competing unfairly with the locals for job opportunities and social support systems. This will eventually lead to serious internal disorder and unrest between local workers and these hordes of illegal immigrants. Can you imagine how the United States would have appreciated a well controlled southern border – where they also experience a similar influx of Mexicans into their country?"

Connie smiled and said in her best American accent, "You telling me baby"

Grant added, "On the other hand, official glut and corruption is growing and the so called 'Gravy Train' picks up passengers at an alarming rate."

Connie placed the dishes in the zinc, "I think you are right Julius. We read about these things in the papers every day. Speculation has it that a few years down the road in this direction could wipe-out the capital and other resources of this so-called Rainbow Nation."

Connie looked at him. The serious nature of their discussion brought them back to an official level – and she felt vaguely sorry about that. There was, however, the promise that their relationship could grow more meaningful. Last night they shared an experience of an intimate nature. She was confident that in some way they bonded. Connie brought her thoughts back to the issue at stake, "Are you prepared to share with me the implication behind what happened last night?"

Grant listened to her earnest request and he did not want to distract her with another academic argument. Now he will have to draw her into his predicament now, "OK. Connie I am. But, on one condition only: Do not discuss this with anyone - not until I agree that you may do so. Not even with Marlene Brooks."

"Is it that serious?" Her eyes widened.

"I am afraid it begins to look like it." Grant told her about the phone call, which prompted Peter to upgrade their security system. He took the crumpled note from his pocket and she read it several times.

"This was written by an amateur." Connie looked up at Julius, feeling uncertain, knowing they stumbled onto something larger than they anticipated.

"Or is it a deliberate deception?" Grant kept an open mind and thought about his oncoming discussion with Kurtz later that morning.

She shook her hair into place, "I don't think so."

Grant clenched his fists on the table. "I am determined to get behind this silly game. I do not scare easily and I hate it if people fool around with me." Connie saw how decisiveness settling in his eyes.

Connie stood up. "Just before I leave, I want to assure you that if you are going through with this, you can rely on me. For what it is worth. I will keep my word - and my eyes and ears open." She liked the warm trust that developed between them.

Grant walked with Connie to her car, "Sure as hell I am going through with this - and thank you for your support. I think I am really going to need it."

36.

WHEELS WITHIN WHEELS.

JOHANNESBURG AIRPORT HOTEL

Akbar Assad looked at the printed message he received from the receptionist and wondered why the sender did not leave a voice mail instead. Then again, it was clear this note was hand-delivered here at the hotel. Now, who could this Yusef person be? Perhaps he was somebody from the travel bureau or the car-rental company. Had Assad been familiar with the South African dialling codes he would have recognized that this was a Pretoria number.

Assad decided to postpone his return call till later in the evening - or even leave till the morning. He went up to his room and settled in an easy chair, took the remote control and selected an entertainment channel. In Dubai he missed the wide choice of television channels and topics offered in other countries however, the M-Net channel that beamed per satellite from South Africa to Dubai offered him enough entertainment. On the other hand he had little time to spend in front of the box but, he always tried not to Miss Patricia Ndlalosi's news commentary. Assad thought she was the most beautiful girl in the world. Her light butterscotch complexion and - sometimes she displayed just a little hint of a cleavage - drove Assad wild.

Her programme had not yet started so Assad took his toilet bag to the bathroom and studied his face in the mirror. He gave special attention to his full black moustache and tried to judge how much attention it needed. His decision was short-circuited by a phone call.

"Yes. Who's this?" He was always careful before identifying himself.

"May I speak to Mr. Assad from the Gulf News please." The accent was Indian.

Assad paused for a while. This must be Yusef, "Who wants to speak to him?" He stayed cautious - Faber's picture flashed somewhere in the corner of his mind and it made him uneasy.

"Yusef Minty, sir."

"And are you Yusef Minty?"

"Yes – Mister Assad, I presume?"

"Yes. What do you want?" Assad was tired and his irritation rose.

"It is about dispatching your mail sir." Yusef sounded young and uncertain and Assad relaxed a little.

"Where are you now?"

"In the foyer, Sir - may I come up to your room please?"

"Wait for me right there - I will be down in a few minutes."

Assad was a little doubtful because he still tried to define exactly his involvement in the covert project of forwarding technical information to a destination somewhere in the UK. He began to doubt if this was a first-rate thing. It felt to him as if he was slowly being drawn into something he had little control over.

Assad had only one personal contact with The Agency. He could still recall the Saturday morning when two well-dressed Arab gentlemen came to see him at his apartment in Dubai. That was about a year ago. They wanted to talk to him about an article he wrote. In this story he speculated on Gadafi's military objectives. It was well written and hinted at some commiseration from him as a writer. He tried to objectively speculate about Gadafi's possible interest vis-à-vis that of the Gulf States.

Assad and his visitors had a lengthy discussion and he answered many questions and eventually the real purpose of their visit surfaced. They wanted him to relay all the information he gathered as a journalist, to them – at a fee of course. They said they were agents for a data bank that gathered and interpreted military technology information for the benefit of potential buyers of attack helicopters. Assad could see no harm in doing that. If they wanted straightforward information, which could be picked-up at any military show or from a brochure, or the internet, as journalists do, so what? And to be paid for a few minutes' 'retrieval effort' was money from home - both of which he lacked. Money and a place he could call 'home.'

Thereafter Assad had regular calls from the younger of the two men – big burly Ben Ahlib and eventually he agreed to assist their fact compilation services. Initially he also rationalised that it could afford him an exclusive source for stories. What he also expected was that they would at some time in the future they would request him to write some material that could support their aims. However right now, all he had to do was pass on all the information about military systems or hardware that came his way. He thought nothing of it and faxed through whatever he came across his systems – that is all the information he picked up from brochures or notes during interviews therefore eventually went to the mail-contact addresses provided to him by Ahlib.

Assad's diligence prevailed when regular substantial amounts were credited to his bank account so he stuck to this menial task and from time to time received calls from Ahlib - who thanked him for his contributions. They never referred to his compensation and Assad was sure 'Ahlib' was not the man's real name. He could not find Ahlib's telephone number in the directory or from any operator's number-enquiry service.

Once he asked Ben Ahlib directly for his phone number and Ahlib responded glibly, "I travel extensively and in areas where cellular phone services are mostly out of reach. I can, however, leave you with a voice-mail service number so, if it is really urgent, you will get a quick response from me – and that, I can assure you." Ben Ahlib gave him a number in London. A girl's pre-recorded voice simply asked callers to leave a message. All he had was this answering service in London and a fax number in Dubai - and now a young man named Yusef Minty who offered him a surface mail or courier service from South Africa to his contacts. This offer came from an Indian person! Something did not add up.

Assad recognized the young man in the foyer from his black uniform with the letters SDS on his breast pocket. "Good evening Sir. I am Yusef Minty from Speedy Delivery Services" "How did you know where to contact me?" Assad tried to sound indifferent.

"My Boss, Mr Abdul Hitam asked me to hand this note to you personally." Assad took the note but did not indicate that he wanted to open it, "Your Boss, is he also… of Indian origin…like you?" Assad smiled but the answer was important.

"No Sir, I am just a driver - my Boss, he is a partner in the business. And he is Malaysian. A very, very, rich but also a religious person and a honest and good man, Sir." The young man wanted to impress the foreigner before him, who obviously had some influence.

"So, he is a Muslim - yes?" Assad indicated that he wanted to leave, "Do you need to wait for an answer from me?"

"No Sir - thank you and good night, Sir."

Minty glanced at the reception desk, turned on his heel and walked through the revolving door. Back in his room Assad looked at the neatly typed note. It simply read,

Dear Mister Assad,

On behalf of The Agency I want to welcome you to South Africa, the land of opportunity for the brave-hearted. For the duration of your stay in South Africa you must refrain from mailing any letters or fax notes to your number in Dubai. Call the mobile number printed on the envelope and ask for Yusef Minty. He will collect all materials from you at your hotel. Hand it over to him personally. He is trustworthy and will bring it directly to me. Do not return to Dubai with any documents, other than editorial notes in your briefcase. Tear up and flush this note down the toilet.

Kind regards
AH.

Akbar Assad was totally confused but nevertheless followed Abdul Hitam's instruction. He lowered the seat cover of the toilet, and sat down, deep in thought, for a long time. He thought mostly about the document he had lifted from Rosemary Barnard's desk - a deed that contributed to his strange circumstances.

Assad stood up and took the document marked "Top Secret" from his briefcase. He read through it superficially - understanding little of the jargon, theories and calculations that obviously explained the operational analysis of the system. An interesting paragraph caught his eye, "Military helicopters are more and more sophisticated and are now dedicated under various configurations, to various missions. The development as far as air-to-air warning and surveillance systems are concerned, has been rapid. A lot of the assault helicopters in service today are equipped with air-to-air missiles. It is therefore of the utmost importance to detect missiles as early as possible. The name of the game is – 'first seen, first shot.' This newly developed system will give the Martial Eagle a clear edge over any other gunship flying today."

Something told Assad he had in his hands the most valuable piece of information to date. "Mr. Ben Ahlib - or whatever your name is - I think when I send you this info you will be really happy. Or rather - I will courier it out with Abdul Hitam's service. This, my friend, looks like the most up-to-date relevant technology concerning surveillance systems," he thought out aloud. For a moment it occurred to him that for the first time he would pass on material that he did not use in an article written by him from any well-known source.

Assad secured the file in the small safe fitted in the wardrobe and then took a much needed shower. Twenty minutes later he was fully dressed and sat in front of the television again. Patricia's program has started. The beautiful black girl read her news commentary with a formal English accent. He looked at her every facial expression, the movement of her lips, the fluttering of her eyes. He was nearly besotted with this girl, locked in the tube like an exquisite little tropical fish in a big clear bowl.

His phone rang - the interruption was a call from the foyer.

"I am ready when you are," said John Molape.

"Give me ten minutes and I will be right down. I have just one more thing to attend to."

Assad had to look at Patricia Ndlalosi's program - for just a few minutes more while in Pretoria, Abdul Hitam stood on the balcony of his luxurious penthouse apartment and spoke to Ben Ahlib in Dubai, "It's done - our Golf News reporter's brief case will be empty!"

37.

Wild Game Cuisine and Game Correspondents.

Randburg, South Africa

The exclusive African restaurant with its layout which was a train station from the late nineteenth century, surprised Akbar Assad.. The staff's dress complemented the era. Four dining saloons stood on tracks amid signals and old-world railway equipment. The ticket office served as reception counter and brass band music was interspersed by a hailer who announced fictional departures to well-known African destinations. En-route to these fictional destination special dishes was offered. The platform between the carriages was lined with buffet tables that carried the most exquisite African dishes. At first Assad was taken aback by the offerings of steaks and goulash made from elephant, crocodile, wild boar, and hippopotamus meat. Then he saw the table with eastern foods and halal dishes - with the result that he had never before enjoyed a similar eating experience.

"Would you like to visit the bar first, Gentlemen?" Molape looked at Assad, who declined.

"Your table is number nine in dining saloon three - please follow me." A smiling waiter with a drop-handle moustache and top hat took them to the saloon reserved for non-smoking patrons. They ordered fruit juice and made their way to the buffet where Assad looked at the wide range of prepared food and shook his head in amazement,

"Whoever invented these creations must have been very hungry at some stage." He looked with dismay at the selection of zebra and giraffe steaks, which could be complimented by various snake sauces.

Molape appreciated his sensitivity about food, "Yes certainly hungry, and for that matter not very religious." He decided to join Assad at the dishes that offered meals prepared according to his religious dietary laws.

When they returned from the dessert table and ordered coffee, Assad judged the moment as opportune to tie Molape down as an extended source of information for The Agency. He started in a roundabout way, "I presume you would not be unwilling to add to your income by acting as a freelance or special correspondent for The Gulf News?"

"Can we talk about this for a while?" Molape was eager but cautious, "What must I do and for how much?"

Assad smiled reassuringly, "Sure. You see it all depends on the information or comment we need to compile our extensive supplement on the most important attack helicopters of the world." Assad's thoughts ran back to the discussion he had with Ben Ahlib at Dubai airport shortly before his departure. The unfathomable man gave him a perfect reason why it was necessary to obtain information in the way The Agency required. It was a well-known fact that some countries that the United States viewed as antagonistic towards the interests of America and their alliances, were in the past supporters of the ANC movement during its years of opposition to and struggle against Apartheid rule. Although many heads of these states and Nelson Mandela were good friends the structures in South Africa still needed to become more amiably for these countries to interact more open and frequently at all levels.

Molape tasted his hot coffee carefully, "Why don't you ask your government to talk to President Mandela, or whoever, to open the channels for you. That way, I think, you will get whatever information you want."

Assad's smile stretched his moustache, "No it is not that easy. Even when countries are engaged in technology alliances, the owners of that technology are very reluctant to share their knowledge."

Over the past months, Molape came to understand the covert culture of the defence industry and said. "Perhaps it is a form of built-in security."

Assad hoped his arguments would convince Molape that what he required was perfectly normal and legally acceptable. He picked up the young man's reluctance and realized shallow arguments and the promise of a good fee alone would not easily convince him, "Yes, but there are a lot of prerequisites for countries to operate successful technology partnerships and, a lot has to do with their interests and the views of their alliances in the world community."

Molape looked at the bottom of his cup like someone who was about to read future events from tea leaves, "I can understand that because in South Africa, our history and mostly the recent past played a vital role. The world communities, as you call it, still need to get used to the new alliances of an ANC-led government for South Africa. Eyes popped when Castro, Arafat and Gadafi attended President Nelson Mandela's presidential inauguration. But I can assure you that at this stage it is unthinkable that South Africa will share its technology and intellectual property with any government except perhaps with a bona vide potential client."

This remark widened Assad's eyes. For a moment he thought Molape could read his thoughts or picked up a message in the bottom of his cup or perhaps through hidden voodoo or other black-magical power. Molape interpreted Assad's reaction as the result of the insight he gave him into South African politics and culture. They sat in silence for a while, ordered more coffee and took up their subject again.

Assad looked at the imitation gas lamps above them, "I suppose there is no shortcut for us poor journalists. We will always have to sniff out the most ordinary information as a result of how things are structured in the armaments marketing environment."

"Talk to me about the fee." Molape was not yet ready to assist Assad and, as he believed, the leading newspaper of the Arab Emirates - The Gulf News.

To Assad this was the tricky part of reaching an agreement and, he thought much about how he would handle the situation when it came up. Now he was unsure how to address the fee structure and tried to postpone his answer, "If you are happy by what my Editor offers you, will you assist us?"

Molape looked at him. The dim interior of the saloon car painted their surroundings in a patina coloured milieu - like the setting of an old movie and old African township music played in the background, "What if you ask me to supply you with classified information? Or stuff I am unable to lay my hands on?"

Assad waited for this, "Well, then you simply refuse!"

"And for understandable reason you stop the payment of the fee?"

"Not really because it is difficult to put a price on the availability of technical information – and it is not like we are playing the role of spies, you know." Assad leaned forward and spoke in a hushed voice, "In the meantime you are still devoting some of your time to find out about something that could be used in an article. Not so? Remember we are paying you for your time and effort and, not for the content of the information or how meaningful it may be for an article." Assad's smooth lying made him feel embarrassed but fortunately the faded lighting hid his discomfort.

Molape relaxed, "Makes sense. Whatever you are paying me - must I see it as a regular or fixed retainer, then?"

Assad nodded, "You may call it that and - our payments are usually made in advance"

Molape had difficulty in holding back the most important question, "What will my fee add up to?"

Assad looked him straight in the eyes and leaned forward against the table, "It will be two thousand US dollars per month and the first payment will be for three months in advance."

"What!" Molape sat up straight and his eyebrows jumped, "Hell Assad, in our currency it means twenty thousand Rand!. We talk of a first drop of sixty thousand Rand here!"

"In international terms it is not a lot of dough - it is your rand currency that is so weak, my friend."

Molape shook his head in disbelief and delight, "Hell! It is still a substantial good fortune for a salaried man in Africa."

Assad smiled, "Shall we call it a deal?"

Molape nodded intensely and drew the attention of the patrons close to them with his loud outburst of laughter, "I like your generous offer man..." He brought his face close to Assad and spoke softly, "...and your payment arrangement."

The agreement was sealed and to Molapi it sounded like winning the lotto when Assad invited him, "Come to my hotel room tomorrow evening and I will give you the first instalment - in cash."

"Make it in South African Rand, please." Molapi rubbed a money sign with thumb over his fingers.

"OK – it will be done." Assad waived an indication that the deal was sealed.

Now, I still don't know what my first assignment will be?" Molapi's eyes signalled a question.

Assad said; "Neither do I. When I confirm our arrangement with my Editor, I will ask him about it." The lie came glibly from the budding young mole.

"Good!" Molape was still smiling. He tapped his feet to the sounds of the throbbing township piece of music.

"Tomorrow evening I will give you a fax number where you can contact me. It will not be The Gulf News number, though." Assad said indifferently.

"Why not?" Molapi was not used to working with twisted communication arrangements.

By now Assad has swiftly developed into a fluent and effective liar, "It will be a fax number at my girlfriend's apartment. In that way I will be sure that whenever you contact me she will pass it on to me - wherever I am working on this old globe." Assad suddenly was painfully aware that he had no girlfriend, "And talking about girls, if you are really so pleased with our future arrangement – how about organizing for us a couple of nice girls that we could take to a show and a late night dinner, - you know."

Molape smiled, "Good idea. It has been a while since I took my fiancé out to burn the town. What type of girls do you like? Black, white, Indian? - unfortunately I do not know any Arab girls!" He roared with laughter at his own remark.

"Earlier this evening I saw a beautiful black girl reading the news commentary. She is my type you know - big smile, nice teeth, big tits." Assad gave him a slow, long wink.

"You mean Patricia Ndlalosi'? - I met her a few times at news conferences and television interviews that I arranged for my Boss. If she is your type of girl, I think I know what you will like. I will come up with an interesting and lovely companion for you." Molapi returned his slow, long wink and they laughed, finished their coffee and left the dining car. Assad wanted to hit the sack as soon as possible.

38.

PROMISES - PROMISES.

KEMPTON PARK, SOUTH AFRICA

Akbar Assad ordered breakfast from room service and then he called Yusef Minty. They arranged that Minty would come to his room for his first mail pick-up. It took the messenger just over an hour before knocking on his door. He greeted the eager, friendly boy and handed him the top-secret document. He smiled as Akbar slipped him a generous tip and wondered if he would ever get to meet the mysteriously Abdul Hitam.

The bubble-lined envelope he picked up at the hotel's Business Centre was properly sealed. Assad suppressed the urge to attach a note for Ben Ahlib – even considered slipping his visiting card in the envelope. Then the memory of Faber's heavy hand on his shoulder made him decide otherwise. By now the document must have been reported missing by Rosemary Barnard and he would not want to leave his fingerprints all over this delivery of information. Assad wiped the sweat from his forehead and wished he was out of the country by now.

The rest of the day he was in the hands of the Southern Cross Electronic Corporation, known as SCEC. A most attractive Afrikaans girl who, like most Afrikaners, spoke good English took care of him. Sue Hartmann was well informed and eager to please. Fortunately Assad had no difficulty to pronounce her name and all day long they communicated well. They visited several of the Group's subsidiaries - which all were suppliers to the South African armaments industry. Assad acquired a fair grasp of the excellence of South Africa's high-technology industry. By noon he understood how this small country with only a handful of scientist could produce world-class defence systems. His notes referred to their commitment and dedication, and that tenacity and good systems management was their secret. Lunch with his attractive host and the top management of SCEC was most pleasant. He promised Sue a follow-up story when they exhibit their Sight Helmet and Firing Control-System for armoured vehicles in Dubai.

Assad returned to his hotel shortly after four that afternoon and slumped over his laptop. He drew up a report on his progress to date and wrote an outline of the SCEC article. He still had to account for the real purpose of his visit. A secretary at the hotel's business centre faxed the printout to his editor and he hoped the trenchant old man was too busy to bother him with instructions to cover additional material.

Later on Assad asked the concierge, "Please recommend a nice restaurant in this vicinity that offers a good show and an intimate dance-floor,"

The attendant was eager to show Assad catalogues where traditional food was served and together they selected a venue and made a booking at the Capricorn. Assad exchanged a large amount of dollars for South African rands, bought the evening papers and took the elevator to his room.

The phone rang as he entered his room and the radio-alarm flashed to 8:14pm. Assad ignored the phone and reached for the television's remote control. He switched to the news channel, while the phone kept on ringing, hoping to see Patricia Ndlalosi again. Instead, the newsreader was a polished little white man with grey hair. Totally frustrated Assad pressed the mute button and lifted the receiver.

It was John Molape, "How was your day, Assad."

"Just fine - I was at Southern Cross." Assad sounded bored.

"Smart lot of white jackets they got out there. That company has one of the highest IQ's per square meter, in the country, you know." Molapi tried to inject some enthusiasm into the evening.

Assad tied to live up to the moment, "Yes and I was impressed. Say - can you come

and pick up your... eh...envelope?"

"Yes, but..." Molapi sounded hesitant.

"But what?"

"I have the girls with me." Molapi could not hide his excitement.

"What!" Assad started to warm up to the occasion.

Molape was impishly quiet for a while, "I thought you were serious when you suggested..."

"Aah -yes of course - I 'm just a little surprised - that's all."

"Good, - I will ask them to wait in the lounge for us see you in a bit." Molape dropped the phone and took the elevator to Assad's room. He knocked and Assad opened the door immediately, turned to his briefcase on the desk and pulled out a stuffed envelope with only the hotel's logo was printed on it. He bowed and handed it to Molape.

Assad looked at the envelope in Molape's slightly trembling hands, "Do you want to count it first?"

"Is it in South African currency?" Molapi regretted his regrettable question.

"Yes - and the fax number is also in there."

Molape slipped the envelope into his inside jacket pocket, "Shall we go?"

On their way down to the lounge, Assad structured the evening, "This evening I will be the host. I booked a table for four at a restaurant close by - it stages a floor show and has a small dance floor."

"So did you hope there would be girls to meet?" Molape felt they were becoming closer.

Assad just smiled and rocked on his heels and followed Molape to the lounge. They walked to a small nook where two black girls sat sipping sodas. They were exceptionally beautiful. The girl with her back turned to them, turned and looked up at Assad. He stopped dead in his tracks - overwhelmed. It was Patricia Ndlalosi!

39.

An Arabian's Night.

Nico's Night Club, Boksburg

Assad could not believe his eyes or good fortune. Just hours ago Patricia was to him just a beautiful face and soft shoulders untouchably preserved in a glass television tube. Now she was standing here in front of him – in real life! Patricia stood up and took his hand and her touch was soft and warm - like her smile and voice. Her appearance impressed him and her full but petite body surprised him. Blood rushed to Assad's ears, which started ringing so intensely that he feared his hearing would fail at any moment. Then she spoke to him in that well-known pleasant voice and all his feelings of distress vanished.

"Hello Assad.. I am pleased to meet you - on the way here John told me so much about you. I am sure this is going to be one of the more pleasant evenings of your thousand-and-one Arabian Nights - or am I now out of context here?" Patricia threw her head back and laughed most contagiously. Assad admired her even white teeth and laughed because she did – he still could still not believe his good luck. It changed his mood and he immediately turned into a humorous and pleasant companion.

Assad still held her hand and stood a little closer, "I am delighted -may I call you Patricia?"

"Sure you do - those who know me a little better call me Pat." She directed him to the chair next to her.

Assad caught a whiff of her perfume and the ringing in is ears turned to music, "I got to know you on television as Patricia and that's how I would like to call you. I enjoy your program tremendously and try to never miss it. Do you need to write your own copy?" Assad laughed and could not remember when he last felt so excited. All the stress of the visit and his hidden agenda was gone.

Assad and Patricia found each other extremely appealing and they talked non-stop all the way to the restaurant and through most of the evening. They were enchanted with their opposite backgrounds. He was born in Alexandria in North Africa and she in Cape Town. They thought it most extraordinary that two people, one from the southern tip of Africa and the other from the northern edge of the continent, coming from totally different cultures, could find so much to talk and laugh about. Their chemistry worked like magic.

As time progressed, John Molape and his lovely fiancée, faded from their perception and they were later like part of the décor and surroundings that created their delightful evening. Later on the charmed couple could not even remember clearly when John and his fiancé decided to do the understandable right thing - to leave early. This allowed the enamoured couple to explore the night and each other. When the couple returned to their table after a long session of close dancing, they found a note from John - wishing them well. They sat and held hands -for them the evening had only started.

Many hours later Assad adjusted the pillows and cradled Patricia's generous breasts in his hands. She lay with her back against him. Her eyes were closed and he kissed her ear tenderly and held her tightly.

"This is a wonderful dream -not so?" Assad could still not believe that he made deep and forceful love to this extraordinary, beautiful woman - barely hours after he had seen her for the first time in real life. He was so lucky!

"No my gentle Arab friend, this is not a dream. Unfortunately I need to be honest with you - this will only be a single pleasant African night." Patricia laughed softly and stroked Assad's cheeks slowly with her sensitive hands.

Assad decided it was a dream and he was also afraid that at any moment she would float out of his arms and through the screen, to be locked away forever and out of his reach in the cold glass tube. He drew her still closer to him, feeling how her warm softness enfolded him. As much as they talked all evening just as little was said since Akbar locked the door behind them. The afterglow of their lovemaking suspended them in a balmy slumber.

It was close to daybreak when Assad hugged Patricia and kissed her goodbye. He stood at the hotel entrance and returned her wave while a cold loneliness enfolded him in the winter dawn - he felt bereft and forlorn. The knowledge that he may never meet her again darkened his mood while he walked slowly through the revolving doors where the warmth of the quiet foyer failed to reach the coldness in his heart. Assad was suddenly a very lonely man.

He also did not see or hear the departure of Faber's faded Volkswagen where it left the shade of a tree in the hotel's parking lot. A cigarette glowed in the stout man's beard as he glanced at the hotel entrance in his rear view mirror and said aloud, "You are living farken dangerously Mr. Assad -bloody dangerously mister Arab lover"

-oOo-

KEMPTON PARK HOTEL

Back in his room Assad's loneliness prevailed and he did not know what to do next. Should he try to sleep some more or take a hot shower and go down for an early breakfast? Ben Ahlib's call from Dubai made up his mind.

"Hello, who do you want to speak to?"

"Am I talking to Akbar Assad, right?"

Hello, Ben." He did not expect Ahlib's call this early and he was not in the mood to talk to the brash man at this hour.

"You OK?" He was more sensitive than Assad gave him credit for.

"Yes my friend - what's up?" Assad's tone was guarded as he continued, "Please remember there is a two hour difference between Dubai and Johannesburg."

"I am sorry my friend I woke you but, I just wanted to thank you for the birthday card you mailed to me. I am looking forward to read your good message and enjoy the illustrations."

Assad picked up on the coded message and tried played along. He sighed for it was clear that Ahlib knew that the file with technical information was on its way, "I am sure you will like this one very much - you will find the pictures most enticing too."

"Good- good and, how is our little brother doing there - does he like his new job?"

Assad knew that he referred to John Molape, "Yes - he is very keen and is happy with his working conditions and pocket money." A nice way to describe the role of an agent provocateur that facilitated an information leak at a large fee, Assad thought.

"That is most encouraging. Ask him to find out how an eagle spots its victim in the dark of night. Some knowledgeable South Africans should be able to tell him how they do it."

Ahlib left it to Assad to pick-up his coded conversation; "Is this for your study of African predators?"

"Exactly my friend and now I am going to leave you to sleep again. Goodbye."

Assad tapped with the receiver on his left hand while he tried to resolve the underlying task for John Molape. He knew enough about attack helicopters to figure out Ahlib's instruction. Slowly he replaced the phone and sat on the edge of the ruffled bed where, minutes earlier, he was still suspended in a haze of love.

He addressed himself in the mirror, "The eagle is the Martial Eagle. The victim is another helicopter or a tank. To spot it at night you need… what?…radar?…yes…and…of course! A night sighting system! To spot the foe in the dark – that's it!"

Assad stood up and looked out of the window where the winter sun painted the hotel's garden a pastel grey, "Mr. John Molape, your first task will be to get hold of the design material of the Martial eagle's MSSS – or its sophisticated, multi-sensor sighting system - as if you won't know that, my good African friend."

40.

ADAMANT ALLIANCES.

NORWOOD, JOHANNESBURG

Shortly after nine, Connie left Grant's home and headed north towards Pretoria. Grant was relieved that he could share his burden with someone he could trust. If only he could say the same after he had had his talk with Johann Kurtz this morning. It was about time for Kurtz's arrival. Grant shaved, took a shower, and was ready for their meeting when he heard the intercom call from the front gate. Grant activated the gate and went outside to welcome the CEO of Africair Corporation.

Minutes later they were in Grant's study, drinking coffee from large ceramic mugs. Both men were acutely aware of their awkward agenda and bridged the gap with some small talk. Grant decided to leave it to Kurtz to steer the conversation. He realized he knew very little about the big man sitting opposite him and at this stage it was pure intuition that made him trust Kurtz. What he could gather from Africair's annual financial report was that, despite setbacks in the international attack helicopter market, Kurtz and his management team produced satisfactory results.

Kurtz carefully placed his mug on the small table beside him, "Please turn on your radio, Grant - I want you to listen to an interesting news-bulletin."

Grant gave him a puzzled look, leaned forward, took the remote control from the coffee table and aimed it at the music center; "You need to wait a while for the next bulletin to come-up."

Kurtz took the remote control from his hand and paged to a music station and then turned up the volume somewhat. He leaned towards Grant, "Just a precaution. You may have several bugs hidden somewhere in your home."

Grant pointed towards his phone, "I have enough reason to believe you."

"Tell me about your recent experience." Kurtz stretched out his long legs and looked at Grant with concern. He was a good listener, especially before he had to make a decision that could have serious consequences.

Grant too sat back and knotted his fingers behind his head. He gave Kurtz a brief account of the phone call and he told Kurtz in a strained voice what happened to his Siamese cat.

Kurtz heard from the awkward and forced tone in Grant's voice that he was really still sad about his pet's undeserved death but he said that he did not assign a high degree of seriousness to the threat itself.

Kurtz said, "Whoever is playing this childish game may be an amateur, as you put it Grant, but he or they could also be serious. Let us not under-estimate them for one minute."

Grant looked at him with close attention, "Perhaps, up to now, I regarded this too long as a sick joke. My son also warned me to be careful - he does not even know about last night's episode. However, he was so perturbed by the intrusion into our home he engaged a friend's security service to sweep the house and upgrade the alarm system."

Kurtz took a silver cigarette case from his pocket, "May I."

"Sure, go ahead." He declined Kurtz's offer to join him and pushed an ashtray towards him. "Now where do we go from here, Johann?" The two of them were now on a good first name basis.

Kurtz blew a slow smoke trail towards the curtains, "The question is, at what stage we should involve the police?"

Grant stood up, "What about right-away? I don't want to look over my shoulder all the time you know!" Grant realized that for the past weeks he had to cope with little sleep and too much strain. Perhaps a proper break will encourage him to get on with the necessities of life again.

"Yes, perhaps we should but, as you know our police force carries an overload. At a rate of around ten criminal killings and more than two-hundred house breaks per day, it is no wonder."

Grant took his chair again, "Don't forget that every thirty-five seconds a woman is raped in this country. Against that background, I think the death of my cat and the silly threatening note is perhaps not significant. So, how do we approach the whole blasted affair?" Grant hoped that his annoyance would push his sadness aside.

Kurtz sounded very serious, "Let's be honest Julius, the person or persons or even movement behind this has its connections with Africair. Most likely it is somebody close to the corporation's top level thinking and operational plans. I think you are posing a threat to their internal plans and they want to stop you from interfering. They hope to scare you - perhaps even get you out of the way!"

"Do you suspect a hidden agenda has developed within Africair?" Grant asked.

"Yes - even outside the company. This is something with political roots." Kurtz pinched his nose between his forefinger and thumb, "For quite some time now I am aware of something sinister going on. It is all still very vague but I have a feeling that shortly something will surface."

"Since when did you sense this – hunch that something was going to happen? What made you so doubtful?" Grant wanted Kurtz to open up.

Kurtz crushed his cigarette. He was silent for a few moments, as if he was evaluating where this discussion with Grant is going, "The death of Gareth Williams was what placed me on the alert."

Grant did not react to immediately to his bland statement. He realized that they were going to miss out on the brunch he promised Kurtz so he stood up and limped to the kitchen. After a while he returned with more coffee and a plate stacked with an assortment of biscuits. "Pardon this lousy meal replacement" he said and picked up their discussion, "I knew Williams from an interview I had with the man, many years ago when he was still a British rugby hero. But I will tell you about that later."

Kurtz helped himself to the meager lunch substitute as Julius called the plate of snacks, "Julius you may think I am over-concerned about what happened to you but - I have a good reason to be. During the years of Apartheid when we all believed that a well trained defense force equipped with superior weapons systems would be the only acceptable method to save the skins of white people in this part of Africa, it was my job to supply the South African Air Force with its aviation and logistical needs. In those days anything, legal or illegal, could be considered viable - as long as the cause of white domination was promoted, sustained or protected. Any rule could be made, any obstacle could be removed. Many so called obstacles had to die for the so-called 'Cause of the

216

white Afrikaner.' Apart from eliminating the ANC and other political groups, which were comfortably all branded as communists, there was also no hesitation to wipe out resistance amongst their own people. As a journalist you will know what I am talking about. I really saw ugly underhand things happening under Botha, Vorster, Fouche, Strydom, and their fanatical Afrikaner supporters during the years when Apartheid was at the height of its power. But one day, those things will be brought into the open. Then it will not only shock the world, but also the majority of Afrikaners who were kept in the dark about these things and blindly supported their leaders."

Kurtz took time to light another cigarette while Grant looked at him and that thought this morning he had a good chance to get to know more about this man who did not seem to care too much about politics – yet he was clearly a brilliant avionics engineer and a good businessman.

Kurtz continued, "Amongst the small band of existing rightwing Afrikaners, there are small fanatical groups that still believe it is possible to reverse the political dispensation to what it was before the ANC took control. They think they can overthrow Mandela's government and reinstate Apartheid. On the other hand there are also those amongst them who accepted the new dispensation but they still want to scourge the technology of the country because - they fear it will be directed against the white man. They fear that the military technology that was instrumental in the white man's suppression of the masses to keep Apartheid in place - may now become the means for a reverse application of these military capabilities"

"And what is your position now?" Grant asked.

"Well - my role was to keep the South African Air Force in the sky from where they could fight the border and bush wars. Now that the war is over the need for a well-equipped air force has diminished but there is still the maintenance to be done. South Africa now has an unsophisticated Defense Force without an enemy. On the other hand we have a sophisticated armaments industry, still producing like hell. To retain jobs and generate revenue from the massive capital investment in this industry, we need to export the over production. That's my role now - maintaining capabilities and driving the international marketing of products and services."

Grant had one biscuit too many and pulled a face, "I can understand your concern for the industry and your emphasis on international marketing. In that regard you can rely on my support - no matter what kind of political sentiments is in the air."

Kurtz sat forward and looked somewhat anxious, "Julius, tell me - do you really want to continue with your assignment? Now is the time to declare your non-involvement my friend."

Grant was somewhat surprised and looked straight at Kurtz, "Listen Johann, I have been through a few rough spots in my time. Right now I am as curious as only an old news hound can be and on the other hand, I share your marketing philosophy and would do all I can to assist you. If in the process we uncover the order of the business of this scorch-the-earth group, as you call them then - so be it."

"Thank you Julius. Perhaps we could still end up with a relationship that is something more than a client-consultant understanding." Kurtz offered his hand and the two men shook on their newly established understanding.

As Grant walked Kurtz to his car he hesitated for a moment and said, "When we are leaving for the Cape with our planning session, I will tell you why I think Williams was murdered. I still need to check up on a few things that previously seemed to be harmless. I have enough reason to believe that his death was not an isolated incident."

Before he left Kurtz said to Grant, "By late this afternoon you will receive a fax from our security department. Kramer has drawn up a travel and accommodation plan for our trip down south - he plays it strictly according to security rules. He never allows the whole team to travel on the same flight. I saw that you and a few others have been placed on the early flight to Cape Town this Friday morning. You will stop over for two nights in Hermanus - a small coastal resort about an hour's drive from the Cape Town International Airport. On Sunday morning your party will leave for Arniston Bay - where we will be meeting at the Overberg Flight Testing Center. Oh-yes, your companions will be Chubby Wilson, John Molape and Rosemary Barnard."

Grant smiled; "Sounds pretty relaxing - I can do with some good clean air and the sound of surf in my ears. See you there, Johann."

After Kurtz had left Grant strolled around the garden for a while, thinking about their conversation and the many things that were left unspoken. It was close to noon and the temperature rose to a pleasant seventy degrees. He started whistling to the tune of "Phantom of the Opera" when his cell phone's buzzed. It was Peter calling from the airport.

41.

LAST REQUESTS.

JOHANNESBURG INTERNATIONAL AIRPORT

Assad sat in the foyer of the Holiday Inn and tried to concentrate on the editorial comment of the Financial News but his mind wandered off and replayed the intense love-making with Patricia Ndlalosi. It disturbed him somewhat that he may actually not have another opportunity to make love to this beautiful African woman again. For the rest of his time this erotic experience will always be just a memory. He would never be able to share his experience with anyone he knew. But then again, - how many acquaintances did he really have? How many friends could you have if you are a roaming journalist? Contacts – yes he had a large network of those but - really no friends.

Suddenly his life became an mixed framework of cultures and he questioned himself, "Am I still a devoted Muslim? When last did I pray - never mind upholding the daily demands of my religion. God, I have become a cold, fast moving, internationalist," he said to himself aloud behind the paper.

"Can I help you sir?"

Assad dropped the paper in his lap and looked up at the friendly bellboy and he realized his loud exclamation brought on this attention, "Ah …yes, please call me when the driver from Africair arrived."

"He just did sir -he is waiting for you in the driveway. Please follow me, sir."

Molape waited for him in the car with a mischievous glint in his eyes, "Hello Akbar how was last night?" He laughed softly.

"Fine, just fine my friend." They fumbled through the African custom of shaking hands. The routine of hand movements was a totally strange practice to Assad and the custom annoyed him thoroughly.

He said to Molape, "I do have an important instruction for you."

Molape nodded in the direction of the driver, "Let's go to my office and attend to our important matters." Molape again winked at Assad. He was convinced they shared an experience the previous evening that allowed him to think they were good buddies now. He knew very little about Arab customs but, then again, Assad was not your usual kind of Arab person.

Molape closed the door of his office behind them. Assad sat opposite him while Molape tried not to run off on a tangent, "Business before pleasure is the rule of Johann Kurtz here at Africair." He pointed a finger at the floor above him. "What is the instruction, Akbar? Or rather, what is it you want to know?" Molape began to understand what was really at stake.

Assad looked at Molape and decided that he would never get used to the way the black people of Southern Africa pronounced English words. They have an accent of their own. Akbar sounded like Auwkber, the word 'focus' came out as 'fuck-us', and 'category' would sound like 'key-taag-oh-ree'; 'Negotiate' would be pronounced as 'nee-goshi-ate'. 'Visa-bull' is something you can see and 'faf-oh-ret' is simply your favourite something; When you switched on the 'red-ee-oh' you made use of an instrument that received a broadcast. A 'Cape-apple' is not a fruit from the most beautiful place in Africa but referred to your capability to develop technology or anything else. Assad smiled and shook his head.

Then he became serious, "John, I urgently need information about two systems. Firstly, I want all the data you can lay your hands on about the workings of the Martial Eagle's MSSS."

Molape looked at him and then stared out of the window, "I think that stands for Multi-something- sight-system. Man if you're not an engineer or an aviation guy, these acronyms and codes can get you confused." He threw his arms in the air. "That's why I find Tom Clancy stories too complicated - because of my lack of military background."

"That's close enough: Multi Sensor Sighting System." Assad leaned forward and scribbled the words on the pad in front of Molape, "The market for combat helicopter sights is limited. A little exposure to the effectiveness the ME is in this area could entice new clients to take a serious look at it. Should this result in a potential sale, just think of the important contribution you as a communications practitioner could make to the bottom-line of Africair's business? If you could facilitate publicity for this system, you surely support the marketing effort. And you know what it is. Top management always see communications people as business expenditure instead of a profit centre."

Molape smiled. Here was a chance to kill three birds with one stone. He could generate publicity, advance the marketing effort, and show he earned the generous fee he received the previous evening, "This sounds a little complicated but I will try my best. I do have a few good friends here at Africair who are always willing to assist me with catching up with my lack of background about everything in this industry. As one guy said to me - in the past everything done here was very top secret – to the extent that we ourselves did not know what we were doing.'" He laughed out loud at own his little jibe on the process of demystifying the armaments industry.

Assad sounded like a man under pressure, "OK my friend, but try to be snappy in getting this little bit of information." He tried to make it sound like an easy task.

"Right, Akbar, I sense that you are working to a tight dead-line." Molape accepted that his new acquaintance wanted to stick to a business-like mode, "But remember slowly-slowly catches the monkey."

"Well, John, this is how you can make up for the advance I gave you last night."

Molape smiled and winked slyly, "And what a romantic evening it must have been for you! My girl friend noticed that there was so much love in the air that we had to slip away so that you guys could get on with the serious matters of affection. I am sure you appreciated our sensitivity -you were just a great couple my man!"

Assad became annoyed and uncomfortable - he hated to be embarrassed, "Listen John -that was last night - this is now. Like you guys at Africair, I don't mix business with pleasure."

Molape looked at him with a mock smile. He was uptight because it took quite some convincing and an expensive piece of jewellery, "With compliments from Africair and the aviation industry" - to lure Patricia on such a short notice into a blind date with his Arab friend. She called him just this morning to say that the only reason why she agreed to help him out was because she wanted revenge. She recently discovered her boyfriend, who is a member of a rock-band, had a wild fling with one of the back-up girls after an open-air concert in Soweto. She said, "In any case - the skinny little man was a lousy lover. And John - everything of that conceited little friend of yours is small. Men are such predictable creatures - however, I have an excellent excuse to feel good this morning. When my boyfriend hears about this, and he will, he will sing a different tune! - or perhaps even compose a new rap number!" Patricia is a tough girl who obviously has been around, Molape thought.

"Let's forget about Patricia Ndlalosi. What else did you want to know? You talked about two systems."

"Oh yes. I also need to know all about the Martial Eagle's Night Sighting System or NSS as they call it. As far as my knowledge goes, it has been upgraded recently. Apparently the Africair entered into a technology agreement with a French company to achieve greater accuracy. Somewhere you should come across a booklet or report that will give us an idea of how it gives the Martial Eagle an edge over other attack helicopters. I am also interested in who your French partner is - I believe they designed the multi-dimensional role that this the system plays during an attack. Especially the anti-tank firing role when missiles are set ablaze. Also, if you could get stuff on the anti-aircraft role the system play when the turret cannon is engaged - so much the better. Look for anything lying around - I will decide if it could be useful for the purpose of our editorial piece."

"Like what?" Molape realized Assad knew more about helicopter technology than he was prepared to admit. But then again, if you want to write a meaningful technical article, you should have a good technology background.

"Like the ground-support role and so forth - anything you can lay your hands on."

"All right my friend, it sounds straightforward enough to me. I will look for a suitable starting point." Molape expected a more complicated assignment and was somewhat comforted.

"Start your search with Rosemary Barnard. I found her more accommodating than those other tight-lipped guys with their white jackets - they are an introverted bunch of nerds. Not so?"

Assad's sudden conceited attitude annoyed Molapi; "Yes - over the years Kramer's security department properly zipped their mouths."

The two communicators dedicated the rest of the day to general information gathering about Africair, its services and commercial ventures for the civil aviation industry. Assad also convinced Molape to take up a two-page advertisement in their upcoming special supplement. They selected a stunning photo - taken over Table Mountain - of the Martial Eagle in an upside-down pose at the pinnacle point of a loop.

While they were still running their meeting, Grant called in and apologized for not being able to join them at lunch so Molape and Assad decided to have lunch in the management dining room. By six 'o clock they wrapped up their work and Molape drove Assad to the hotel to pick up his luggage before dropping him off at the airport.

"Shortly after I filed my story in Dubai, I will be off to London and Seattle - but don't hesitate to send the info to the fax numbers I gave you."

"I will do so – and see you at the Lankawi Air Show next month in Malaysia?" Molapi waived at his new media friend.

"Most probably - and then we could look for some Asian fun." Assad winked at him, "Goodbye my friend and thank you for all your hospitality and future assistance - you will not be sorry."

"Goodbye Akbar. On your next visit I will show you more of this beautiful country of ours – like Cape Town and the wine lands"

"That's a date" Assad waved to him and followed the porter into the departure hall of Johannesburg International Airport.

John Molape left in a hurry - he wanted to get his home and girl as soon as possible. With all the extra money in his pocket, he had lots to do. He was so caught up with all the exciting new possibilities that awaited them that he did not notice the poster of the late evening edition of "The Johannesburg Star." That read:

POPULAR TV PRESENTER DEAD.
GAS EXPLOSION KILLS
PATRICIA NDLALOSI

42.

FALSE EPITAPH.

DUBAI

Exhausted from the previous night's romantic experience, Assad slept all the way on the flight from Johannesburg to Dubai. He was so worn-out that he did not even ask for any refreshments or a newspaper. Before the plane left the runway Assad was sound asleep and doing so, never read about Patricia Ndlalosi's untimely death.

In a late news item the evening paper reported that during Patricia's lunch break, a gas explosion in her apartment's kitchen instantly killed the popular television presenter. The Soweto Fire Chief speculated that a faulty gas stove regulator might have caused her apartment to fill with gas during her absence. The explosion may have been caused when she struck a match to light the gas cooker or even a cigarette. As a gesture of empathy with the many black people who did not enjoy the comforts of electricity, Patricia refused all privileged treatment as a result of her status and also made use of gas and battery powered energy. She frequently addressed the lack of power-supply to the homes of the people who were disadvantaged by Apartheid and, regularly monitored progress in this regard on her television programs. Her supporters were left deeply shocked by the loss of the person they came to love and admire.

Assad's flight landed shortly after daybreak. He was still drained from the eight-hour flight as he went through the tedious customs procedure and he found the sudden change from Johannesburg's cold dry air to Dubai's hot dry air quite formidable. Two hours later he walked into his apartment, which had a magnificent view of the city's high-rise central business district - situated on the opposite bank of the Creek. Assad stood under the shower for a long time to soothe his aching muscles and then slipped on a silk robe and took to his computer.

For about six hours he worked on the abundance of material he had gathered and was amazed at the shape his articles took on. It was new data and he wrote fluently. He was confident his articles would please his obnoxious old editor. Assad printed out three copies and slipped two of them in his briefcase. He left the third set on his desk and said aloud, "Perhaps Ben Ahlib would like to read these."

Around five o' clock that afternoon he reached the offices of "The Gulf News" and filed his material. Fortunately his editor already left for his home, so and he handed his copy to a sub-editor who promised to look them over before passing them on to the Old Man - as they all referred to the Editor. Assad then took the elevator to the administrative offices and picked up his flight tickets for London and Seattle. He glanced at the itinerary, which told him that his flight to London was due for departure at noon the next morning - he had to report at the British Airways terminal by ten. All he needed now was to catch up on some sleep.

Assad hopped onto a water taxi and crossed the Dubai Creek towards his apartment. The *abra* slowly puffed its way through the waterway traffic. There were many traditionally shaped *dhows* that lined up on the banks of this waterway. Some were on their way to Iran, East Africa, or India. The seawater inlet wound its way through the heart of the city. Assad always enjoyed the experience of sitting under the canopy of the wooden raft and watching the modern skyline of the city from the historic quarters on the banks of the Creek.

They passed a number of old 'wind-tower' houses that reminded modern Dubai of its graceful traditional architecture that pre-dated the arrival of electricity and air conditioning. Most of these attractive buildings are in the city's Bastakiya district and the vents or wind towers of these old houses faced in all directions and drew every breath of cool air into the interior of the homes -thus affording some relief from the intense desert heat of summer.

At the water-taxi terminal Assad stepped off the *abra* and walked the short distance to his apartment. He was very thankful to step out on the tenth floor and now only had his bed in mind - he wished that he could sleep forever. A few paces from his apartment he came to an abrupt standstill. The door stood slightly ajar. He heard how the elevator doors close behind him. Assad was nervous - he never left his place without locking up properly. On tip toes he approached his front door and with an outstretched arm slowly pushed the door open - too suspicious to enter.

Then he decided to press the doorbell and see what would happen. He waited at the entrance, ready to flee. He played the chime once more and heard somebody moving slowly, with a heavy step towards the entrance.

Ben Ahlib filled the door. He held a large mug in his hand and chewed on something. Whatever it was, bulged the black stubbles on his cheek, "What took you so long?"

"How did you get into my place? I cannot remember giving you a key." Assad was not at all friendly or pleased with this turn of events. For a moment he regretted that he allowed himself to get involved with this "silly network-stuff." Suddenly it being a straightforward journalist doing an honest day's work, looked very attractive and an uncomplicated way to earn a living. In God's name - why did I get sucked-up in this shady business? My salary as a senior writer is ample to make a comfortable living here in the exciting Pearl of the Gulf, Assad thoughts raced through his tired mind. He looked at Ahlib with anxiety written all over his face.

"In a country like the Arab Emirates, with its virtual crimeless environment, it is easy. Not a single developer of high profit property ever invests in four-lever locks. So if you are from my part of the world it is very easy to gain entrance to apartments here in Dubai." Ahlib took a master key from the inside pocket of his grubby garment and dangled it close-up to Assad's face.

Although prepared to accept to the awkward situation, Assad was still very aggravated. He did not like the power game the big Egyptian played, "You could have asked for a key - I am quite willing to provide you with a duplicate. I have pretty few secrets in my place and those that I do not want to share - I hide in my laptop under a password."

Ahlib swallowed loudly, "I have here in my pocket the stories that sat on your desk. But perhaps you need to tell me about those passwords as well, OK?"

"Not on your life - that is not part of our arrangement." Assad was tired, frustrated, and now furious.

"Listen young man - here I make the rules. If need be I will wring those silly passwords out of your brain or break eight of your ten fingers so that you have just enough left to type them out for me," Ahlib said while standing closer.

Assad kept his nerve and tried to demean the Egyptian with a stiff-upper-lip English approach, "Listen old boy, you may look and sound powerful and superior but if you want, I also have sound resources that could change your mind you know. Say old boy, have ever heard of the good old saying that declared that the pen is mightier than the sword? I doubt it - by the look of things."

"My power is stronger than yours." Ahlib responded in an undeveloped way.

Assad realized that the scruffy man, apart from a personality - also lacked intelligence. He could only focus on one specific task and nothing more. He got his instructions from somewhere else and outside of those parameters he had no other requirements to meet. Assad continued his mockery of the dumb giant, "You know old boy, the wise also say that every live wire is plugged in somewhere. If you over extend the application of your power in - let's say a shocking manner - there will always be someone who will cut your power supply, you know," Assad felt very on top of the situation and grinned at Ahlib.

Ahlib dropped the mug, which bounced and coffee stained the ivory shaded carpet. With remarkable speed he lunged forward and clenched Assad in a tight bear hug, "And I think it's time to cut your air supply, little man," he hissed through white spittle in Assad's ear. Ahlib's sudden attack caught Assad off guard and he hung motionless in the grip of the giant.

Naked fear took hold of Assad - never before in his life was he subjected to physical violence. His last and most serious shuffle with another human being was in primary school. He breathed laboriously and tried to shout but Ahlib buried his face halfway under his armpit in his foul smelling shirt. Ahlib awkwardly danced backwards with his unwilling partner who now kicked in all directions with his legs dangling. They smashed against the heavy front door, which slammed shut with a bang that reverberated down the long passageway. Ahlib added power to his clutch and shuffled with Assad towards the lounge. Assad managed to kick the giant full on the shin. It made the Egyptian roar with pain and he staggered forward and fell on top of Assad – so that the air from gushed from his lungs. All along during their scuffle, Ahlib was careful not to bruise him in any way.

"Listen here you little bastard, this was in any case not a courtesy call. Your role is played out, thank you - you are going to commit suicide." The smell of garlic filled Assad's nostrils as he tried to yell. He kept on kicking furiously and tried to free his arms. Then he bit the Egyptian in the armpit and gritted his teeth into the man's flesh. Ahlib moved a callused hand under his armpit, grabbed Assad by his moustache, and jerked him free from the bleeding wound. Assad sucked in air but was stopped short when the large hand closed over the lower part of his face. Ahlib rested his full weight on Assad, held him in the deadly face-clamp and pulled a large cushion from a loveseat while Assad again tried to bite him and kept on kicking.

The soft cushion swiftly closed over Assad's face. Ahlib held it there for a long time. A raging buzz sounded in Assad's ears and his lungs jerked in vain for air at his choked-up nostrils. Bright figures and spots, like the screen saving pattern of a computer, slowly filled his blackened vision and exploded in his mind. Then the intricate screen saver pattern changed to icons of a naked Patricia Ndlalosi. Her image came closer – and passed through the pupils of Assad's eyes. Patricia's icon sank into the depths of his mind and - somehow he saw how she smiled and signalled him to follow her. The pattern dimmed slowly and eventually Assad floated with her into a darkness where they dispersed to nothing. The frail reporter's kicking seized, and he slept forever - as he wished for just a few minutes earlier.

Carefully Ahlib checked for a pulse beat. Assad was dead. He stood up and looked at the man who now looked like a small fragile boy. Ahlib had a numb sensation of someone who accidentally sat on and suffocated a small kitten.

He spoke to Assad as if he was still alive or just sleeping, "May I now have your passport and flight tickets Akbar?" Prior to the journalist's arrival he had enough time to search the apartment thoroughly. He found the printouts and a few useable publications. He walked over to Assad's briefcase and opened it, "Good thing you did not lock your case. Not much here except extra copies of your stories and - o-yes! Ah! - here are the travel documents."

Once the Egyptian was satisfied that he took the most important documents he switched on the television and waited a few minutes in the dimly lit apartment for the eight o' clock news. From time to time he looked without emotion at the body of Assad and then at his huge hands that had ended so many lives. This too was just another job well done. He was nearly finished with his task. He had an appointment in the old sector of the city to have his photo placed in Assad's passport. The piece of artwork had to be finished by midnight. That way he would have enough time to clean up and catch Assad's flight. All that was then left to do was to exchange his briefcase for the balance of his lucrative fee as mediator of The Network. All very easily done Ahlib thought and the inferior feelings that Assad stirred up in him slowly dissipated.

The opening sting of the newscast sounded. It was time to stage Assad's suicide. Upon his arrival at Assad's apartment, he placed on Assad's laptop a printout made from the website of "The Star" in Johannesburg - that covered the death of Patricia Ndlalosi. He had it delivered to Assad's hotel room just before he left for this meeting with Assad. This was an essential step to ensure that police will link Akbar with Patricia. Ahlib took from his pocket a crumpled, faked note that had to create the impression that it accompanied the printout and read the contents:

My dearest Akbar,

It took me a long time to write you this last note. I decided to give my fiancé another chance and hope our relationship will take off again. I think I still love him. This evening when he comes to me after his Soweto-gig, I will have a superb dinner with candlelight (what else with no power) waiting for him.

I know this will break your heart. I will pray to God that he sends you another woman, more beautiful than I, to make you happy and comfort you. If you really care for me, please do not try to contact me again. Please do not make it difficult for me. Allow me to make my amends.

I will always reserve a fond corner of my heart for you.

PN.

Ahlib stuffed the note in Akbar's shirt pocket. Assured that most of the tenants in the opposite building would by now be watching the main evening news, Ahlib carried Assad's body to the balcony. He placed him in a sitting position on the banister and then slowly toppled him forward. Assad floated down while his garment billowed and flapped like a failed parachute. Ahlib did not look down to where the unfortunate writer landed. Preparing for the murder during the day he calculated that the body would drop into the dense foliage of the garden. It could take the landscape services days before they would find him. With the possibility that someone could have spotted Assad's, fall, Ahlib grabbed his briefcase, left the apartment and locked the door behind him. He ran down the stairwell to the second floor where he parked his car. With open windows and load music he drove slowly out of the building and then headed towards the old sector of the city.

-oOo-

HARRODS, LONDON

The following day Ben Ahlib sat cafeteria of Harrods, in London - ordered coffee waited for the arrival of his contact person. After a while a distinguished looking Englishman with a short umbrella hanging from his arm walked up to him and said, "I believe it is hot in Dubai."

Ahlib nodded and replied "Yes, but not as hot as London"

Satisfied with this pre-arranged response the Englishman took a seat opposite Ahlib and without a word he produced a thick envelope and pushed it towards Ahlib – who stared at it in silence.

"I presume your task is now completed and you may leave now. Just push your briefcase towards my feet and I will take care of your delivery."

Without saying a word or opening the envelope, Ahlib weighed it in his right hand and then carefully slid the bulky packet in his jacket pocket. He then slowly shoved his piece of luggage towards the feet of his caller. The big Egyptian stood up and looked absolutely worn out while he slowly pushed his chair under the table. Ahlib stooped and said in a soft voice, "Thank you and good day Mr. Collins."

43.

GAMES LOVERS PLAY

WALKER BAY, SOUTH AFRICA

The rain stopped and the air was still - it was neither hot nor cold. The low clouds hung over Walker Bay like a fluffy substance coloring the placid Indian Ocean in a soft tint of blue denim. The waves seemed to be in no hurry to reach the shore. The surf had no need to pound the rocks – and gently slapped around their sharp, unperturbed black edges. Across the bay a misty window opened in the dark clouds and hung above the low-lying blue mountain range. The setting sun was allowed only a few minutes to peep out from under the dense nimbus cloud blanket and for a brief moment painted the window on the dark blue horizon with the full spectrum of a hazy rainbow. Then the wine-red glimmer sank into the ocean. The multitude of flowers amidst the rocks lost their color when dusk came but - the fragrance prevailed. In the twilight the barely audible murmur of the ocean and the far-off harbor lights indifferently substituted the scenery. The scratchy repetition of a lonely cricket recited the start of a long African night.

Julius Grant and Rosemary Barnard took in the scenery from the hotel terrace where they sat on an old wrought iron bench. For a while now, they have been silent and enjoyed the impressive natural splendor surrounding the town of Hermanus. During the two hour flight from Johannesburg to Cape Town and on the way to this dainty old town they exchanged only generalities about politics, sport and their travels. Chubby Wilson, who grew up in the wine-lands of the Cape, brought them straight to the Marine Hotel. While they preferred to enjoy the cool evening air John Molape and Wilson sat in front of the log-fire in the lounge where they were enjoying their third round of draughts. They followed the sporting events on the wall-mounted television and discussed the Saturday matches that were lined up. They were relaxed and looked forward to the weekend. The prospect of having a few days free before the grueling planning session also allowed them to plan a trip through the wine-lands.

Grant enjoyed the company of Africair's ergonomics engineer. Rosemary looked at the bay and said softly, "Every now and then you have a perfect evening like this. It is Hermanus' way of ensuring that you will return again." She knotted her fingers around her knee and placed her heel on the seat of the bench.

"Then you have been here before?" Grant asked and looked at her profile silhouetted against the dark clouds. He admired her classic lines and long-limbed built.

She shook her short hair in place. "I grew up in Worcester, and as you would know, it is an average-sized town, and just about an hour's drive from here. That is if you follow the route over the Hottentots-Holland Mountains and past the Teewaters Kloof Dam. My parents were teachers there and for all of my school years we came here to holiday during April or over Christmas and New Year."

"How did you spend you breaks during your years at University?" Grant still knew very little about his companion because she was also not one to talk easily about herself.

"My father was a mathematics teacher and later on he took up a teaching job with the Engineering Department of the University of Witwatersrand," She said.

Grant looked at Rosemary and guessed her to be in her early thirties "I suppose that played a role when you decided to become and avionics-engineer?" Grant asked.

She smiled, "Yes, to the extent that as the child of a professor, I had free tuition - it was one of my Dad's perks."

Grant stood up and to Rosemary he looked very tall, "Let's take a stroll. Then you can show me your little town and the board walk or someplace where you had your first kiss," he invited.

Rosemary blushed easily but liked Grant's relaxed and easygoing manner - she also found him extremely attractive. "You remind me a bit of the man I lost on the slopes of Table Mountain."

"Oh that sounds like a tragedy. I feel sorry for you." Grant wondered if she ever married.

"Some time ago my quite boyfriend and I accompanied a group of youngsters on one of these regular Table Mountain climbing expeditions. During this two-day outing I was very much attracted to a well-build young man and I openly flirted with him - while my boyfriend did not like it one bit." Grant saw how small little devils danced in her eyes.

"So the poor fellow committed suicide by jumping off a cliff?" Grant pretended to be shocked.

"No! Fortunately he did nothing so dramatic but he tried to get back at me by paying too much attention to one of the other female members. Perhaps he just tried to hide his jealousy – yet afterwards he avoided me and a few months later he told me that he was going to marry the willing girl."

"Just like that?" Grant looked at her with disbelief.

"Well, he made her pregnant and perhaps that was good enough reason to marry her." Rosemary looked quietly at the moonlit ocean - signifying that she wanted to get off the subject of her past.

"My goodness and so - you never married?" Grant realized that he displayed bad manners and wished that rather should have bit his tongue, "Pardon my rudeness - I should not have asked."

"Not to worry Julius. To put you quickly into the picture, I later married an overweight, dull engineer, flirted again with somebody exciting, was caught out and got divorced. Fortunately there were no kids in this short marriage - but I think I learnt my lesson."

"So?" Grant wondered what she gained from the experience.

"And, so I decided that with my life-style I should rather dedicate the rest of my time to my job and - here I am." She opened her arms and gave Grant a playful coquettish smile.

Rosemary led Grant on a narrow path that winded along on the edge of the cliff. From time to time they stopped to admire the scenery in silence. They were very aware of their closeness and often looked and smiled at each other. Grant realized how much he needed a break and wanted to enjoy every moment as much as possible. They walked past a point called Roman Rock where the narrow path twisted away from the cliffs towards a block of holiday apartments. They deeply inhaled the smell of *fynbos* shrubs as they walked through the shoulder high foliage.

On the corner of Protea and Sea Streets, Rosemary leaned against an old-fashioned lamppost.

"Are you tired?" Grant asked. He was concerned and felt a new sincerity growing for his companion - and he had to admit to himself that it could be really easy to flirt with her.

"Who me? - not at all," she answered. She looked up at him. "You see this old lamppost? Well, it is not a fake -it has been here since electricity came to the streets of Hermanus."

"OK and what's so special about it? I saw a number of similar ones around the hotel."

"Yes, but those are replicas - this one is for real." She stood close to him. And?" Grant slanted his head.

Rosemary held out her slender hand, looked up at Grant and smiled sweetly, "Here, on an evening like this at about this hour, for the first time in my life a boy took my hand.".

Grant stood closer, took her hand lightly and asked; "In a way then, history is repeating itself."

Rosemary looked down and slipped her hand out of his. "Come I want to show you another spot."

They walked eastwards down Protea Street towards their hotel. Where Protea ran into Main Street they joined the cliff path again. She turned off towards the ocean and came to a bench right on the edge of the cliff where they sat down. Grant noticed the short turn-off earlier in the evening and wondered where it would lead to. He was silent as he sat close beside her while they looked at the ocean and listened to its soothing murmur.

Rosemary spoke first, "This is where I had my first kiss. Right here on this selfsame little green bench."

Grant was afraid that she would see and hear how his heart boxed his lungs inside his chest. He cleared his throat and turned to her. "Would you mind if history repeats itself again – here and now?"

Rosemary looked at him closely and slowly shook her head from side to side. Grant leaned forward and kissed her tenderly. She pulled him closer to her and whispered, "I suppose not and I also won't mind you know. It will feel like the first time since - it has been a while since a man kissed me." This time she took the lead and kissed Grant with loving intention.

Grant looked over her head at the rollers, which slowly ran into the cliff wall below them. "Perhaps there is magic in this place," he said.

He followed her back to the hotel and was very aware of her perfume and the gracious movement of her slender body.

They arrived in time for dinner and came across Wilson and Molape in the lounge. By this time they consumed a good number of draughts and laughed easily at their own jokes.

Grant tried to be casual. "Don't tell me you guys are drinking beer, here in the land of grapes and good wine?"

Wilson speech was slurred -it would be some time before he needed to be back in the cockpit and he wanted to make the most of the "booze recess," as he called moments like these. "Listen here mister Granth, I wash brought up in this part of the world. From birth my mother altered my bottl'sh containing cow'sh milk with some wine throughout the day. It made me a good baby and I schlept right slugh the night." His eyes rolled a little, "So sche and ma' ol' man had enough time to make four more bambinou'sh like me. All of us looks the sjame. Each one of ush had hish own handy little thing-a-ma-jig to play and pee with." It took them a long time to stop laughing while Rosemary and Grant just stood there smiling out of courtesy.

Molape was still holding his pose. "Today is beer-day - tomorrow will be wine-day. Tubby promised to take me on the wine route tomorrow and we hope to end up in his favorite bar outside Stellenbosch. Apparently he 'banked' all his pocket-money there as a student." Again long drawn-out laughter followed.

The men declined Grant's invitation to join them for dinner, "We wanted to go over to the pub, play some darts and we'll grab something like a bar-bite right there -then off to bed. We will see you guys after breakfast on Sunday," Molape said and put his arm around his colleague's waist. They swayed a little, laughed and staggered to the men's room.

Grant and Rosemary went through to the dining room. It was very large and airy with a Mediterranean atmosphere that overlooked the Indian Ocean. They were placed at a window and both of them still felt a little awkward with their hearts were occupied over what happened while they were out walking.

Rosemary tried to casually break the ice. "This hotel was started by the Luyt family, back in 1905, you know. As late as 1985 the Marine was re-opened after extensive renovations," she explained.

"And what a beautiful place it is - my room is sea-facing." Grant ordered them a bottle of rosé wine from the Nederburg Wine Estate.

The wine, candle-lit table, and soft music played on the old grand piano re-kindled their romantic feelings. For most of the evening they spoke of fond and sentimental things that happened in their youth.

Grant was amazed with Rosemary's knowledge of whales, "In this part of the world whale-watching is a big tourist attraction. People come from all over the world, between June and November, to see them. Especially the Southern Right whales that stop over here to calve and nurse their young before they move northwards to Mozambique and Angola."

"I believe at times they venture quite close to the coastline?" Grant remarked.

"Oh yes, they do - they would play and show themselves just behind the breakers. Other species like the Humpback whales and Bryde's whales stay slightly further offshore. However, they and the so-called killer-whale or Ocras with their striking black and white coloration are to be found all year round. However, sighting them is extremely rare." She said.

Grant filed their glasses with rose wine, "What would be the size of a Southern Right?".

"They are between twelve and fifteen meters long and weigh around thirty to sixty tons."

"And the cows come here every year to calve?" Grant asked.

"No - Southern Right females produce calves on average once every three years." Rosemary sipped her wine and smiled at Grant.

Grant wanted to know more about the giant creatures, "And how long do they keep their calves here before they take them out to the ocean?"

"About four to five months."

"Are they actually strong enough in such a short space of time?"

Rosemary still remembered how she enjoyed her father's conversation about sea life, "Well, calves feed on about six hundred liters of milk per day and grow about three centimeters per day!"

Grant said "I believe there are not many left?"

"Well - between 1908 to 1963 - thousands of whales were killed in South African waters alone and - they were nearly exterminated. Since they are protected, their population grew at about seven percent per year – however there are some concerns that lately the protection program has been neglected"

Grant made a quick calculation. "That means their population doubles just about every ten years." He tried so stay with the topic in order to hide his yearning to be with her.

"Yes - so there are still a large number around here - we can go out and do some whale-watching tomorrow." Rosemary said with a smile in her green eyes.

They left the dining room and Rosemary held on to Grant's arm. They took the stairs up to their rooms on the second floor where she pulled him to a standstill in front of her room and opened the door. From the radio they heard Laurika Rauch singing the Jacques Brel song 'la tendresse'. Grant held her close and looked down at her attractive face, and whispered; "So, will we go whale-watching in the morning?" For a second time that evening Grant's heart throbbed uncontrollably while he asked the question just because he did not know what their next move would be.

"We could go out and do that or laze at the heated pool right here at the hotel." She pressed her warmness against him and smiled, "But right now I would like to invite you for coffee – or something?" She gestured towards her door.

"May I suggest that we have it all in my room, instead? Then you can leave when it suits you - otherwise you may have a man in your room that does not have the courtesy to leave or perhaps do not want to leave." Grant still held her close.

"And I will have to call the manager to get you out - is that what you mean?" She stood tip-toe and kissed him on the cheek. "Allow me a moment to freshen-up and I will join you Jules."

He liked the nick-name she used for him and tried to even up, "OK Rosy - see you in a bit!" This time he kissed her full on the mouth. The evening held endless promises.

44.

A DUMB OYSTER.

WALKER BAY, SOUTH AFRICA

"Well, you can say all you like boss, but I do not trust all of them. Tubby Wilson is perhaps harmless, but John Molape is too pally-pally with that bloody Arab. Rosemary Barnard can still not account for the missing copy of the Air-to-Air Warning and Surveillance System. She is also too lovey-dovey with this Grant Englishmen and you know how we feel about him. He succeeded in bluffing his way past Kurtz and becomes more and more important in the Africair structure," Christian Faber said and snorted through his beard.

"How do I know so much about this? True to my job, boss, I followed them all day. Right now Molape and Wilson are in the bar of The Marine Hotel, here in Hermanus and they are just about pissed out of their minds by now. Barnard and Grant went up to their rooms - as a matter of fact the lights in their rooms went on - just a moment ago."

Faber stood up to his neck in the *fynbos* shrubs opposite the Marine Hotel's sea-facing rooms. He spoke softly on his mobile phone and continued, "How do I know that their lights went on? Listen Boss you don't know it but I am also a good spy, you know - I am watching them through my binoculars from opposite their hotel. There - there - Barnard just walked into Grant's room, and she hugs the Englishman. And if that is not a farken hot French kiss I have never seen one. Now they are chewing at each other real good, boss." Faber belched softly and blew his beer-breath skywards. He could hardly contain his excitement and felt somewhat dull aroused by what he saw and described.

Faber was so agog by what he witnessed that he had trouble training his powerful binoculars on the scene above him while he simultaneously pinched the mobile phone between his ear and sweaty shoulder. "Now they are getting real hot Boss - she is unbuttoning Grant's shirt. Whoops! - And there goes her top too. She does not wear a bra! *Bliksem* and you know what boss? – She has a pair of goodies - much larger than I thought! They look like swollen pears! I have never seen anything like it!"

In his excitement the mobile slipped from his sweaty shoulder and disappeared in the undergrowth, "Dammit - where is that bloody thing now?"

Faber found the instrument and was just in time to hear his boss shouting "- and get the hell out of there you bloody nosy dumb oyster and do not ever over-extend your objectives again. What if the police pick you up and charge you with *crimen injuria?* Then our whole plan will be ripped wide open - you bloody old fool. Get back to your hotel in Gordon's Bay. Faber? - do you hear me?" Fischer sounded beside himself with rage.

"Yes boss –sorry boss." The phone went dead. Faber still stared at the window when a softer glow replaced the ceiling-light. Grant and Rosemary Barnard were out of sight. Faber could only guess what they were doing and uttered a high-pitched whimper like a hungry puppy dog. He felt as if his prostate gland could explode with excitement and he was frustrated out of his mind.

45.

Too Close for Comfort.

Walker Bay Hotel Room.

Grant gently pulled Rosemary closer to him and led her slowly to the bed. They kissed tenderly while his hands travelled slowly down her back as he softly caressed her. Rosemary slid out of his embrace and sat on the bed - slightly trembling with anticipation. She had only her skirt on while his shirt hung open. Grant looked her in the eyes while he walked round to the opposite side of the bed where he kicked off his shoes and stretched himself out beside her. His fingers ran lightly down her evenly tanned back again – while they both understood what they were doing. They longed and were prepared to take their flirting a step further. Rosemary rolled over and snuggled up against Grant and they knew how the evening would end. Grant felt the twin pressures of her firm breasts and the outcome of the evening was predictable.

Grant touched her cheek and she moved up to kiss him and they did so – gently at first but then their lips softened and their kissing became moist and intense.

The phone started to ring irritably and they tried to ignore it - but it kept on ringing. Their kissing froze – and Rosemary leaned back on her elbow, "I guess you will have to answer that." The ringing continued like a siren that warned against an overheating passion.

Grant swung his legs off the bed and reached for the phone. He spoke with his back turned to Rosemary, "Yes, this is Julius Grant. OK – connect me". He waited a few seconds –and wondered why on earth would Marjory Brooks want to talk to him –this late in the evening? Goodness, this call is so untimely! His thoughts were still with Rosemary and the vision of her beautiful body burned in his mind.

Rosemary listened hoe Grant's rather curt answers became friendly.

"Oh, - hello Marjory - this is quite a surprise."

Grant tried his best to focus, "No – no, I was not asleep – and not in the shower either."

Grant was uncomfortable "Do I sound - out of breath? No - not exercising - well let's call it some unusual activity -nothing serious though. As a matter of fact you sound tense - what's wrong?"

"What!" Grant became tense. "What happened to Peter?" Grant listened in silence. "Is he out of immediate danger - stabilized? OK - I will rush home immediately'

"Where are you phoning from? Oh - from the hospital. Can I talk to him? No? - OK I am glad that Connie is prepared to do that. Please tell her that I appreciate her help very much indeed and - of course your kind assistance too,"

, "Ok. Tear it open and read it to me." Grant sat listening for a while "It does not make any sense whatsoever to me."

"Now please tell me as much as you know about the whole incident and what happened to him." Grant seemed less perturbed while he was silent for a long time - listening to Marjory's encounter of what happened to Peter - as far as she could gather from a policeman.

"Thank you very much for all your support and please keep in touch. I will call Connie at regular intervals on her cell-phone. "Bye Marjory"

The beautiful romantic evening faded out of his comprehension. Grant turned to Rosemary and saw that she was fully dressed. Grant heard from the tone of her voice how her romantic inclination towards the evening fell apart, "Let's go out and have a drink somewhere - then you can tell me what happened," she said.

"OK. It's all about Peter. He was mugged and severely wounded - but there are some ugly circumstances around this whole thing. Let's go." He pulled a sweater over his head and they went downstairs.

Grant's expectation that this wonderful opportunity would spice up the weekend were stranded like a fragile fishing-vessel on the rocks of Hermanus. He also now realized that he was on a course where there was no room for fun and games or sideshow flirtations. He was in the midst of the ugly games that weapons mongers play. He realized that in this industrial sector trouble happen at any time and more often than usual. This was an out-and-out dangerous industry to be caught up in, and he found it had hard to calm his pent-up frustration and keep his mind on the real purpose of his involvement.

But there was no turning back -not now, not even with his son in a Johannesburg hospital. Then he thought with concern about an article that he read on the worsening conditions in South African hospitals and the issue of a shortage of medical staff. Highly qualified South African doctors left the country in droves and relocated to the USA and UK. In Houston, Texas alone there were close to two thousand medical practitioners – from the country that gave the world its first heart-transplant. Now, Cuban doctors were imported to replace them. The writer of the item said the physicians, who obtained their qualifications from the Russian Medical Bureau, were not even allowed to practice medicine in the USSR. Perhaps the Russians were protecting the position of their own physicians - or because their training of the Cubans was of a sub-standard level. Grant's concern for his son grew and his by wild irrational thinking threatened to spook him out of his mind.

They went down to the resident's lounge where the fire place still radiated some warmth. Grant ordered port and they sat in opposite chairs. For a few moments Rosemary looked at and listened to the large stinkwood clock mounted beside the fireplace. She moved her eyes to Grant and said softly, "In Lankawi circumstances may allow us to continue where we left off this evening." She reached for his hands, "I am very much attracted to you Julius but - I must also be honest with you. I did warn you that I am a notorious flirt and perhaps this evening with its romantic foreplay, wonderful surroundings; wine and good food got me in a mood to take things a little faster and further - than usual."

Grant replied after a while, "I fully understand that, Rosemary and it also accounts for my behavior. I am really sorry about the untimely phone call and what it did to our evening. But right now I am very troubled about what happened to my son."

"Tell me about it," Marjory looked at him with eyes filled with sympathy.

"Before I left home, I took my Range Rover to a service station for an oil change and general check-up. Peter promised to call for it this afternoon and take it back home for me. As he arrived at our gate, a van stopped behind him. Four men jumped out and dragged him from the truck. He was badly beaten up and during his scuffle with the thugs he sustained four knife wounds - one of which damaged his spleen to such an extent that it had to be removed. He lost a lot of blood and right now his condition is serious but apparently he is out of danger. My partner, Dr. Marjory Brooks, spoke to him after he regained his consciousness. His first words were 'Tell my Dad I am OK.'" Grant stared into the fire and Rosemary saw how a dampness covered his eyes.

To help him deal with the shock she decided to make small talk around the incident. "How did Marjory hear about his ordeal?"

"I am not sure -but somebody called the police and an ambulance. Marjory's home and the Police Office are both close to our home. It was rush hour and I suppose a passer-by made the call. From Peter's mobile phone's address file the police selected phone numbers and started calling. Marjory was the first to answer while I had mine shut down - for obvious reasons." Grant looked at her and managed a smile.

"Marjory then rushed to the hospital despite the fact that she had to officiate at a function this evening. But she did call my assistant, Connie, who promised to stay at his bedside - all night despite the fact that he is now out of danger recovering from the operation."

They ordered more port and talked for at least an hour. Rosemary suggested to Grant to call Connie on her mobile phone. He agreed and got an immediate answer. Connie convinced him that Peter was in a stable condition but she insisted on staying at his bedside till morning. She wanted to talk to him as soon as he came to from the effect of the anesthesia.

Grant refrained from telling Rosemary of the envelope that the Police found in Peter's pocket, together with his diary and other personal belongings. The note was addressed to Grant and was marked "Very Urgent." He asked Marjory to read it to him. The note simply said "Mister Grant, if you are so lucky to survive this serious treatment by the hit men, you know you had your very last chance to change your mind." He was also not sure he convinced Marjory when he denied understanding what the note was all about. Whoever attacked Peter must have thought it was he who was driving the Range Rover.

Rosemary leaned over to Grant and kissed him lightly on the forehead, "Goodnight my dear friend and please call me at anytime if you need any help - or me. OK, Jules?"

"OK Rosemary - thank you for a lovely evening. I am so fortunate to have had you by my side - while this happened"

Rosemary sensed that he wanted to be alone. She pinched his cheek, smiled, and left.

Grant stayed behind for a while longer, thinking about the ugly event. It was clear the attack was aimed at him. Unfortunately Peter became the victim of whoever wanted him out of the way.

46.

THE TESTING RANGE.

AFRICA'S MOST SOUTHERN TIP

It was about noon when the foursome travelling from Hermanus arrived at the Overberg Testing Range. Wilson drove the two hundred kilometres with Molape in the passenger seat Grant and Rosemary sat in the back and were mostly quiet and dozed off at times. It was a foggy day and they listened to the casual music and news bulletins that came from Radio Good Hope. Wilson tried to stay awake by trying to make conversation with Molapi. The excessive wine-tasting tours and pub-crawling took its toll.

Grant was so absorbed with his concern about Peter's condition he could think of little else - even after Peter recovered to such an extent that Connie could pass her phone to him so they could exchange a few consoling words. For the second time, as a result of his doing, a close member of his family got hurt. What made it worse was that Peter warned him against getting involved in the "dirty-tricks-business," as he called it.

During the trip Grant had a long telephone discussion with Marjory about his presentation in the morning. She carefully explained to him how President Mandela's program would fit into the overall program. She also pointed out the necessity to reveal during his talk the President's involvement in such a way that the premature knowledge of his presence at the show would not pose an unnecessary security risk.

They passed through the control gates of the testing range without a hitch and approached the small inn on the site that was available only for the clients of the Overberg Testing Range, or OTR as it was referred to. OTR was situated about twenty-five kilometres north-east of Cape L'Agulhas, the most southerly tip of Africa. The range covered a vast area that allowed for the unhindered flight testing of weapons with an extended firing range and the site was also equipped to launch low-earth-orbiting surveillance satellites. OTR was an ideal remote open-air laboratory to test long-distance missiles - launching them over the Southern Atlantic Ocean in the direction of the South Pole. Here the South African weapons industry tested the combat readiness of their air-to-air, ground-to-air and ground-to-ground weapon systems.

With a wry smile Grant thought how, only months ago, it would never have been possible for him as a journalist or for Molape as a member of the ANC, to be allowed near this site. Now they entered the previous heavy guarded facility - and nobody even asked for an ID. They booked in at the pleasant and tastefully furnished inn where each received a note that called for their presence at six in the Dolphin Breakaway Room. The purpose was to structure the agenda for the two-day planning session - or *bush-counselling* as it was called in Afrikaans. The term *bush- counselling* had become the accepted word in many South African languages for this type of strategic planning meetings. It became known when the previous Nationalist government used it for its many planning and discussion sessions before and during the negotiations with the ANC.

The receptionist mentioned that most of the top members of management had arrived during the morning. They all left again on a site-seeing tour of the majestic rock formations running into the Indian Ocean in the vicinity of Arniston Bay.

Chubby immediately suggested to Molape a bar lunch at the Arniston Hotel - about ten kilometres down the road, "where there is a long counter with a unobstructed view over the magenta southern sea. You also need a bite of the hair from the dog that bit you yesterday." He laughed out loud and slapped a pain-ridden Molape on the back.

Grant decided to run through his material again while Rosemary promised herself a workout in the small gym to be followed by a long hot bath. They both decided to order lunch from room service instead of going to the dining room.

Julius Grant was the last person to enter the Dolphin Room where about twenty people were present who were served coffee, tea and soft drinks. The tables and chairs were arranged in a horseshoe pattern. The room was abundantly equipped to execute a workshop of this nature. At the top end of the table there were three chairs, now being taken up by De Witt, Fischer with Kurtz in the centre. The event was regarded as Kurtz's workshop and De Witt would attend only this one evening's session. As expected, the chairman would give a motivational speech. Kurtz mentioned earlier to Grant that the old man would also call for support for Grant's strategic plan. Despite his growing dislike for the old Afrikaner rogue - Grant sensed he would need all the support he could get from this team - some of whom he began to develop his reservations.

Once they were all settled around the table with their papers before them, De Wit raised to begin his talk. Grant was not particularly interested in his discourse and while he was talking, took the time to study the people around the table. About seven of them were unknown to him and he guessed they were the secretarial and security back-up staff who would not be present during their planning session. So he concentrated on the people who he judged could play an important role in his life over the next four months leading up to the ten-day Lankawi Air Show in Malaysia.

He looked them over one by one and suddenly realized that those role players whose agenda it was to get rid of him could be amongst them – and up to now he did not know exactly why they wanted him out of the picture. He mission was to enhance the marketing position of the Martial Eagle. Should the Malaysian deal be successful it could secure their jobs for many years to come - so why then was he in their way? It just did not seem to make sense -or was this part of the thinking that all possible advanced weapons should not be left by the white government in the hands of a black government with questionable international associations? Like, for instance, the timely dismantling of the country's nuclear weapons capability - shortly before the takeover of the ANC led government? For a moment Grant entertained thoughts that he wished he could classy as most unlikely. That is - what if somebody worked from the inside to support of an outside agenda that is aimed at also taking apart the country's attack helicopter potential. Grant decided - for the time being - to at least park the idea somewhere in the back of his mind.

Grant tried to assess - apart from Kurtz - which Africair officials he could develop some sort of affinity or at least a good rapport. He started with De Witt who was influential, extremely wealthy and well connected - with the defence forces and members of all the South African political groups. De Witt served on many corporate boards and also had a hand in the rugby administration of the Gauteng Lions. He and his wife, who severely disabled, led a very private life and they never appeared in public. Grant somehow had a gut feeling that De Witt and Marjory were on closer terms than they would care to admit. But that's fine, he thought - it proved to be a good business connection.

Kurtz? He was sure he knew the man well enough by now. He was a smart aeronautics engineer and also no-nonsense businessman. He approved of the new South African political dispensation and wanted to get on with his job.

Fischer. Now here is a dark horse Grant thought -if ever there was one -but he had too little to go on. Up to now all he got was a cold shoulder and snide remarks from the big Afrikaner and he did not like his domineering personality. It was also clear that he made it a full-time job of stepping on Kurtz's heels.

Jack du Preez, sitting close to Fischer, was a quiet brooding man who kept mostly to himself. He would regularly walk off to one side and feverishly puff on a cigarette. He avoided casual conversation and was continuously making notes or tapping away at his laptop. Du Preez was not the usual test pilot-type. He also noticed that none of the staff was too keen to seek out his company - perhaps for Chubby Wilson who would do so from time to time. Wilson on the other hand was a good-natured happy-go-lucky - but solid type of person. Grant enjoyed the few short conversations he had with Wilson.

Molape sat doodling on the pad in front of him - legs outstretched and periodically would stifle long yawns. He came over as being nonchalant and bored with all the old white regime stuff -as he called it. During their first chat he told Grant that, although his appointment was looked upon as a political correct gesture, he wanted to believe that he was there as a communicator with suitable qualifications and experience. Grant appreciated Molape's openness but hoped that he would more effort to keep in touch with him. Grant was sorry he missed out on the lunch with him and the Arabian journalist from the Gulf News - whose name he could not remember now.

Grant caught Rosemary's eye and she gave him a compassionate smile - signalling her understanding of his concern over Peter. For a just a brief moment a vivid picture of her, bare-foot and wearing only a short skirt, flashed on the monitor in his mind. Grant liked her very much but warned himself - not to fall in lust with her. He still felt a little guilty about their one-night stand. Goodness! What a painful unpleasant way to refer to their interrupted evening. Anyhow, Rosemary was the one person he could count on as a friend. She also knew all about helicopters and the tough, razor-sharp international marketplace. She was indeed a person of many talents, Grant mused.

His gaze moved on to Kramer who was a regular well-programmed old-styled security personality. His hairdo and suit said it all and his light-blue eyes had laser-cut qualities. He seldom made statements, except when delivering a well-prepared report. He could ask a continuous stream of questions and could easily beat any Scotland Yard detective to the narrative. Kramer was cold, to the point and was a closed person - full of political, country and corporate secrets. To Grant the Kramer-mind resembled a computer with many folders, each closed under a different password.

And then there was his sidekick, Christian Faber. Grant disliked the man and found his overweight, alcohol-bashed, bearded appearance most repulsive – despite of the fact that to this moment he never spoke a word to this nasty - piece of work! Grant shuddered every time he looked at the man with the green watery eyes. Fortunately he would only be involved in a subordinate manner in the program and will only tend to the security arrangements of the planning session.

Grant's attention returned to De Witt when he heard his own name mentioned. He nodded his acknowledgement and tried to smile at the old man who invited them all for a cocktail and dinner after the meeting.

Then Kurtz took over and ran through the program point by point for each day. Grant noticed he structured the agenda in such a way it would afford attention to every angle mentioned in the strategic plan, which he passed on to him a few days earlier. Kurtz scheduled Grant's presentation to be the first point on the agenda for the following day and he admired the CEO's tidy management style.

Under general discussions a few items were added that were mostly administrative stuff. When Jack du Preez spoke he got everyone's attention – perhaps because he talked so seldom, "I had a special request from a

Vietnam disabled American helicopter pilot for a ride in the Martial Eagle at the Lankawi Air Show. Could we please include him in a flight as part of the show plan?"

Kurtz looked at him and smiled. "Sure, it's all part of show business offering rides to prospective clients and - of course to people who merits a flip. What is you pilot friend's name?"

Du Preez hesitated for a moment before replying, "Boddington. Brian Boddington - an American who now resides in London."

47.

GRANT'S GRAND STRATEGY.

MISSILE TESTING RANGE, ARNISTON BAY, SOUTH AFRICA

Grant placed the transparencies for his presentation in a neat pile next to the overhead projector. The previous evening he went to bed shortly after dinner and was well rested and prepared. The attentive group in front of him relaxed when they saw his calm appearance while he took a sip of water before starting his address.

Grant used the opportunity to look every member of the team in the eyes. For a fleeting moment he again wondered who was friend and who was foe and then focused his attention on his presentation. "My presentation will cover two things. Firstly I will address a few questions as a back-drop to my strategy, and then will hopefully provide some answers as to how we could better our position in the attack helicopter market."

"I would like to ask three basic questions." Grant flashed his first transparency. It read:

1. The successful competition: How and where are they positioned?
2. What current international interests and conflicts need to be considered?
3. Is Africair operational ready to execute a 'big' and extended attack helicopter order?

"We know who our competition is and how they outstripped us to the order book. But they all have a few things in common. Firstly, they have been in the marketplace for many years while we are still battling to get our first attack helicopter order. Secondly, they have good networks to render logistical support and thirdly, they have the support of their air forces and their government. We have the back-up of the South African government in the name of Minister Joe Modise, our Defense Minister, but virtually nobody else." Grant allowed time for a response to on his statements.

Grant continued, "As far as international interests are concerned we have a number of things to take into consideration. As a result of the anti-Apartheid actions and intensive arms-embargo's, the South African armaments industry had to develop on the lines of comprehensive self-sufficiency. Because it was not possible to do component acquisitioning on the open international market, it was imperative to develop complete weapon-systems."

Laughter and a few complementary wisecracks followed when Grant said, "I am not referring to the good old bad days when we stole technology from the Americans, the English, Israel and oh-yes from the Frogs! Not to mention our stiff-upper-lip friends who criticized the Apartheid policy severely in the United Nations but smuggled hardware in containers to our shores under carefully worded consignment-notes that described the content as 'furniture' or 'medicine'".

"Now we find that the world realizes that perhaps our weapons industry kept the Apartheid Regime in power for much longer than was necessary. With our new reconciliatory frame of mind and a community and with no enemies, we are without a distinctive role to play as a regional force in Africa. The international community, and especially those countries that are our competition, hold the opinion that we do not need a comprehensive armaments industry in Africa any longer".

Kurtz responded; "Sure, but we need an aviation industry to sustain our place in civil aviation. Our military technology can serve as a source to keep the big airlines flying to our airports and make use of our ground crew and maintenance facilities".

Grant agreed and added; "Yes, but in the international arena we have a sensitive concern that we may supply weapons to countries that are being barred from buying their needs from the traditional suppliers. I need not to mention who those countries and their controversial leaders are".

Grant allowed them a while for his remark to sink in and continued; "So we will find that apart from the normal competition around product preference, we will also be up against a very strong lobby-force who routes for the eventual break-down of the South African high-technology industry to a mere component-manufacturing level." Once he made this remark he realized that there may also be a local, covert movement with a similar objective.

—Grant took another sip of water and tried to be as brief as possible," Looking at the question of our preparedness to execute a large order - we need to make sure that we consist over enough working capital, manufacturing facilities and on-line component suppliers to support our product. What concerns me most, however, is the huge loss in skills that the country is experiencing right now. We see clearly in the media how headhunters and personnel groups from Canada, the UK and Australia are running recruitment campaigns here in South Africa. We must prevent at all cost, any signals on these topics, that could spark an international media debate."

Kurtz called for a tea break that also gave Grant the opportunity to make a quick phone call to find out about Peter's progress. Before he spoke to his son he had a most encouraging discussion with his physician, who assured him that the human spleen is like tonsils and that one could have a normal life without this organ. But what pleased him most was how impressed Peter was with Connie. Apparently the admiration is mutual - because she became a regular visitor and even brought him flowers - something that Grant did not even considered doing. Now he was sure his son had all the motivation he needed to get well. He sounded very enthusiastic an it set Grant at ease.

Grant continued his presentation. "During this week we will have to pay close attention to those actions flowing from my strategy. " Grant displayed a rather busy transparency. "I will call it my ten-point-plan." He gave the following directions:

1. Run well-coordinated advertising, promotions and publicity campaign;
2. Put–up a spectacular two-helicopter air show. Fly two Martial Eagles;
3. Let the South African Air Force (SAAF) officials be present at Africair's pavilion at Lankawi Air Show;

4. Strengthening product confidence by supplying the SAAF 12 Martial Eagles over 5-year period. (Endeavor to close an upside-down deal by renting them choppers so as to avoid exuberant defense budgeting.);

5. Sponsor the Training of 24 Martial Eagle pilots.(Representative of the South African demography i.e. Black, White, Coloreds, Indian)

6. Enter into a technology partnership with a Malaysian aviation company.

7. Create an operational agreement between the SAAF and the Royal Malaysian Air Force (RMAF)

8. Train a core of pilots and ground staff at no charge for the RMAF

9. Make an official announcement of the above – carrying an embargo for the opening day of the Lankawi Air Show.

10. Arrange for President Nelson Mandela and Prime Minister Datuk Seri Mahathir of Malaysia to sign letter of intention at the Lankawi Air Show. (Followed by an up-market social function for the media, government official SAAF and RMAF officers, suppliers, and potential clients from other international forces)

Grant allowed the team to read through his ten-point-plan and to think about his suggestions. "Please run through this carefully and jot down your remarks and questions for discussion. I am confident we will be able to work out potential solutions for all your concerns. As a matter of fact, this is why we are here - not so?"

Grant listened to the soft murmur amongst them and saw that the team was eager to tackle the problems and work out the procedures; "OK? Shall we start at the top?"

Kurtz, who had the benefit of pre-knowledge about Grant's strategy, opened the floor, "As far as point one, three, five and eight is concerned, I think you are really giving us some very good new ideas there. Part of it can already be covered with the existing budget but of course we will need to increase our investment and adjust our unit price accordingly."

Jack du Preez stood up. "Mister Kurtz it seems to me you think that taking an extra helicopter along won't cost us that much more. Point two alone will just about double our cost. I would like to ask Mister Grant why he thinks it necessary to take two Martial Eagles. I think it's a silly idea. Perhaps most of the other points will add somewhat to our expenses but will not do much more than that. They therefore do not come to too much."

Grant was a little surprised by Du Preez's slight flare-up – and he wondered why? Then he caught a glimpse of Chubby Wilson's pleased expression and he knew the reason instantly. It would give Chubby an opportunity to skipper his own aircraft while it would mean Jack du Preez won't be the only big star of the show any more. Or does it mean that this closed-minded man had something else up his sleeve?

Grant decided to make a mental note of his reaction; "None of the other attack-helicopter participants are doing that. There is even talk of the Americans not demonstrating their Warrior in South-east Asia, any longer. We want this Malaysian contract more than anything else. Think of the consequences for all of us - should our bid fail again to secure us a contract to supply our ATH system?" Grant drew a dagger-finger across his throat and added "We will have to cast more bread on the water this time."

Mark Fischer slowly shook his head from side to side, "Points five and six looks like reasonable sales gimmicks but why the supply of Martial Eagles to the SAAF while they won't have a budget for them for a zillion years to come?"

Grant sat on the corner of the table and replied, "Mark, for precisely that reason I suggested the unusual option of renting of the aircraft instead of ordering them. We have three Martial Eagles as EM's available at this stage. Let's develop one of them to client-ready-status and let the SAAF fly it all over the country on an hourly-fee and based on direct cost. For the purpose of the media we can state that this is the first delivery of a potential extended contract - to be considered by the SAAF and Africair. We could then use that decision as a basis of confidence and run a media publicity drive to gain extended international coverage - so as to convince other potential clients. It could also play a role in the decision-making process of the Malaysian and other forces. It will show that our own air force has so much trust in their own country's product, that they are buying it. What better endorsement do we want? The forces of other countries are buying everything that their defense industries produce. Especially, all their top of the range technology-systems - like attack-helicopters!"

John Molape supported Grant. "Mister Kurtz, I have, as you know, a personal ear with our president. I am convinced that if I would sit down and carefully talk the situation of the Martial Eagle though with him during a social occasion, we will have his consideration for points nine and ten. President Mandela is on a good footing with Prime Minister Mahathir. By the time Joe Modise approach the President, he will have thought about it and perhaps give us his support."

Fischer exclaimed sharply, "Listen here John if you can twist Mandela's arm on this one, my friend, and secure a contract, than you have done enough for Africair. You won't need to put in another day's work. We will pay you to do nothing more for the rest of your time!"

Molape gave Fischer a long emotionless stare - not saying a word. Grant was surprised by Fischer's snide response and wondered what was going on in his mind.

Kurtz ignored this remark and looked at his watch. There was still about ten minutes to go before lunchtime - yet decided to call for a break. As the group got up from their chairs he requested Fischer and Du Preez to stay behind to have a word with him.

Rosemary whispered to Grant, "I think that for the first time we are properly focusing on our show-related marketing effort.".

Grant turned, took her by the arm and led her towards the wide verandah covered with vines; "Thank you Rosy but do you really mean that?"

"Most certainly Julius - what it will require though, is that all of us, for a change, will need to get off our backsides and work like hell on many fronts in order to shape your plans - before the show starts"

Grant placed his foot on the low verandah wall and rubbed his painful ankle. "I am not so sure. I think there may be some hidden opposition in that conference room and most likely half of the ideas will be argued into oblivion."

Barnard looked at the closed-door of the conference room, and then turned to Grant;. "Can I ask you a question? You do not need to answer it ".

Grant leaned forward; "Go ahead."

"My guess is that Kurtz asked you to let him have a copy of your presentation or written strategy, a few days before this session. If he did not come back to you with any suggestions to adjust it - he accepted it as it stands. He would also have discussed it with De Witt. So, my dear friend, both of them will back you up. That is the way Kurtz does things around here. Am I right?' She looked straight at him with eyes that carried nothing but pure logic.

Grant came to also trust her along with Kurtz. "Yes. You are right. Kurtz phoned me beforehand and assured me of the chairman's approval. He said De Witt committed himself to personally tend to those actions that are politically-inclined. Hence the Chairman's plight that I should receive the team's support".

Rosemary nodded towards the closed door of the Dolphin Room. "I believe that right now - Kurtz is turning a few minds behind that door".

Grant did not respond. He began to understand something of the top management culture that Kurtz has cultivated over time. It was an executive style based on plural decision-making and twin-executive decision-taking. He looked at Rosemary as she rested her hand on his knee. "Let's see what's for lunch".

48.

GO FOR IT.

CONFERENCE ROOM, MISSILE TESTING RANGE, SOUTH AFRICA

Grant finished his light lunch and pardoned himself from the company of Rosemary Barnard, John Molape, and Chubby Wilson. They all made complimentary remarks about his presentation and he would have preferred to stay with them a little longer, but he wanted to run to his room and call Peter again at his bedside in the Johannesburg Academic Hospital. Peter was in a positive mood and assured Grant that he was in good hands. All he wanted was to be back at his job and have a normal routine as soon as possible. Peter was, however, a little unhappy because he had to accept that with this occurrence, his rugby-season came to an early end.

Peter sounded on top "Dad don't you worry - I can understand that you need to be at your planning session. Here in hospital I am safe – I think. Remember they are not after me - they want you out of the way. Think about that as an important factor of your strategy. "

For a while Grant stood looking out of the window at the faint blue hills in the distance and decided to talk to Kurtz and arrange his early departure - despite Peter's assurance that he was in a good situation. He looked at the bedside-clock and saw that he still had about twenty minutes before he had to return to the conference room. He decided to lie down for a few minutes hoping to catch a power nap but just then there was a knock on the door - it was Kurtz.

"Molape told me you came up to your room - can I come in?"

Grant opened the door wide, "Hello Johann – sure, I have a request to put to you but please - you came to see me and I suppose you wanted to discuss something?" Grant could guess what it was about.

"When you return to the discussions this afternoon, you will find full support for your strategic plan. So you can go therefore ahead and talk us through your detailed tasks and actions that are necessary to make your plan work."

Grant gestured Kurtz towards a chair and said; "I am glad to hear that - perhaps you addressed the resistance and now we could expect less flak from certain individuals?"

Kurtz smiled and said; "Let's just say I brought about some consensus".

Grant relaxed and smiled; "I like the way you put it".

Kurtz sounded a little mischievous; -"Well - there are ways and means you know".

"Suppose so – and more so when you are the boss?" Grant smirked in a friendly manner.

"Whatever" Kurtz tried to be formal again; "Grant, I think I've developed a clearer picture since we had our discussion at your home".

"And?" Grant's right eyebrow lifted.

Kurtz showed concern; "I am convinced there is something irregular developing and I am pretty convinced that there is also an attitude of vindictiveness - even opposition that is growing"

"Coming from?"

Kurtz thought for a while, looking at the distant mountain range; "Fischer, Du Preez and perhaps a few others - whom I cannot name yet." Kurtz decided not mention his vague distrust about the chairman. At this stage it would just not make any common sense to speculate about De Witt.

"I suppose all is directed against me?" Grant knew what the answer would be.

"Yes of course - remember your cat?'"

Grant looked at him and said evenly, "Yes and now my son"

"What? What about your son?". Kurt sat forward, fumbling for a cigarette.

"He was mugged when he brought my car home from the workshop. His assailants were under the impression that they were launching an attacking me. They assaulted and wounded Peter pretty badly - took off with my Range Rover - making it look like another car highjack. But they left a note with Peter." Grant gave him a full rundown of the event up to the discussion he had with Peter a few minutes ago.

"And why didn't you tell me about this? Kurtz sounded upset.

Grant said simply, "I did not want to bother you before we started the planning session."

Kurtz was upset, "Good Gracious man - this is terrible. You should have told me immediately".

Grant turned from the window, "Perhaps I did it on purpose"

Kurtz was at a complete loss, "Why?"

Grant sat on the bed, looked at Kurtz, "To see if something would leak out while we are here. In that way we could be sure that there is a connection with some entities present at this meeting."

Kurtz agreed, "That makes sense - who else from Africair knows about this".

"Only Rosemary Barnard and I asked her to not mention it to anyone. She promised that she would do so - although she does not understand why I requested this."

"And she will". Kurtz sounded convinced. "She is a solid person".

"But so far I did not hear anything yet". Grant started to doubt his own decision - or if there was any connection at all.

Kurtz held his hand on the door handle, "OK -let's keep it that way and keep our ears open. Is this what you wanted to talk to me about".

"Yes and I wanted to know if I could leave this afternoon - after I ran through my detailed action plan? I think the rest of the session you could do without me. There will surely be follow-up working sessions but, I would like to go back - to be with my son." Grant followed him to the door.

"Sure as hell man! Actually you should have done that in the first place. I could have slotted you in at a later stage. On the other hand it was imperative to start-off with your strategy so - I appreciate what you did. This is really what the meeting is all about. But, yes - we can take it from here."

"Thank you Johann." Grant felt a relief from his guilt.

Kurtz looked at his watch. "It is time to go – and on my way down I will ask Faber to arrange transport back to Cape Town's airport, for you".

Back in the Dolphin Room Kurtz ploughed right into the hard work; "Guys, we have less than five months to do a hell of a lot of things simultaneously. Grant here is going to hand out his detailed action-plans that support his strategy and then he is going to leave it to us to finalize the commitments and operational detail."

Grant took them through the all commitments. He covered the overseas travel, the advertising and promotions programs, the timing of tender documentation and government interactions as well as the flight demonstrations, show staff training, letters of intent and a host of minor detail - which if neglected, could jeopardize the carefully comprehensive plan.

When he answered several questions he left the meeting with a feeling of deep concern. Whoever was against him and his plans or in favour of a hidden agenda, knew exactly what the Africair plans were. Yet right now he - and Kurtz - does not yet have anything more than threats, attacks, and a bad omen to go on. Grant felt like an untrained, blindfolded boxer who entered the ring against a world champion.

In the entrance hall Faber and a tall young man waited for him. The youngster stepped forward with a long stride and took Grant's hand; "Good day and pleased to meet you Mister Grant - I have read many of your articles in the newspapers. I am in charge of OTR's transportation and while I need to go to Cape Town to pick up clients from London - you are most welcome to ride with me."

Grant sounded relieved; "Thank you and, it's great of you to wait for me. Please allow me to get my bag in the room"

On his return Grant found the young man and Faber waiting for him at the car which was parked at the entrance to the inn.

Faber, who has not spoken a word yet, took the bag from him and dropped it in the BMW's boot. He turned to Grant, "Good day Mister Grant - safe trip and I hope your son will recover soon." The bearded man slammed the lid down and walked off.

With that Faber said enough to convince Grant that he was the originator of the recorded phone threats. Grant looked at the man as he moved out of sight and said aloud; "I knew I heard that voice somewhere! - and how did he know about Peter?" Grant muttered several subdued profanities as he and stepped into the car.

49.

PRE-DEPARTURE INTROSPECTION.

JOHANNESBURG ACADEMIC HOSPITAL

Upon his arrival at the Johannesburg International Airport, Grant walked straight up to the Avis counter. Till this moment he gave little thought about the loss of his Range Rover and accepted that it would never be recovered. Almost all expensive cars stolen in the republic of South Africa are being shipped within hours over the border and sold somewhere in Central Africa at a below market price. He decided to take-up his claim up with the insurance company in the morning - however he doubted if he would have the time to replace it before he left for Lankawi. For the time being his aged Jaguar XJ-Six, which had no export market value, just had to suffice.

Twenty minutes later he left the airport and took the circle-route to the Johannesburg Academic Hospital. It was well after eleven, but he could not postpone a visit to Peter till the next morning. The night nurse on duty was most helpful and asked Grant to follow her to Peter's bed. She told him that they moved him to a private ward and that his family and friends could visit him at any time. "He had a visit from two members of the Police Hi-jack Squad - earlier this evening," she said.

"How long did they stay? Grant asked.

"I am not sure - but it was less than thirty minutes. I was on my rounds administering medicine when they were with your son - but on my return they have already left."

They reached the private wards and she carefully opened the door to Peter's partially darkened room. Only a night-light shone while Peter was asleep. "I am going back to my office now and leaving it to you to decide if you want to wake him up." She smiled at Grant, closed the door and left him – staring at his son's bruised face.

Grant sat down on a narrow bench that stood right next to the high-leveled hospital-bed. He held his eyes on his son and heard his labored breathing. The attractive lines of his profile were distorted by his swollen cheekbones and lips. His one eye was severely blackened and he was in need of a shave and a haircut. He became deeply moved and his heart and eyes filled with compassion for his son. He had the urge to hold and kiss him like when he was a small boy and battled with the pain of a broken arm or an illness.

Grant wrung his hands and kept his eyes on his boy. He felt so inadequate -the quality of his life fell dismally short and it was the result of his indiscretions and shortcomings - despite his deep commitment to his family and career. Now his son was suffering as a result of his involvement with the Martial Eagle affair. Peter was such a fine understanding person - who always cared so much for the people around him. He always believed that he could change the circumstances and environment for the better. He was involved in many projects and actions aimed at serving the less fortunate. And, he never talked about his good deeds. Now his good son just lay there and suffered as a result of his father's inconsiderate ways. Grant's failed to calm his disconcerted conscience.

For a fleeting moment Grant thought he could understand what Peter tried to explain to him - of what it took God to send his son Jesus to this incomplete world in order to give everyone the option of an eternal life. The only pre-condition was to believe in Jesus. "That's the problem with Christianity," Grand whispered, "for some of us it is just too simple a solution to believe in."

Grant's troubled mind just could not be calmed. He reminded himself that he did not even arrange to send his son a get-well card and flowers. He did not even pray once - for his save keeping and recovery. What sort of a man is he really?

Grant regarded the planning session at OTR as a rushed, unsatisfactorily exercise and - he also allowed himself to get drawn into a silly flirtation with Rosemary Barnard. While, just a few days before his little love-adventure, he had the feeling that he was ready to let go of Anna's memory. He even allowed himself a steadily growing attraction towards Marjory Brooks.

Grant whispered to himself, "Hell! I acted really irresponsible again. What if anybody saw us and uses it against me? Especially slobs like

Faber or that caustic Fischer! And - I also did not get round to a good discussion with de Witt and Kurtz at OTR".

Grant sat in the still of the night with the hospital-sounds muffled behind the closed door. He could not remember when last he structured his thoughts into prayer, but he wanted to do it now. For a long time afterwards he sat there looking at his son and reviewed his life. It was around three in the morning that Grant's mind was made-up. He tore a page from his notebook and wrote to Peter:

My dearest Son,

I was here with you for a few hours of this night. I did not have the heart to wake you but I had enough time to think about a lot of things. I am so very sorry for you - forgive me for what happened to you. I should never have allowed you to drive home in my car -not with the type of criminals we are dealing with now. I just hope that one day I can make it all up to you again. You will be surprised to know that this evening I prayed for your good recovery.

See you later in the morning – say at about ten-o-clock.

I love you my son.

Dad.

50.

Pre-departure break-up

Du Preez's Home, Kempton Park.

For the various teams committed to stage the exhibition of the Martial Eagle Attack Helicopters, the months preceding the Lankawi Air Show in Malaysia passed as swiftly as weeks. The fact that two aircraft would be on display asked for double the effort in terms of preparation and qualification of the two aircraft, their crews as well as the maintenance and logistic support. It also required the renting of two huge Russian Antonof Cargo Carriers. Kurtz kept closer than usual an eye on progress and called for numerous countdown meetings, which frustrated the hell out of the likes of Fischer and Du Preez.

Apart from the official preparations, there were many social functions to be attended to create a good liaison with politicians, government officials and, officers from the department of Defense to drum up their support for the marketing campaign. In the meanwhile Fischer, Du Preez and Faber also had to spend long hours during the night and weekends for the purpose of the WAC's Technical committee work. They had to review the planning of the ME's technology demise that now suddenly required much more careful planning and attention to detail.

On top of it all, Jack Du Preez spend many hours on his lap-top planning the destruction of the ME and how to cause the fatality of Nelson Mandela and Thabo Mbeki - who was to become South Africa's new president in 2000. This colossal arrangement of destruction and death also had to synchronize - with his suicide plans.

It was days away from spring and the warm Saturday morning gave Jack du Preez all the time he needed to do his planning where he sat under a thatch-covered pergola alongside his pool. He unplugged his phone and switched-off the mobile which lay beside his PC. In no way he wanted to invite distraction while he was adding the finishing touches to his brutal plan. Du Preez tried to anticipate how to deal with all possible developments that could interfere with his wicked intentions.

Although Du Preez's new comfortable friendship with Lillian Pretorius, made his home feel at times less empty or cold since the death of his young wife - he lost all interest in his life here and - the lack of good homemaking began to show. He also declined when Lillian offered to tend to the housekeeping of his home - perhaps because he was afraid that this could bring them even closer together and that he wanted to avoid that at all cost. Their sexual relationship was good enough for now and only served as a crutch to get him to the big final moment of his life. He had no family, apart from his elderly sister with whom he lost all contact. Perhaps he could somehow make it up to Lillian – like by adding her to his final will. He was adamant that nothing should come between him and the sworn commitment he made - to revenge the murder of his wife and their unborn child.

It was around three in the afternoon and Jack was so immersed in his task that he did not hear when Lillian's car pulled into his driveway. She had a front-door key of Du Preez's home and planned a pleasant surprise for him. Once inside, she placed the snacks, scotch, and greeting card on the dining room table. Through the window she saw where Jack where he sat at the pool and she appreciated the absence of pets that could have alerted him of her presence. Then she went to the main bedroom and slipped on a scanty brief and covered her large breasts with a see-through chiffon wrap. Lillian looked at her appearance in the full-length mirror and decided to kick-off her sandals. She went to the liquor cabinet and placed two glasses, ice, soda water and the snacks on a silver tray and carried it out to Jack.

"Hi! Stranger - it's been quite a while since I saw you last. Busy? - or are there other attractions around?"

Lillian placed the tray on the table next to his PC, kissed him lightly on the cheek and then curled up on the chair opposite him. She waited for him to look at her and notice her tanned cleavage - that showed clearly through the transparent white fabric.

Du Preez briefly looked in her general direction, "Hi Lillian. How are you doing?" He sounded bothered and continued tapping away at the small keyboard. He did not give the impression that he noticed her intimate attire or appreciated the refreshments she brought. Lillian gave him time to finish with the thoughts he was turning into characters on his screen. For some time now she intended talking to him about the future of their relationship. She gave him enough time to take the lead but, somehow he always stopped short and pulled back in his closed way of communicating - shutting her out of his innermost feelings. Du Preez just kept on working.

"May I fix you a drink my darling?" She hoped that he would eventually notice the card.

"Later, old girl - much later. Can't you see that I am tied up right now?" It was really the first time he was so abrupt with her.

Lillian tried to gain his attention without words and was confident that this time she would succeed. Slowly she dropped the wrap stood up, stretched her body and showing the lines of her well shaped bosom and walked to the shallow-end of the pool. In the meantime Du Preez just continued at the keyboard. She then slid into the water up to her neck, "The water is a little chilly but refreshing - would you like to join me? Come and see what it does to my boobs". She had an inviting smile and was ready for him.

"Shit Lillian, can't you see that I am bloody busy and not in the mood for booze or sex right now?" He was annoyed and restrained himself from becoming furious. He looked at her with an irritated scowl.

"But it is four days now that you have been sitting in front of that toy of yours - scarcely noticing what's going on around you, Jack".

"Nothing else is more important. What I am doing here I prefer above anything else"

Lillian stood up in the shallow water - her body taut from cold and anxiety, "Does this include me too?"

"Listen we have an arrangement - so don't bother me now. As and when it suits me, or us - we can have fun. OK? Now let me alone. Pour yourself a drink or - if you want to leave – OK - I'll call you later."

Lillian stepped out of the pool and with her wet body and tears running freely down her cheeks she went back in the house and got dressed. She knew now for certain that Jack du Preez was still not over his wife's death and that he had no intention to take their relationship any further. Perhaps she knew this from the beginning - but was too afraid to admit the possibility that theirs was just a sexual involvement. She got dressed, picked up her keys and while walking back to Jack, unhitched the front-door key from her key fob.

Du Preez looked up at her when she came round the pool towards him, "So you're leaving. OK - see you sometime later". He did not rise to greet her but glanced occasionally at the monitor.

Lillian's mind was made up, "Listen here Jack du Preez - there will not be a sometime-later. This shallow relationship has been going on for too long now. I think it's time for us to part. That is if we are not seriously allowing our relationship to become more - complete". There was a built-in opportunity for him in her remark. Now Du Preez now had the chance to take her in his arms and explain to her - a lot about him and what he thinks of their future together.

Instead he just sat there and looked at her with a strange contempt in his eyes, "Perhaps it's time for you to find another bed partner. I do not think we need to take this any further. We both know what we only want each other to alleviate our prevailing sadness. What more do you want?"

Lillian's temper flared-up and she knew this was the end for them. She gave a step towards the table, took the flat screen in both hands and hurled the humming portable into the pool, "Now you can take a skinny dip with your wretched computer." Then she threw the key at him and ran off.

Du Preez jumped up shouting a string of well-used swearwords, "Get the hell outa here, you bitch!' He ran to the edge of the pool and looked at his computer as it bubbled down to the deep end of the pool.

Du Preex ran after Lilian and shouted, "In any case - I have all of this copied on a disc!" He then followed her into the house, "That's right! - rush off and pick-up another young stud at the club's bar – you cheap old tart!"

Lillian stopped at the gate leading to the driveway and turned to him. She was so furious that she doubted if she would ever cry over this episode in her life, "This time I will make sure that it's someone with more reach than your lousy bloody five-inch little wiener - you arrogant bastard". She backed-out out of the driveway in a zigzag fashion, running over shrubs while burning tire-marks on the tiles of the driveway – just to remind Jack du Preez of this afternoon for a long time to come.

The scrawny test pilot went back and stood at the edge of the pool and looked at the distorted image of his laptop, "Now isn't this a farken mess! You bloody lousy over-boobed bitch. Do you know what you did to me! "

Du Preez swung round and ripped the bottle from its expensive package. With one swing he opened it and gulped down several large mouthfuls - wiped his mouth with his arm. Only then he noticed the card that Lillian left him. He opened it, and read the words aloud;

Hi Pal,
I missed you. Is this a time to talk – about us? Or what? L.
xxx

Jack du Preez threw the card on the table and took two more swigs - looked up at the clear late-afternoon sky and talked to the heavens. "Or what? Or what? It's time for revenge! That's what my dearest family in heaven. I am doing it for you and our baby, sweetheart".

Du Preez took another careless swig and he wondered was it whiskey - or tears on his cheek? "The bloody sun is too bright" He slid his sunglasses on and looked up at the sky again and said barely audible, "First I need to kill all those evil bastards! Then - then I'll be joining you my darlings! That's what".

51.

Pre-departure Contemplation.

Africair Offices at Midnight

Mark Fischer sat cross-legged with his feet resting on the desk in his Africair office. Two hours before midnight was not unusually late for him to still be at his workplace. Now he had to think through a few peripheral but very important issues and actions before attending the final detail-planning meeting of the WAC – later in the week. It was absolutely imperative for him to be on top of the situation and run through the Committee's agenda without referring to notes. He had to direct the WAC's objectives to finality without depending on paperwork. With a man like Jack du Preez, whose subliminal self was honed like a blood dipped bayonet, you do not take the chance to appear anything else - then being in control. Fischer knew he had to ride out this meeting aiming at their objectives as if it had become a natural part of him - like riding a bicycle or making love to a woman.

Fischer endured many forlorn and risky moments in foreign countries when his duty was to smuggle illegitimate acquired weapons technology for the South African Defense Force during the period when a total arms-embargo was enforced against the country. When confronted in a tight spot, he would play a theatrical game that sharpened his rational capability. He founded out that it allowed his thinking to work at its best when he conducted a thinking session by talking to himself in Afrikaans. It was quite safe to converse in this way, because very few people outside of Africa spoke or even heard of his mother tongue.

"Let me get a global view of the situation as it stands now." He altered his sitting position somewhat. "Right now the objective is plain - or perhaps very complicated. Depending from which point of view you would like to look at it".

Fischer reached for a brandy flask from the bottom drawer of his desk. He slowly unscrewed and the cap and filled it with brandy. He dripped the measure on his tongue, allowing the invigorating fluid to cover his taste buds, while he breathed the palette slowly through his nose. The warming substance ran down his throat and immediately comforted his empty stomach.

He spoke to his invisible companions again, "The objectives are clear gentlemen. We must destroy the political influence of Mandela's ruling ANC party and prevent that South Africa's high technology or aviation-warfare capability fall in the hands of the president's undesirable international friends. Because they are either communists or terrorists or both! "

"Shit!" He said in a different voice and followed, "Listen, it is only a matter of time before this bloody black government will be so committed to their old friends that words alone will not hold the bonds of comradeship strong. Mandela will be forced to do something more or exercise substantial proof of his gratitude - by shipping out deadly armaments stuff to all the new pariah countries. And it will happen shortly. You wait and see - I am reading the early signs".

. "Are you sure?" He asked in a mocking voice and answered; "Oh yes my friends. You will see that at first Mandela will start by playing a sort of international game that will confuse and upset the Americans and all their UK and European buddies. Slowly but surely he will be siding openly with Cuba, Libya, Syria, Iraq, Iran, North Korea and of course Big Brother China. Brothers and let me tell you - China is a future giant super power that is slowly but surely growing into a position of strength by peacefully getting involved in widespread international economic networks. South Africa does not know it yet but we will form part of the subversive plan to create a balanced opposition for the Americans and their allies. The only thing viable that Mandela has to offer these pariah allies is the output of our comprehensive, independent armaments industry to strengthen them and supply terrorist cells harbored in these countries".

"And if so, how do we achieve this? What can we do to prevent this move" Fischer played his eulogy-game like a puppet show, by asking the self-directed questions in various animated voices.

"Easy -by making use of a kamikaze-minded Attack Helicopter pilot like Jack du Preez".

"And how is he going to do this?" Again the animated voice teased a possible question.

"By smuggling a live missile onto the Martial Eagle's weapons-platform, and during the demonstration flight, launching it at point-blank-range into the VIP stand at the Lankawi Air Show. Poof – and gone are all our current political heroes. That's how. Sweet and simple".

"Apart from President Nelson Mandela and Vice-president Thabo Mbeki and Prime Minister Mahathir of Malaysia and their companions and staff, who else will die in the process?"

"Unfortunately - also our own superman CEO, Johann Kurtz - and of course our new friend, Julius Grant. The bloody Englishman will be there with Dr. Marjory Brooks, who will be accompanying President Mandela and his party. It will be quite an impressive funeral procession"

"But Grant had his merciful chance to get out of it. Faber, the farken fool, tried on his own to scare the bloody Pommy out of this, for his own good health. But instead of backing-off he also drew his sexy partner onto the scene. But, Grant is set on being a communications expert, an industrial hero, a lover and heaven knows what else!"

Fischer thought for a while about Faber's indiscretions of the past. Once again he nearly ruined their plans with his personal plot against Grant. As a result of his hit-teams success with Gareth Williams, he became too confident and tried to become a one-man operator. Fischer was in a desperate spot when Kurtz confronted him with Grant's suspicion and story about the attack on his son. Fortunately the young rugby player he is recovering. Hopefully the Police will be too inundated with the spate of vicious crimes that is now all over Johannesburg that it will take them a long time to put two and two together. And there are other means to distract them, if necessary.

"Once Du Preez thumbed the firing-button, what happens to him and his co-pilot?"

"They will fly out from the commotion and confused-filled stadium, and rush-off to a nearby uninhabited small island. From there the escape operation will kick-in."

"What will happen to his co-pilot who most likely will be Chubby Wilson?" The voice-animation made Fischer cough, and this time he took a swig straight from the bottle. "If Du Preez cannot convince Wilson there and then to play along for the good of the western world, he will have to pay the price. He is in any case a tame English-African with no deep patriotic sentiments towards the country."

"Talking about being patriotic, who else can you rely on, except Jack Du Preez?"

"Of course there is Christian Faber. He owes me one for getting him back into the Africair Company. I also kicked his balls purple as plums for the dumb things that he did. Then there is Miss Glynis Botha, who keeps me up to date with what goes on in Kurtz's office. Very few people know that she is the younger sister of Faber's wife. As a matter of fact she introduced Faber to her. There was talk that she was actually in love with Faber when he was still young and a debonair helicopter pilot. But as soon as she found out that her sister and Faber was set for a shotgun-wedding, she became the aloof person she is now, and never married."

"Who else?"

"Now let me think. The rest are a small cogs but I've got their support. I am referring to Gert Smuts of finance, Willem Niemand of production, and the like."

"What about Fredric Kramer, the super security man?"

"I have a question mark over him. He is a good Afrikaner and churchgoer, which knows his job and is loyal to the interests of Africair. How he really feels about the new black government I don't know. Perhaps his training in the Department of Information, which conditioned him to hate the ANC and all communists, could make it possible to get his understanding and support for our cause. But on the other hand he has a strong conscience and may have his own ideas of what is true and right. We will have to watch this guy. He is the wild-card in this game."

"What about Rosemary Barnard".

"Listen mister alter-ego, you're asking a lot of questions tonight. However – that's always good. When I walk into that meeting, I need to have done all my thinking. Oh-yes! You mentioned Rosemary Barnard. Now let me see. Faber said he is sure Grant has the hots for our beautiful little engineer. I must say, I wouldn't mind measuring my dipstick in her pretty little sump. But that would be like messing up one's own the nest. Not so? In any case – back to the serious business - she is not much of a concern to me. She is one of the boys but not part of the politics. Like many of the other members of the Martial Eagle-team, she keeps to her discipline. That's it. I doubt if she's got anything to spill during their pillow-talks."

"What about our racial corrective action candidate - John Molape?"

"Well, that bloody boy is a bloody fool. He is the token of Africair's affirmative action approach to please the government. He still knows sweet-all about a lot of things here and he thinks to be a public relations person you must be friendly and everybody's pal. Fooling around with reporters, like that Arab from the UAE, is what makes him happy. By arranging a little publicity, he hopes to make a huge contribution towards the companies bottom-line. Like all black people who are being pushed into senior positions in companies and government nowadays, he will take a long time to catch-up. And sure as hell also make a few costly blunders in the process that will conveniently be covered-up. Like Barnard and the rest, we just need to side-track him – which will be a easy.'"

"Coming back to the Lankawi Air Show, where will you be Mister Fischer, when all this havoc and disruption takes place?"

"I will inform Kurtz, a few hours earlier that I need to escort Dr Herman de Witt to meet a Malaysian Aircraft Manufacturer for lunch at the De Tai Hotel, on the opposite side of the Island."

"And - what then?"

"Instead, we will wait in front of the hotel, on the beach, where Faber will pick us up in a rented light transport-helicopter and whisk us towards the meeting place with Du Preez. There we will destroy the Martial Eagle, and if need be – conveniently also Chubby Wilson with the steel bird he loves so much – if he does not want to play along. From there it's a thirty-kilometer flight to the Island of Penang and its International Airport. The rest will be an easy exit."

"And why take Dr de Witt along? Can you trust this shrewd old businessman?"

"Hey man - wake up – De Witt is the main brain and the paymaster, you dumb ass! Shut-up now, you're asking too many questions."

Fischer laughed harshly at his contorted humor and sounded like a ventriloquist addressing his cloned puppet. His one-man-one alter-ego meeting was over. He stood up switched off the lights and locked the door. He had only twenty four hours before meeting with the members of the Technical Committee of the White Afrikaner Concern at the Kempton Park Rugby Club.

At the lower end of the passage Kramer sat in his dark office. The glow from his computer screen lit-up his distraught face. He shook his head in disbelief as he switched-off his monitor which also had a built-in, concealed a listening device - which networked with all the monitors of in Africair's workstations. He could not believe what he heard, despite the suspicion he had about Fischer.

52.

FAMILY AND FRIENDS.

CASTLE WALK RESTAURANT, PRETORIA.

Julius and Peter Grant sat at the bar in the Castle Walk Restaurant in Pretoria, which was close to the homes of Dr. Marjory Brooks and Connie Heyneken. It was a pleasant Friday evening and the 'Walk' that served excellent food in a warm atmosphere was very crowded, busy – and noisy. They drank colas and watched the front door for the arrival of their companions. Grant experienced that since Peter left hospital their father and son relationship developed an attribute of profound trust that allowed them to discuss topics - which they avoided in the past.

Grant was not at all surprised when Peter told him that he thought Connie was a sweet person and that he hoped their friendship would develop into something more than just a good relationship. He referred only once to his girl-friend at Oxford University for whom his interest was clearly on the wane. Suddenly he developed a number of reasons why he was going to postpone his trip to England. To Grant the signs were clear, and at least something positive resulted from this hideous experience. Grant wished that things would turn out well for Peter and Connie. He vowed to himself never to think or talk again of the incident he had with Connie and his old cat, Kieter. Like his pet - that memory was now dead and gone.

"What's the age-difference between you and Marjory Brooks, Dad?"

"What a surprising question, Peter". Grant avoided his son's eyes and fixed his attention on the wide glass-doors of the restaurant.

"Is it more than five years?" Peter persisted.

"Not really - or rather I am not at all sure. But why are you asking?" Grant had to face his son now.

"Because, somehow I have a feeling that the two of you could become more than business-partners".

Grant saw the mischief dancing in Peter's eyes and the marks of his injury still somewhat visible, "Don't be silly Peter - what sort of a thing would it be if father and son are simultaneously courting the ladies of Meyer, Brooks and Associates? Hmm?"

"It would be nothing much to anybody, but it could mean a lot for our happiness - something of which we had very little since Mom's death." Peter had a firm wish that his father would free himself from the loyalty to his mother's memory. He wanted him to understand that as his only son, he would not object if somebody new would enter his life.

Grant looked at his hands and then up to his son as he tried to formulate a suitable answer.

"Good evening gentlemen - our apologies for keeping you waiting so long". They did not notice the arrival of Marjory and Connie that somewhat startled them. They laughed at their own awkwardness and also because they realized that they were indeed very happy that their attractive companions arrived. Father and son complimented them on their appearance while a waiter led them to their table. The evening was young, the music romantic, and the expectations high. There were already signs of early spring in the air and with the childish game of Faber now identified and out of the way, Grant was in a relaxed and merry-making mood. For once he looked forward to a weekend and decided to take it easy for a while.

Once they have studied the menu and discussed the wine order, Peter asked, "Is this a farewell dinner for all you lucky people who will be travelling shortly to Malaysia?"

Connie was quick to react, "No Peter - we are celebrating tonight"

"Celebrating? What?" Grant sounded like a boss talking to his secretary, busy filling him in on a new item added to his schedule".

Connie gave Peter a sweet smile and then turned to Marjory Brooks, "Can you think of any reason to celebrate, or is this just one of those rare get-togethers?"

Marjory, who sat next to Grant, leaned over to his side, "A good friend of mine always says that if you do not celebrate your success, any success for that matter - it would walk away from you. So let me suggest a reason for a festive mood this evening. How about drinking to Julius' Malaysian project? Dr Herman de Witt told me that he and Kurtz are very pleased with your strategy and that at all levels, things are falling nicely into place" Marjory smiled and signalled to Grant to lift their wine glasses.

Everyone said "Cheers" but there was some lack of enthusiasm. Grant realized that only Marjory did not have any knowledge of the threats that he received and what was really behind Peter's unfortunate experience. Connie kept her word and did not speak even to Peter about the whole matter. Peter on the other hand, kept a professional distance from Grant's official matters and would only talk about it if Grant would insist to discuss matters pertaining to his work. In any case the whole silly threat thing was settled and it would serve no purpose at this stage, to tell Marjory about the all the trouble they encountered.

Grant wanted to back off from the topic but Marjory continued, "I feel sorry that you will not be sharing in the fun Peter, while in a few weeks from now we will be in the middle of all the excitement. Your dad will then be interacting with all the important defence officials and aviation industry media while I will be at the side of President Mandela and hobnobbing with all the important politicians over there."

Connie pulled a sad face. "While this poor little back-room girl will be running around like mad, trying to patch-up secretarial and admin things so that the Brooks and Grant partnership looks good in the eyes of the media, all the big brass and the rest of the south-east Asian world."

Peter looked at her shook his head - he thought this was the right moment to surprise them all. He placed his arm around Connie and said, "My boss granted me six weeks of convalescence leave. So, I was hoping to fly over to Lankawi and join you guys on the last day of the show. For some time now I wanted to visit that part of the world, eat their wonderful food and do some scuba diving and under-water photography at the Pulau Payar Marine Park. After all your hard work, it would be grand if you guys wanted to relax a little - amidst the charm and splendour of the tropics." Peter extended his general invitation but his whole being betrayed that he would rather have Connie alone there with him. She gave him a smile but did not respond.

Marjory asked. "Sounds just great, but where on earth is this park you're talking about?"

"It consists of four smallish islands about a three-hour boat journey south of Lankawi and about thirteen kilometres west of the mainland of Malaysia. It's breathtakingly beautiful coral gardens have the reputation of supporting the largest number of coral species in that country. Although there is no accommodation available on the islands, visitors have the option to camp in the great outdoors."

Peter still held Connie's hand and he looked down at her, while talking to them, "What do you guys think of that?"

Grant looked at Marjory and he winked at her ever so slightly. "Afterwards the two of us will have some wrapping-up to do. On the other hand Peter knows that I am not the picnic and camping type - what do you think Marjory?"

Marjory took a long sip from her Chardonnay and looked at them with a sparkle in her eyes, "You are right Grant. If all goes well, the two of us will then have lots of re-planning to do. I think by that time the so-called back-room staff will need a rest. How about granting our colleague an all-paid official holiday - that is if she would want to help Peter through the last phase of his healing and assist him with his tanning in the tropical sun?"

Connie let out s shriek and kissed Peter on the cheek. "I think that would be just wonderful."

Grant lifted his glass. He was extremely pleased with the way things developed for Peter and Connie as well as for Marjory and himself, "Now let's drink to that!"

After dinner Connie and Peter decided to see a film show at the nearby Menlyn theatre complex where they hoped to catch a late screening of "Independence Day". The obvious happy couple took leave from Marjory and Grant at Castle Walk's entrance. They were obviously not at all interested with what Marjory and Julius had in mind for the rest of the evening.

For both Brooks and Grant t was an awkward moment. Since they met it was really the first time that they were alone – and with time on their hands. Grant wondered if it would be appropriate to stretch the evening a little further with his boss and decided to let her guide them through this evening, "Any suggestions for what's left of the evening?"

Marlene smiled up at Grant and he was unexpectedly very aware of how little he knew about Marlene Brooks' private life. He wished that she would open up to him. Grant smiled as he looked at her black hair. The glimmer of the neon signs gave it a near gunmetal shine. What a silly comparison, he thought. It was also the first time that he saw her in casual dress. Her red and blue chequered top was tugged into smartly fitting blue jeans. The shirtsleeves were folded back and she wore no jewellery. Her v-neck top allowed him to be very aware of the rounding of her ample bosom and her make-up complimented her tanned face and brown eyes.

While Grant openly admired her beauty she said; "Well, seeing that all you can offer is your nice smile and no ideas, I suggest we go to my place. I am quite a bartender you know. If you like, I could serve you a liqueur or make us some Irish coffee. How does that sound to you?"

Grant smiled; "Sounds excellent to me. I will drink whatever the doctor prescribes."

Marlene stood on tiptoe and kissed his cheek. "OK partner, follow me to my apartment building. I will meet you in the foyer and help you to get past our grumpy old security man".

53.

Just a Friend of Mine.

Marlene's Pretoria Apartment.

The décor of Marlene's apartment had a modern touch and was evident of her fine taste. She favoured large paintings that depicted South African beach and mountain scenes. The music cabinet was a sophisticated electronic installation and produced professional sound. Grant sat on the love seat and looked at her where she was selecting a CD.

"I suppose your music taste will be Andrew Lloyd Webber or something similar or do you prefer the classics?" Marlene asked over her shoulder.

"That's OK and I can listen to classics, if it is not too heavy - but I don't mind listening to country music".

Marlene turned to him with a few CD cases in her hands, "That's a surprise. Where did you acquire your taste for country? I thought your upbringing was very English."

"My mother was Afrikaans and she liked country. I can remember her playing records of Ernest Tubb, Roy Rogers, Gene Autry, Roy Drusky, Patsy Cline, Faron Young and the like."

"And do you really like to listen to that" Marlene smiled but was somewhat surprised.

"The CD-players in my cars are loaded with country music, and yes I listen to it - if Peter is not with me. He likes to listen to southern gospel-stuff. Perhaps his is also a sort of country taste. What do you prefer?"

Marlene still looked surprised and then at the albums in her hands, "You, an Englishman, and you like country music. Still sounds strange to me? "

Grant raised his shoulders and smiled while she said; "Well, I prefer Verdi's music and the like, but perhaps this evening we could compromise by listening to the rock music of the all female Belgian Group - Vaya Con Dios. Have you heard of them?'

Grant nodded and the rich sound and voices gave just the right background to their togetherness. Marlene went to the kitchen and after a while retuned with two the glass-mugs filled with whipped cream on their Irish coffees. She took place next to Grant and for a while they sat in silence and listened the popular group and the words of their song; 'Still a Man'

'Call him anything you can
A sinner or a saint
Call him a boozer
A winner or a looser
He is still a man.

Grant turned to Rosemary, took her hand, and said, "Now you know my whole history from day one but please tell me all about yourself - I know very little about you".

Rosemary squeezed his hand slightly and realized that she could easily come to like this man very much and the memories of Meyer were rather vague right now. It is seldom that she still thinks about her deceased friend, and suddenly she had the urge to take Grant into her confidence and tell him about her past. Or rather as much as what will be good for their friendship.

"Where shall I start?" she asked.

Grant smiled, "Right from the beginning with 'I was born ...'"

Rosemary moved closer to him and took his hand in both hers. "Grant, some of what I am going to tell you are not all very pleasant and I trust you to keep it for yourself. For what I am going to tell you will leave me a little, shall I say, - vulnerable?"

Grant stroked her arm, "Buddha said, 'A good friend is someone who keeps his friend's secret, a secret'. You can rely on me to do so Marge".

She had a dream-like look in her eyes while she gave an account of her early circumstances, and Grant decided not to interrupt her story. Marjory Brooks' mother was the daughter of a Greek immigrant that owned a convenience store in the small mining town of Barberton. Her mother fell in love with the son of a staunch, wealthy Afrikaner attorney who was also a political and church leader. Their love grew and she fell pregnant at the age of nineteen. When her lover told his father that he wanted to marry her - all hell broke loose. It was unheard of in those days that an Afrikaner boy would marry a foreigner - let alone someone from Greece. Like most non-Germanic nations, Greeks were not regarded as suitable human material to be assimilated completely into the Afrikaner community.

To silence matters and dissolve the embarrassment that the son caused his family the attorney confronted her mother's parents with a pre-conditioned unrealistic huge amount in settlement of his business. Her grandparents could accept the unreal big offer – only if they also accepted to leave town. If they refused, they had to face the consequences of financial ruin as a result of the termination of their bank's credit facilities. The attorney was a member of the board of the bank where they operated their business account, and he would make sure that their overdraught facilities be cancelled and called up with immediate effect. However, should they accept the offer and leave town immediately, a separate trust fund would be created that would take care of the education of their daughter's baby - until her twenty-filth birthday or – until no further funds were required to ensure the child's career.

Marjory still held on to Grant's hand. "My grandparents were then not only forced to sell their business, but he did so in the best interest of his family. My mother was her parent's only child and the small family then moved to Cape Town where I was born and raised. I never knew my real father or who his family was, and my mother never talked about him. She told me it was not important because my father died in the meantime – shortly after I was born.

"Did your mother ever married later on?" Grant was trying to find out from where she got her last name.

'Yes. She married David Brooks when he was still a young medical student. I think she also loved him very much. Unfortunately he died in a car crash before he even completed his studies. I was too small when he died and I can't really remember much of my stepfather. At least from him I got my last name. Shortly after I graduated my mother died and from then on I was pretty much on my own".

"So you never heard anything about your own father's family again?" Grant saw the teary glimmer in Marjory eyes and it filled him with compassion.

"Not really. At my mother's funeral I heard with great shock, from a distant relative, that for a time being, there was some gossip that my biological father may actually still be alive and married to an Afrikaans woman. Rumour has it further that He became a wealthy businessman and inherited the family fortune that his trenched old lawyer father accumulated. I decided that as far as I am concerned he died, and I was not interested to find out anything about my family's ill-fated past. On the other hand, because I was also an only child, I inherited enough from my mother to enjoy the independent life I am living – to this day.

Marjory did not tell Grant that she was also told that the availability of abundant funds for her to complete her studies, and the comfortable inheritance she received from her mother was in fact her father's way to make up for the unhappiness of their youth - with money. Marjory therefore had the good prospect to concentrate full-time to her studies until she had completed her doctorate. It also allowed her to go on an extended international travel program abroad. Upon her return she still had enough capital to form the communications practice in partnership with Arnold Meyer.

Grant thought the moment was right to talk openly. "What can you tell me about Arnold Meyer?" As a reporter, Grant knew about Meyer's anti-apartheid articles that appeared in several local and international media. He was an amateur golf champion and on his way to be good possible follow-up for Gary Player. Then a terribly tragedy struck - he was killed during a media visit to the Angolan border war zone.

"I suppose you know how he was killed and that he had a passion for good sportsmanship, fellowship, and peace. I think that is why he was such a popular golfer. But on the other hand, he was also defying the Botha government with his activism, which he referred to as - "Stop the Bloody Border War' which he ran on behalf of the 'Mothers of South Africa'.

Marjory continued told Grant more about Meyer and how he was of the opinion that the border war was not about fighting communism but about fighting the ANC, and what would result from the end result of their aims. He was in favour of a democratically elected government for South Africa. Despite the fact that, should a black majority take over the government rule, it would lead to the demise of the Nationalist Party and the equality of all the races in South Africa. In his eyes the border war was really a off-premise racial war. On top of that, he said that greed also played a role. Many industrial and financial suppliers to the armament industry had strong political party links - who benefitted financially For this reason they wanted to drag out the conflict as long as possible"

When she became silent Grant asked, "How did you feel about his sentiments?"

Marjory thought for a while and the carefully tried to sum up how she saw matters, "Taking my own background into account and how my family were also, to certain extend, the victims of racial undertones, it's understandable that I sided with his cause. But what really made me realize how vulnerable you can become when you have an alternative point of view, was when Arnold received those many subtle 'warnings' and 'advice' from several influential government figures, to cool his political sentiments. But because of his popularity as a promising golf player, it was clear that the Security Police could not easily lock him up under the ninety-day act, or get him banned out of the country - as they did with so many other journalists and writers. Perhaps you could remember know someone once wrote a letter to the Editor of the Johannesburg Star, and speculated that there is the possibility that Arnold was the victim of a complot by the Civil Co-operation Bureau - and in what happened to him was perhaps how they helped the Security Police to get him out of the way"

Grant did not want the conversation to lose its budding intimacy and trust, "As far as I know the CCB's original job was to manage all misinformation, discredit and intimidation projects aimed at the then banned ANC. But, hey, I understand what you are talking about".

Marjory thought for a while and then added, "Yes I know but there were allegations of killings against the CCB that came forth during the 1990 Harmse Commission's inquest into the murder of the Wits University academic, David Webster. I will not be surprised if the Mandela government decide, in the near future, to also look into the circumstances that shrouded Arnold's so-called 'death by enemy ambush'.

Marjory sensed Grant's unease over the political nuance that crept into their conversation and leaned over and pressed against Grant, "Let's be naughty and have another round of Irish Coffees. OK".

286

Grant took her face in his hands and kissed her lightly on the lips. She pulled away and stood up.

In the background the Vaya Con Dios group sang
'Maybe things will get better, if I learn to be patient.
What I wanted was love and not imitation.
And I know it; we're heading for a fall"

They drank their Irish coffee in silence, sitting close together. They both knew that they were also heading for something - a better partnership or perhaps a more intimate friendship? Could they venture love?

"Were you and Arnold lovers?" leniency sounded in Grant's voice.

"Yes and no. His death came too early - so I guess he was just a friend of mine" Marlene was teary and Grant wondered if she perhaps did meet up with her biological father – sometime in the past. However he decided to leave it to her to talk about that at the right moment, if and whenever she would be ready to do so. Right now he felt deeply sorry for her. She had a terrible life of sadness through a series of untimely deaths of her loved ones.

They sipped the last of their coffee in silence and in deep thought. The similarities in their emotional lives were foremost in their minds - she lost Arnold and he lost Anna. They both understood what each other had to endure because they both lost something good, solid and valuable. They lost the advantage to trust their vulnerability to someone who is prepared to do the same – without being concerned about it.

They looked each other in the eyes, seeking confirmation for their thoughts, tenderly embraced and whispered;

"Marjory?"

"Julius?"

They moved still closer and while Brooks and Grand kissed The Vaya Con Dios group sang;

"Something's got a hold on me.
Yea, Yea, it must be love"

54.

DEAD MAN'S SILENCE.

KURTZ'S OFFICE, KEMPTON PARK

Julius Grant exceeded the speed limit of a hundred and twenty by thirty kilometres per hour on the freeway to Africair. The mid Monday morning traffic and absence of patrol cars allowed him to reach the aircraft manufacturer in record time. Kurtz phoned and said that he had a few urgent last minute things to discus and finalize before their departure for Malaysia.

Apart from the normal organisational issues, Grant also had a few questions to put to his new corporate friend. He still wondered about Faber's real idea behind the silly little game that he played. Was it really a game? And why is Faber also part of the team going to Malaysia? He also wanted to know more about the role that Gareth Williams played in the past. As yet Kurtz has not spoken a word about this man's mysterious death and what his real mission would have been.

A young security guard passed him through the steel gates without asking as much as a question. Faber was nowhere to be seen -perhaps he too was busy packing for the oriental air-show. Miss Glynis was more stuck-up than usual. To hell with you old hag, Grant thought and walked right past her into Kurtz's office, not waiting to reply to her request if he would like to be served some tea.

Kurtz was on the phone talking to De Witt. He nodded to whatever the Chairman was telling him, looked up at Grant and signalled him to the conference table. In the meantime Miss Glynis brought tea and flatly ignored Grant. He took a good look at her and wondered what on earth made the poor old thing ran off the rails - she looked like the typical soured old spinster.

Kurtz hung up and came to the table and said to Grant with a smile, "Let me show you how to pour tea" He took a seat opposite Grant, served the tea and stirred his with rapidity. The porcelain cup rang with the sound of a travel-alarm. He was clearly in a hurry and under some stress.

"That was the Old Man that called - he is a cunning old fox you know. Since we had our meeting at the testing range he has tied-up a few neat business knots for us. He also got the total support of Mandela and Mahatir of Malaysia to sign a letter of intent at the air-show, right after the Martial Eagle made its demo flight in front of the Royal Suite of the stadium. So your plan for a big media conference right after the show - to witness the main figures signing and shaking hands, is on. You can now go full blast ahead with your news releases and media invitations. I also want you to spare no cost with the social function afterwards."

Grant and Kurtz then ran through the program blow by blow to ensure that they tied-up all the loose ends. The detail action list covered twenty pages. In between they made calls and drew-up faxes for Miss Glynis to transmit to just about all four corners of the world. Grant called his office several times to dictate tasks to Connie or alert Marjory on certain developments or movements and placement of dignitaries. It was just before lunch before they could close their files and sit back for another cup of tea.

This time Kurtz stirred his tea very leisurely. He ran his thoughts over the ground which they covered. "I think we've got it all in the bag now. Do you agree Julius? It looks if something is still bothering you."

"As far as our project is progressing, I cannot complain. I had wonderful support from just all the people here at Africair and that always makes things easier. But you are right. I still need to know more about a few things." Grant left his tea untouched and instead poured a glass of water.

"Like?" Kurtz slanted his head.

"Like what is the sense behind what Faber tried to do".

Kurtz then called Miss Glynis and asked her to hold his calls and arrange lunch for them at the management lounge, he returned to Grant; "Faber works for Fischer. I confronted him and said we see this whole damn thing in a very serious light. Fischer said that it sounded to him like a joke and that he would look into the matter. A few days later he turned up with Faber here in my office, requesting to hear the voice-message that you heard. I told them that I did not have a recording but that you clearly recognized Faber's voice. They took this as a strong point of departure and pointed out that Faber did not even know where your home is. They said they would do nothing to hinder you as they see you as perhaps a valuable partner to save our company and the aviation industry of this country. They were sorry to hear about your son Peter and offered to assist with the investigation of the whole matter."

"Do you believe their story? I mean to say the way they put it, makes me looking a little silly." Grant sounded very sceptical.

"No I do not believe that this is a joke. I believe they are up to something sinister. I have heard too many rumours of right-wing activities trying to undermine or scupper the South Africa's armaments industry. I tried to scare them into caution by saying that we wired your house for protection and appointed an independent security firm to patrol and protect your property." Kurtz was clearly embarrassed by the incident.

Grant responded with a crooked smile, shaking his head; "The truth is that I did make such appointments. Peter arranged for a friend of his to replace our burglar system, but that is all we have done. The whole affair sounds ridiculous."

Kurtz said quickly; "When I returned from our planning session I visited Peter in the hospital. He told me about his friend's security company who did your installation. I made contact with that firm and arranged for the full security service, which includes regular car and helicopter patrols and much more".

Grant was surprised. "Thank you Johan, but what would the cost of that come to?"

"For you my friend – absolutely nothing. Africair picked-up the tab and I am not going to discuss this any further and I do have my good reasons for doing so."

Grant shook his head. He was clearly impressed by the way Kurtz ran matters. All he could do was to thank him for his concerned effort.

Kurtz asked; "Any more questions?"

Grant leaned forward; "Yes. What can you tell me about Gareth Williams? I know nothing more apart from what I read in the papers."

Kurtz thought for a while; "I will try to tell you in as short as possible way what sat behind the Williams visit, as seen from my point of view. But I must warn you that the maze of the international armaments industry is a perplexing world with networks of deceit and delusions and kick-backs - as if I need to remind you about this fact"

"I have learned that much many years ago from my father, who was an editor of Jane's Defences Weekly Magazine". While Grant spoke, he only then realized the depth of his father's remarks that he made at times when he talked at their dinner table about the trends in armaments sales around the world.

Kurtz continued; "Let me give you my picture of how things stand at this stage, as far as South Africa's armaments production is concerned. I will also show you how it ties in with the so-called informal or private visit of Gareth Williams to attend the Rugby World Cup finals". Kurtz looked at his watch and decided there was enough time before lunch to fill Grant in on the situation.

Kurtz told Grant that the newly democratic elected majority black government of the New South Africa inherited a bag full of bad and good things from the Apartheid Regime. One of these legacies was the very competent and comprehensive armaments industry that was earning annually up to five billion dollars in foreign exchange. They were selling mostly to markets that were not fully serviced by American, British, French and German manufacturers.

Kurtz continued; "Soon after FW de Klerck legitimized the ANC and released Mandela from jail and even before the outcome of the elections, the World Powers realized that shortly, in historical terms, there would be a black-led government in South Africa. They would then become the owners of a sophisticated armaments industry with an immense production output. You and I know that our industry produces more than three hundred types of systems, weapons and equipment. Virtually anything, right up to a nuclear bomb, can be bought at our armaments-supermarket. They also realized that with the active border war coming to an end there would be less demand for this output and that exports may be the answer for the South Africans."

Grant remarked, "I suppose that accounts for the recent flooding of South African military wares on all the international defence trade shows and, not only for the reason that South Africa is welcomed back into the world market fold".

"Exactly! The critical question now is - who will be their most important clients". Kurtz enjoyed the strategic exercise.

Grant knew the answer; "I suppose all those countries that do not have access to the capabilities of the Americans and their former Western Allies".

"Correct. And it is clear who they are." Kurtz raised his thick eyebrows.

Grant changed his posture to relieve the pain in his ankle. Someday I have to do something about this stiff joint of mine - I cannot go on limping around for the rest of my time, he thought quickly while listening to the Africair CEO.

Kurtz continued, "Suddenly the free world had a problem on their hands. How to contain the South African situation is the big question now."

According to Kurtz the biggest threat was the independence that the industry developed during the years of market isolation. "So you see, on the one hand the arms embargo supported the Anti-Apartheid movement, but it also hatched a new monster to reckon with. I know, in world terms, the South Africans only have an insignificant point five percent of the armaments market. But should we get a few large orders from oil-producing countries and embark onto a technology and production exchange-program, this young monster could develop into milliards of Spielberg-sized creatures. And this, my friend, is not public knowledge".

Grant leaned with his arms on the table, "So what is the option now for the Americans, the Brits and their international friends?"

Kurtz told him that the world powers are looking at a number of approaches and options. It would be unwise to overtly start a movement to dismantle the industry, so as to eliminate the possibility of an African source that could supply negative intended forces. Forces, which in time, would demand costly war-efforts to halt them from attaining their destructive or terrorist supported objectives. What could go unnoticed or be tolerated by world opinion was to apply the powers of sheer competition to knock the South African efforts out of the armaments marketplace.

Kurtz expanded; "You know when we would for instance bid against the Americans for, say a transport helicopter contract, they are economically so powerful that their offer could include a few helicopters with training-packages for free, which makes it impossible for us to equal theirs". The corners of his mouth dropped and he raised his hands as a submission to despair.

"What other hidden possibilities are there to get us out of the marketplace?" Grant knew from his days as a journalist that under the surface there was always an undercurrent that carried a story behind the story.

"Several. Countries like the USA and Britain use their Presidents and Royalties to smooth relations between their industries and the forces of potential buying governments. Then there is always the possibility of undercover action, which is really criminal and, could take on many forms. Like threats, sabotage, terrorism and even murders. Remember what happened to Gerald Bull, the guy who assisted us with the development of our howitzer - that is still matchless in its class? He was killed surreptitiously in front of his Paris apartment, some years ago." Said Kurtz

"Did this approach tie-up with the death of Gareth Williams?" Grant's straight question silenced Kurtz for a while.

"Yes and no. Gareth Williams was not only a seasoned military man but also a brilliant political and international business strategist which is a rare combination of qualities to be found in a single person. He had a good insight on post-Cold War world developments and interests. He was of the opinion that there could be a good compromise between all these approaches towards South Africa. To eliminate the threat that was build into the comprehensive capability of the South African armaments industry he suggested that the state-owned manufacturer, namely the Denel Group, privatize and that one of the major international weapons manufacturers of the world take up shares in the South African company. In that way they would have representation on that company's board and have control over the manufacturing programs and the clients to whom the country would sell their weapons of mass destruction.

"But that would still leave them in a position as total system suppliers. On the other hand, what's in it for the New South African Government?" Grant had an idea what it could be but he wanted to hear Kurtz's argument.

"That was exactly the reason for Williams' visit. He was actually here, not to attend the football match, but to convince the South African Minister of Defence, Joe Modise, of the benefits in selling the South African Government's shares in the Denel group." Kurtz looked up at Miss Glynis who entered the office.

"Mr. Kurtz, Mr. Jack du Preez phoned to remind you of your luncheon date at the manager's dining room with him and his American guest from Miami." She waited for his response.

"Tell Jack I will be there in ten minutes and I am brining Julius Grant along."

Grant waited for Kurtz to continue, "The immediate benefit is in the vicinity of three billion dollars cash for this government for the value of its shares. It could also mean that Denel and its new international partners could do joint marketing, which could save many thousands of jobs for the local industry.

Grant voiced his agreement, "And this is what this government desperately need now. South Africa desperately needs money to relieve the housing shortage and create jobs for our people through large civil projects to upgrade the infrastructure of this country. We still have an unreal, unheard of unemployment figure of forty five percent, you know".

Kurtz eventually came round to Grant's question, "Who-ever killed Williams wanted to stop him and what he stood for. He was earmarked as the person to even the playing field for the privatization of the country's armaments industry. Now, I am afraid his talents and this opportunity is just about lost"

Grant leaned forward and asked softly, "Who were his killers?"

Kurtz looked at Grant now eagerly awaiting his answer. Somehow he knew that whatever he said now would influence Grant a great deal, "I am honestly not sure and it makes me most uncomfortable. It could be just a normal car-jack fatality - that is a daily occurrence here in Johannesburg; It could be an international political plot; or a market-related hit-job as I described to you. Or, maybe even an Afrikaner right-wing plot to prevent outside interference. Whichever way you look at it, what we are left with is a dead man's silence."

Grant looked at Kurtz for a while. He just knew that the man was not hiding anything. "What made you think it could be right wing stuff?"

"A reliable informant told me last week that he does not have a leg to stand on and he does not want to mention names, but he has a suspicion that right here in Africair there are key right-wing supporters that may be contemplating disruption. What it would be, he could or would not tell. But he heard whispers in the assembly plant of the Martial Eagle and he does not like it one bit, he said. He will, however, keep me posted"

Grant smiled. "Who is this man or your informant as you called him?"

Kurtz sighed, eyed Grant from under his lowered eyebrows and said softly, "This he, is actually a woman".

"Rosemary Barnard?" Grant's eyes widened.

"Yes" Kurtz crossed his lips with his forefinger, requesting Grant's confidentiality.

"It is time to go, Sir" Miss Glynis entered the room so quietly that they were not sure how long she stood there behind them or how much she heard.

Kurtz, now clearly nettled stood up briskly, "Let's go and have lunch with Jack du Preez and his visitor. I think you should also meet Mister Brian Boddington from Florida. He is a disabled Vietnam Veteran who was also a helicopter pilot in that war."

55.

THE MAGIC OF MALAYSIA.

FLIGHT TO SINGAPORE.

Julius Grant always enjoyed flying eastward with Singapore Air. The flight from Johannesburg to the island city comprised of only business and economical classes but the seating was comfortable. Grant thought that the outstanding service by its flight attendants and the excellent menu made it one of the world's best carriers. For several reasons he preferred it above the Malaysian Air services - despite the longer flight and obligatory step-over at Singapore.

Grant paged through his diary, which Connie Heyneken updated in detail before they left Johannesburg. From Singapore it was a two-hour hop to Kuala Lumpur where Connie arranged several appointments for him with the Malaysian newspapers, a radio station and their main television network.

It was Grant's third visit to the Malaysian Peninsula with its more than one-hundred hundred islands. He has never crossed the South China Sea to the eastern provinces of Sabah and Sarawak on the Island of Borneo - but hoped to visit them someday after the air-show. To Grant there is nowhere in the world a country as exotic as Malaysia. The sheer fabric of the country, like their batik, is multi-coloured and multi-hued. He admired the singleness of purpose in the national vision of the richly mixed populace of Malays, Chinese, and Indians that united them to strive towards becoming a fully developed nation by the year 2020.

Grant was fascinated by the country's impenetrable evergreen rainforests that covered the greater part of central Malaya. The historian J Kennedy of the University of Liverpool told him that, in prehistoric times, this peninsula was described as a bridge which was used by successive generations of migrant peoples in their passage southwards from the Asian mainland to the island archipelago of South East Asia.

Kennedy remarked that as a result of the dense and mountainous tropical jungle the settlements were almost exclusively coastal based. To a large extend this is still the trend. Should one take into account that Malaysia is a comparatively small country, a little larger than England, while only about a quarter of its area offers normal habitation, it is understandable why the country and its cities give the impression of being densely populated country.

Of all the cities Grant preferred Kuala Lumpur, or KL as the locals called the old town. He loved to go for long walks in the city of muddy rivers. And he particularly enjoyed the delicious food that was served in the many small street café's in Petalang Street. He promised Connie that he would take her there for the best cuisine experience of her life, let alone sauntering through the maze of this popular marketplace.

Their flight-plan would bring them to Singapore at just after six in the morning. The connection flight would land them at KL International Airport at around eight o clock. Their first meeting was scheduled for ten-o-clock at the offices of the "Financial News" with Editor John Toot. Then a lunch date with Eric Wang of "The Star", followed by the radio and television interviews during the late afternoon. At about Sunday-noon they would fly to the island of Lankawi to join the rest of the Africair team.

Africair's technical, communications and marketing teams arrived at the small Island during the previous weekend. They had to assemble the show stand and exhibitions. The technical team, who flew with the Russian Antonof aircraft that transported the two attack helicopters in a semi-knocked-down status to Lankawi, would by now be doing final test-flights to have them ready for the opening ceremony that was scheduled for the following Tuesday morning.

It was close to midnight and the flight attendants folded the movie-screen back and prepared the cabin for the remainder of the night before they would wake the passengers for breakfast. Grant watched them through sleepy eyes yet admired the blue paisley patterns of their uniforms that tightly wrapped their petite figures. He wondered what would happen to any of these girls, should they gain only a few pounds in weight? Perhaps the overweight girls will be forced to join the ground staff or perhaps risk being fired?

Beside him Connie tried to adjust her sleeping position. She dozed off shortly after dinner. Grant knew that she and his son went to a house party the previous evening and because Peter only returned shortly before daybreak – she must be a little pooped-out. Connie told him that she and Peter have become really good friends since they met in the hospital and that they were looking forward to their planned scuba-trip to the islands.

Just before he dropped off to sleep, Grant left his seat to visit the toilet facility but had to wait for a vacancy.

He looked back towards his seat when behind him, a voice asked; "Are you still awake?" He turned and stood face to face with Fredrick Kramer the chief of Africair's Security Department.

"Hello Fred - this is a surprise. I did not know that you were also booked on this flight. How are you doing?" Grant looked at him and thought he had a stereo-typed appearance that would easily qualify him in as the character of an intelligence official in a spy movie. His shiny-creamed hairstyle and pencil-thin moustache suited his cold blue eyes that squinted guardedly through horn-rimmed glasses. Kramer wore a conservative patterned suit with a corporate tie. The built-up heels of his shoes did not do much to improve his height. Grant wondered into which type of personality pigeonhole he should sort Kramer. He decided to approach him in a tentative and objective manner until he was sure of what this man's loyalty was like. By now Grant has learned that there were diverse categories of dedication to duty in the cadres of Africair.

"I am just fine Grant. I saw you leaving your seat and followed you, hoping that I could have a word with you. That is to say if this is a good time for you - otherwise I would like to speak to you before we reach Lankawi" Kramer beamed an air of importance.

"Now is as good a time as any. But let me first answer to Mother-nature's call and I will be with you".

"There is an empty seat next to mine - if that's OK with you to join me" Kramer signalled.

Grant looked a little puzzled, "Sure".

In the meantime Kramer peeped behind the kitchen's curtain and ordered coffee for them while he waited for Grant before making their way to Kramer's seat, in the economical class.

"How come you are on this flight? I would have thought that you were with the rest of the team in Langkawi by now". Grant asked and wondered what Kramer had on his mind. It was his first opportunity to have a conversation with this man alone.

Kramer took a careful sip from his cup and said, "I had to tend to business that turned up unexpectedly. On the other hand, during an international trade show my task seems to be fairly simple. All I need to do is to coordinate my team's security activities with that of the host country, or as in this case, the Malaysian security police."

"So your team is there already?" Grant added to the small talk.

"Yes and Faber is running the show until I arrive". Kramer did not sound too convincing.

"Oh. And what are their activities, as you call it". Grant still lacked interest in the moment.

"They patrol and guard our exhibition stands and the area's where our aircraft are parked. I need to assist the Malaysian authorities with an inspection of dangerous weapons and must sign-off a declaration which states that none of our exhibits carry or are charged with live ammunition of any calibre." Kramer sounded on top of his delegated responsibilities.

"Have you had any problems of this kind in the past?" Grant tried out of politeness, to keep the conversation going while their coffee lasted.

"Bar petty theft of television monitors and personal things like cameras, not really anything worth mentioning. Except maybe . . ." Kramer shrugged his shoulder as if what he thought was an exception not worth mentioning.

Grant persisted "Except what?"

Kramer turned to Grant. "The occasional loitering of unauthorised persons in the exhibition stands. We had a few instances where we caught persons who hung around our equipment and whom we caught during the night, going over our hardware"

"And who were these persons – souvenir hunters?" Grant pretended to be ignorant.

Kramer placed his empty cup in the seat pocket in front of him, "We never really could to establish that for certain. Invariably we turn these trespassers over to the local authorities and - never hear a word again. So they could be over-zealous competition, petty thieves, souvenir hunters - or whatever".

"Like industrial spies?" Grant smiled at him but he maintained his serious expression.

Kramer looked at his hands; "Perhaps yes, but most likely - well trained saboteurs".

Grant gave him a look of disbelief and Kramer quickly explained, "Why do you think there are so many flying disasters or mishaps during international air shows? We all tend to accept it is because the show pilots are reckless in their effort to show-off the capabilities of their aircraft or trying to make a name from themselves. Perhaps that is so but over the years there were too many cases written-off as so-called pilot's-error or faulty execution of a complicated display-envelope. On the other hand stringent supervised aviation mechanics are in most of the cases, quite confident that some form of sabotage must have taken place - or played a role".

Grant remembered several mishaps that took place over the years at Farnborough, Le Bourghe and at several displays in the USA, but still asked, "Are you serious?"

Kramer knotted his hands fingers his head; "Yes I am afraid that is the case. At this stage we have displayed the Martial Eagle at more than ten air shows abroad, and also put them in service at shows and ceremonies in South Africa - in the recent past. In all of these demonstrations we made use of the same attack helicopter. Although this machine received the best logistical support possible, by now it could have developed some undetected mechanical or electronic weakness after all these many hours. On the other hand, the South African chopper is a new bird in the cage and it most certainly poses tough competition out there for other machines in its class. I have met and listened to some of these so-called marketing agents trying to sell their gunships. To them selling these gunships is deadly serious business."

"Is that true?" Grant looked at Kramer and thought about the many cloak and dagger stories that he heard about that were connected with international arms acquisitioning.

Kramer tried to smile, Present company excluded - I am convinced that some of those guys selling these mechanical slayers are killers themselves".

Grant tried to sound unconvinced; "Do you have any evidence of any incidents?

Kramer studied his hands again before looking Grant in the eyes, "I am afraid so. During the UN Arms-embargo, South African's got hold of a lot of foreign technology in various , how shall I say - underhanded ways".

Grant tried to sound not too informed because he sensed that Kramer enjoyed the power brought about by the privilege of having secret knowledge, "I know about some of those clandestine deals but do not accept that it necessarily bore a criminal element".

Kramer leaned towards Grant and whispered, "Oh it's quite real. But the actual reason for my delay in departure was brought about by an unbelievable piece of information that I picked up. It confirmed a growing suspicion that I have had for some months now. I have little to go on, but there may be some foul play looming at this Lankawi show. Unfortunately it sounds so bizarre that right now, nobody would believe me".

"Did you share your suspicion with our guys at Military Intelligence?" Grant's asked.

"What I found out is so serious that I wanted to unearth more facts before I register my suspicion. But on the other hand, nowadays things are much different than it was under the old Apartheid Regime. I must confess that despite all my years of training and networking, I am progressively losing trust in my resources and secret service support systems. And what is most disturbing is that this tendency is growing amongst the old Afrikaner networks. There is a conception taking form that says that we, the security fraternity, are kissing up to the new black government, to save our jobs. In some cases that may be true, and this could result in a shocking exposure of some ugly and grotesque methods that the Apartheid Forces applied in the past. In short, I am afraid that old Father Tutu and his Truth and Reconciliation Commission are one day going to have a field-day." Kramer smiled in a crooked way and said 'You media guys are going to have a lot to write about when these stories pop the surface."

Grant looked at Kramer in silence and wondered why he trusted him with this information. He now clearly succeeded in putting him on the alert again. Just as he started to enjoy being content with himself, Peter and Connie's new friendship, and naturally - with the new and kindly feelings that started to develop between him and Marjory Brooks. "Tell me more about this bizarre omen you picked-up" Grant asked.

Kramer stood up and stretched himself in the isle, then bowed down to Grant and said in a hushed voice "My friend, at this stage I can't tell you anymore. Because you are a highly regarded as a communication man I do not want to teach you how to suck eggs. I am quite sure that in your briefcase you have several versions of draft news releases that are each one based on several anticipated outcomes that could happen during this show. Some of them will most certainly be exciting business success announcements. But I am sure, that a smart and experienced communicator like you will also carry well contemplated statements and appropriate announcements - should the Martial Eagle be involved in any form of mishap or disaster. Am I Right? So - magic or mayhem awaits us in Malaysia. Of this I am quite convinced. Please excuse me now. On top of all these concerns to take care of, I also have - a running tummy." Kramer pulled a face and walked down the aisle.

Grant returned to his seat. His hope to catch a little sleep was now out of the question.

56.

SNAPSHOTS AND SHARKS.

STRAIT OF MALACCA

John Molape's last day of his life started out with much excitement. The weather was perfect and he looked forward to the specially arranged photographic-session from the open door of the light helicopter that his friend from Dubai, Akbar Assad chartered. He hoped that the weather would hold during the early morning, to allow him taking shots at various angles from the aircraft. He again checked the contents of his camera bag and zipped close the side pocket, where he stored the file with the information that Assad asked him to 'pick-up' and bring to Langkawi.

Molapi had to use all his skills of pretence to get hold of the original documents that contained the technical data and drawings on the workings of the martial Eagle's MSSS or Multi-Sensor-Sighting-System and the NSS or Night-sighting-System. The armaments industry was a new and unfamiliar environment to him and he was still not familiar with all the military acronyms and, he knew it somewhat annoyed Assad. But, at least he was at the point of making a first important delivery and that would compensate for the large fee he received for his supposed free-lance work.

Fortunately he had the support and understanding of Rosemary Barnard who tried to explain to him in layman's language, how these systems were developed and operated. She gave him the documents and said, "Now take these files and go through them and try to understand as much as you can on your own. Bring them back here at about closing time this afternoon and tell me what you figured out. Then I will fill you in, the easy way. Take this shopping bag to carry them to your office and for God's Sake, don't let that Faber-creature see that you have them. If he traps you with those, you'd better tell him that you stole it from files in from my office. If you declare that I gave them to you, I will deny it and say that you always came over as a snooping little 'Tokoloshe'. Molape laughed heartily at her comparison of his six-foot-five frame to that of the little voodoo gremlin referred to by African people. She continued with her mocking; "remember, I will not defend you in any way. As a matter of fact I will rather pray that you develop at least seven types of most painful drawn-out cancer. Do you hear me my friend?" She kissed him on the cheek and pushed him out of her office.

It was a dicey job to make photocopies of the files without creating suspicion in the copy -room. Then he had very little time left to rush back to his office and scan the material. Needless to say he walked into Barnard's office shortly after five with very little general knowledge of the systems. He dispatched the document on the MSSS in the manner dictated by Assad. Here with him he now brought the documentation on the NSS.

Molape went down to the foyer of the Sheraton Lankawi Resort, where he stayed for the duration of the air-show. He was to a certain extent a little annoyed with the way Assad treated him. OK, he regularly received those fine amounts deposited into his checking account and as a result could enhance his life-style but, he did not succeed in getting hold of Assad personally. All he received was a few cryptic fax-messages, transmitted from various public locations. But he was sure that seeing him again this morning and having their meeting face to face will straighten things out again.

He immediately spotted the big Arab waiting for him in his flowing white garment at the entrance of the hotel and walked up to him. "Good morning Sir. I am John Molape from South Africa. The message I received from the front desk said that Mister Akbar Assad would arrange transport for me to the airport."

The big Egyptian bowed and said. "May God bless you sir. I am Ben Ahlib and will take you to meet with Akbar Assad at the helicopter".

"OK, let's go" Said Molape and swung his heavy camera case over his shoulder.

They drove swiftly along the winding road past Padang Matsirat towards the airport. Molape enjoyed the scenery of lush tropical forests with its rich bird-life and the scenes of padi-fields that contoured into the limestone hillsides. At the airport an unmarked Hal Chetak helicopter with two crewmembers awaited them. A lanky man, wearing an impeccable suit and large sunglasses walked up to Ahlib and without greeting Molape said in good English to the Egyptian, "May I have a word with you.?"

They walked towards a small Subaru car and stood alongside it talking and gesticulating for a while. It was quite clear that they discussed the flight-route. Ahlib took a long intensive look at the man before him and asked, "What happens if he does not want to hand the information over to me?"

The Englishman said, "Listen here Ben, the fee I am paying you is so enormous that I do not want your problems to become mine. I want the data on the Martial Eagle's NSS and that's it. And I want it in my hotel room by this evening. So go and have your fun and sort Molape out. OK?"

Ben Ahlib looked towards the helicopter and saw the pilot talking to Molape. "I will deliver the data to you but, as far as your big fee is concerned, I want to tell you here and now that this is the last mission I will be doing for you. I have a premonition that I need to walk away from your network. No more requests to Ben Ahlib. Do you understand me Mister Collins?"

Douglas Collins opened the car door and hissed; "We shall talk about that again - after you supplied me with the info."

The pilot asked Molape to board and he chose seating close to the sliding door. A while later Ahlib hopped on board and while the wining of the engines increased, cupped his hand to Molape's ear and shouted, "Mister Assad send a message saying he had to file a story and that he will be waiting for you when we get back after the photo-session".

Molape was clearly disappointed and wished to call off the outing but the Hal Chetak was already airborne. Ahlib shouted in his ear again, "We will be flying eastwards over the Straits of Malacca, and then circle the Islands of Singa Besar, Dayang Bunting and Tuba. We will allow you enough time to take nice photos of the high tumbling waterfalls, and other scenes. Then we will fly over the small islands before returning to the airport."

They kept at low altitude over the Straight for about twenty minutes. The sliding door was open and Molape hitched the seat belt around his lap. He gave it enough slack so that he could place his feet on the step-rail and lean forward. Next to him Ahlib did the same.

While they gradually gained height Molape thought again about his arrangement with Assad \, and somehow the unexpected absence of the journalist's made him somewhat uncomfortable. Now he also speculated about what would happen to him if Assad does not treat the information in an indiscreet manner when writing his news articles? Surely Faber and his boss, Fredrick Kramer will start to investigate the leak. Can he trust Rosemary Barnard should they put her under pressure? For the first time, he is seriously doubting why he got involved or doing this. Was it really for good product publicity in the interest of the company or, was it for the money now burning in his mind? Or has he been cunningly sucked into a sophisticated spy-network? Who are these people here on board with him? He never met any of them before in his life. Can he trust them? Especially, this brute of a man sitting behind him! Molapi decided to stall his negative thoughts and enjoy his new camera work.

For about an forty minutes they flew over the islands off the Lankawi coast and circled the most beautiful nature spots. Molape relaxed and plied his high-quality photographic equipment to good use. He took extraordinary shots of the Lake of the Pregnant Maiden on the Isle of Dayang Bunting. He read an article that this glorious fresh water lake is where, according to local tale, a couple which had remained childless for nineteen years drank water from the lake and subsequently she bore a baby girl.

Molape signalled to Ahlib that they could return back. He used up a thirty-six roll and was happy with his takes. Ahlib went forward and spoke to the pilot who changed course in an easterly direction, away from the islands towards the Sumatra Peninsula. He returned with head-sets and clip-on microphones and gestured to Molape to don them. Over the headphones Molape herd Ahlib's accent, "Have you brought the documents for Mister Assad"

Molape nodded, "Yes, why do you ask?'

"You must give it to me now!" Ahlib held out a hand.

"Why?" Molapi looked annoyed because of the interruption of his photo excursion.

"Because - I am telling you to do so!" Ahlib's eyes started to fare-up.

"I'll give it to Assad when I see him upon our return because I don't know you and that is that". Molape grew weary and felt how the stress built up in him.

"Listen here Molape, I am Assad's boss. So you give that information to me. OK?".

Molape instantly knew something was wide of the mark here. Why would Assad send his Boss to pick him up at the hotel? "Sorry Ben, or whatever your name is, I don't believe you"

"Listen my pretty black boy, I don't care if you believe me or not - just let me have those papers. You hear me!" Ahlib shouted at the top of his voice.

Calling him a pretty black boy outraged Molape and coming from an Arab made it worse, "Sorry but I do not have it with me. So take me to Assad and everything will work out just fine, you bloody ugly Gypo!"

Ahlib held on to the seating rail and grabbed Molape by his shirtfront. He jerked him close to his face and hissed. "Pass on that camera case of yours and let me see for myself, black boy!"

Molape clutched his case with his right hand while he tried to rid himself from Ahlib's grip. Ahlib jerked his head forward and opened a gash above Molape's left eye. Blood immediately started to flow over his eye and cheek down his collar. With his left hand, Molape brought his camera up in a short jab and broke the Egyptian's nose. Ahlib roared with pain while blood spattered in the draft that flowed through the cabin and covered their shirts and the inside of the helicopter. At that moment Molape realised that this fight could only end one-way. His death!

These bastards had no intention to let him see dry land again. Despite his bewildered mental state, he realized that his earlier suspicion was grounded and surrendering this valuable information would not save his life. It would mean that by giving the documents to Ahlib, despite the fate awaiting him, he would complete a job that he opted for under false pretences. He was indeed spying on his own country's technology! Molapi decided he would not die as a traitor, never mind how long or short his life would be.

He looked down at the water and saw that they maintained a low altitude and frantically remembered that Chubby Wilson called this flying under the radar-detection. Ahlib bashed Molapi's head twice more and jerked at his camera-case. Molapi threw the camera-strap over Ahlib's his head and started to choke him. The thin leather slid through his skin and again the Egyptian roared like a wild boar in a fight to death. Molape heard on the headset how the pilot shouted in a foreign language and it deafened his hearing. He had to prevent Ahlib from getting to the classified file and at any moment he expected Ahlib to pull out a weapon of some kind. Blood flowed profusely over Molape's face and he began losing his sight. Now he was fighting desperately like a blind man. He became aware of the excruciating pain that burned his face as if the skin was being sliced from his head.

Ahlib shouted an instruction to the pilot who banked steeply to the left and locked the Hal Chetak in a tight turn. The door opening was now a gaping hole under Molape. He felt how Ahlib released the seat strap and knew the strong man was going to push him out of the helicopter into the shark-infested water, miles away from land. Molape took his last decision. He will not allow them to get the file and, what's more, Ahlib is going to join him down there amongst the sharks. Molape released his grip on the camera strap and while Ahlib's gasping seized he shoved the camera-case in the arms of the blood-covered Arab. Ahlib eagerly grabbed the case with both hands, momentarily losing his anchor to the seat-rail. Molape then lunged forward and circled Ahlib with his muscular arms and wedged the case between them. Molapi then shut of his mind and like a pro-wrestler, flipped Ahlib and the camera case with him in a powerful backward summersault. While the whirring sound of the rotor silenced their screaming decent, they plunged into the waters of the Malacca Strait.

The pilot circled and flew very low over the boiling spot where they immersed. The bleeding bodies swiftly pulled shark-fins towards the swirling pair like an Electro-magnet. The Hal Chetak hovered for a moment and then turned east - leaving the blotch of blood and popping limbs in a hurry.

57.

FINAL COUNTDOWN.

THE DATAI HOTEL, LANKAWI.

While Molape and Ben Ahlib were devoured by sharks in a blood discoloured tropical sea, Grant and Connie's flight from Kuala Lumpur touched down at Lankawi Island's Airport. The flight offered only economy class and they were served a small snack which had to suffice till dinner. Grant was quick to assure Connie that their hotel, The Datai, was one of Malaysia's most luxurious. It was situated on the north coast of the island and has been built in a rainforest with the Macincang Mountains as backdrop. The Hotel's Beach Club is situated on the edge of the deep blue waters of the Andaman Sea and served authentic Thai cuisine. A variety of other restaurants served Malaysian and Western specialties. He promised her a super dinner that would make–up for the strange gastronomic experience they had the previous evening in KL's Petalang Street.

While they rode in the taxi to the hotel Grant thanked Connie for her assistance with the media in Kuala Lumpur. "Apart from the television interview I think that the rest of the media contacts also went very well. Due to your good preparations we can be assured of good coverage on the Martial Eagle. The fact that Mandela will be attending the official opening on Tuesday morning puts our products immediately in the limelight. Our timing to see the media in advance and giving them all the background, photos and captions, will give us the edge over those companies whose PR people did not do the same".

Connie smiled and said; "I saw that you were not very impressed by the television anchorman or woman in this case. But I also noticed how you extended your answers to cover questions that she did not ask". Connie appreciated the opportunity to be in the company of a person who knew how to handle the media in a professional way and also have the technique to handle difficult questions.

Grant looked at their tropical environment and said; "Well I suppose you know that during a media interview it is always important to start off with the reporter's question but somehow cross over to your own agenda. I always allow the media to go for the answers they want, if it is appropriate for me to comment on the topic, but I always make sure that my message somehow comes through".

As they approached The Datai Hotel's entrance Connie asked, "What is our POA this evening?"

"Goodness you sound like our military clients - what does POA stand for?"

"It means Plan of Action, Sergeant". Connie laughed and pumped Grant in the ribs.

He played along. "Well Rookie, I will let you go on a Sunday-afternoon pass but be sure to report for duty at seven this evening. Rations will be served at the Beach Club".

"OK Sergeant".

"You're dismissed - private"

Grant had a good many calls to make and he wanted to work through his action log, minute by minute until the closing day of the show. He also longed to call Marjory but she would be incommunicado while travelling with President Mandela - whose itinerary called for a stop in Singapore and Kuala Lumpur. Grant would only see her for the first time when they arrive at the opening ceremony on Tuesday morning - at about ten-o-clock. While Grant paged through his notes, the phone rang. "Yes Connie?"

"Hello Grant, sorry to disappoint you – this is Kurtz speaking".

Grant wondered what was the reason for Kurtz's call; "Hi Johan. How are you doing?"

Kurtz sounded relaxed, "I'm good man, when did you arrive Julius?"

Grant looked at his bedside clock, "About an hour ago - what's news".

"Well you should know! So far we got good coverage on television and I must congratulate you on the comprehensive article in this morning's New Straight Times". Kurtz still sounded easy

Grant also eased-up; "Thank you, Johann. As we have arranged, you will have a full audience at Tuesday's media conference, after the opening ceremony. How do things develop on the business and political fronts?'

"Just fine Julius. It is now confirmed that Mandela and Mahatir will sign the letter of intent for the exchange of aviation technology between our countries". Kurtz said.

Grant could not help to sound optimistic; "Good! - and on the business side of things?"

Kurtz cackled like Scrooge Duck; "Excellent! It looks as if the agreement between Africair and Malaya Aircraft Corporation could be signed by as early as Wednesday. Herman de Witt phoned me this morning - by the way he is still in Singapore, and trying to arrange a meeting with Malaya Aircraft Corporation's chairman for Tuesday. For his appointment he may need to fly on Tuesday to Georgetown, the capital of the island of Penang. It will mean that he will miss part of the Lankawi demonstration flight for the two country leaders, but I suppose in this case it is a matter of business before ceremonies. I have arranged for a helicopter to get him there – hopefully on time."

"Sounds good man!" Grant felt relieve to hear how his carefully planned strategy and action plans gradually turned out.

Kurtz had more o share, "But the best news of the day came in the form of a fax that I received from General Kriel from the South African Air Force. He is going to make a statement tomorrow confirming that our Air Force ordered ten Martial Eagles. Defence Minister Joe Modise informed the Cabinet that it would be rental-based as you suggested, but no reference will be made of that part of the arrangement in the official statement. So he said we may go ahead and quote him in all of our future marketing presentations. We have a client man – and for that matter, a good product reference!"

"We should drink to that, Johan" Grant was very pleased with the way the whole build-up to a potential mega partnership and supply deal was developing.

"Absolutely, my friend! - we must celebrate our success!" Kurtz was a happy man.

Grant could hear the excitement in his voice and was thankful that everything went so well for them. "All we need now is for the Royal Malaysian Air Force to sign us a contract".

"If that happens, Julius, you owe us a big party with a big bang. I mean with your forthcoming massive commission and residual income for many years down the line, you will be able to afford a swanky booze-up". Kurtz sounded as if he regained his long-lost enthusiasm for the chopper business.

Grant also laughed. "Let's not count our little eagles before they're hatched"

Suddenly Kurtz regained his usual stoic calm, "Which reminds me of a little hitch that we have encountered as far as the RMAF is concerned".

"How come?" Grant sounded worried.

Kurtz thought for a while and sighed, "One of their senior air force generals has his doubts as far as the crash-ability and survival-ability of the Martial Eagle is concerned. And, you know, perhaps he is right. All we have is our claims of competence based on our superior design. But the Martial Eagle has never been battle tested. On the other hand, our competition, the American Warrior has a long history and many incidences where these capabilities were proofed over and over in combat situations. In this area we are at a loss because, financially it was asking a little too much - to destroy a Martial Eagle just to confirm our claims that our killer-machine is based on a superior combat design".

Grant groaned; "Hell no! That is unthinkable! I can appreciate that crashing an eight ton attack chopper is not the same as running productions cars with dummy drivers slap-bang into a concrete wall full of measuring devices." Grant experienced a sinking feeling and thought that the general, whoever he may be, was just trying to be difficult. He told Kurtz so in no uncertain terms.

"I can understand your frustration Grant, but you know the failure of any kind of weapon or military system, is the last thing that any army or nation could afford. The price usually comes in precious human lives. On the other hand, there is the possibility that our competition, who monitors our every move and claim of excellence, may have planted this idea in our dear general's mind."

"Yes I suppose that is a possibility. May we be spared that - but I am afraid that until we have realistic evidence of a test of some kind or the ME's crash-ability becomes evident, we will just have to do a better selling job". Realising the importance of a lack of testing results in this area, caused Grant to lose some of his excitement.

Kurtz listened to the tone in his voice and replied, "Hey man, I think you are not always aware of the enthusiasm that your new communications and marketing approach injected into Africair. And look at the results with our own air force supporting us! I can't thank you enough for what you have done so far".

"Thank you Johan". Grant still sounded somewhat despondent.

"Cheer-up my friend and remember our countdown-meeting tomorrow afternoon".

"Will do" Grant tried to snap out of his flat mood.

"Julius, before you hang up - have you made contact with Molape yet". Kurtz sounded concerned.

"No. Why?" Grant thought that Molapi was busy with his direct media communications entertaining program.

"He left his hotel this morning and we haven't been seen since". Kurtz said

"Maybe he's exploring the island or arranged a fun outing with one of his many media contacts" Grant offered. "Maybe you're right Julius" Kurtz still did not sound too content.

58.

ADMIRE THE VENOMOUS BIRD.

ISLAND OF LANKAWI

Brian Boddington cursed the low-lying clouds that capped the Island of Lankawi with a dark blue ceiling. He looked so much forward to this day. To secure a flip this Monday morning in the Martial Eagle took time, and he had incurred a lot of expenses by making a special trip to South Africa to make the necessary arrangements. Unfortunately, as a result of stationary ground tests, he missed the opportunity to fly in the South African chopper while he was in Cape Town. However he appreciated the trouble that Jack du Preez took to fit him into their already tight demonstration schedule.

The shuttle of the Radisson's Lankawi Hotel took him right into the hanger where the Martial Eagle was parked next to a large number of other rotary-aircraft – all of different manufacture. Jack du Preez was there to greet Boddington and walked up to the side-door of the van and rolled it open.

Boddington vented his frustration from his wheel chair while still sitting in the back of the van; "Up to now the weather was clear, but somehow just after dawn this muggy tropical started to build-up."

Du Preez tried to sound jovial; "Hi! Brian. You farken old moaning bastard! Today you will be flying in a machine that eats tropical storms for breakfast". The driver of the van assisted Du Preez, to lift Boddington out on to the hanger floor and left the two men who laughed loudly and energetically shook hands.

Boddington respected the stern-faced man from the moment he met him in South Africa. They shared in the tough hardships that war-seasoned helicopter pilots have endured. Somehow they both appreciated the permission for this flight that they pried out of Kurtz during a lunch they had together at Africair's dining room.

"How's things man?" Boddington looked at the sinewy airman before him with a longing to be in his shoes, instead of being tied to a wheelchair.

"Just fine Old' Buddy. And how are you doing?' Du Preez looked at him with searching eyes.

"I am looking forward to the flip man - when do we hop?" Boddington wheeled towards the Martial Eagle.

"Right away Brian. We are just waiting for the Ground support to pull her out on the apron". Du Preez was eager to show the Martial Eagle's capabilities to the American pilot.

"And what does the weatherman say?' Boddington indicated skyward with his thumb.

"To blazes with the bloody weatherman. War doesn't care if its shower or shine - you know that. I mean to say it was not very far north from here that you had it out with those bloody Vietnamese bastards! Not so?" Du Preez severe attitude broke through his thin jovial mood.

"Yea, you're right man. I sure do know all about flying in this type of weather". Immediately Boddington knew why he was so uptight. It was on a morning like this that he left base for his last sortie. Little did he know what price he had to pay that day, only hours before he was to return to his family and home in Florida? The bravery award that he received afterwards from the President of the United States was for the lives that he saved that day, and not for the legs he lost. Now he was about to fight a war of a different kind in the form of an act to prevent future wars that may be waged as a result of South Africa's willingness to sell technology and weapon-systems, like this chopper, to America's potential adversaries.

Du Preez asked; "Would you like to take off your jacket?" The humidity was high and the heat topped ninety Fahrenheit.

"No Jack, I am OK, Jack. Just get me into your bird's cockpit" He could not take off his windbreaker because then the thin personnel-mine tightly strapped under his left arm would be showing.

To prevent the explosive device from interfering with the Martial Eagle's avionics, he replaced the magnet-attachment with about two hundred grams of sticky modeling clay. From the information and technical drawings that Du Preez gave him, he worked out the exact position and measurements where he wanted to position the time-set bomb.

During his visit to Africair's assembly plant, Du Preez went in detail through the design factors and operational characteristics of the Martial Eagle. The ruggedly built attack helicopter belied its state of the art technology. Its capability to engage in high mobility warfare with a wide range of potential threat and intensity scenarios allowed for various mission types. The Martial Eagle's avionics and weapon system gave it a multitude of attack flight-performance options. The aircraft-systems bred into the gunship with its fully integrated digital management and logistic system fulfilled the requirements needed to survive in high-intensity operations in high threat environments. It had all the potential to fulfill a stated mission successfully in any type of war against any type of weapon-system in any kind of weather.

Brian Boddington came to admire the ugly machine that was he was supposed to hate to the point of destruction, and he yearned to fly the South African chopper just once - before exploding it to bits and pieces.

Getting the crippled man into the front cockpit was much easier than the ground support staff expected. With his powerful arms Boddington lifted himself over the front cockpit-sill and lowered onto the seat. Boddington waited for Du Preez to settle into the rear cockpit from where he would run flying operations. Boddington felt close to tears when he inhaled the familiar smell of the inside of the helmet and wondered if he would ever get over his earnest desire to fly again? It burned inside him like the exhausts of the twin-engines - now heating-up on either side of the fuselage.

While strapping in and clearing out of sight of the ground crew, Boddington unzipped his jacket, opened his shirt, and slipped the small flat bomb to the floor of the cockpit. He extended his arms down the sides of his thighs and kneed the putty to a soft sticky pulp. The intercom crackled in his ears; "Are you OK old Buddy?" It scared him somewhat but then he realized that Du Preez could not see him from his elevated rear position.

"Doing just fine, Jack. Perhaps I should have taken your advice about the jacket, but I am unzipping it though" said Boddington

"In a moment the air-con will kick-in - then you would long for a pair of flight-overalls Skip"

"Shit – it sounds good Buddy", Boddington replied, and thought that it was long since somebody called me skip!"

"Brian - let's fly this piece of the fantasy" Du Preez turned his converse to the control tower. It gave Boddington time to concentrate on planting the deadly device, now lying on the cockpit floor behind his heels, in the best obscure position

Boddington dropped his head between his knees and pushed the bomb under the seat right back to where it glued on to the anchor beam of the seat. He positioned it close to the automatic crash box from where fault and failure detection of the helicopter operated and carefully avoided the switch that engaged the manual time-delayed detonation switch of the deadly weapon.

In his mind's eye he could see what the result could be should he accidentally activate the device. In the sixty seconds that the device's time-setting would allow them to vacate the target area, it would be impossible for him and Du Preez to clear from the helicopter to safety, and that would be no fun at all. Boddington grinned at the thought while he tried to wipe the sweat from his neck with his shirt sleeves. The remote detonation control unit that was designed to cause the explosion and destruction of the martial Eagle was craftily built into the armrest of his wheelchair. He planned to set it off in the next day or so, whenever the opportunity proofed appropriate. He hated the thought of destroying this technological marvel, but consoled himself with the fact that he would execute the destruction at a moment when he was sure that no lives would be in danger. That will be when the Martial Eagle would be by standing on the apron, by itself - which will be most likely during a lunch-break or - whenever the moment is right. For this purpose he will position himself in the VIP lounge – that overlooks the helicopter parking locale.

Boddington strapped up and tried to concentrate on enjoying the Martial Eagles special demonstration flight.

59.

SHOW TIME.

LANKAWI INTERNATIONAL MARITIME AND AEROSPACE EXHIBITION

"This is only the forth Lankawi International Maritime and Aerospace Exhibition or the LIMA-Air Show, as it's referred to. Although this island is fast becoming one of South-East Asia's premier meeting and exhibition destinations, it is still a long way behind the air-shows staged at Singapore, Dubai, Paris, Farnborough and not to mention all the top American venue's" said Brian Walters.

Grant was glad that he ran into his old journalist friend who was perhaps one of the foremost aviation and military writers of the day. Walters frequented all the major trade exhibits and was very knowledgeable when it came to aviation shows. They stood opposite the Africair display, which formed part of the South African Pavilion. A heavy tropical downpour drummed on the roof of the large metal hanger where the exhibits from many companies from all over the world were set up. He looked at Walters and said, "That's true Brian, but I feel that participating in any military air show without the presence of American attack helicopters, is like playing in a game room. On the other hand, we had to be here in the light of the near final phase of our bid for to supply choppers to the RMA."

Grant noticed that there was less international representation than during the previous Lankawi show and asked, "Do you really think the Lankawi show venue has the potential to promote to the level of say, a Farnborough?"

"Julius, I think it is highly unlikely. As you know Farnborough has not only been a show venue but for more than ninety years it has been a major site for continued aviation research and development activity. From the days when flying machines were textile and cane structures to today's fly-by-wire aircraft, Farnborough played a significant role in the aviation industry. Then there is also its traditional link with American aviation. You will remember that on October the 16, 1908, the Texan Samuel Franklin Cody became the first man to fly an airplane over British soil."

Grant smiled because one could always rely on Walters to come-up with an interesting titbit, "However what concerns me about this show, is the absence and non-participation of the American Warrior Attack Helicopter"

"You're right and it is the talk of the day about why the American skipped this show. On the other hand your Africair Company has an overwhelming presence with this large show stand, with its spacious and luxurious chalet for entertainment. Not disregarding the fact that you have two Martial eagles for air-displays and demonstrations." Walters gave him a wink.

"Oh yes, and for a very good reason too. Our choppers are lined up as a major attraction for tomorrow morning's opening ceremony" Grant returned the wink.

Walters laughed and nodded skyward "If weather permits" and added "but with the abundance of publicity for the Eagle that you facilitated I am sure a little weather won't steal your show".

"We will still have Mandela and Mahatir on the Grand Stand though, and they would want to see something". Grant looked up and listened to the increased sound of the falling rain.

"You're right Julius. For your part I hope the weather holds, despite the old Chinese proverb which I just thought out" Walters gave him a mischievous glance.

"What does your Chinese wisdom say, Brian?' Grant played along.

"Man that makes big splash perhaps went overboard". Walters laughed out loud and slapped the back of Grant's head and walked off.

Grand laughed at the seasoned writer's remarks but also felt how concern started up in him. Perhaps, everything is going just too well? Grant shook his head, immediately discarded the thought as silly and negative, and then made his way to the stalls where the military publications exhibited.

The first person he bumped into was Jack Kerrigan. They knew each other from the days when they were rivals. He was then a reporter for Jane's and Jack was with Defence News of Washington. In the meantime he started up his own series of publications and was well represented at air-shows with his Military Training Technology magazine.

"Did you see that I have Mandela on the front page of my issue's special supplement that covers the Lima Show?" was the first thing Kerrigan asked Grant.

"Yes I received a copy in my hotel room this morning and thanks for the coverage that you gave our Martial Eagle. How are you Jack?"

"Just fine, buddy. Unfortunately my dearest Conni couldn't make it this time but she sends her love." Kerrigan was very in love with his beautiful wife.

"May I do the unprofessional thing to thank you for the coverage you gave us in your issue" Grant squeezed his arm.

"Oh sure, but I did not exactly do you a favour. Your release was well written and well ahead of my deadline. But then I see you're also covered in Jane's, all the Alexander Shepherd Publications, and the rest of the aviation books. Not counting the exposure you had in local media. I can see that your inputs in the Africair stable are making a difference. For the first time in that company's history they have a renowned agency and a workable advertising budget. Now they are getting somewhere."

Grand thanked him for the compliment and walked past the many colourful stalls that displayed aviation equipment and systems from most of the world's major companies. Thousands of visitors walked slowly along the narrow passages and admired the stands, staffed by eager young salesmen and attractive women. Video monitors talked about products and loudspeakers bleared Malaysian music. A favourite seemed to be a song from their their hit star, Amelina who sang her song titled "Asyik. "

The exhibitors who regularly frequented the international military show-circuit over time became friends and after hours made the most of the many cocktail parties and fun that this environment offered. Grant knew enough about the world of military shows where clients are being treated and media enticed to witness demonstrations. Tons of printed matter finds their way to offices and board rooms as well as - bedrooms and classrooms on open days for the general public and students.

"Here comes mister Corporate Image" laughter arose from the circle of men and women that were gathered at the counter of Jane's Defence

Weekly magazine. Grant recognized the voice of Christopher Foss of Jane's as the heckler. With him was David Silverberg who had just joined Jack Kerrigan's outfit but still had writing ties with Armed Forces Journal International. Sharon Denny of Defence News and Paul Beaver with his camera crew, who had interviews with Grant, enjoyed his temporary embarrassment. Karen Herder from Defence News walked up to Grant and gave him a hug while he kissed her on the cheek and looked at the men.

"Don't ask me to kiss anyone of you bloody scruffy lot." They stretched out and greeted him, each with his own wisecrack or teasing remark.

"I suppose you guys are only kissing up to me as a result of the generous advertising space we took up in your lousy publications?" They booed and playfully pushed Grant around. It was clear that he enjoyed their goodwill and that they loved to tease him with his decision to leave the media world and move to the 'other side' as they mocked him.

"If you have enough Scotch and South African beer at your party after tomorrow's signing ceremony, we will perhaps consider attending your booze-up" Laughter erupted again at the remark from Shenilla Mohamed from Gulf News - whom everybody knew did not use alcohol.

"As if that is so important to you guys? There will also be enough genuine American Diet Coke for you, Shenilla" Grant smiled and wondered where was his colleague Akbar Assad. Grant regretted that he could not meet with Assad and Molape back in Johannesburg. For a fleeting moment he also realized that since he arrived, he has not yet seen Molape around. Initially he thought he would get on very well with Molapi, but somehow he was not able to get him more involved in the communications strategy and action programs. It was as if Molapi was always occupied with an unknown side-agenda of his own.

Grant spoke for a while to his friends from the media, glanced at his watch and realized that he had very little time left to get to the Africair Chalet to be in time for Kurtz's final countdown meeting. "OK, I'll see you guys tomorrow then".

Grant went back to their show stand where Rosemary Barnard issued him with a large umbrella with the corporate logo printed on the panels. From the hanger he sloshed through the heavy rain to the chalet that had an unobstructed view of the apron and runways. The four-roomed layout was filled with staff and catering people putting the final touches to Africair's media function where the guests of honour would be President Nelson Mandela and Prime Minister Dr. Mahatir.

Connie Heyneken met him at the entrance, "Here are a few notes for you. The rest of your documentation and notes as well as the latest faxes that we received from the South African Media are upstairs in the conference room. The meeting is about to start and some of the chaps are already there."

Grant took the stick-on from her, read them at a glance and said, "We have an arrangement that during the show, John Molape would take care of all the media inquiries from back home. May I have a quick word with him before the meeting starts?"

Connie pulled up her shoulders, "He has not turned up yet. From what I heard he went off on a photographic excursion with one or other Arabian or Malaysian journalists. I can't vouch for the story thou."

The small room was filled to capacity when Kurtz walked in and said, "I hope our thinking will not be as cramped as this little cubicle. This reminds me of how you get six elephants in a Morris Minor."

"How?" Asked Chubby Wilson.

"Three in front and three in the back" replied Kurtz in his normal official manner.

"Luckily there are no elephants here' replied Kramer and laughed at the CEO's dry humor.

"Only a few dirty pigs" Fischer was quick with his snide remark.

Kurtz ignored his reply, "Where is John Molape?"

Silence was the only response.

"Does he know about this meeting Miss Glynis?" Kurtz tried again.

Her eyes popped behind the fishbowl lenses, "He got the same notice like everybody else. As a matter of fact he also did not respond to any of the messages that I left for him at the hotel".

Kurtz was annoyed and wondered about the man's punctuality, "Go and get him, wherever he may be." Kurtz looked around the tabled and nodded at Kramer. "Will you please take notes Fred?"

The group went through the lengthy and detailed action list. It took them about two hours. Everything went according to plan, except for a few minor details, that could be followed-up or rectified. After they have dealt with the final point on the agenda Kurtz looked at the people around the table. Everybody longed to get out of the small stuffy conference room.

Kurtz held up a finger, "One final word. We had a request from Chubby Wilson who will be flying the second Martial Eagle to support Jack du Preez's demo. He requested that Rosemary Barnard join him in the front seat of his cockpit in an observer capacity.'

"What? - Johan, are you out of your mind?" Jack du Preez exploded with a face taking on a deep red glow. This could jeopardize or at least complicate his plans to a large extend.

"No, I am not. I am still so sound of mind to realize that Rosemary never before had the privilege to fly in our machine, and I think after all the many years and how much of her contributions went into the development on the ME - she really deserves it." Kurtz made an effort to smooth his sarcasm and hide his feelings of ill will towards Du Preez's and his continued disgruntled remarks.

"So did hundreds of others who worked on the development of the ME. Must we let them also be flipped around? It would take weeks and will be not only impractical and costly but bloody boring" Du Preez stood up and indicated that he wanted to leave.

Kurtz raised his big hand and stopped him. "Listen here Du Preez - tomorrow is Rosemary's birthday and I decided she could fly along - and fly she will"

Jack du Preez gave him a long tight-jawed stare, "OK boss - just as long as I am alone in my chopper." He turned on his heel.

"Not so fast Mister du Preez" The sarcasm bit through Kurtz's words. The rest of the meeting was stunned and sat in a state of hesitant anticipation. "You will also have a passenger, thank you."

Du Preez turned back abruptly and nearly shouted, "What?"

"Yes Sir. I decided that Mister Brian Boddington can fly again with you tomorrow."

"Hell man! But we . . ." Du Preez realized that despite the fact that Kurtz promised Boddington he would consider to arrange for him to fly in the ME he did not confirm the previous days outing with Kurtz. And Kurtz surely found out about this – unscheduled flip – and he as

CEO has the last word on who may and may not fly in the Martial Eagle.

"But what?" Kurtz cornered him.

"But it would be a risk - he is not an employee like Barnard." Du Preez got out of his tight spot real quick.

"At the previous Farnborough show you had a member of the British Royal Family aboard the Martial Eagle - can you still remember that Jack?" Kurtz asked sharply.

Jack du Preez was nearly beside himself. He walked out of the room and left the chalet by the front door. He walked through the rain to where the Martial Eagle was parked on the apron in front of the chalet. He was not aware of the warm rain falling on his bare head and shoulders. "You bloody bastard. Now you are confuculating my plan completely. I have been waiting for months to do my thing, - but I will still do it - you bloody jerk. So OK - if that is what you want, that is what you will have - and Brian Boddington's death on your conscience. He will just love dying in a helicopter. Brian baby - here comes your chance to hit the grandstand – and the headlines!"

Grant stood on the balcony of the chalet and looked down at Du Preez as he walked in the rain towards the helicopters waving his arms with frustration.

"Here is this afternoon's Kuala Lumpur Star, Grant. Look at your article -it covers four columns and I must say your photo right there makes you looks real good." Said Connie

Grant took the paper that was opened on page three from her and glanced at the copy. What also caught his eye was small item in the bottom-left of the page. The headline read. "*Show Suicide.*"

The news item told the story of a pilot's body that was found in a light transport helicopter. Apparently it landed on a small uninhibited island where the pilot clearly committed suicide. The aircraft belonged to a small charter company that operated from Georgetown on the Island of Penang. No further details were available.

60.

FAMILY SECRETS.

TANJUNG RHU RESORT, LANKAWI

Rosemary Barnard walked into room 469 of the Radisson Tanjung Rhu Resort, slammed the door shut with her heel, and threw her umbrella and briefcase on the floor. She rubbed her eyes and with a few brisk movements stripped naked, looked at the shower and then at the queen-sized bed. She was tired to the bone and chose the bed. I am relieved this day is behind me, she thought - and flopped backwards on the soft bed.

The first days preparing for a show were always hell-on-wheels. Just to get everything in place, and ready - in time for the show-evaluator's appraisal required a backbreaking effort. Rosemary positioned her against the large pillows and rubbed the itchy red lines caused by her brassiere and panties. She noticed for the first time the prints on the wall and stared disinterested at the framed scenes.

At the third of forth ring of the phone Rosemary realized that she had dropped off in a very deep sleep. A glance at the bedside clock told her that she was gone for more than an hour. She moved slowly across the wide bed and stretched for the phone.

"Is this a bad time or what?" Grant sounded unsure.

Rosemary smiled and stretched, smiled and said in a soft voice, "Hi Julius - when you call it is always a good time - or the promise of a good time." Her laugh was also soft – and contagious.

"I hope I didn't drag you out of the shower." Said Grant

"No - but I am stark naked and will be in the shower shortly - why?"

A vivid picture of Rosemary, as she was with him in his hotel-room in Hermanus flashed against the inner-wall of his mind, and he asked, "Well we kind of had an agreement to take some time off here on the island. But up to now it was such a mad rush and we did not have time to even talk yet. What do you suggest for this evening?"

Rosemary sighed. Grant placed the ball neatly in her court and she was not sure what to say, "I accepted that you may want to go with the rest of the Africair team on the Moonlight Bay cruse which the organizers of the Lima Show arranged for the exhibitors."

"My assistant Connie is apparently going, but this evening I am not in the mood for that kind of outing. Do you want to go on this trip?" Grant asked.

"Well to be honest, I took a nap when you phoned. The program says they would be leaving in about ten minutes. So, I think we have really missed the boat and also the chance to have cocktails, listen to music and watch the tropical sunset." Rosemary did not sound at all regretful.

The ball was back in Grant's court. He still felt terrible about the romantic interlude he had with Rosemary in Hermanus, but also thankful for the interruption that smothered their passionate feelings that evening. Now he was a different man and perhaps falling in love with Marjory Brooks. Grant hesitated with his response.

Rosemary sensed his discomfiture and decided to came to his rescue – and set him free, "Grant, this evening we do not have to take off where we left off in Hermanus. My, but I sound silly -what I wanted to say is that we are friends and I sincerely hope we could stay that way."

Grant breathed a near audible sigh of relief, "I appreciate your honesty Rose, and you will always be very special to me. In the meantime I will think of a place where we can have dinner. In under an hour I will pick you up at your hotel - OK?"

"I have perhaps a better idea. I am dying to see your posh resort. Why not arrange a table in any restaurant of the De Tai and I will take the shuttle and meet you there - OK?"

"Good thinking - take your time. I will make arrangements here and wait for you." Replied Grant, relived that they solved the awkwardness of their romantic interlude.

"Julius."

"Yes Rose?"

"I have a few interesting military and family secrets to share with you."

"Now you're burning me up Rosie" All of a sudden Grant's interest in the evening ahead flickered up for totally different reasons than when they started their converstion.

"See you in a bit, Julius."

About an hour later Rosemary met Grant in the foyer of the De Tai Hotel. Minutes later they were in the most exquisite surroundings with a menu in their hands that baffled their minds. It took them some time to work through it. With the assistance of an Indian waiter who formerly worked in a hotel in Durban, South Africa, they were able to make fine decisions and enjoyed their dinner.

"Tell me about those military and family secrets. You know they say that only people who can't keep a secret always craves to hear one." Grant was not only interested in the story to follow but it also made for good platonic conversation, and Rosemary Barnard was always pleasant company to be with.

"Perhaps nothing what I tell you would be news to you but in any case, the circumstances under which I heard this was most interesting - perhaps even laughable." Rosemary looked at Grant and knew that she would always be attracted to him, perhaps because he seldom spoke about himself and yet he could be great fun to be with - like the weekend they had together.

"How come?" In the background a band consisting mostly of Philippino's played Moon River and a young man sang in a voice that tried to imitate Frank Sinatra.

Rosemary leaned forward, "Last night we returned very late to our hotel - it was like past eleven. The men invited us for drinks down at the bar but I declined and went upstairs to my room. Glynis Botha, whose room is adjacent to mine, invited me in for coffee and I sort of thought I will make a quick stop-over. Shame, sometimes I feel so sorry for the old spinster."

"I've heard this is really the first time that Kurtz took her on an overseas trip?" asked Grant while unfolding his napkin.

"Yes and I think she finds it all a little overwhelming, to say the least." The waiter brought their first course and they were pleasantly surprised at how good it was.

Rosemary continued, "To make a long story short, instead of coffee we drank some of the South African wine which Molape placed in our rooms. It was not long before I noticed that the Pinotage had the better of Glynis and she became a little tearful as she told me about herself and her disillusionment with life in general"

Rosemary told Grant about Glynis' affair with Faber that went wrong many years ago. That for a time she was also secretly in love with Kurtz but never allowed it to show. How Fischer who knew about her secret love intimidated her and placed pressure on her to inform him about Kurtz's actions and the content of certain classified documents.

"But what spooked me, and that is why I would like to hear your opinion, is the whispers, as she put it, that she overheard. Glynis said it scared her to the extent that she is going to resign as soon as she arrives back in South Africa."

Grant indicated to the friendly waiter to re-charge their glasses "what spooked our old girl Glynis that much?'

"First of course the military secrets that she leaked, and I hope Glynis was not telling me a brave wine story - but I doubt it. According to her there is a serious plot by a Right Wing Afrikaner Group to sabotage the South African armaments industry and also assassinate Nelson Mandela and his designated successor, Thabo Mbeki. Apparently they are afraid that the new government will secretly supply weapons to countries that are terrorist friendly. They are of the opinion that the dismantling of the South African's nuclear capability, just before the current Mandela government took over, was not precautionary enough. Glynis is sure that they plan to go into action quite soon while they are abroad. Perhaps even now, while they are touring here in South East Asia." She looked wide-eyed at Grant and waited for his response.

Grant shook his head slowly. "You know Rosemary this sort of story has been doing the rounds since the release of Mandela from jail. But I must concede, it may be the sort of revenge that they perhaps could contemplate. You saw the mess they made with their futile attack on Homeland President Mangope, a few years ago. All in all, I would not be too concerned about these rumors."

"But what worries me Julius, is that she said people or high-ups, as she referred to them, from Africair may be involved. And she added that she has good reason to belief that it is not just talk." Rosemary's concern grew – as she recalled her conversation with Glynis.

Grant became interested, "Did she give you any indication who might be involved?"

Rosemary took a sip of wine and said, "I tried to get names from her but she said I am free to guess who is involved – but she would not mention a single name. For a moment I thought she was afraid that her room was bugged so then I started whispering names while she said nothing. But she nodded agreement when I mentioned Fischer, Du Preez, and Dr de Witt. She shook her head sideways to all the other names that I mentioned, and that included yours!"

"Thank you for your trust in me my dear? Grant laughed at her slight embarrassment.

"I started with the most unlikely persons and mentioned your name first". Marjory said that even if a bugging system were running, there would be no evidence of her calling names. I did the entire name calling and she responded in silence."

"I can see she is used to work in an environment where secrecy is a high priority."

Grant just shook his head but was disturbed by what he heard - especially because De Witt was also mentioned.

While they waited for their coffee Grant led Rosemary to the dance floor. They spoke about their Hermanus encounter and how rudely their evening was interrupted. Grant held her tight while they danced but somehow they knew that there was no magic in the evening that would lead to another flirtation. Back at the table regret set in and somehow caused Rosemary to lose her sparkle for the rest of the evening ahead, and she asked Grant to take her back to her hotel.

Grant read her mood and dropped Rosemary off at the well-lit entrance of the Tanjung Rhu Resort. It was a few minutes before midnight and he walked with her to the foyer. "I will think about what you said. Did Glynis report this to anybody, like Kurtz for instance?"

"Not to Kurtz - she is too fearful of him as her boss. But, she said that she told it earlier in the day to the only other trustworthy person in Africair."

"And who would that be?' asked Grant with a crooked eyebrow

"Fred Kramer – our security guy"

"And what was his response?" Now Julius was really caught up by Rosemary's account.

"He told her to keep quiet and tell it to nobody else. He would investigate it she said."

Grant relaxed, "Well, there you are. Things are in hand and I don't think you and I should be bothered. We have a busy day ahead of us and we will also be celebrating your birthday." Grant looked at his watch and took her in his arms and kissed her brow, "It is after midnight so it's really time to wish you - congratulations my dear friend"

Rosemary pulled back and looked up at him, "That's exactly what Kramer said to Glynis. He also said to her not to worry or doubt Herman de Witt. He mentioned to her that perhaps the only questionable thing De Witt did was to make sure that the Africair communications contract was awarded to his illegitimate daughter - your partner Dr. Marjory Brooks."

When Marjory saw how Grant's eyebrows jumped she added, "When I asked Kramer what he thinks about that - he calmly stated that this is the way Afrikaner networks operated. He also added that he believes in leaving well alone - because you all are doing such an excellent job and that the results are overwhelmingly promising."

Grant's heart skipped several beats. He held his breath for a long time. He did not want Rosemary to find out how stunned he was. He brushed her cheek and said, "It's late Rosie -good night birthday girl"

.

61.

LIVE AMMO.

LANKAWI SHOW GROUNDS

"So, Mister Communications is still having his way with our quite little avionics engineer." Christian Faber threw his zipper-bag, stuffed with brochures, on the passenger seat and slid behind the steering wheel of the small Nissan van, just as Grant and Rosemary Barnard entered the Tanjung Rhu. He was pleased that they did not spot him coming out of the resort. Faber took a narrow side-route with very little traffic - apart from the occasional moped cycles - that ran directly south towards the Lankawi airport, which was adjacent to the show-grounds.

Faber was nervous. All evening he refrained from any drinking so that he would not run the risk of bungling his midnight mission. And it was tough – a night without alcohol in his system was boring and made him restless. He flashed his security pass to the guard on duty and had no problem entering the airport and show grounds. The Nissan van rolled up to Hanger B, which accommodated the South African pavilion. Faber had keys to the small entrance that was positioned in the hanger's large sliding door.

"Hell but its dark in here" he whispered while only a dim glimmer came from the scattered night-lights. Faber closed the door behind him and gave his watery eyes time to accommodate to the semi-dark surroundings.

"I should have brought a farken flashlight - Dammit." Faber mumbled while he shuffled slowly towards Morton Engineering's exhibit of their G 12 Automatic Cannon. This was an extremely reliable combat proven weapon that was installed in several South African Defence Force armoured cars like the Ratel 20 IFV. These cannons could be installed upright, sideways, or even upside-down without affecting their performance. Due to its low recoil forces it could be fired from virtually any platform. Re-arming could be done either hydraulically or manually. It used standard HS820 ammunition. For exactly these operational friendly characteristic and it's compatibility with logistic support from ground-forces, it was also integrated onto the weapons platform of the Martial Eagle.

Faber emptied the bag and placed the printed material on a marketer's desk. He then took a large piece of cheesecloth from the bag and knelt down at the canon. He stood in this position for a few seconds and sweated profusely while listening for sounds of movements in the hanger. It was deathly quiet with only the tin roof that creaked at times. Assured that he was alone in the structure he placed the fabric on every third round in the steel belt and slipped the shinny projectiles out of its cage and into his bag. It took him less than five minutes to select and remove the ammunition. Then he went into the little office and brought back a box of blank rounds. He polished each of them before sliding them into the empty cages.

Faber congratulated himself on his plan to successfully smuggle live ammunition - in this manner - into the show area,. He slipped the live-rounds into the magazine when they were still in back in South Africa. When the Malaysian Security Team did their inspection-rounds with him - as head of show security - he made sure that he pulled only blanks for their tests. "I can thank my lucky stars that the Lankawi show security officials did not yet have trained ammunition snifter-dogs." Faber whispered to himself.

Minutes later Faber locked the small steel door behind him and complemented himself, "If you're good, you're farken good." He carried the bag with much care and drove over to the hanger where the Martial Eagle was parked. He entered in the same manner except that here it was much lighter in the aircraft hangar. Several rotary aircraft were parked in the mid-sized structure.

Faber walked past an Italian A 129 Mangusta - a helicopter that the Augusta Manufacturers were yet unable to sell to any other defence force - except to the Italian Air Force. He then took a glance at Eurocopter's Tiger - who also has had no selling success anywhere outside of France. "Hey man - selling attack helicopters is a bloody difficult job, man." He shook his head and walked on.

Faber stopped in front of the Martial Eagle. He was glad that Africair received an order from the SAAF but that's all, he thought. So they are in the same selling status as the Italians and the French. However, it is good that the Malaysians are now looking at the comprehensive bid that Africair presented. But they are dragging their feet and it may take years before they come to the point of actually acquisitioning a number of these bloody choppers. Faber's mind re-played the results that he heard at the marketing meetings.

"We Afrikaners will help you bloody Malaysians to make up your mind. Tomorrow we will give you a good demo by killing your Prime Minister with these little punchers" Faber held the bag with ammunition up to the Martial Eagle as if showing it to a live animal. "Here you are my birdie. I'm going to feed you with the stuff that kills Heads of States" He smiled and let out an ugly chuckle.

Somehow Faber felt a surge of pride at the thought that he is playing such an important role in the WAC's assassination attempt. "And to proof it - I have right here in this bag a deadly big bullet with the name of Mandela written all over it." At once he knew that after this dastardly undertaking he would never cry again for his boy who was killed by the ANC in Angola. Faber was convinced that this deadly intention was in a way his personal contribution and revenge for the death of his son, and the many young white boys who were maimed or lost their lives in vain - during the senseless border wars of South Africa.

Suddenly, the barrel of a Z.88 pistol rammed into the back of Faber's neck, "To whom are you talking old fart?"

Faber nearly had a stroke. His sudden accelerated heartbeat caused him to cough rigorously. He became dizzy and thought he was going to suffer at least a heart-attack. Then he realized that his stalker spoke in Afrikaans. He relaxed somewhat but did not move until the barrel left his neck. Behind him Jack du Preez sniggered softly as he slowly turned around.

Faber was furious, "To hell with you Jack - you nearly . . ."

"You are losing your edge old man." Du Preez pushed the pistol back under his arm.

"What the hell are you doing here?" Faber asked and placed the bag on the floor and wiped the sweat from his face with his bare hands.

Du Preez stood tall, "Checking-up on you - what else? Do you think I would fly into tomorrow's exercise depending on you alone? - While, I am not even sure if you know how to arm the Eagle's canon-system? That is something I do not want to find out too late, old Grandpa."

"Who else is here with us Jack?" Faber whispered while looking in all directions.

"Only the devil old man" said Du Preez and whispered "As you suggested old fart, let's feed this farken hungry predator."

Du Preez opened the two ammunition bins of the chin-mounted cannon. Their capacity enabled a maximum of seven hundred rounds in a ready-to-fire configuration. The dual feed system enabled the loading of ammunition combinations for more than one mission type. On the left side for soft targets and on the right side to penetrate any armoured vehicles that may be encountered.

The ammunition could be selected from the different bins on a burst-by-burst basis - to cater for different target characteristic. The ammunition belts were pre-linked with any of the combination of rounds. "Let's charge the belt on the left side." Du Preez said in a voice that sounded strange to Faber.

62.

PREMONITION.

THE DATAI HOTEL, LANKAWI.

It was just after seven-o-clock when Connie Heyneken and Julius Grant waited for their turn to be served at the breakfast buffet. She found Grant unusually quiet this morning and thought that perhaps he was also stressed out about the opening-ceremony.

Connie tried in vain to make conversation, "From an organizational point of view, everything's running just fine. But, perhaps it's my female intuition but something is bothering me. Maybe it is because I had a silly nightmare about your poor old cat and the death threats that you received in South Africa." Connie searched Grant's eyes for a message that would alleviate her concern - but he did not respond to her remark.

After a while he replied, "Kurtz uncovered that little 'Let's scare Grant' game. So I think you shouldn't be bothered. As far as today's program is concerned, I think we are past the point where we can worry about anything now. We did what we could. If something does go wrong, and like at any good wedding reception, something invariably does, we'll act as competent as possible - to try and save the day."

Grant tried to put Connie at ease without betraying his own feelings of insecurity around the Africair project. It came with Rosemary Barnard's revelation that De Witt was Marjory Brooks' biological father. He spent sleepless nights thinking about what Marjory told him how and what she went through as a young person - re-thinking his relationship with her, and analyzing her every word and action pertaining to Herman de Witt. He somehow always had the feeling that some form of non-business-type of understanding existed between them. Grant also regretted his previous snide remarks and his reference to De Witt as a stubborn old Afrikaner bull. His mind was all night long caught up in a confused turmoil.

"Have you heard anything from Marjory?" Connie asked.

Grant snapped out of his depressing thoughts, "Yes and no - I mean while I had a work-out out in the gym she left me a voice-mail message" Clark thought about the mixed feelings she added to his disposition. In a voice that carried a great deal of warmth she told him that she missed him and looked forward to whatever fun was in stall for them, after the air-show was over.

"What did she say or was it all very private?" Connie pinched his arm.

"No - not at all. She said that the Mandela and Mahathir's flight would depart from KL at nine this morning and will land about twenty minutes before the fly-past starts. They would motorcade from Mahathir's official plane directly to the Grand Stand. And as arranged, from there they will come over to the Africair chalet for the signing ceremony, the press conference, and the social function." Grant sounded less keen about the day ahead.

They chose a table in a window-nook but were so occupied in discussing the day's program that they did not take any notice of the tropical splendour outside their dining room. It was a perfect day for an air-show.

Grant sounded formal, "I think we should get to the chalet as soon as possible - I still have a few phone calls to make. In the meantime while you, I, and the rest of the Africair staff will tend to the preparations for this afternoon - De Witt, Kurtz and Marjory will be with the entourage of the Heads of States in the Grand Stand. I was told that at some stage during the fly- past, Faber will pick De Witt up and take him to a transport helicopter. Apparently he needs to attend a business meeting - in Georgetown, on Penang Island - with the Chairman of Malaysian Aircraft Corporation."

Connie buttered her toast and asked, "I gathered that much from the program" She learned long ago that Grant preferred to form a clear sequential picture of his day ahead and would talk through it in vivid terms - as if believing that whatever he sees in his mind's eye - will without doubt come to pass.

To show that she gave attention to detail as Grant expected from her Connie added, "I thought their departure would be a little untimely. But, what surprised me most, was that Christian Faber will fly them to Penang Island - while just last night when we were having cocktails during the sunset cruise - somebody from Africair said his pilot-license was revoked ages ago?"

Grant stopped chewing his bacon, looked at her, and asked "Are you sure?"

"Yes - why?"

"That's strange." Was all that Grant said - but did Faber's unusual responsibility add to his discomfort?

- o 0 o –

LANGKAWI AIR SHOW

Jack du Preez asked Brian Boddington to meet him at the outdoor display of the Martial Eagle, which was positioned on the apron right in front of the Africair chalet. He looked at the tough-faced pilot as he rolled up to him in his chair with the slanted wheels. Somehow he was not sure if he really liked the ex-Vietnam pilot. He definitely did not like Kurtz's idea to take him onboard this morning's demo-flight, but that's how fate sometimes plays a final role in a pilot's life, he thought.

For many months Jack du Preez waited for this day. This morning he cleared every scrap of evidence in his room, briefcase and laptop – that could reveal what he was really up to. He had very left little meaningful information on his new notebook - destroyed the last of his three-and –a-half inch discs, credit cards, and personal notes. In his wallet were only a few ID cards and he left only his clothes in his hotel room.

But, Jack also dreaded this day and was filled with trepidation to enter into the unknown dimension of after-death that now gradually loomed bigger and bigger towards his soul. But then he took a final look at the picture of his pregnant wife - taken only a few days before she was raped and killed. He lit her photo with his cigarette lighter. The last of the flame distorted her lovely smile – blackened out her image – while Jack du Preez's soul departed from the life in his body. Somehow his mechanically driven being went on to believe that he would see her smile again - shortly.

Du Preez looked impassively at Boddington wheeling towards him. Right now he felt nothing for nobody or anything - like so many times when he prepared for a dangerous sortie during the bush-war. "Today I am going to execute my M-Plan – that is – killing all the M's; Mandela, Mbeki, Mahatir, masses of people and me. Oh yes, and now also the latest addition to his list of victims - Mister Boddington. But none of this it would make-up for my lost woman and child – you cold war-hungry bastards of this world!" The noise of aircraft on the ground and flying above him muffled his embittered words.

– o 0 o –

Brian Boddington shielded his eyes from the sun with his hand as he looked up to Du Preez. "What? Is this final? Is it decided by whom-ever - that I could join you during your air-display?'

Du Preez's voice carried an edge of cold empathy for the man whose life he was to end in less than an hour, "Yes old Brian - this is Kurtz's idea of a special treat for you. You will be going through the whole envelope with me. You and I will run this schedule - to the very end."

"You mean the barrel-role and the loop too?"

"Yes the whole routine and – much more my friend." For a moment there was a glistening of melancholy in Du Preez eyes - before cold antagonism returned again.

"Hell man! Are you sure?" Boddington initially thought that this new development would interfere with his plans to destroy the ME. But then again - the answer was right here under his left arm. He would set off the on-board time bomb soon after they have landed and when nobody was close to the aircraft. Furthermore it could cast suspicion away from him - or would it? Why does he get that old familiar on-guard sensation? On the other hand the moments he had in the Martial Eagle were like being a whole pilot again. He looked down on the people around him and people looked up at him. When you are in a wheel chair people do not even always look down at you. They simply ignore you and speak to everybody else – right over your head - treating you on the same level as a child. I certainly would like to have a last flip in this mean looking African machine - before I blow it to smithereens, Boddington thought.

Du Preez waited patiently for Boddington to work through his long train of thoughts that reflected in the faraway stare that held his eyes, "Yes Brian - you're booked for the next flight. Now - go and have a piss and be back here in thirty minutes".

"You bet!" Boddington swung round and wheeled swiftly to the restrooms.

- o O o -

Boddington also welcomed the opportunity to make a call to Douglas Collins's cell phone just to bring him up to date with the latest development.

"Well Brian, you came thus far. The whole exercise is now in your hands. If you want the rest of your fee, you know what to do. Otherwise - it's goodbye to $250 000 my man." Collins challenged him and continued in his haughty manner "But remember if you don't deliver today - it would not help me too much. I had a round of talks with the Malaysians yesterday. I get the feeling they are really starting to cotton-on to the bloody African's chopper, you know. Main reasons are the preparedness of the South Africans to share their technology, and even put up an assembly plant right here in Malaysia. And with the South African currency at its lowest against the dollar, they have the costing structure in their favour too." Collins was not particularly happy with the way his marketing effort progressed in Malaysia.

"I begin to understand why you want to retard their marketing process." Boddington said and thought by himself that the two hundred and fifty thousand dollars that he has already earned is a lot of money, and perhaps he reached the stage now where he could pull off the demise of the ME - for a much nobler reason. The idea that, for once, he would be doing something really worthwhile for the benefit of this world, made him feel for the first time in his life - really superior.

Collins continued, "But, not all is hopeless. General Abdul Hamat of the RMAF doubts the survivability or crash behaviour of the Martial Eagle. It does not have the combat track record of The Warrior. But those are my problems - all you need to do – dear Brian - is to get that African chopper out of the way today. From tomorrow onwards – for the rest of your time - you can live a fat and happy life." As usual, Collins intensely infuriated Boddington.

Boddington slammed his mobile dead and said out loud, "To hell with you Collins - all the money in the world will still not replace the lost value of my legs - you conceited English bastard!"

63.

WALKIE-TALKIES.

LANKAWI AIR SHOW

Rosemary Barnard felt something cold slithering down the back of her neck and shrieked while she swung around. It was Chubby Wilson who tickled her with the thin chain attached to his sunglasses. He grasped her in his arms, and kissed her on the mouth. "That's to say happy birthday, you sexy thing."

"Oh! Chubby! You little beggar - you shouldn't do this to me" She shrieked and laughed.

"It's nothing compared to what I am going to do to you – much later in the day. You better watch out my girl." Chubby said with a ever hopeful twinkle in his eyes.

Rosemary said, "Kurtz told me that I will be with you in your ME. It's a wonderful birthday present you know - I fell really, really privileged." And she gave the stocky pilot a hug while he smiled cross-eyed at the ceiling.

"But, my dear - I am talking of something I want to do with you much, much later in t the day- or rather this evening." Chubby stayed hopeful.

"Like what?" she posed in an enticing way.

Chubby took her hands and looked up at her, "If I you bring you down safely – could we celebrate your birthday with a special candle-light dinner?"

Rosemary looked smilingly at his friendly freckled-face. She knew for a long time that he was dying to take her out so - she kissed him on the tip of his nose, "That's a promise, Chubby."

Before he could swoon about his unexpected luck Rosemary said in a serious, quiet sort of way, "But business before pleasure my friend, I have something to tell you that is bothering me – tremendous more than I would like to admit."

"Talk to your pilot baby." Chubby was a happy man.

"It is something Glynis Botha told me that's troubling me. But, apparently it does not bother Fred Kramer or Julius Grant, but somehow I am not at ease – sixth-sense stuff – you know." Rosemary played out the circumstances that bothered her as she set it out to Grant. However she did not tell Chubby about the De Witt and Brooks' relationship. Perhaps she refrained to do it for the sake of Grant's company.

Chubby took Rosemary's elbow and led her to the high chairs at the counter in the briefing room. He looked around to see who might be within hearing distance. Then he lowered his voice. "I attended the flight briefing-session here, just a few minutes ago. It was clear that Jack du Preez will be totally in control during the execution of our flight-plan. You know, he has been the star of the show at many air displays and gained the reputation as a kind of Prima Donna helicopter pilot. The fact that we entered two ME's - for the first time - frustrates the hell out of that trenchant man. The role we will play when it comes to this morning's flying demo will be very much back-drop stuff. You know - like what back-up singers do for a rock star."

"My Goodness Chubby - what are you trying to tell me?" Rosemary asked in a soft voice.

Chubby responded somewhat desperate, "Well, in the light of what you just told me, I am convinced that Jack du Preez has an evil agenda of his own. And that perhaps he has been working on it for many months. We all know he is embittered enough to execute his plan, whatever it may be." Chubby then told Rosemary about the appalling mock attack game that Du Preez played at the Rugby World Cup Final at Ellis Park. He concluded "In the light of what you told me - I think he has a dirty plan up his sleeve - and it may surface during this morning's display. Fortunately it is not one of us who will be with Du Preez in his chopper. I feel sorry for his guest passenger - but all in all - I feel like a fool because I can not substantiate my story."

"What do you suggest we do?" Rosemary knew she could rely on her extra-sensory alertness to react soon enough - should a threat develop during their flight. But she wanted to know how Cubby would approach their possible dilemma.

"I really don't know. All we can do is listen to his radio and do whatever is possible when he does whatever he plans to do. At least we will be mentally prepared when he does something out of the ordinary." Chubby thought he sounded a little off-centre with his summary of what they could anticipate.

Rosemary had a more practical suggestion, "I think we can trust Fred Kramer. Let's tell him about our suspicions and ask him to provide us with radio-intercom sets so that we can stay in contact with him and report to him directly if we pick-up anything irregular. In that way we could communicate for a while with the ground without using the Martial Eagle radio frequency."

"Splendid -let's go. Kramer should be in the chalet by now." Said Chubby and slid off his chair

Rosemary grasped his sleeve and held him back, "Chubby - let's ask Grant to also carry a radio unit - despite the fact that he has with him a cell phone that is programmed with speed-dialling to Kurtz and who-else is important." Silently she hoped that the new GSM Mobile networks - that was still a very new and an untested communications medium in South Africa and Southeast Asia -would have roaming capability on the Island of Lankawi.

Chubby nodded his agreement. While they rushed to the chalet he wondered if they had enough time to convince Kramer and get him to supply them with two-way radios.

They found Kramer and Grant on the balcony of the chalet. Grant held a pair of powerful binoculars to his eyes - looking at the Grand Stand opposite them. They took the two men inside and sat down at a table. They were a distance from the next occupied chairs where marketing personnel had a discussion with two Royal Malaysian Air Force officers.

Kramer and Grant listened intently to their theory. Grant who knew about Rosemary's concern and gave her a slight wink. "I think it could do no harm if the two of us had radio contact with you guys in the second ME" Kramer said.

Kramer asked a few questions and then said, "Let me think." He was well aware that time was of the essence and he thought about the many unanswered questions he had about the remarks from Fisher that he taped through the Africair computer listening devices. Suddenly a few incidences fell in place and now made sense to him. Without telling them about his experiences he declared, "You are making a lot of sense to me. I will make sure that we get those radios within a few minutes -we just need to synchronize the frequency and keep them switched on.

"Good!" Chubby breathed a sigh of relief and looked at his watch. They had only twenty minutes before they had to report for departure preparation"

They all rose simultaneously and pushed back their chairs. Grant held up a hand. "Wait - I suggest that we only use this when Chubby hears something and initiate the contact between us. If nothing happens - we did not lose face. Just remember that if we engage in idle chat - the ME's radio frequency hopping capability will pick up our communications, and translate it immediately to Du Preez's chopper."

Chubby's eyes widened, "Hell Grant you're right! I should have remembered that - I admire you for reminding us. Fred, he's right - no contact until absolutely necessary. And in the light of what Grand said - we will have only a few seconds before Jack knows what we're up to"

"We will all wait till you start talking Chubby - come down-stairs so that I can give you the radios" Kramer led them to his storeroom.

64.

HEADS OF STATE.

THE GRANDSTAND AT LANKAWI AIR SHOW.

Grant returned to the balcony of Africair's chalet. He trained his binoculars on the Grand Stand - just in time to see how the Prime Minister of Malaysia and President Nelson Mandela of South Africa took up their seats. Mandela was accompanied by Vice- President Thabo Mbeki and his Minister of Defence, Joe Modise. They had a very large entourage of South African government officials and Grant had difficulty spotting Marjory Brooks amongst them. There were countless greetings and introductions amongst the VIP guests and it took some time before they were in their allocated seats. Eventually they came to order and Grant spotted Marjory sitting next to Mandela's communications officials - with whom she had a good working relationship.

Marjory wore a light blue dress and her dark hair rested loosely on her shoulders. Her beauty filled Grant with mixed emotions - and he was certain that he was falling in love with her. - But he could not understand why she did not never trust him enough – to tell him all about De Witt being her biological father?

Grant's binoculars were glued to his face and he longed to call her on her cell phone at this moment - but right now he could not bring himself to do so. For a long time he took in her every movement. Not once did she as much as look at De Witt - who sat just behind her with Kurtz on his left. Grant decided that he had nothing in particular to say to her right now - other than to hear her voice and please his own budding affection for her. Despite his doubts that grinded against his earnest feelings of compassion for her. He decided that he would not bother her with a call right now - she could call him instead.

A few minutes later the show's announcer introduced the Premier of Malaysia, Dr Mahathir bin Mohamed - who was born in Kedah and trained for the medical profession in Singapore. He became Prime Minister in

July 1981 - when he took over from Datuk Hussein who retired for as a result of his ailing health. Mahathir was an energetic politician who was well known for his enthusiasm and support of the Malaysia's National Economic Policy. He especially encouraged economic development through industrialization and welcomed international partnerships that could help his country along its path to become a fully developed nation. He was praised for the role he played to elevate Malaysia's into a position of respect and dignity in the international politics of South East Asia and beyond. Through his efforts Malaysia was elected in October of 1988 to become a non-permanent member of the Security Council at the United Nations.

As a member-state of ASEAN countries, Malaysia was promoting as much self-help schemes for the region as possible. Mahathir was the main-drive behind the Lankawi air shows. In his speech the Prime Minister defined the huge export market of the Pacific Rim with its extreme appetite for aerospace goods. He welcomed the competition between European, UK, and US companies to gain a foothold in these markets. Then he directed a special welcome to South Africa for its preparedness to not only satisfy this market but also to contribute in terms of beneficial partnerships between private companies.

Mahathir called President Mandela to the podium and introduced him to the spectators. He praised the man who personally endured so much for the liberation of his country and announced that after the opening ceremony, Malaysia, and South Africa would sign an agreement of technical co-operation. Mahathir declared the Lima-sow open and moments later an eight-Hawk formation of Britain's Red Arrows rocketed over the Island and painted the clear skies in the official colours of Malaysia – and in doing so created a spectacular opening scene.

Grant rested his binoculars on his chest and rubbed his eyes. He replaced his sunglasses and saw how the two Martial Eagles taxied out to take up their positions to fill their slot in the air display to follow. They were the last item of the opening ceremony and were to underline the important presence of President Nelson Mandela, his misters and officials.

Kramer read the concern on Grant's face and wanted to let him understand how vulnerable they were for any mishap that may happen,

"I hope our radios remain in the stand-by mode this morning. To tell you the truth Julius, the security network here in Malaysia is not yet on the same level as at other military shows. Anything could happen and we are not well prepared and do not have the infrastructure of a local air force on standby to handle a major crises or catastrophe of any kind."

Grant heard his tentative remark and tried to make light of the situation. "Well with a pair of binoculars, a radio and a cell phone on my belt-clip - I have enough toys to keep me busy. Just hope they won't hamper me."

"I can see that you are not at ease Julius. But at least I have several other support options lined up - should we need to act swiftly." Kramer lit a cigarette and looked up at the vertical climb of the British Red Arrows right above them. There were seven other types of aircraft to perform before the Martial Eagles would sign-off the program.

As the roar of the Hawk-engines faded, Grant heard his cell phones ring. He looked at Kramer - smiled and said, "This is Grant"

Marjory talked in a hushed but clearly strained voice, "Hello Julius". She did not wait for him to return a greeting, "Shortly before the Martial Eagle show I need to leave my seat for a while. So sorry – but I will miss out on the M.E's display, signing ceremony, etc."

Grant focussed his binoculars on her and saw that she bowed forward while talking into the handset. Her abruptness reminded him of a similar conversation they had at Ellis Park - many months ago. "Whatever it is that you need to do - can't it wait a few minutes?" was Grant's impulsive question.

"Apparently not - Dr De Witt asked me to walk with him to his car to discuss something very important -before he leaves for Georgetown." She sounded a little regretful.

For the moment Grant lacked the qualities of a boon companion, "'OK -there will be other shows." But not if I can help it Grant thought.

"Julius I am very sorry about this -could you perhaps record the demo flight for me on video camera - please?" she whispered.

"Right now our video camera is in my car which is parked behind the Grand Stand - but OK - I will ask Connie to fetch it for me so that we can do some amateur camera work." Grant promised.

"Thanks Julius and - Julius - I love you – see you in a bit."

65.

EVERYBODY ON STANDBY!

BIRD'S-EYE VIEW – OF THE LANKAWI AIR SHOW

From the aft cockpit of the ME, Jack du Preez looked down at the layout of the show site below them. They were parked at a thousand feet up for two minutes and then made a wide circle at hundred and twenty knots while burning up a continuous four hundred and twenty five k's of fuel per hour. Chubby and Rosemary followed Du Preez and Boddington ten meters above and fifty meters behind them. They waited for the Control Tower's instruction to start their demo routine. On the apron the wide bodies of the McDonnell Douglas C-17, in its familiar olive drab and the Russian Antonof AK 5 dwarfed the other aircraft.

"What do you see down there Boddington?" Conversation did not mean a thing to Du Preez anymore but he had to fill the waves with sounds that would put the security monitor's at ease.

"Lots of lovely flying machines, pal." Boddington enjoyed the flight so much that he almost forgot about the lethal device under his seat that carried the potential of awful death and destruction.

"Yes - worth billions of farken dollars while lots of poorly paid air and ground crews are standing around them, and many onlookers – who are here because they are unemployed and are trying to escape from the question burning in their numbed minds – how do I feed my family this evening? ." Money, means and any form of compassion have just lost all its meaning to Du Preez.

Boddington thought about his bank balance that could swell with another two-hundred-and-fifty-thousand dollar within a few hours. Funny, he thought, if you acquire a lot of money in a short period of time, how quickly it loses its significance. "You're right, Julius, poor bastards".

They flew in silence for ten more minutes more, looking at the blue and white beach-line and forests of the island. They were two men - committed to destroy the Martial Eagle and not knowing - or aware of each other's secret agendas. Two men embittered by the relentless blows of life - that scarred them body and soul and ripped to pieces the quality of their lifes. Both were reckless in their undertakings. Both were unconcerned about the outcome of their deeds. Both were emotionally uninvolved with their after-event life - be they dead or alive.

At that moment - Du Preez felt the presence of his wife, and I his mind's eye saw the colour of her hair - blue eyes, and her smile – somewhere in the heaven and clouds that formed on the western horizon. He was also so close to her now - could it be that her soul is sharing this cockpit with him? He dedicated so many hours of his life in this seat and now he is about to give it his last hour too. He wished that he had brought Linda's photo with him instead of burning it this morning. But that's OK - he consoled himself - because she was in the clouds and with him here at the controls. "Not too long now, my dear – not too long"

"Repeat that" Boddingtons request crackled.

Du Preez jerked out of his stray thoughts, "They will call us any moment now." He tried to correct himself.

o 0 o –

GROUND VIEW, LANKAWI AIR SHOW

Grant leaned on the railing of the Africair chalet and looked first in the direction of the two Martial Eagles that hung like fat tropical mosquito's in the distance and then at the people below him. There were large numbers of men whose uniforms designated many air forces from around the world. The crowds stood still and looked up at the air display. Temporarily the stationary exhibits lost their attraction. Like any big match event, an air-show has its own atmosphere and attraction that never failed to excite the spectators.

With the cold war something of the past, new participants from communist countries added to the diversity of all military shows. For the first time it was now possible to see touch and admire equipment and defense-systems that, not so long ago, belonged to the enemy. Much of the saying that said - friends and enemies are never forever - became true. At shows like these it was sometimes difficult to understand why it was necessary to spend so much time, energy and capital on things that now seem to be superfluous.

Grant followed Connie as she careened her way through the crowd towards the car park. She was not particularly keen to leave the air-conditioned chalet to brave the heat and humidity – just to go out there and get the video camera. She was concerned about the ruinous effect that the high humidity would have on her hair and make-up - but said nothing about these concerns - that are important to women – but not to a somewhat ignorant male like – Julius Grant.

Grant saw how she caught the eyes of the young men that she passed on her way - some even turned round and stared at her. At once Grant thought how fortunate his son was to have met such an attractive and pleasant person. On top of it all they shared the same religious sentiments. Grant smiled - he knew this was definitely a story with a happy ending. "Thank you God for *something* that is working out well in my life." With this speed-prayer Grant realized that Peter's happiness was of more importance to him than his own. Then - for a moment Grant asked himself – is what he now feels for his son a manifestation of what Peter tried to explain to him how the Heavenly Father loved his Son? Grant decided that in future he wanted to develop a more meaningful relationship with his loved-ones.

About a hundred yards behind her he saw Fischer walking in the direction of the Grand Stand. He was talking on his cell phone and gesticulated emphatically to his unseen listener. What a strange man, Grand thought. What an awkward lot of people Kurtz had brought together and surrounded himself with at Africair. Sometimes he thought of them as a conceited lot of Prima Donnas'. He was sure they were not always like that - perhaps it was the result of years of the pressure to work under covert circumstances - towards soul-breaking deadlines. Most of the company's executives became conditioned introverts - as a result of working with information that for security reasons were limited to only a restricted few.

"What a stuffy work environment it must have been" Grant's thought slipped out audibly. Beside him Kramer - the prime guardian of company and international covert interests could not hear him above the blast of a Russian Sukhoi Su-37. Yevgeni Frolov - Sukhoi's test pilot - just pulled out of a daring Stop Cobra and Summersault maneuver - that had the spectators gasping in awe.

349

o 0 o –

GETAWAY CHOPPER WAITING AT LANKAWI AIR SHOW

Sweat ran from Christian Faber's red cheeks, soaking his dense white beard and colored his flying overalls dark-wet. Heat, high humidity, and excessive drinking caused him to dehydrate like an out of shape boxer warming up for a fight. He was anxious to fly again - and an important mission it was to be.

He never dreamed that he would ever form part of any operation again - it felt as good as the days when they scrambled to go all out for the Angolan's. This Langkawi Mission came along just when he thought that he was forever tied down to factory flights. That was what they called unauthorized flights from the assembly hanger over the fields adjacent to Africair and back. They dared these flips when Kurtz was out of town and Faber knew Fischer always looked the other way – which allowed him to somewhat retain his flying skills.

Today's mission was coded as L3M. It stood for Langkawi Mission to Murder Mandela. Faber convinced himself that he did this for his son's sake. He did not dare thinking anymore about the good or moral reasons for doing this – because Fischer told him not to break his head over things of a higher-order, as he called it. He said, "Faber, all the thinking and planning has been done. All you and you need to do now is to get your part of the job done. And don't you marinate yourself with too much brandy - old boozer, you can drink yourself into a stupor after the show."

Faber ran through his briefing and re-motivated himself aloud, "Up to now, I, Christian Faber - one of the country's best transport-chopper-pilots - did not mess-up anything. I am the one who's going to do the real important smart flying here today. I will take the bosses to the small uninhabited island of Pulau Dangli to pick up Jack du Preez up. Then with Jacks help we'll flip over to Penang's Georgetown International Airport. By the time they all here realize what has happened - that bloody Mandela and his baboons will all be dead and, we will be on our way to Namibia – where their families – and a new life - will be waiting for them."

How glad those Nigerian guys will be to hear that old Mandela is dead. He annoyed all Nigerians with his condemning them for how they were dealing with the political undercurrents and problems in their country. Bloody blacks in any case haven't a farken clue of how to run a country. In the near future we'll give them such a lot of grieve in South Africa they will come begging for Apartheid-rule again. My boys, this is only the beginning of all the muck that will be flying your way like from now-now!"

Faber stood at the open side-door of the Bell 206 L4 that Fischer rented on behalf of Africair and was alone with his tangled-up thoughts and weird ideas of political matters. He kept on talking to rid himself from the stress that was building up inside his chest like a hot-air balloon. He looked at the forty-two feet helicopter and said to the machine, "Listen here you American Baby. Today I'm going to knock 110 knots per hour out of those 557 horses that's tied up in your Allison engine. And don't you give me any start-up farken problems. OK?"

Faber hopped on board, checked their luggage and then moved forward where he pulled a Vektor R6 Assault Rifle from under the co-pilots seat and checked the magazine. It was there for just in case Fischer ordered it. The R6 was a shorter version of the famous South African R5 that was designed as a counter weapon for the AK-47. Littleton Engineering Works in South Africa developed it for use by the security forces that had to work in confined spaces. It weighed less than four kilograms and with its folded stock - had a length of only 565 millimeter of which 280 millimeter belonged to barrel. It was just the right piece of iron that Faber needed now.

Faber folded the R6 and hid it again. He looked at his watch and then to the sky. From where he was parked behind the hanger he saw the two ME's coming in fast at low altitude for a first run past the Grand Stand - as if they wanted to impress the VIP's.

"Our passengers will be here any minute now" he said to the silent helicopter. "Time to warm up my American Baby" Faber's face screwed-up in a devilish grin as he listened to the whine of the ignition and saw how the ten-meter rotor-blades above him slowly came into motion.

66.

DEATH LOOP MANEUVER

CONFINED AIR SPACE, LANKAWI AIR SHOW

Jack du Preez flew the Martial Eagle directly towards the Grand Stand of the Lankawi Air Show at a speed of one hundred and twenty knots, altitude one-hundred-and ten meters. He stayed in contact with Chubby Wilson in the ME behind him. Now and then he would comment on manoeuvres for the sake of Boddington - who sat incommunicado in the weapons-control cockpit in front of him. His communications were harsh and staccato-like. This was a mission without a respectable outcome for Du Preez and Boddington - only the American did not know it yet.

Du Preez banked sharply to his right around three hundred meters from the Grand Stand and the media commentary boxes,. They flew parallel with the two temporary bleacher structures and Du Preez looked down at the rows of important visitors in the organizer's cubicle as they rushed past the Grand Stand. The stone cold South African was unattached to his surroundings as if he screened a video program. From the commentator's box sounded the description of the ME's capabilities and the demonstration routine that was to follow.

After they attended the final flight-planning session earlier, Chubby commended to Rosemary, "So, Du Preez would perform the whole routine while we fill in only during the fly-past, and other low-level demonstrations. When Du Preez performs the Barrel Role and do The Loop Maneuvers - which he developed and is a first for an attack helicopter in the eight-ton class, we must stay out of site from the Grand Stand. This would allow Du Preez all the exposure that he needs to maintain his ego"

The two ME's were applied masterfully to display their maneuverability. They made reverse flights, side-to-side swerves, handstands, and spirals. The spectators were very impressed and the applause of all who were wearing aviation uniforms was spontaneous. They could understand why the South African attack helicopters received so much attention. As a result of their flexibility, these machines were set to become the dominant force on especially the anti- terrorist battlefields of the 21st century. Certain schools of military strategists projected a future development in combat scenarios that will vastly differ from the traditional battlefield status and therefore advised Commanders in Chief to strengthen their attack helicopters capability.

The show commentator cited Peter Donaldson of the Defense Helicopter Magazine, who said - that although an attack helicopter that was devoid of armor protection and lacked the speed, payload, and range of a jet fighter or bomber, it could employ a wide range of weapons to carry out various missions. Their missiles could destroy bunkers and bridges or stop a massed armed assault. On the other hand they were sophisticated suites of sensors and communications which made them very capable reconnaissance platforms. These information-gathering operations could be applied very effectively during day and night and in most types of weather. The attack helicopter could even play a role to discourage an angry civilian mob by firing warning shots of blanked ammunition.

Jack du Preez switched on all the communications systems of the Martial Eagle. The communications suite was now ready for flying under normal and attack conditions. Boddington saw how the controls showed that the two V/UHF transceivers with its associated logic converter units, were operational

"This is it Guys - your captain is going to show you a jolly barrel roll and then a loop like you have never seen and never will witness again - do you read me Wilson?"

"I read you Jack. Is this another display of your Ellis Park-type of games?" Chubby Wilson sweated under his helmet. He hoped to needle Du Preez into an admission or indication of some kind as to what he planned in his evil mind.

"No my pal - this is for real. Adios Wilson and Barnard - enjoy the rest of your careers at Africair!"

Chubby and Rosemary were stunned. They saw how Du Preez's ME corkscrewed sideways into a Barrel Roll and then jerked up into a steep climb, with the ME's belly to the Grand Stand. With shock that nearly made him puke, Chubby Wilson gauged the diameter line of the loop —

anticipated the lowest point and suddenly realized what the manic South African test pilot was about to do!

o 0 o –

Grant and Fred Kramer followed the Martial Eagle's routine through their binoculars. They were amazed at the machine's agility and Du Preez's flying skills. It was clear that by now, after so many demonstrations, he could run the envelope blindfolded.

Suddenly the two-way radios of Grant and Kramer crackled and they heard Du Preez's high-pitched voice "Are you warmed-up Faber?" They dropped their binoculars and jerked simultaneously as if the units on their hips exploded. They reached for their equipment like cowboys for their six-shooters in an old western movie.

"Hot as hell Jack and my Yankee chopper is whirling - where are my passengers? And where are Kramer and that bloody Tommy" This time Grant had no problem recognizing Faber's heavy accented reply.

Du Preez cackled, "Fischer, De Witt and the woman left the grand stand and they are on their way. Right now they're driving past the chalets heading your way -they should turn-up any minute now. Kramer and Grant are at the chalet waiting to join the politicians - so, forget about them"

Only then Grant and Kramer, who exchanged puzzled gawks, realized that instead of Wilson breaking the silence - it was Du Preez talking to Faber on the same frequency as they were locked on with Wilson and Barnard.

"So they are also connected with two-way radios to short-circuit the Martial Eagles comms-systems!" Kramer shouted unnecessarily. They were at a loss as to how to react.

Du Preez crackled again "Faber! Don't you wait-up for me –just get the hell out of this place old buddy -cheers, it's been good to know you -over and out! "

Grant reacted first - switched his mike on and barked, "Du Preez, Wilson, what the hell's going on?"

Du Preez was already off the air but Faber was still linked up with the unit in his hand. He could still not comprehend Du Preez's last remark - while in the back-up ME Chubby and Rosemary were equally dumbfounded.

Chubby retorted in a high pitched voice, "On completion of his loop at near ground level, Du Preez is going to crash his ME right into the Grand Stand. Oh! Oh! And there's no time to vacate the seats!"

Faber, now completely confused, shouted, "Stay out of this Grant or you will get killed you farken Englishman!"

Grant then saw how the Africair van rushed past their chalet with Fischer driving his passengers towards the waiting helicopter - to be piloted by Faber.

"What about his American passenger? Let's cut Du Preez off." Barnard shouted.

From where Grant and Kramer stood they saw where Wilson and Barnard in the second ME hung above the Grand Stand and then looked up to followed Du Preez's ME that neared the pinnacle of the loop.

"OK. We're going to fly right into his line of flight!" Wilson yelled.

Wilson hopped the willing ME over the rooftop of the grand stand to appear suddenly before the surprised spectators. He gradually moved the chopper five hundred-yards away and waited for Du Preez - directly blocking his corridor and hoping that the agitated Du Preez will be forced to change his fatal course. Should Du Preez reach the bottom of the loop - that was already unthinkable dangerously low - he would be forced to continue upwards, or fly strait on and crash into Wilson and Barnard's helicopter. Barnard realized the consequences and finality of Wilson's plan and tore the air with an abrupt high-pitched shriek.

o 0 o –

"We've got to stop Faber!" Grant shouted.

"Let's go! This is going to be dangerous Grant - here, take my pistol. I'll get another in the office on my way down." Kramer knew that Grant was exceptionally capable with a firearm.

On their way out of the chalet, Grant and Kramer pushed and rammed through the unsuspecting guests of Africair that stood on the balcony. They upturned tables and flower-arrangements as they scrambled through the well-prepared conference area. They jostled down the corkscrew stairs and Kramer grabbed a pistol from under the arm of a startled security officer.

Grant stuck the Magnum in his belt and threw off his jacket as they ran out the front door of the chalet. The spectators shouted curses of dismay and surprise, as the two men rushed after the blue van with Fischer and his passengers. Grant's stiff ankle shot pains up his leg that exploded in his groin. His lungs burned from the muggy tropical air and his mind was raw with agony about Marlene Brooks' role in this whole mess. Suddenly his whole life, which seemed so promising a moment ago - turned into a horror picture.

Kramer ran past Grant and shouted, "Try to stop Fischer - I am going to command a helicopter for us to follow them!" He hopped over the fence and ran towards the pilots that stood by the small helicopters that were parked on the lawn between the aprons.

Grant envied the man's speed and pushed himself harder. Ahead of him through the unsuspecting crowds that stood looking up at the ME's display, Grant saw how the blue van rounded Hanger 9 where Faber was waiting in the warmed-up Bell helicopter. He knew that he had to get to them before they departed. The loose gravel between the hangers slowed Grant up and made running with his pain-racked body nearly unbearable.

Grant reached the end of the lane just in time to see how Fischer pushed a struggling Brooks through the side-door of the Bell 206. De Witt, who was already seated, grabbed her wrist and jerked her into the noisy machine. Grant ran as fast as he could towards them - waived his arms and shouted in vain at the top of his voice. Fischer stepped on the helicopter's side rail, turned to Grant with a Z.88 in his right hand. At a distance of thirty yards with Grant rushing towards them Fischer aimed at him. Grant saw the slight whiff of smoke - heard a cracking sound while his feet left the ground. He spun to the cement floor as the searing hot bullet tore through him - taking flesh from the left side of his ribcage and inner-arm.

Grant screamed with shock yet he felt no pain. He rolled over and saw how the Bell gradually lifted off with Fischer still trying to get into the light chopper's open door. Grant lay on his back while blood seeped through his shirt. He rolled over on his side, rested his elbow on the concrete floor while he pulled the Magnum from his belt.

"This is also going to hurt a little Mister Fischer." Grant said as he aimed along his outstretched arm. The 9-millimeter steel bullet left the barrel and smashed into the back of Fischer's knee. He jerked backwards - lost his grip and slid from the door railing. Fischer grabbed his knee with both hands - pulled himself into a ball and dropped the three-meter to the runway floor. He hit the surface like a kid bombing into a pool. The sudden absence of Fischer's weight caused the Bell to shoot upwards and Faber nearly lost control.

Grant stood up, swayed a little and trotted past the squirming Fischer towards where Kramer was waiting for him at one of the parked helicopters. As he limped past the wounded Fischer he heard him uttering the most disgusting Afrikaans swear-words. Grant gave him a disdainful look and shouted, "It's OK you'll live you bloody bastard"

Kramer shouted and indicated to Grant to follow him to a McDonnell-Douglas 520N that was warming up for take-off. He ran towards the light helicopter - climbed aboard and then stretched out a hand to pull Grant aboard. Once inside the chopper Grant tore off his already bloodied shirt - rolled it into a ball and pinched it in his bleeding armpit. As they cleared the roof of Hanger 8, Grant saw the Bell with Faber, de Wit and Brooks on board, heading north - straight towards the small island of Pulau Dangli.

Behind them Jack du Preez's Martial Eagle completed the loop, fifty meters above the runway and eighty meters from Cubby's hovering chopper that created a deadly obstruction on his suicide course.

67.

FURY FLY-PAST.

MAIN EVENT: LANKAWI AIR SHOW.

Brian Boddington saw how Chubby Wilson's Martial Eagle filled-up his windscreen while the distressed young man's yelling hammered his eardrums as he begged "Jack! – have you lost your mind! - pull-up! - pull-up! - pull-up!"

Boddington heard his own voice breaking as he shouted, "Hey man! Are you out of your mind?" Suddenly it was Vietnam all over again. He sweated profusely and could not discern between the morning above the rice-paddy, the here and now in the reality of this Malaysian moment, and the anticipation of their inescapable doom.

At the last moment Du Preez roared his ME up, passing inches from Wilson's chopper's whirling rotor-blades. The downward drafts from the two heavy machines intertwined and disrupted the air-flow. It shook Wilson's helicopter to near uncontrollability and they were drawn into a descending spin. An infuriated Wilson jerked at the controls and regained control.

The spectators were on their feet, overwhelmed by the daring and most entertaining display by the two Martial Eagles.

"Chubb, this is your last warning -get out of my way, pal!" Du Preez shouted while he banked sharply to his left, turned around and again started to lined-up with Wilson and Barnard.

The American regained the control of his judgment as he heard the fanatical Du Preez's warning and shouted, "Jack! Land this wretched chopper - your game is over."

With widespread eyes Boddington tried to read the complicated and strange Control and Display Unit (CDU) in front of him. He cursed himself for not making a proper study of the layout of the Weapon Systems Officer's cockpit. He knew that the South African disengaged the intercom and could not read him. He had to get back on the air, and nervously typed at the hierarchy of hard and soft keys arranged on the borders of the green faced instrument panel. Several displays lit-up. The hard key for the weapons system selection and monitoring told him that Du Preez had his 20-mm cannon enslaved to his Helmet-Mounted Sight and Display. He had engaged this deadly weapon in standby-mode.

The focus of Boddington's eyes shifted from the cockpit's Multi-function Displays to the visor-display - which formed an integral part of his helmet. He was now part of the 'Eyes out of Cockpit' design-philosophy of the Martial Eagle and also confused with the cluttered readings on his helmet visor. If only he knew where the Emergency Engine Cut-off switches were located - so much new developments were integrated in helicopters since Vietnam! To read about new technologies was not the same as operating them in a moment of crisis!

Du Preez was back on the air again and roared like a demon. "You're also going down Wilson - never say I did not warn you buddy! - and,' then Du Preez continued in a throaty singing voice, "happy last birthday dear Rosemary!"

Boddington felt how the ME slightly shuddered as the nose-mounted canon under his feet exploded and spouted intermitted rounds into the fuselage of the Martial Eagle below them. He shouted in vain, "Dammit Du Preez! You're going to kill those kids!"

The live ammunition that were covertly transported into the show grounds with the sole purpose to end the lives of Mandela, Mbeki and others, now ripped through the fuel-tank and hydraulic structures of Wilson's chopper. Like Chubby, Rosemary knew exactly what the demand of the damage caused by these projectiles would require from ME's Crashworthiness System.

As an avionics engineer who, for many years have been dedicated to the development of the Martial Eagle, Rosemary was as acquainted with the guts of this ugly machine, like that of her own body. The fuel-system components and pipe-work of the ME's was designed to carry out and accommodate crash loads in a way that would avoid possible fuel-leakage. The hydraulic operated components of the aircraft would be kept at a constant pressure by single solenoid valve, under all conditions. They were included in each of the main systems to isolate damaged components - in the event of a leak. Rosemary trusted that the landing gear would perform well and decrease the impact of their crash-landing – she was convinced that their landing would be severe but contained.

Rosemary knew where to locate the Emergency Engine Cut-off Switches. She also could understood that Wilson would do the instinctive male-pilot-thing by trying to fly the crippled bird to a suitable landing-spot - while the damage called for a hard landing right now! She knew for certain that the design could accommodate a severe landing and then -without hesitation - she snapped the EEC. They whirled down - while Wilson cursed like the son of a devil - as he stared and heard - in horror - the furious activity of the warning and indicators systems around him.

o 0 o –

Brian Boddington looked down at the grounded Martial Eagle and saw how the two pilots scrambled feverishly out of their cockpits. Ambulances and fire engines rushed from all corners of the airfield toward them. Du Preez elevated to a height of one hundred meters and rounded the side of the Grand Stand.

"The plan of the WAC failed but mine will succeed!" Du Preez's harsh, demonic voice had a metallic effect and rung in the American's ears like shocking bad rap-music.

"Cheerio! - my Yankee friend. Brace yourself for a spectacular landing on Mandela's lap. Let's go and kiss Uncle Thom a fond good-bye!" Du Preez made a wide turn and rounded the stand and flew over the parking lot, en route to the grand stand.

Boddington then knew for certain that in this flight he was going to lose more than a pair of legs. He saved ten lives in exchange for his well shaped pair of struts but, today, he would pay the ultimate price while at the same time dozens - perhaps hundreds of important and valuable people material would be wasted. "What went wrong with the values, ethics, politics and religion of the far right-minded Afrikaner males?" Boddington asked himself.

"No time for thinking metaphysical stuff now old man" he said to himself aloud, while he released his seat-straps and reached for the personnel-mine under his seat. "You've got to stop this mad assassin."

It was difficult to free the bomb from its hardened glue-base and his fingernails cracked and broke in the process of getting the lethal weapon onto his lap. Boddington looked forward and gauged that - should he flick the manual trigger now - in less than thirty seconds they could be right above the parking lot where there were very few people - because everybody ran from there to get a glimpse of Wilson's crash-landing.

The American detonated the bomb - closed his eyes and in a calm voice - started to recite the Lord's Prayer.

o 0 o –

Connie Heyneken unlocked and opened the back door of Grant's rented car. She waited a while for the heat build-up to escape from the car and then reached for a large bag that sat on the back seat and then, from it she removed Grant's video camera.

As she locked the car again she saw people running and heard sirens in the distance, "Now what's going on?" She asked herself, "I hope nothing serious is going to upset Grant's program".

Her attention was averted by the sudden appearance of the Martial Eagle that flew very low over a cluster of trees and banked above the entrance to the parking lot. It was Connie's first experience of an international air-show and she had no idea that this was not part of the air-demonstration routine. She swung the strap of the camcorder over her shoulder and walked back to find Grant.

With the key of the car still in her hand she heard a loud percussion and looked up. What she saw made her drop the camera. The front part and cockpit of the Martial Eagle disintegrated. Small fragments of metal, flesh and blood spat in all directions like a burst of thick red paint from a spray gun.

"Oh! No! No!" Connie cried while she saw how the stump-nosed ME hung motionless for a few split second before it plunged down on a parked passenger bus about fifty meters from where she stood. The explosion that followed sucked the air out of her lungs and burning shrapnel scattered over her like wedding confetti - igniting the grass and cars all around her. From the burning wreck of the bus the gas tanks of adjacent parked cars ignited and exploded in an ever-widening circle.

"Jesus - help me!" Connie cried a desperate prayer as a burning piece of vinyl stuck to her dress. The heat melted the polyester-cotton material and with desperate jerks she ripped off her dress. Out of desperation she started running through the burning vehicles - expecting to die any moment from the ensuing explosions that followed her. She howled as she stumbled and fell - bobbed up again, and ran out of the parking lot towards the back of the pavilion. Like a football player diving for a touchdown, she slid under a long catering counter. She busied her mind with only one point of attention - to get away from the gas explosions of the cars parked close to where she was hiding. A nearby explosion lifted her from the ground and a beam of the counter caused gash behind her left ear. As soon as the angry outbursts stopped, Connie managed to get out from under the counter and crawled hands and knees towards the door of a store room - which she spotted at the end of the counter. She was bleeding profusely and was only slightly aware of the burning sensation that wrapped her bruised breasts and ribs.

"Got to get out! Got to get out!" she muttered in a daze while two men wearing Coca Cola jackets - rushed to her aid. They lifted the half-naked girl and ran with her into the store room - while behind them the parking lot turned into a hellhole of flames.

68.

TROPICAL HELL

Grant's face screwed up with pain as Kramer cleaned his wounds with a disinfectant while they chased after Faber - now escaping with De Witt and Brooks. Africair's Head of Security was clearly not well trained - when it came to administering first aid. Nevertheless he tried his best to stop the bleeding and covered Grant's upper-left arm with the scant bandage and tape that he obtained from the MD 520's first-aid kit. Through his near closed eyes Grant followed the Bell helicopter in front of them - he hoped that by concentrating on Marjory Brooks and Herman de Witt and trying to understand their presence under these traumatic conditions - would take his mind off the burning pain.

Grant nodded his thanks to Kramer and threw his bloodied and torn shirt behind the rear seat of the helicopter. He looked back in the direction of the airport that disappeared behind the tree-covered mountains. On the horizon he saw a thick column of smoke that billowed into a large black mushroom – and on top of his pain – it sickened him to the stomach.

Kramer followed his gaze and shouted, "All hell must have broken loose back there!"

Just before they lost sight of the airstrip they saw how the Martial Eagle of Wilson and Barnard went down. Grant shook his head and replied, "It must be Chubby and Rosemary's aircraft that caught fire -can we hope that they are - OK?"

"God forbid! If I understood Du Preez's conversation with Faber correctly - they had an arrangement to meet somewhere - and I think that is where he is leading us now." Kramer checked his pistol - trying to hide his concern.

"I think you're right. He also asked Faber not to wait-up for him. So if he does turn up - we are in for a hell of a party!" Grant said with sweat and pain covering his face.

Knowing Faber's background and reflecting on the scraps of information that he picked up over the last few weeks troubled Kramer. He wished that he had shared his suspicion earlier with the people he could trust -like Kurtz and - perhaps this tough Englishman here beside him. "Grant, I am afraid with Faber around, there will be enough manure in the fan to plaster us." He wanted to prepare Grant for what may happen –a grim confrontation.

Grant nodded towards their Chinese-Malaysian pilot and asked in his best Afrikaans, "Can we trust this little Asian?"

Kramer smiled. "Yes - Paul Yeo is an old acquaintance and a very capable pilot. This is the second year he is flying for Africair."

Grant noticed that they gained speed as they crossed the Langkawi northern shore at Telok Yu. - they were gradually catching up with Faber's helicopter - that slowed down to search for a landing spot on the small-uninhibited island of Pulau Dangli. Suddenly Farber's Bell swayed and jerked inordinately and Grant shouted to the pilot "Paul! Get as close as possible!"

At first they could not understand what caused Faber's erratic flying pattern - then Grant saw how Faber stuck the muzzle of the R6 Assault Rifle through the open window on his side. Intermitted white puffs signaled that he was firing at them. For a second time in a matter of minutes Grant experienced the total vulnerability - of being a target. Their helicopter shuddered under the occasional hits from Faber's rifle - that sounded as if an invisible ice pick chopped the holes in the their MD 520.

Paul Yeo saw no warning lights and knew the damage was superficial – so he kept his cool and pulled the aircraft up to a level that positioned them at an angle that made it impossible to be fired at by Faber – who also had to concentrate on his flying.

Kramer placed his hand on Grant's shoulder and pointed at Faber's helicopter -it was clear that a struggle broke out between him and Marjory Brooks. She tried to wring the weapon from his large fist. Faber had to choose between the R6 rifle and flying the aircraft. Reluctantly he released his grip while shouting an instruction to De Witt. He tried to free his thick finger from the trigger-case, and in the process discharged a burst of rounds. Sparks filled the cockpit as the shelling perforated the Bell's avionics-panel.

"They are going down" Paul Yeo shouted. They saw how Faber held on to the combined grip and with his thumb on the height-hold selection button. He tried to maneuver a soft landing in the shallow magenta colored water that surrounded Pula Dangli.

"Stay with them!" Grant shouted while he saw how De Witt now wrestled with Brooks to get hold of the rifle. She jerked the R6 towards her and the steel butt hit De Witt between the eyes. The old man cupped his hands over his face and fell backwards he seemed to be knocked unconscious. The next moment Marjory Brooks pushed the firearm through the window and it dropped with a splash in the calm water.

"That's one helluva brave and smart colleague of yours, Grant!" Kramer accepted that the Englishman knew all along about De Witt and Brooks' family relationship.

"You're telling me." Grant said without enthusiasm. He could hardly digest the fact that De Witt was Marjory's biological father - let alone their involvement with Fischer, Du Preez, and Faber's diabolic plan. But whatever the circumstances might be - it looked as if she must have been forced into accompanying them on this flight. Otherwise she would not have endangered her life to prevent Faber from firing at their helicopter. The thought filled Grant with some hope and determination to get her out of this impossible situation as soon as possible. Suddenly his heart sang again and he felt no more pain.

o 0 o –

Grant saw how the Bell aircraft fluttered down into the shallow water about fifty yards from the shoreline. The helicopter bounced once like a ball and landed on its side - while it sunk gradually with steam filling the air.

"How deep is it here?" Grant asked Paul Yeo.

"About six feet Mister Grant" The young Chinese pilot circled the spot where the Bell lay on its side in the clear water.

"Drop me as close as possible" Grant rammed the door of the MD 520 from its hinges and stood on the landing rail. Yeo parked about four meters above the partially submerged helicopter while Grant kicked off his shoes and as they dropped into the water he saw the heads of Faber and Marjory where they bobbed-up. They held on to the rotor-blade that pointed upwards.

"Land on the beach and wait there for us - Fred cover me!" said Grant before he dropped from the railing. On his way down felt how the pistol slipped from his belt and as he struck the water and disappeared beneath the surface, realized that he the now had to face Faber unarmed.

Grant stayed under and swam in the direction of the helicopter. He reached the undercarriage of the aircraft and slowly worked his way up to surface –where he leveled about ten feet from Faber and Brooks - who were looking in the direction of the beach where Fred Kramer and Paul Yeo landed. There was no sign of De Witt.

"Your silly little game is over, Faber. You may just as well come with us." Grant saw that Faber held Marjory from behind. The bearded man treaded water and turned round slowly.

Faber had his left arm around Marjory's middle and held her tightly against his barrel-shaped chest. The other arm was around the rotor and in his hand he held a knife - close to Marjory's throat. "Oh no Mister Grant -you should have stuck to your communications job. Now be a good boy and swim with us to the shore - I need your helicopter to make a getaway."

"That will be the day you bloody pig" Grand stood on the side of the helicopters cabin -he was up to his armpits in the water.

Marjory pleaded with him through tears, "Do as he asks Julius - he has already stopped me from getting my . . . De Witt out of the water. He was unconscious and surely he drowned by now!" She managed to control her sobs and fear.

"Now listen to your boss Grant. You go ahead and tell Kramer that I want his chopper. As long as you behave - and do as I tell you -I will let the doctor-lady stay behind with you."

Grant stood there and cursed the pistol that now lay somewhere on the seabed.

"Please Julius - do as he asks." Brooks had regained her self-control - she gave Grant an encouraging look.

"Faber, if you as much as hurt her in the slightest way - I will kill you with my bare hands." At that moment glimpses of his battered son and his cat hanging from the showerhead flashed before him - and he shouted - in Afrikaans - so that Faber would clearly understand how serious he is, "That's a promise -you bloody piece of no-good low-life."

Grant turned from the Afrikaner and his captive and swam towards the waterline with even strokes. Halfway there his feet touched the sand and he waded up to Kramer and Yeo.

"Now what?" Kramer asked.

"He's holding Marjory hostage - he wants this helicopter. He promised to leave her with us if we obey his orders so - somehow we must stop this stupid bloody man." Grant had difficulty containing his anger.

"Let him go Grant - Yeo have already radioed a message to Air Traffic Control at the show and gave them our location. They alerted a police chopper - with medical support -and they are on their way. Incidentally - Wilson and Barnard are OK - but Du Preez and the American died in a horrible crash - which turned the car park into an inferno"

Grant's legs ached and gave way. He sat on his haunches. "The car park! Connie my assistant - I asked her to fetch my video camera from our rented car. Did they say anything about her?"

Kramer shook his head slowly as he looked over the water. "No"

It took Grant a while to get over Kramer's shocking account of the catastrophe at the airfield – so he forced himself to concentrate on their current critical situation.

"And what if Faber flies off to another destination?'" Grant looked over his shoulder to where Faber and Brooks slowly paddled towards the waterline.

Kramer turned to Yeo, "Contact the mainland and ask for support and an interception of - whoever flies off from this piece of land." The Chinese pilot ran to the small helicopter and slid behind the controls.

"Kramer, Kramer -look at me - where's your pistol?" Grant's voice turned into a whisper with urgency.

"Under my arm". Said Kramer.

Grant hissed urgently, "Hide it in your belt - behind your back - and keep it out of sight from Faber. Quickly - before they reach us."

"Now don't do anything . . ." Kramer warned.

"Shut-up man and just do it." Grant was adamant.

Kramer frowned - but obliged with an inconspicuous movement.

Grant turned and looked at the clumsy shuffle of the dripping-wet couple in the shallow water. Faber stayed behind Brooks and Grant saw that there were bruises on her throat and arms. Her chiffon dress clung transparently to her beautifully shaped body. Grand swore under his breath.

Faber snorted water from his bearded face, "I saw your pilot tinkering with the radio. So they are already on their way to get me. Therefore I have changed my mind Grant. Your pilot will take me to Penang and the doctor-lady will now accompany us. I will ask the little Chinaman to radio to ATC the consequences for your boss - should they try to stop me. OK?"

Faber panicked and his mind was in turmoil as he accepted that Fischer probably fell to his death and now with De Witt drowned, and while Du Preez did not yet turn up - he was in a bad place. He knew very little of their escape plans - once they landed at Penang. He became desperate and played for time -but he felt like a rat that ran up the mast of a sinking yacht.

"Faber - you can just as well give up right now. No ways will you be able get away from Malaysia on your own. Do the right thing now you bloody old goat and surrender to your security officer – Mr. Kramer." Grant hoped to bring the man to understand his hopeless situation and bring his - ridiculously plans – to end.

"Shut up Englishman and keep your trap shut - do you hear me? Or else . . ." Faber pushed the knife up under Marjory's chin, severing her smooth flesh. Immediately blood started to run down her throat and between her breasts. Faber walked backward dragging her towards the waiting helicopter.

Grant bit his lip. He realized that this man was totally out of sync with reality and - another word from him could be fatal for Marjory. He kept a close watch on their movements and every time Faber glanced backwards, he moved closer to Kramer. Faber reached the open door of the MD 520. He stepped carefully on the railing and stooped to pull Marjory on board. For a split second his head was down - the midday sun shone on the red bald patch of his head.

With one flowing movement Grant stepped up to Kramer – he pulled the 9-mm pistol from his belt - straightened his arm - squeezed the trigger and the bald patch exploded. Faber fell backwards into the helicopter with Marjory scrunched up on the sand. She sobbed uncontrollably as she looked up at the dead man's feet that swung from the open door above her.

69.

ORDERS MAKE THE HEART GROW FONDER.

KUALA LUMPUR GENERAL HOSPITAL.

Grant and Marjory Brooks sat in the waiting room of Ward 38 in the General Hospital of Kuala Lumpur. They were alone and waited for the return of Connie Heyneken from the operating theatre. On a large coffee table in the middle of the room, an assorted number of outdated Malaysian and English magazines were stacked up.

The latest 'New Straight Times' - that Grant brought with him - lay on top of the pile. The bold headlines, photo's with long captions and many articles and items captured the disastrous occurrence which took place at the Langkawi Air Show. It covered most of the front page and three more pages were dedicated to the disastrous outcome that the two Martial Eagle's grave crashes brought about. Reports said that many vehicles were demolished and a number of temporary exhibition stands were damaged. Fortunately very few persons were injured – and no deaths were reported apart from the crew of one of the Martial Eagles

Dozens of journalists - who syndicated their news coverage of the dreadful events at the Lankawi Air Show - to more than three hundred international media – gave the incident instantaneous worldwide coverage – something that certainly would have - pleased the deceased test pilot – Mister jack Du Preez.

"Mishaps during air-shows are not unusual occurrences." - Grant said to Marjory, "But I suppose the proportions of the Lankawi disaster that happened up-close to a stand - packed with international spectators and the entourage of the Malaysian and African politicians - puts this occurrence in a news-class by itself".

"There is also enough material there for many investigative journalists to come forth with in-depth stories with not only a human or military nature, - but also with a political slant." Marjory said while she lightly touched the flesh colored band under her chin.

Grant placed his hand on Marjory's shoulder, "You're so right my Darling. Already a main article speculated what would have been the position for South Africa - if Mandela and Mbeki died -only months before the election. It could have thrown the country into apolitical turmoil - something that we thus far were spared."

Marjory, who still had many things to deal with – officially and personally - said, "Dr. Christian Bernard gave South Africa – and the world – its first heart transplant- that lead to wonderful outcomes that saved many people afterwards. President Mandela gave the South African nation a heart transplant of a compassionate nature – the reconciliation of the people of this country. Just think if this horrible intention succeeded – what the outcome would have been for this wonderful country - and its good-natured people.

Grant stood up to stretch his legs and painful body. The bandage around his ribcage was a little too tight for his liking. He stood before Marjory and looked down at her lovely dark hair. She looked so youthful and lovely in her flowery halter-neck dress. Grant was indescribably grateful that they came through their ordeal safely. He longed to hold her and tell her how much he loved her - but it had to wait for later. The depth in their eyes said it all.

Marjory looked up at Grant and asked him tenderly, "Are you OK Julius?"

Grant took her hand. "Yes Marjory - but right now I am concerned about Connie. The doctor said she might retain a number of small scars from the shrapnel that pelted her body. The head wound may keep her here in hospital for a considerable time." Grant continued, "It all came as a terrible shock for Peter and I am glad that he could alter his arrangements so that he could arrive here this evening."

Rosemary pulled Grant gently down to the seat beside her and rested her head on his shoulder. He placed his arm around her and kissed her on the forehead. Just then Johann Kurtz walked in. "Oops! Am I intruding? Or is this a top-secret management meeting?" He laughed and greeted them in a heartily manner.

Brooks and Grant did not respond – feeling a little embarrassed Marjory simply said, "Hello Johan. It is kind of you to come over - just to be up-dated on Connie's condition."

Grant also tried to respond, "According to the papers and last night's television newscast, you did an excellent job at the, now famous, news conference."

Kurtz smiled, "It was easy - all I had to do was to select the right option of your many news-releases - which you prepared as contingency statements for when things goes wrong. I now realize that to be a good business communicator calls for the capability to do crisis anticipation to the point of near clairvoyance. Grant you were really well prepared and I am very impressed with the high level of your professionalism."

Grant became uncomfortable, "It was really an all-in-all a team effort."

Marjory squeezed Kurtz's arm, "I want to thank you also for informing President Mandela about - my abduction - and your advice to him to skip the news conference and leave immediately for KL. That was the absolutely the right thing to do - under those circumstances.".

"I still can't understand why you hired two very expensive communications consultants who did not even bother to turn up for the final media occasion." Grant said - winking at Marjory.

"Yes. Instead they were flying around the islands like two love-birds, doing sight-seeing" said Johan with a smile.

"Oh Johan, you're a bully" Marjory gave him a hug.

"Perhaps I am - but I am also the bearer of good tidings. Firstly, Mahathir and Mandela will appear on television this evening for a comprehensive interview on the consequences of the disaster for the two countries. To clear the air - they will announce that a technology agreement was signed. It will be done during this day at Dr Mahathir's offices. This agreement will smooth the execution of future business with Malaysia. It means that a technology transfer could solidify fledgling commercial relationships."

Grant sat down and wiped his brow. "Thank goodness for small mercies"

"Talking about mercies my dear friends - now I want to give you the really good news." The big Afrikaner looked enthusiastic and pleased with himself.

"Good news?" Marjory and Grant asked at simultaneously.

"Yes my dear friends and good colleagues. The Royal Malaysian Air Force will be announcing that - pending the outcome of a very thorough investigation being conducted right now - they will press ahead with a first-stage order for eight Martial Eagles. Apparently they are now totally convinced of the demonstrated effectiveness of the Martial Eagle's crash-worthiness. Ultimately the Malaysian Government will extend the order to a total of twenty Gunships! In return they want us to train Malaysian technicians in South Africa over the next three years. Ultimately they will - with a technology transfer - take full charge of helicopter production in Malaysia."

Grant's opened his mouth without saying a word.

"Good Gracious Johann! We're talking of about seven billion dollars!" said Marjory while Grant was still speechless.

"Yes guys — as a result of your contribution our company is well grounded for many years to come — and we are also happy that the two of you who are — rightfully going to earn large fees. Not taking into consideration - the personal price you had to pay as a result of your involvement - we are grateful that you helped us to facilitate a breakthrough in this tough market.

Rosemary kissed and hugged Kurtz - then she turned to Grant. "You've done it partner!" She placed her arms around him and held him very tight. Over her head Grant looked at the smiling Kurtz - with an expression that simultaneously reflected delight and pain.

Behind them Connie's medical doctor cleared his throat. They looked at him — very tense and ill at ease. "Your friend, Miss Heyneken came through quite well. We had to do a lot of stitching-up. Her head wound is particularly severe - and we will need to keep her here for several days. She is not critical and she is recovering from the anesthesia. She's asleep right now - so I suggest that you come back this evening - say around seven. By then she would be able to talk to you."

He gave them a slight bow and turned to leave when Marjory stopped him, "Pardon me doctor -will she be badly scared? "

The slender man gave her a calculated glance and said quietly, "Around some areas -" while he indicated to his chest, "- it may be necessary to do a little cosmetic surgery in a few places. But she will still be a really beautiful woman." He gave Marjory a reassuring smile and left.

- o 0 o -

Grant and Rosemary left the parking lot of the Kuala Lumpur General Hospital and entered the freeway junction of Tun Razak and Tun Ismail. They turned eastward and traveled through the exquisite surroundings of the city. At the Sultan Salahhuddin and Kuching interchange they took the Putra Street exit and drove past the World Trade Center to the Pan Pacific Hotel.

"Let's go up to our rooms and freshen-up before meeting Kurtz." Marjory suggested.

"I am OK dear so let's meet here in the foyer in - say fifteen minutes? In the meantime I will make arrangements for lunch and a small conference room in the Business center" replied Grant while Marjory kissed him on the cheek and left.

The meeting with Kurtz was filled with enthusiasm despite the dismal overtones - brought about the surprising turn of events - and the deaths of De Witt, Du Preez, and Faber. They discussed the ensuing commitments that they had to deal with. As far as the legal and technical investigations were concerned, they left it to Kramer to give them a firm understanding of their commitments before they leave Kuala Lumpur.

Shortly after five Kurtz took leave and Marjory agreed to meet Grant that evening at Connie's hospital ward, while he would pick Peter up at the airport and bring him directly to the hospital. They relied on Peter's devotion to Connie, to allow them to wrap-up their respective business commitments during the days ahead.

"While I am at the airport I will also tend to our travel arrangements" said Grant before he left.

Grant was aware of the slight tension between him and Marjory - who did not yet talk to him about her relationship with Herman de Witt or -how she felt about his death. When he told her that he was sorry about De Witt's tragic fatality, she just looked away and simply said. "We can talk about that later, Julius - when I am ready to do so"

70.

THE FAMOUS FLY FIRST CLASS.

FLIGHT TO LONDON.

Grant followed Brooks down the aisle in the first-class section of the British Airways flight to London. The past week has not only left him traumatized but also bereft of energy. He had the urge to sleep for days. At least he was going to make the most of it during this flight, he thought. And after this trip he will have enough money to squander time as he pleases. The thought consoled him as he limped behind his attractive companion. "Now I've got to get this blasted stiff ankle fixed" he muttered to himself.

They were allocated first class seats three rows from the front. A very distinguished looking gentleman in his mid forties occupied the window seat. All around them people were aware of their presence as a result of the abundant exposure they got from the media. They tried to act normal and pretended not to notice the nods and whispers.

Rosemary asked him in a very sweet way if she could have the isle-seat instead and Grant had no problems to be seated next to their travel companion - who was engrossed in the pinkish colored London Financial Times. It carried small filler on the front page, which read "Africair successfully closed Helicopter deal with Malaysian."

The man next to Grant slowly folded his pink paper and said, "May we have a pleasant journey together, sir."

Grant gave him a blank stare -a talkative companion was the last thing he wanted on this long flight, "Same to you, sir." Grant replied politely and then turned to make small talk with Marjory.

His companion was unrelenting, "The name is Douglas Collins. I doubt if we had the pleasure of meeting."

Grant responded abruptly. "Grant is the name -Julius Grant." He sounded a little like Bond – James Bond - and Grant thought that his was a silly remark

"Good - call me Doug -everybody does."

"Hi Doug" Grant set back and closed his eyes.

Beside him Douglas Collins reflected on the events of the past fourteen days. He was not at all pleased with the outcome of the Lankawi spectacle. He hated to admit failure to the South Africans - who scuppered his bid for the lucrative Malaysian contract. But what infuriated him most was Boddington's dismal failure while the media made fair reference to Du Preez's unfortunate passenger who was first crippled by a helicopter crash and then killed in his favorite gunship. As a result of the covert nature of the involvement of Boddington, Collins did not come forth as a relative and did not contact his wife or relatives. His destination was as usual undisclosed and he also dreaded facing the family who would be waiting for him at Heathrow Airport. And - after he would be done with the tedious and careful lying about where he was - at the time of the tragedy, he would still have to accept the loss of the part-payment that now would be a console to Boddington's widow. All that money would sure alleviate his sister's sadness and eventually make her a happy widow - at his expense!

"Anything to drink before we depart, Sir? Asked their flight attendant.

Collins had to think for a while. "Yes my dear. Johnny Walker - Black Label please."

In the meantime Collins continued his mental frustration. He could not understand or get a good explanation about the death of Africair's Chairman and some of his staff. He had a nagging suspicion that there could have been a hidden objective of a conspiracy by another opponent of the Martial Eagle System. If so - who were they? - Why is the whole matter dealt with so many conspiracies of silence by the authorities of both countries? Especially by the spokesperson for the South African contingent of the board of enquiry - Frederick Kramer

"Here's your Johnny Walker, sir".

"Thanks - this will do me a lot of good" murmured Collins.

Collins looked out at the ground staff preparing their plane's departure and thought about his own network of demolishers, as he nicknamed them. He really did not care about any of them. To him Ahlib, Assad, Molape, and Eric - his Asian agent, were small operational cogs in his armaments trading structure with its cloak and dagger strategies. However - he was, just a little bit sorry about the fate of his obnoxious brother in law. He can just imagine how his sister would be all in black - snot and tears by now. But on the other hand - against the loss he made this week, what pleased him a little was that he no longer has to pay the rest of Brian Boddington's fee.

"Ladies and Gentlemen - welcome aboard British Airways flight ..." interrupted Collins' thoughts

But what irritated Collins the most was that his network misread the importance of this bloody Grant fellow who now sat here right next to him - basking in his success while sipping his Scotch. It called for a fine effort from his Asia entity to arrange seating for him next to Grant and Brooks. He planned to do his utmost to establish - as much as possible - what the couple's movements would be in the following months. Just before he left his hotel Collins tasked his London entity to follow Grant's trail and await further orders. The only reason why his hit-squad should demolish Grant now would be to render him the personal pleasure of retribution.

"Please fasten your seatbelts and do not - - -." the enouncement continued.

Collins leaned over to Grant, "I've read all about you're ordeal Mister Grant. May I sympathize with the unfortunate deaths in your client's company? But I want to hastily add my congratulation with your contribution to successfully secure the South African's bid to supply all those sophisticated Martial Eagle Attack Helicopters to the RMAF."

Grant detected a slight innuendo of sarcasm and turned to Collins. "Oh, thank you sir. Seeing that you know all about our ordeal, I believe you will appreciate my getting some sleep and not being much of a conversationalist. OK?"

"Much obliged Mister Grant - but one last question. You are well known as a journalist - what are you going to do now that you have achieved this objective?"

Grant clasped his hands behind his head and closed his eyes. He gave a deep sigh as Marjory curled up her legs and rested her head on his chest, and then he said, "From now on I will be a retired writer touring the world, Mister Douglas Collins." Grant fell asleep even before they left the runway.

Collins smirked and made a cryptic note in his small diary while he whispered, "My dear Mister Julius Grant, there is no such thing as a retired writer - there are only poor, wealthy - or dead writers."

The end

EPILOGUE

Dear Jack,

While I was busy working on the book there was a newswire item that reported the intention of the Royal Malaysian Air Force to purchase eight attack helicopters from South Africa. .According to the report the Malaysian Defense Minister, Syed Hamid Albar, apparently indicated that the final number of aircraft to be purchased would only be determined after negotiations between the Malaysian Government and the South African manufacturers. That number could be as many as fifty helicopters

This bit of news made me happy – because it sounded like the good outcome I had in mind for this book. As a result I was quite confident that my storyline was reasonable and quite plausible. I was confident that you would find it real good; even perhaps a little entertaining

But a few years later, shortly after I wrote "The End" at the bottom of the last page, another news item was brought to my attention. A South African political correspondent reported that after the attack helicopter manufacturers failed to win a bid for the Turkish Air Force, the company decided to abandon their gunship because it was not commercially feasible. And that after more than a billion dollars was invested in the development of this most superior flying machine.

The correspondent of this article mentioned that the managing director of the South African firm was of the opinion that their attack helicopter could not compete with other major defense manufacturers as a result of critical economic factors. However, a spokesperson for the company said that they were pleased that their marketing strategy was excellent and that they had the support of the South African Government.

To me this was the sting in the tail of the real world! If there would have been any truth in the objectives of the antagonists in my fictional story, they would have had good reason to celebrate the termination of this absolutely superior attack helicopter.

This correspondent's news article made me feel as if I ended my story - perhaps a few chapters too early ?

Jack, thank you for reading my book and I hope to see you soon.

Holtz Hauzen,
My Beach House, South Africa

CHOPPERS TO DIE FOR:
ABOUT THE WRITER AND THE BOOK

The author is a retired communications practitioner and correspondent for military magazines. His career was devoted to the management of strategic and general corporate communications pertaining to the South African banking, gold mining, and armaments industries.

This is a work of fiction by the author, describing vivid imaginary situations and events. The fictional characters that the writer invented do not represent specific living persons or views. Where places and incidents, as well as the names of particular prominent and well-known persons are mentioned in this novel, it is the product of the author's imaginative and fictional making of the relevance of these persons and locations to enhance the narrative. The objective was to augment this exceptional story with its line-up of fictitious characters with a sense of authenticity to create a new and yet un-plotted novel genre: the unrevealed circumstances behind South Africa's Apartheid Curtain and what took place within the country's extremely guarded armaments industry.

Holtz Hauzen is the pseudonym of the writer of Choppers, who now lives in the USA and in the meantime became an American Citizen.